ELYSIUM

A SOOTHSAYER NOVEL

ALLISON SIPE

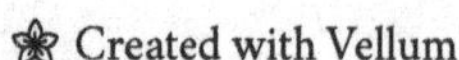 Created with Vellum

ALSO BY THE AUTHOR

SOOTHSAYER SERIES

Soothsayer

Avalon: A Soothsayer Novella

Trivium

Le Fay: A Soothsayer Novella

Elysium

REALMS SAGA

Realm of Flames & Steel

Realm of Stars & Shadows

BOOK PLAYLIST

If you like to listen to music while you read, then you're in luck! We've created a playlist just for Elysium on Spotify and you can listen here:

*"Not I, nor anyone else can travel that road for you.
You must travel it by yourself.
It is not far. It is within reach.
Perhaps you have been on it since you were born, and did not know.
Perhaps it is everywhere -"*

— Walt Whitman

VIOLET IN THE DARK

*My hold on reality blurs as the outside world becomes fuzzy
and distant.*

*A heavy pressure squeezes my body like I'm being forced into a
tiny box.*

Fear prickles through me...

I don't want to go...I push against the darkness.

I don't want to die.

CHAPTER 1

 IVIAN

PUFFY, over-stuffed storm clouds moved across the sun, throwing a shadow over the lake that made gooseflesh rise on my skin. The surface of the water shifted from a calm sapphire blue to a dark midnight black. This battle was far from over. The wind picked up, rustling the hair off my face as Robert's eyes searched for his Violet.

"I... it's too hard-" Violet's words were barely a whisper in my head as the sensation of her essence faded into the background. She should have died upon waking me, but still she held on. What strength she must have to accomplish such a feat.

"It's really you, Milady?" Robert said, clearing his throat. A sharp pain shuttered through my heart as Violet's emotions warred within me. Robert looked as if someone had let the air out of him as his eyes traced my face. Realization dawning on him that Violet was no longer the woman standing before him.

"Yes. Violet succeeded in her quest to wake me," I supplied.

"I thought… I didn't realize…" his Adam's apple bobbed up and down as he let out a shaky breath.

"That I'd take on the body of The Waker?" It's an unfortunate part of the process that always leaves loved ones confused and feeling betrayed. "Your Violet is strong and though I don't know how she's survived, she has." I tried my best to reassure him again.

"How can I be sure you're telling the truth?" His fingers twitched like he wanted to touch me, but thought better of it.

"You're bonded, are you not?" I asked, as an unfamiliar thrill of Magic unfurled in the pit of my stomach.

His eyes widen for a fraction of a second. Surprise washed across his face that I was aware of their connection.

"We are," he blurted, composing himself.

"You understand, your *Artognou Magic* can only be accessed if both parties are alive?"

Understanding flickered across his features as he squared his shoulders. He held my gaze and his fingers curled into a fist as I waited to feel the connection between them.

"I see." Robert kept his eyes averted from mine.

I'd met bonded pairs before and been close to their Magic on numerous occasions, but I've never experienced the raw, unbound nature of the bond for myself.

The wind rustled my hair as the tall grass moved against my trousers. Gooseflesh crawled across my skin as every nerve in my body fired at once.

The raw, untamed Magic poured through me, taking my breath away. It was unlike anything I'd ever experienced before, warm, powerful, and hungry. It tasted like pure freedom.

Robert took a step toward me and reached for my hand; Violet let him take my fingers as another wave of energy pulsed through me at his touch. The heat began to crawl up my skin from where his hand held mine, and Violet's strength pushed me toward him.

"Violet," he breathed. "Don't give up." His thumb traced a circle on the back of my hand.

"I won't," she replied. Violet's words pierced through my head as if she was standing right next to me.

Tearing my hand from his grasp, I tapped into my Magic, shutting them out and fortifying my claim on this body.

My stomach turned as Violet faded into the background once more. I hated silencing her, but there was much to be done and I couldn't afford the distraction.

This will be rather interesting, I thought, as another sharp pain flashed across my chest.

"Your bond is young, untested." I kept my Magic close to the surface. "But strong."

A heaviness settled over my heart as Violet's spirits fell.

"Forgive me, Milady." Robert inclined his head as the last shred of their Magic dissipated within me.

"There's no need to stand on ceremony, Vivian will do."

Robert squeezed his eyes closed and exhaled. "Will Violet make it out of this?"

I studied the sharp edge of his jaw, the tension in his shoulders, uncertain of what I should tell him. Not a single person had survived this long, but the reality of her death, while she was still so close, would be too hard for him to accept. That much I knew from experience.

Robert opened his mouth to speak but was cut off by someone yelling his name.

"Robert! Oh, thank God, I was worried you..." a woman came to a stop next to him, her brow furrowing as she took in the pained look on his face. "What's wrong? Did you guys find The Lady?" She turned to look at me and her eyes widened.

"Violet?" She squared her shoulders as her eyes held mine.

"Brett, meet The Lady of the Lake." Robert motioned between Brett and myself.

Brett's head swiveled to look at Robert, and she whispered, "What happened?"

Sparks danced up and down my fingers as my eyes caught three figures jogging across the open field toward us. "Do they belong to you as well?" I asked, taking a step forward.

"Yes," Brett shouted, "There's no need for your defenses." Her eyes fell to my hands and I let the Magic die with one last crackle.

"Whoa, what's with the *X-Men* eyes, Violet?" One of the men joked with a playful smile.

"Ethan." The woman who shared his features nodded her head toward Brett and Robert.

Brett shot him a warning glance, and he looked at me and Robert.

"Allow me to introduce myself," I started. "The title you'll know me by is The Lady of the Lake, but you may call me Vivian."

"This is a joke, right?" The bronzed skinned woman looked at Robert for confirmation.

He folded his arms over his chest, and without looking at me, he said, "I'm afraid she speaks the truth, Elodie."

"But Violet? I mean, is she...?" The tall, broad shoulder man asked.

"Jake," Brett scolded the man.

"In my experience," I interjected. "The host is destroyed upon my entry, but Violet has survived within this body."

Everyone looked at each other, fidgeting and trying not to stare as I spoke.

"And Morgana?" Jake asked.

"She's escaped, for now." Anger bloomed in my chest, hot and furious.

"We need to get out of here before they regroup," Brett recommended.

"Where's Lila and Annabel?" Jake searched the group for their face.

"Lila didn't make it," Robert said.

Again, Violet's emotions bubbled to the surface and guilt pierced through me.

"I'm sorry, brother, Lila was complicated, but I know you cared for her."

"Jake, there's something you need to know about, Annabel." Robert's voice broke, and he couldn't meet his brother's eyes.

"Not here." Brett grabbed Robert's arm.

"Putting it off, won't make it any easier." Robert whirled on Brett. "He should know."

"Tell me." Jake's eyes darted between Robert and Brett.

"Annabel." Robert closed the gap between him and Jake and placed a hand on his brother's shoulder. "She's gone."

"What're you — no." Jake shook his head and stepped away from Robert.

"She's been gone a long time," Robert continued. "Since the day Ian took her."

"No, no, we got her back, we saved her." Jake's brow furrowed and his hands balled into fists.

"The woman parading as your wife showed us her true form and killed Lila right in front of us." Robert's voice was devoid of emotion.

A flash of a memory skirted through my mind. A blonde woman shifting into a redhead. A blade across another woman's neck and Violet's hands covered in the victim's blood as she held her.

Brett stepped forward like she was approaching a wild animal and said, "Ian told us, our Annabel, the real Annabel," she hesitated. "Was killed by his hand the day he took her."

"No," Jake argued. "Why would they take her, if they were just going to kill her, why? It doesn't make sense," he yelled at no one in particular.

"I don't—"

"You're wrong," Jake growled at Brett.

I stepped forward, wanting to help him see the truth of their words. Reaching out my hand, my fingers brushed against Jake's temple. A rush of Magic coursed through my torso and Violet's memory played between us. The woman playing his wife slit Lila's throat, then shifted from Annabel to her true form.

Jake's eyes met mine for a fraction of a second. I watched the heartbreak work its way from his chest and into his eyes as his knees hit the soft earth.

Looking down at his hands as if he was staring at Annabel, he uttered her name softly and I could feel the tiny cracks in Violet's heart open up. She knew pain and loss all too well, it would seem.

"I'm so sorry," Brett whispered. Kneeling next to Jake, she wrapped her arms around his shoulders.

"I too am sorry for your loss." I took a step toward them. "But we must move to a more convenient location."

"No," Jake barked. His face contorted into a mask of pain and anger. "I held her in my arms, cared for her, loved her."

"You didn't know," Robert argued. "None of us did."

"I should have known," Jake shouted as his eyes filled with tears. "I should have—"

"Stop, you can't do this to yourself. Anna wouldn't want you to blame yourself." Brett gripped Jake's shoulder.

Jake's eyes met hers as a tear trailed down his cheek. "If it was Matty, you'd blame yourself, wouldn't you?" He snapped.

Brett's mouth opened and closed.

"It's not my wish to rush your grieving, but we must take our leave in the event Morgana returns," I said again.

"I need to… bring Lila home." Robert moved away from the group through the tall, thick grass, and Brett pulled Jake to his feet. Following Robert, the others whispered among themselves as I scanned the open field. The chill that hung in the air was more than just the weather turning. I could feel the darkness in my bones with each step I took. Something was lurking out there, something sinister and not of this world.

Robert came to a stop, and the others halted a few feet away, giving him the space he needed. As he knelt down in the grass, I moved toward him, pushing past the others. Lila's body was no more. Only a pile of black ash remained on the blades of grass.

Robert laid his hand on the ash, the glint of something silver catching my eye.

"I'm so sorry," he said under his breath.

I knelt next to Robert, placing my hand on top of his and said, "Whether you brought happiness or pain, may your soul yet win delights on this, your death-day."

"Thank you," Robert said, without looking at me. His fingers pushed the ashes aside, and he picked up the silver ring and stuffed it in his pocket.

"It's not safe here," I reminded him. "We need to seek shelter." I scanned the dark clouds holding steadfast to the horizon.

Nodding his head, he stood and turned to face his family. "Let's go home," he said.

I held my hand out for him to grab.

"For those of you who wish to return," I held out my other hand. "Robert, if you'll please picture home in your mind." I nodded to him.

Ethan and Elodie grabbed onto my arm while Brett and Jake held onto Robert.

The Magic inside me unfurled like a rose blooming, slow and easy. *"Auferetur."*

Within the blink of an eye, we were home, wherever home was for Robert and his comrades.

A dizzy spell washed over me as I took in the furnishings. It felt like someone had taken hold of my intestine with a death grip. I could feel Violet more prominently again as the edges of my vision blurred.

"They're back," a voice shouted, and a pair of arms wrapped around me.

"Jake? Jake, what's wrong?" A worried female voice called after him.

"It's been a long day. Leave him," Robert said.

"We'll go." Ethan nodded and he and Elodie followed Jake.

"Thank God you're safe." A tiny woman with short dark hair held me at arm's length, then let go of me like a hot coal.

The pain in my abdomen sharpened, and I slumped against the wall, letting out a heavy breath. Holding out my hands, they shook as I turned them over.

"Are you okay?" Robert grabbed my elbow to steady me.

"Of course." I cleared my throat. "Just out of practice."

"Is this normal?" Violet's voice rang in my head.

"Nothing about this is normal," I replied.

"Vivian, is that you?" A familiar, gentle voice said from somewhere above me.

"By the stars. It's you." An overwhelming sense of relief washed over me.

"Ahh, my dear Vivian. It's been quite a long time. I was afraid you wouldn't recognize me."

"You two know each other?" Robert's eyes caught mine and his brow furrowed as he tried to work out how I could know anyone in his world.

"You could say that." I shrugged and took a ragged breath.

"Your face may have changed," I said through another spout of dizziness, "But you can't hide the stench of your Magic." I did my best to hide the pain in my voice as Violet grew stronger.

"Good to see, The Lady of The Lake still has a sense of humor." He held his arms out to me.

"You and I both know I was always the humorous one, Merlin." I stepped into the circle of his arms and my legs went out from under me as darkness fell over my eyes.

VIVIAN IN THE DARK

Something is...different...wrong.

I could still hear their worried voices as I fell

deeper,

and deeper

into the darkness.

Save me Merlin.

CHAPTER 2

IOLET

"Is she okay?" Robert's voice broke through the fog.

"I'm… I'm okay," I said, pushing myself back on my feet.

"Violet?" Graham looked at me, confused.

"Yes," I sighed.

"It's you," Robert whispered. "Vivian said you-"

"You can't get rid of me that easy." My voice cracked as I held onto Graham's arms a moment longer to steady myself.

"How's this possible?" Brett's eyes danced over me.

"Thank God, you're back." Becky wrapped her arms around me.

"I'm not sure how long it'll last," I admitted, as Vivian's presence overwhelmed my senses.

"Unfortunately, it won't," Graham interrupted our reunion. The tiny shred of hope I'd been harboring popped like a balloon at his words.

"What do you mean?" Robert asked.

"Before we get into that, did she," Becky pointed in my direction, "call you Merlin? As in the wizard with the pointy hat?" Becky mimed a pointy hat over her head.

He grumbled under his breath, clearly not a fan of the description, as everyone waited for an answer.

"Is it true?" Brett stepped back with a new light in her eyes. "Are you really, Merlin?"

"Indeed, I am." He smiled.

There was a noticeable shift in the air, and everyone seemed restless at the change.

"But that would mean…" Brett's eyes shifted from Merlin to her siblings.

"All this time?" Robert said under his breath. "Why didn't you tell us?"

"What's to tell?" Merlin waved him off. "You lot know me just as well as Graham. Besides, a name isn't what makes a man and I'm still the same person I've always been."

"That explains how you were able to teach us about our *Artognou Magic*," Robert realized.

"Indeed." Merlin smiled down at me.

"Does this mean you can help with what's happening to me?" I asked.

"I don't have all the answers, but I'll do everything in my power to fix this." Merlin's cool tone sent a chill down my spine.

"She's going to have to live like this?" Robert looked down at me helplessly. "Shifting between herself and Vivian?"

"For the moment, yes." Merlin's voice was grim as his eyes held mine.

"Can you fix them, split them apart?" Brett asked.

"Vivian needs a body to survive in this realm. Without it, she can't sustain her life-force and she will fade back to Avalon."

"And all of this will have been for nothing." I let out a shaky breath.

"This might be a little morbid, but can't we find another

body for Vivian to inhabit?" Brett squirmed as she said the words.

"While that would solve the quarrel between there souls, separating them is less than ideal," Merlin explained.

"It can't be any worse than this?" I pressed my hand to my aching chest.

"Oh my dear, Violet." Merlin's eyes met mine, and they were filled with pity. "The only way to separate Vivian from a Waker," Merlin hesitated and my stomach turned to knots. "Is to kill the host," he finished, without looking at any of us.

I stared at him, shocked into silence. I wanted to cry, I wanted to scream, but all I could do was stew in the knowledge that my death was the only way to free, The Lady of the Lake.

"You're not killing Violet." Robert's grip on me tightened.

"Quite right," Merlin said. "I'd like to avoid unnecessary death at all costs if possible."

"You don't know how to separate us without killing me, do you?" I asked, even though deep down I already knew the answer.

"At the moment, no." Merlin pursed his lips.

"Don't you think, Violet should have known what was at stake before she woke, Vivian?" Robert stared at Merlin like someone killed his favorite pet.

"He did warn me that I'd be lost to, The Lady," I squeaked. "Though, I wasn't sure what exactly that meant."

"And you should have been," Merlin said. "No one's survived waking Vivian before."

"Then how is Violet still here?" Brett asked.

Vivian's restless annoyance bucked inside me. She didn't enjoy being trapped in my body, and her frustration grated against my fragile nerves. The memory of being lost in the cold darkness was still fresh, and no part of me wanted to return.

"I may've had a small hand in your current predicament." Merlin steepled his fingertips together.

"Of course you did," Robert huffed. "But why, to what end?"

"She's family," Merlin said matter-of-factly.

"Oh, for crying out loud," I sighed.

I knew Merlin was part of my family tree, in theory, but now he was standing in front of me, in the flesh, like it was no big deal he was alive.

"I cast an enchantment on Vivian's Ring. When you put it on to wake her, it was meant to safeguard you from death."

The memory of Merlin and me eating cookies and sharing stories in the middle of the night flashed before my eyes. His warning and discretion with the Ring made perfect sense now.

"But why not just tell me?" I wondered. The weak, faint coil of Vivian's Magic stirred deep inside me like a predator waiting to strike.

"I wasn't sure it would work, and I didn't want to give you false hope." He gave me a tight-lipped smile.

"Okay, so I didn't die." A dry laugh escaped my throat. "Now what?"

"I wouldn't say you survived either," Ethan said as he walked into the entry.

"Ethan," Brett and Elodie scolded him in unison.

"No, he's right, I'm not entirely myself," I said. "Everything since the waking feels like a dream that's fading with every passing moment. I can't grab a hold of what's real, what's my memories or hers, it's all jumbled with Vivian."

Robert grabbed my hand in his and the distant flutter of our Artognou Magic came to life.

"While you survived as I intended, there seems to be a rather unusual side effect." Merlin's fingers gripped my chin and moved my head back and forth.

"I think, side effect is putting it mildly." Becky crossed her arms over her chest.

"It's not ideal, but it's better than the alternative. And though, I don't know what's happening to you, to either of you,"

Merlin said. "I can venture a guess that both of your souls are vying for control of the body you're sharing."

"And what happens if one gains control over the other?" Robert asked the question I was too afraid to.

"Can you still feel Vivian? Is she active or dormant?" Merlin ignored Robert's question as he held my face between his palms and looked into my eyes.

Vivian's contentment settled deep in my bones as Merlin stared down at me. She knew him well and though her anger rolled through me, there was also a sense of comfort under the surface.

"She's present in every sense of the word," I acknowledged. "Although I'm not sure how long she'll last." I bit my bottom lip and grabbed my arm.

"Then listen to me." He glanced over my shoulder to the others and back at me. "I don't know how long either of you can live like this." His eyes raked over me. "But if there's a way to save you, I'll do everything in my power."

"So, what now?" Brett demanded.

"Now we find a way to save them both." Merlin gave me an apologetic smile.

"You think you can save her?" Robert asked. Moving to my side, he placed a tentative hand on my back.

"Violet still has work to do." Merlin's eyes met mine. "I'll do everything in my power to make sure she's able to accomplish it."

My head spun and my mouth filled with saliva like I was about to be sick as I leaned against the cool stucco wall.

"What is it?" Merlin's voiced filled my ears.

"Violet, can you hear me?" Robert's warmth engulfed me as his arms wrapped around by body.

"Oh God," Becky gasped as a vision took me.

Shadows flickered across the stone walls on either side of me. The smell of smoke and the heat of nearby flames made it difficult to gather my bearings.

"Tell me where to find it," a shrill woman's voice echoed through the cavern.

I moved toward the voice slowly, looking for anything that would clue me into where I was. Looking above me, I expected there to be a roof, but instead, there were a million stars dotting the night sky.

I'd never seen so many constellations in all my life and I stared at them in wonder, realizing I didn't recognize any of the patterns above me. Where was I?

"Last chance," the voice I'd heard before was closer and held an air of calculated malice.

Taking another step in her direction, I noticed the bulky shadow in the corner. I knelt down to see what it was, and panic tore through me.

His eyes were still open and blood dripped from every orifice. As I walked past him, I noticed another figure laying on his side. Moving closer, his body slumped over as I approached. He wore the same shocked expression as the other man, blood dripping down his face.

A scream tore through the otherwise quiet space and I ran toward it. As I rounded a corner, a large room spilled out in front of me. In the center of the room, Morgana stood over a man, his blood trailing down her fingers, while another woman watched over the proceedings. Every line of her body was harsh and unforgiving and as I looked closer, I realized the other woman looked more like a ghostly shadow than a physical person.

"What are you?" I wondered.

Against the wall, dozens of men were on their knees, watching as Morgana finished draining the life from the man at her feet.

"I'll ask again." The ghostly woman stepped forward. "Tell me where it is, or suffer the fate of your Brothers."

No one spoke or made eye contact with the woman as I stared on in horror.

Her head snapped in my direction, as if she knew I was there.

"We have a visitor," she said, moving closer to me.

"Where?" Morgana scanned the room, murder in her eyes.

"It's a Soothsayer," the woman whispered in disgust.

My skin crawled as she said my title, and bile rose to the back of my throat. How could she know I was seeing them?

"Let's give her a show," she smirked, and turned back toward the helpless men.

Not wanting to watch them murder anyone else, I searched for my Magic.

Morgana sauntered toward the line of men as I put the first mental wall into place. The room blurred in front of me as I struggled to get my Magic to cooperate.

Taking a deep breath, my whole body shook with the effort to shut out the vision and return to the Maxwell's.

The outline of Morgana dragging a figure into the center of the room was the last thing I saw, as his screams echoed around me.

"Violet?" Robert's voice was cautious.

"We have to stop them." My entire body shook as the screams echoed in my head.

Pushing Robert aside, my stomach heaved and vomit burst from my mouth. The sheer effort it had taken to summon my Magic and escape the vision was almost too much to bear. I felt like I'd run ten miles in one-hundred-degree weather, with nothing but milk in my stomach.

I retched again and gasped for a clean breath.

"What did you see?" Merlin asked.

"Is that what that was?" Becky's brows furrowed as she stared at me.

"Death," I said, wiping my mouth with the back of my hand.

Brett waved her hand over the pile of sick, and it vanished before my eyes.

"You look like you've seen a ghost." Ethan's lips formed a hard line.

"I think I might've." I gathered enough strength to push off the wall and stand on my own.

"Here," Elodie said, holding a glass of water.

"Thank you." I took a sip and the cold liquid traveled down my throat, through my chest, and into my empty stomach.

"It's Morgana and someone I didn't recognize." I took a shaky breath.

White hot anger erupted in my chest as Vivian's emotions tore through me like they were my own.

"Ahh," I grabbed my chest, dropping the water. The glass hit the hardwood floor and shattered into a thousand pieces.

"What, what is it?" Becky grabbed my shoulder.

"Vivian. She's pissed." My lips quivered as I bit back the anger. "She know's something." I bit my lip. "At least, I think she does."

"Merlin, fix this," Robert demanded.

"Vivian, can you hear me?" Merlin pushed Becky and Robert out of the way and forced me against the wall.

My chest tightened and my lungs suctioned together, making it impossible to catch my breath.

"Yes." Vivian's answer escaped my throat as I fought for control of my body.

"Who was it, who did Violet see?" Merlin begged.

Heat spread across my chest and up my neck. I thought I might throw up again.

My vocal cords flexed as if I was trying to cough up a golf ball and a strangled sound escaped my throat.

"Nim-"

"Nimue?" Merlin finished for her.

Another burst of anger jumped through me.

"I think you…" I strained to get the words out. "hit the nail on the head," I breathed.

"Violet, listen to me closely." Merlin cradled my cheeks in his hands. "If we're to stop them, you have to stop fighting Vivian, we need to know what you saw."

My eyes searched Merlin's as I took in a ragged breath.

My hair rustled as a breeze from nowhere passed over me. "If either of you is to survive," he continued. "You must share your body with her for the time being." Vivian's emotions settled to a quiet hum.

A tingling sensation spread through my heart to my extremities, and I could breathe again.

"Good girl," Merlin cooed.

"What are you doing to her?" Robert demanded.

My eyes felt heavy, and I wanted to curl into a ball on the floor.

"Grah-Merlin," Robert yelled and pulled him off of me.

As Merlin released me, my body caved like melted butter on a hot day. I was dimly aware of the fact that a pair of arms caught me before I hit the floor.

"What did you do to them?" Robert asked as he cradled my limp body.

"I aligned the frequency of their souls. It won't last forever, but it'll allow them to coexist in harmony while they transition into this new way of life."

"What does that mean, exactly?" Brett asked.

"It'll buy Violet some time before Vivian is strong enough to take hold again."

CHAPTER 3

 IOLET

"Now tell us, Violet. What did you see?"

"Can you give her a minute?" Robert barked. "She's clearly not herself."

"It's okay." I gave Robert a small smile. "It's important."

"Go on, then," Merlin encouraged. "Tell us what you saw."

"I'm not sure where I was or when, to be honest."

"It's okay. Just start with what you *do* know," Merlin encouraged as Robert sat next to me, keeping my hand in his.

A chill ran across my arms as the memory of blood and fire flashed before my eyes. "They were searching for something." The smell of death still filled my nose.

"Morgana and, Nim-Nimue?" I looked at Merlin for confirmation, and he nodded.

"Do you know what they were looking for?" Ethan asked. His arms folded over his chest and for the first time since I met him, he sounded more like Robert than his joking self.

"They didn't mention it by name." I shook my head and frowned. My visions were notorious for never showing me the whole picture.

"What else?" Merlin asked.

"I don't know," I shrugged. I tried to remember something, anything, that might help. "Stars," I said. "There were more stars than I've ever seen, but I wasn't familiar with the constellations."

Merlin's brow furrowed, and he asked, "Who were Morgana and Nimue interrogating?"

I sighed. "They were all men." I thought back to the people I'd seen. Each one was clad in the same dark leather pants, fur coats, and each one of them was male. "I think I was seeing something that happened long ago."

"Why do you say that?" Robert asked, tracing a pattern on the back of my hand.

"Their clothes, they weren't modern." I shook my head. "And all those stars. With light pollution, it's almost impossible to see a sky like that nowadays."

"It's possible you saw days gone by," Merlin mused. "Is there anything else?"

"No. Yes," I shot up. "She could see me. She knew I was there." My heart hammered against my chest at the memory of Nimue's frigid stare.

"Morgana?" Elodie asked.

I shook my head and said, "Nimue. She stared right at me and called me by my title. She wanted me to watch what they were doing." I shivered as the scream of the man Morgana took hold of echoed in my head.

"She was always in tune with her surroundings," Merlin mused. "While most can't sense a Soothsayer's Magic, she could always tell when someone was dropping in on her."

"You know her?" I furrowed my brow.

In the few minutes I spent in her presence, I'd learned she was the kind of evil that took pleasure in other's pain. If Merlin had intimate knowledge of her Magic, then what did that say about him?

"In a way." His eyes fell, and he moved across the room to the French doors. "The woman you hold inside you is only one half of The Lady of The Lake," Merlin continued without looking at me. "Nimue is the other."

His words hit me like bullets. I couldn't reconcile the woman inside me with the evil it'd witnessed from Nimue.

"What?" Brett and Elodie said in unison.

"How'd they end up as two separate people?" I forced myself to ask the question.

"Her son," Ethan said. "Right?" He turned in Merlin's direction, and Brett looked at him like he was speaking a different language.

"Correct." Merlin stared out the French doors, ignoring the rest of us.

"How do you know anything about her son?" Brett asked.

"Not just a pretty face." Ethan winked.

"Who was he?" I asked.

"One of the best swordsmen I'd ever seen," Merlin smiled to himself. "But even with all his skill and training he couldn't keep death at bay." He let out a sigh and shook his head.

Vivian's emotions squirmed inside me as Merlin spoke. Sadness and unease washed over me, and my heart ached.

"Mordred was all but dead when they brought his body home," Merlin continued. "But Nimue wouldn't accept it. She turned to the Shadowlands for help."

"You can't be serious." Robert tensed next to me, and his hand squeezed mine.

"I am," Merlin confirmed.

"What are the Shadowlands?" I wondered aloud.

"It's a realm worse than death. It feeds on the desperate and miserable." Merlin's nose scrunched up in disgust.

"Realm?" I asked.

"The Shadowlands are not part of our world," Robert said. "It exists outside of what is known in this realm."

"So, like a parallel universe?" I offered.

"In a way, yes," Merlin said. "Though the Shadowlands aren't an alternative to our world. It's more of an afterlife for Magical souls who make bargains with the Umbra-Kai."

"Afterlife," Brett snorted. "If you can even call it that."

"Umbra-Kai?" I asked.

"Warriors of the Shadowlands," Merlin explained. "They have the power to grant miracles, but there's always a price."

"Why anyone would ever make a deal with them, I'll never understand." Robert's fingers laced through mine.

"Desperation brings out the worst in people." Merlin acknowledged. "Hence the split of her soul," Merlin continued. "Vivian, is the pure and good fraction of their soul. She wouldn't bend to the darkness and give the Umbra-Kai the price the Shadowlands demanded to save Mordred."

"But Nimue did," I said through a shaky breath.

"Yes." Merlin's jaw flexed on the word.

Magic pulled at me, and I wasn't quick enough to block the vision. The room tilted and shifted under me and swirled into a thousand colors, reforming around me.

I was standing in the middle of a modest cabin. A small bed nestled in the far corner. A man, still as stone, laid atop the bed with a sheet covering half his body. The shallow rise of his chest indicated he was still alive, though not for very much longer, if I had to guess.

In the middle of the room sat a large table. A woman stood over the books and herbs piled across the tabletop, with a large bowl in front of her.

She looked like Nimue, but her cheeks were fuller and her eyes were a bright summer green, unlike the dark empty pits she had in my previous vision.

Grabbing a knife, she pressed the tip against her wrist until it broke her skin. A bright droplet of blood bloomed on her pale skin, and she dragged the blade along her forearm. As the blood dripped in the bowl on the table, she recited a spell. Her voice was deep and smooth as she spoke, as if her words were running into one another.

"Foolish woman, you haven't the slightest clue what that spell will do to you?" The knife shot out of her hand, tumbling to the other side of the cabin.

"Who are you?" She asked as she raised her shield around her.

"Ambroise," a deep voice said, stepping out of the shadows. "Some know me as Merlin." He was young, handsome, and looked nothing like the man I'd come to know.

"Ahh, of course." She blinked lazily, as if her eyelids had grown heavy.

"Stop this at once," he demanded.

"This is none of your business," she snarled. "And you're not welcome here."

She raised her other arm in one swift motion and with a clipped incantation a blast of Magic hit Merlin square in the chest and he froze on the spot and fell to the floor.

Squeezing her wounded arm, she continued the spell. The drops of blood turned to a stream as it flew out of her.

She was killing herself, I thought in horror.

She finished the spell and closed her eyes as a white shimmer emanated from her chest. Still, she kept herself upright.

Light poured out of her in a steady stream, forming into the shape of a woman. Her ghostly figure hovered above the table, and my mouth fell open.

"Don't do this," the spirit begged.

"I... have... to," Nimue struggled to get the words out.

She placed her good hand on the symbol carved into the wood table and spoke one last word.

The shimmering woman and Nimue screamed in unison as wind blew through the room, knocking everything to the floor.

Getting to her feet once the spell took hold, Nimue rolled her neck from side to side. The wound in her arm vanished, along with her green eyes and soft features. She was harsh and cold, just as I'd seen her before.

"*That's better,*" *she smirked.*

The cabin shifted and swirled around me until the Maxwells reformed in front of me.

"Oh God," I whimpered as a tear rolled down my cheek.

"What is it?" Robert asked.

"How could anyone do something like that?" My eyes searched for Merlin.

"Vivian showed you?" Merlin guessed, and I nodded my head.

"She's ruthless," I snarled.

I sat back down, overwhelmed by Vivian's loss and heartbreak. The others continued to talk, but their words were lost on me as I played Vivian and Nimues split in my head over and over again.

Eventually, Robert helped me to bed. Every fiber of my being was exhausted. My body was depleted, my heart ached and my soul felt like it'd gone through a cheese grater by the time Robert turned off the lights and laid down next to me.

CHAPTER 4

IOLET

This morning was mostly a blur. Though I was feeling more myself, Vivian's constant presence in the back of my mind was unsettling. Robert had picked up on my mood and mostly left me to my own devices until it was time to head to my place. Given my inability to stay in control of my body and the looming threat over the Magical world, we all agreed it would be best for me to stay at the Maxwell's.

"You doing okay?" Robert asked as we pulled away from the estate. "You're looking a little flushed."

"Adjusting to the new normal," I sighed as I stared at out the window. I still couldn't believe I'd survived, though I wasn't wholly myself. Still, I was here, living and breathing.

"You know we'll find a way to save you, right?" Robert's hand reached for mine as he drove. "I won't let anyone hurt you."

"I know." I could feel Vivian squirm under the surface. "I just thought." I looked at our joined hands. "I thought that waking, Vivian, would be the hard part and now…"

"We'll get through this," Robert glanced in my direction as we came to a stoplight. "You have my word that we'll find a way to separate you and Vivian without… killing you." He struggled to get the last part out.

I gave him a small smile and looked out the window as the light turned green. He was so optimistic, so full of hope. I didn't want to rain on his parade, not when he was just trying to help me feel better.

Robert parked the car, and we walked through the gate and up the path to my condo. Butterflies churned in my stomach and I paused as we reached the front door.

"It's been a while." Robert gave me a cautious smile.

"Feels like another life." I turned the key over and stepped inside. The warm, stale air hit me like a wall, and I frowned as I thought about how long it had been since I was home.

Looking around, everything was just as I left it. My camera bag sat in the middle of the kitchen table next to my Walt Whitman photo album. A sweater sat discarded over the back of the couch as if I tossed it there a moment ago and a coffee cup sat on the end table, stale and forgotten.

Tears stung my eyes, and I took in what used to be my home. My safe harbor in a storm. It wasn't much, but it was mine and it was perfect. Bits and pieces of who I was stuck out like a sore thumb and I wondered if I could ever go back. I'd changed so much since Robert came into my life, I barely recognized myself anymore.

"I'll grab some clothes real quick and we can get out of here," I said as I started toward the hall.

"We don't have to rush. I'm sure it must feel good to be home." Robert gave me a small, patient smile.

"Honestly, it's like I'm in someone else's home," I said, biting my lip.

His brow furrowed and his head tilted to the side as he reached out and touched my arm.

"It's just, the person who lives here, who takes photos and can't keep a plant alive to save herself, she doesn't really exist anymore."

"Your world's bigger now and some things have changed. Though, you may not be any better at watering your plants," he eyed the brown leaves of a Bonsai tree sitting on the end table in the living room. "But you're still you. Your life's just more complex now."

"That's putting it mildly," I chuckled.

He kissed the top of my head. "Take a few minutes to yourself and I'll worry about the world ending until you get back." He pulled back and smiled.

"Gee, thanks. That makes me feel so much better." I rolled my eyes and shook my head.

"I'll also see what I can do about that plant," he joked.

"I think it's called the trash."

He faked shock and horror at the idea of throwing away the dead plant.

Heading down the hall to my bedroom, I couldn't help but think back to when Robert so rudely invited himself into my home. It seems ridiculous now, that I was ever upset with him for staying here. When all I wanted was to get back to that.

I pulled a bag from my closet and shoved random articles of clothing into the duffle. Really, it didn't matter what I grabbed, so long as I had the essentials.

Scanning the room for anything else I should bring with me, I spotted William's journal on the nightstand. I smiled as I thought of William's whimsical musing and experiments and I wondered how I ever could have forgotten him.

Sitting on the edge of the bed and plopping my bag down next to me, I picked up the journal. As I flipped through the pages, the familiar handwriting sent a wave of nostalgia through me. Even though I didn't know William personally, he felt like an old friend, someone I could turn to who always had the answers.

I flipped past a couple more pages, stopping halfway through the journal, and started to read. It looked like an ingredient list he'd stopped working on mid-way. Turning the page, I scanned William's words when *Le Fay* popped out at me.

Immediately, I was on my feet and marching down the hall. "Robert," I called out to him without looking up from the journal.

"What is it?" He asked, rounding the corner, a stunning orb humming in his palm.

"This," I said, holding up the journal. "I don't know why neither of us thought of it before."

"Is that William's?" The orb disappeared, and he reached for the journal. "What should we have thought of before?"

"Le Fay," I said, excited. "I remember reading that he and Constance were involved with taking down Le Fay back then."

"That's right." Robert walked away and flipped through the pages. "And I believe there was mention of an artifact or something that Le Fay was after during William's time."

I followed him into the living room.

"That I don't remember, but I still haven't gone through everything," I admitted.

"It's here somewhere." He combed through the journal as he took a seat on the couch.

Sitting next to him, I was close enough that our legs pressed together so I could read the pages he was flipping through.

"Here." He pointed to the middle of a page.

"We fear that Ian," I started to read. "Ian?" My heart sunk into my stomach. "You don't think... he means, the same man who tried to kill me?"

Robert shrugged. "I doubt it, but anything's possible, I guess. Merlin is proof of that."

My eyes darted back to the page, and I started reading again.

"We fear that Ian's another step closer to Elysium. If it is so, Le Fay may be able to carry out Morgana's wishes in her wake. Constance is still trying to uncover her betrothed's involvement, and she hopes to delve into their world unnoticed. Although I am against this plan, if she can confirm or deny that Le Fay does indeed have knowledge of Elysium, then we might have a chance to change the course of history."

"Do you know what Elysium is?" I asked when I finished reading.

He shook his head. "I've never heard of it, outside of William."

"Is there anything else, do you think?" I flipped to the next page.

He held his hand over the journal and recited a spell. The pages flipped back and forth until the journal froze open like a dome. Each page stood straight on its end, and as he ran his fingers across the top of the worn paper, half a dozen of them came to life in a soft yellow light.

"Is that every mention of Elysium?" I looked between him and the journal.

"It would seem that way." The corner of his mouth turned up.

"Let's see what else he has to say." A thrill of excitement ran through me, and I leaned closer.

Robert fingered through a few of the pages, picking one at random. The paper was still glowing when he pressed it down flat so we could both read.

It would appear that Le Fay commissioned the Cook expeditions. Whatever they think they've found is leading them to the other side of the world, outside of our reach and influence. The next fleet of ships is set to sail in a week; if we don't find a way to stop them, we may be too late.

"Cook expeditions? Do you know what he's talking about?" I said, reading the page again.

"I know of the James Cook expeditions, but not any specifics," Robert pursed his lips.

"I wish I could sit William down and talk to him," I huffed. "There's always so much more to his writing than the written words can portray."

"William may be helpful, but he's not gonna spell out the answers for us. His life is already lived, and it's not like he knew we'd be reading this and searching for answers."

"I could try to *see* if there's something else, something more?" I suggested. "Of all my visions, he's always been the easiest to see."

"How many times have you visited William?" Robert studied me.

"Oh, you know, just a few times here and there. He's an interesting person and a lot of fun to watch."

"I never thought of him as fun when I was reading him." Robert's smile reached his eyes. "But then again, what a man writes down doesn't always define who he is off the page."

"I wish you could see him the way I do, the love he has for Constance, the passion he has for his work, and the friends he surrounds himself with." My heart felt lighter as I thought of William and his fun, easy lifestyle.

"Maybe there's a way," he said, giving me a shy grin. "If you're up for it."

"What is it?"

"Do you remember when Merlin was teaching us how our shared Magic works?"

"Of course." The familiar thrum of our Magic hummed deep inside me.

"And do you remember when we connected, I was able to have a vision with you?"

"You want to try to see William? I thought the whole thing freaked you out."

"It wasn't a picnic, that's for sure," he shrugged. "But I'm sure if I got used to it, it wouldn't be so bad."

"We can try," I said hesitantly. "But we should find a better memory to tap into so we can get the most out of William."

"Alright, let's check the next page."

He flipped to the next glowing page and again held the journal out for both of us to read.

Today is filled with bleak news. We thought we attained the location of Elysium, but the coordinates led to a decoy location. Whoever crafted the clues to Elysium knew what they were doing.

"What do you think Elysium is?" I asked.

"It could be anything, really," he shrugged.

"You're not curious?" I furrowed my brow. "I mean, William and Constance are fighting for their world against Le Fay, just like we are."

He opened his mouth to speak, and I raised one finger and said, "Doesn't it make you wonder if it's all connected?"

"Well." He shrugged. "Of course, it's connected through the Le Fay aspect, but their war is not ours. They weren't fighting Morgana, they were fighting her ideals."

"Maybe." I let my fingers brush over the page. "It just feels like it means something more. When you gave me this journal, you said that it would speak to me, that Magic lived in every word. What if William's trying to tell us something?"

He looked at me for a moment considering my words and said, "Or it's a small detail in a war that was fought hundreds of years ago."

"You really don't believe that, do you?" I had to fight not to roll my eyes. "This can't be some insignificant detail."

Since when was I the one trying to convince him that Magic could be at play here?

"I don't deny it might mean something, I just don't think it's our biggest problem right now."

"Well, I can't argue with that," I sighed and looked down at the journal in my hands with a nagging feeling in the pit of my stomach.

He reached out and tucked my hair behind my ear, letting his hand linger on my cheek. "After everything that's happened..."

His voice trailed off and his eyes fell to his lap.

"We've all lost so much more than I could have imagined when I set out on this path. Annabel, Lila and you most of all." He finally met my eyes. "When I… seeing you standing there, the life in your eyes replaced with Vivian's, it was like you died right in front of me."

"Oh, Robert." I touched his arm.

"And Lila," he sighed. "I'm a Healer, Violet."

"I know." There wasn't anything I could say to ease his pain. What he was dealing with was so much bigger than guilt.

"My mentor, Felix, drilled into me that life is precious and that we must always exercise restraint with our gift."

"Every life saved is a life taken," I repeated the words he once said to me and squeezed his arm.

"My appreciation for how delicate life is goes beyond what anyone else can understand."

"I get what you're saying, and I know that what we went through isn't easy for either of us. But Robert, you couldn't have saved Lila."

"And you?"

"I'm still here." I placed a hand on his leg and his eyes held mine with a fury that made me flush.

"You are and you aren't. Vivian..." he blinked and looked away from me.

"Vivian's the only one who can put a stop to Morgana."

"On paper, I get that. But it's my heart that's paying the price for what's happened to you. It's my moral fiber, the essence of who I am that aches with the loss we've suffered, that you've suffered."

"You're not alone in this. You always lecture me about letting people in. You have just as many people who love you and care about you. This is war, Robert. You can't let everything that's happened in the past cloud your judgment and make you question who you are. Not right now."

He let out a heavy breath and said, "And the student becomes the teacher." He smiled and placed his hand over mine. "I'll get through this, it's just gonna take me some time."

I leaned closer to him, placing my hand on his chest and my lips against his.

His hand found its way into my hair and his other arm wrapped around the small of my back, pulling me closer. He was gentle, cautious as he deepened the kiss and I melted against his chest. All the pain, loss, and sorrow poured out of me as I pressed closer to him. The pieces of my heart shattered beyond repair, the hole in my soul, were a little easier to ignore with his arms wrapped around me.

I only meant to give him a quick kiss, but the need burning through both of us propelled me forward. The journal fell to the floor as I slid my leg over his lap and I was straddling him.

His hands ran up the length of my spine as the kiss turned from soft and gentle to rough and eager. The heat of his skin through his sweater pressed against me, inviting me in. Even though we'd only been close like this a few times, I missed it. The heat of his lips against mine, the calloused touch of his hands on my skin.

"Violet," he pulled away half an inch. His lips were still close enough that I could feel his breath mingle with my own.

"Yeah," I breathed.

"Whatever happens next, promise me we're in this together."

He pulled my face to his so our foreheads were touching. "No more secrets, no more lies."

"I promise," I said, and he tilted my chin and kissed me again.

As he wrapped his arm around my waist, he shifted his weight and flipped me onto my back. Hovering above me, he took off his sweater and tossed it behind him. Reaching up, I pulled on his shirt, and that also found a home on the floor somewhere.

Our fingers intertwined as his lips made their way back to mine. This time, it was like a bomb went off. Our Artognou Magic sprung to life stronger than I've ever felt, and I whimpered at the intensity.

"You feel it too?" Robert breathed.

"Mmhmm, but why now?" I managed to get out.

"Our emotions are close to the surface, I'd guess," he said and kissed my neck.

My heart was beating so hard, I could hear it in my ears and every nerve in my body cried out as our Magic itched for release. The warmth of Robert's Magic flooded me and though I didn't need healing, the familiar sensation sent a wave of pleasure through me.

"This is so surreal," I gasped as his finger ran down the length of my arm. Goosebumps covered my arms and chest as his mouth found mine again.

The broken parts of us started to heal and mold themselves back together. I could feel his pain mingle with my own and I knew deep in my soul how much we both needed this. No matter what the future may hold, at least we'd have this one moment in time when everything was at peace.

CHAPTER 5

 IVIAN

BIRDS CHIRPED NEARBY, pulling me from my slumber. Stretching my legs, I was acutely aware of a body pressed against the length of me, warm and content.

"Morning," a husky male voice said above me.

Gently extricating myself from him, the cold sheets against my naked skin made me shiver.

"What's wrong?"

I turned toward him and understanding lit up his eyes. "Though I can't say it's unpleasant waking in your arms, I think it unfair for all involved to pretend I'm still the one you fell asleep with."

He cleared his throat and sat up. "I'm sorry, I didn't—"

I raised my hand, "No need for apologies, we're all getting used to the new order of things," I said over my shoulder, my eyes lingering on his bare chest.

Well done, Violet. I thought.

"We should get back to the others," he said.

"Are they not here?"

"This is Violet's place. We came by to get a few of her things and, well..." he motioned to the bag on the floor, spilling over with Violet's personal items.

"I see." I smiled as I wrapped the sheet around my body. "Is there somewhere I can freshen up?"

"Right, yes, of course." He grabbed a blanket off the bed and wrapped it around his waist. "It's just through here," he said, pushing a door open and revealing another room.

"You haven't seen a washroom like this before, have you?" he asked.

"It's been a while since I've had a body to worry about, yes."

"I think you'll find things have changed quite a bit." He motioned me forward and stepped into the smaller room.

He twisted a handle and water sprung forward like a waterfall into a small rectangular basin.

"You can change the temperature here." He pointed to the other handle.

"Thank you." I let my sheet fall to the ground.

His eyes darted to the ceiling. "If you need anything, I'll be down the hall." He cleared his throat and made his way out of the room, closing the door behind him.

As I stepped under the stream of water, the heat cascaded down my skin and soothed the raw ache in my bones. I closed my eyes and let my head fall back, allowing the waterfall to run through my hair.

Running my hands over my arms, I familiarized myself with this new body. Violet's frame was small, but as I stretched up onto my toes, the muscles in her legs, our legs, flexed and tighten effortlessly. She may be petite, but it was evident she kept up on her physical training.

I reached for one of the many bottles on the shelf to my left. Unscrewing the top, I sniffed at the contents and a delicate aroma of roses wafted from the bottle. With my eyes closed, I could almost pretend I was back in Camelot, walking through the fields just beyond the castle walls.

Pouring the mixture into my hands, I rubbed it through my hair and over my body. As my hand moved over my torso, the raised, smooth skin of a scar gave me pause.

This Waker was different from the others. She was a fighter, a survivor. The simple fact that I could still feel her in the corner of my mind was proof of her strength. How long she could maintain her presence in the body would remain to be seen.

Rinsing off, I turned the knob Robert had earlier, and the water vanished.

Cool air touched my skin as I stepped out of the little room and I relished in the feel of gooseflesh crawling over my body. Droplets of water cascaded down my skin to the rug under my feet as my fingers brushed through my hair. With practiced hands, I formed a plait off of one shoulder and made my way back to the sleeping chamber.

Off to one corner was a wood chest with portraits and other personal items strewn across the top. Opening one of the drawers, I found a few articles of clothing. Unsure of what was appropriate attire, I looked over my shoulder at the clothes discarded the night before. A pair of trousers and a fitted top lay haphazardly, along with undergarments that were much too small for my modesty.

I searched for something similar and settled on a top that showed off the arch of my collar bone and the swell of my chest and a pair of trousers. All of Violet's clothing was much more revealing than anything I'd ever worn before, but I had to admit, the trousers were just about the most comfortable and practical article of clothing I've ever had the pleasure of wearing.

Grabbing the bag Violet packed, I left the bedroom behind and made my way down the hall. Images of people and places lined the walls. I paused at the last one, taking in the unique art of capturing a moment so clearly.

A man looked down at a woman as she touched his face, her smile reaching her eyes as she stared up at him.

"They were Violet's parents," Robert said behind me.

His hair was now neatly in place and the soft scent of his cologne wafted over me.

"It's curious to see something captured so vividly." I touched the edge of the image.

"It's called photography," he chuckled.

"What's so amusing?" I turned away from the portrait and met his eyes.

"Violet's a photographer. Most of these photos are her own work." He motioned down the hall and his lips twitched with the hint of a smile. "It's odd, having to explain a photo to you, when it's Violet's whole life."

"I'm surprised?" I looked back down the hall. "From the feel of her Magic inside me, the scars on her body, I wouldn't have thought her to be a gentle artist."

"She had another life before Magic turned everything upside down." He pinched his lips together and looked at his feet.

"Some of us live a thousand lifetimes in one." A wave of emotion coursed through me as I thought of all those who perished upon waking me.

"Shall we?" he asked.

I took one last look at the couple in the portrait and nodded my head.

Robert led the way and explained the world around me. Time had galloped forward in great leaps in my absence, leaving little that felt familiar to me.

Being called upon is always a jarring experience and never without turbulence. After all, I'm thrust into another person's life, in a time outside of my own. But Violet's world is unlike anything I'd encountered before.

After a short journey, we arrived at his family's home. I was still reeling at how quickly we covered so much ground when Robert said, "I'm sure everyone will have questions for you." We walked up a stone path to a large wood door. "We didn't get much of a chance to talk before you…"

"Before Violet took control," I finished for him.

Without pausing, Robert pushed the door open, and I followed him inside. The dark wood was a familiar sight, and the heaviness in my chest eased with each step. Magic lived in these walls and it made it feel more like home. My body relaxed at the small comfort and the tension in the pit of my stomach eased.

"Took you long enough," a woman said from the top of the stairs.

"Brett," Robert called to the woman. "It's no longer Violet who's with us."

"Oh," Brett took the stairs two at a time. "My apologies."

"Apologies are quite unnecessary," I waved her off. "Remind me of who you are again, will you?

"I'm Brett, everyone's in the kitchen. Why don't we properly introduce ourselves," Brett motioned for us to follow her.

Brett wrapped her arm over Robert's shoulders, whispering something in his ear which made him elbow her and they both laughed. There was a warmth in this home, a camaraderie that reminded me of days gone by in Arthur's court.

"Pay up." Brett held out her hand as she bounced over to a blonde man and wrapped her arms around his neck.

"You placed bets on us, Matty?" Robert frowned.

"Just on when you'd make it back, nothing else," Matty shrugged.

"I'd like to formally introduce you to my meddlesome family," Robert motioned around the room.

"You've met my sister, Brett, and that's Matthew she's wrapped herself around. Jake's our brother, who you met at the lake and this is Becky." He placed a hand on the woman's shoulders.

"I'm basically like Violet's sister." Becky folded her arms over her chest and looked me up and down.

"It's very nice to meet you all," I said. "And I understand it's difficult to look upon your friend's face and know she's not the one who's speaking with you." I stepped forward and placed my hands on the counter in front of me. "There's much about this transition that's uncharted, but I do hope we can find our way through this together."

Five pairs of eyes stared at me without saying a word.

"Ahh, you're back," Merlin's voice rang through the kitchen. "How're you holding up?"

Merlin's eyes met mine and before I could answer, there was a knock on the door. Everyone's eyes shifted at the intrusion, but no one moved.

Another rap at the door and Robert stood. "What now?" He sighed.

Brett was quick on Robert's heels, followed by Jake.

"It's never a dull moment with this lot," Merlin said, extending his hand.

"I've never known a moment to be dull with you," I replied as we followed the others.

"Keep your guard up, no matter who's on the other side," Robert said under his breath as he reached for the door.

"Quite true," Merlin chuckled.

"Though, I do recall it was you creating all the drama for a time."

The front door creaked open and Robert said, "Can I help you?"

"We need to speak with Merlin." A deep booming voice caught mine and Merlin's attention.

My Magic flickered to life, eager and ready.

"And you are?" Robert held his ground.

"We're what's left of The Brotherhood of The Realms."

Merlin dropped my hand and pushed the others aside.

"What do you mean, what's left?" Merlin stepped forward.

"They're gone, all of them. Killed." The spokesmen of the group did his best to hide his emotions, but his glassy eyes gave him away.

"How do we know you're who you say you are?" Jake pushed himself in front of Robert.

The man speaking for the group looked at the others and nodded his head once. Each of them pulled their shirt aside to reveal their chest. Over their left breast, The Helm of Awe was branded on each of their skin. An intricate symbol that only the Brotherhood could bear to carry.

"What's your name, Brother?" Merlin asked.

Though I knew the Brotherhood well, the fear in their eyes sent an anxious chill through my heart. They were not easily run off and if it was true, if they were the only ones left of their kind, then we were far worse off than anyone realized.

"Brother Halvar, servant of the seven sisters." He placed his hand on his chest and bowed his head.

"Welcome Halvar," Merlin said. "Please do come in and regale us with your tale."

Halvar took one step forward and Robert moved to block his path.

Robert's eyes met my own before they flicked back to Merlin. "Are you sure we should be—"

"You can trust them," Merlin interrupted him. "This isn't another one of Morgana's tricks."

The Brothers' eyes shifted to one another with the mention of Morgana's name, and Violet's anxiety fluttered under my breast.

"What is it about Morgana?" I asked, stepping forward.

"It's true, we're not involved with the witch, but our arrival here is her doing."

"Explain," I demanded, as adrenaline burned through my veins.

Merlin turned toward me and pierced me with a stare that would nail anyone else to the wall. "Is it your wish to delay their refuge?"

"I only want to be sure of their intentions," I shot back, unafraid of his temper.

"We've nowhere else to go," a man from the back of the group spoke up.

"Adelram, hold your tongue," Halvar snapped. "My apologies. It's been a trying time for us all."

Merlin looked at me again, awaiting my decision about these men. He may not agree with my assessment, but he learned long ago to trust my instincts.

But was it my intuition that was telling me something was off, or was the dread in the pit of my stomach a result of living with Violet squirming around inside me? I searched their faces, each one somber, each of their eyes haunted.

I nodded my head once and Merlin turned back to the Brothers and ushered them inside.

"Tell us everything," Merlin said as he led Halvar through the house.

Robert moved to my side as Merlin led the Brothers further into the house

"Is there a reason for your mistrust?" I asked under my breath.

"We've been here before," Robert replied, once the last of the brothers turned a corner and were out of sight.

"And we were betrayed," Jake said, sidling up to Robert. "You really think this is a good idea?"

"No," Robert said, closing the door.

"We need to find out if they're telling the truth," Brett agreed.

"I may be able to help with that," I said.

"How so?" Robert asked.

My lips curled up at the corner. "Let me show you." I held out my hand.

Brett reached for my hand, but Robert grabbed her wrist and stopped us from touching.

"What's your interest in this?" Robert asked.

"Robert, she isn't the one in question," Brett snapped back, and pulled her hand free.

"True, but she's not Violet, and Vivian is loyal to Merlin. Why help us, instead of trusting him?" Jake jumped in.

"It's because of Violet I fear something is not right," I said.

"What do you mean?" Robert's eyes searched mine and, for the first time, he didn't flinch at the sight of me.

"I can't be sure, but I've learned to trust my intuition. I think it best we investigate things for ourselves."

"I'm in." Brett reached her hand out for me to grab.

"Anyone else?" I asked.

"If Morgana sent them, I want to know." Jake placed his hand on top of Brett.

"I need you to stay here and keep an eye on things," Robert said to Jake as he nodded his head in the direction Merlin and the Brothers had disappeared.

"You sure?" Jake asked.

"Someone needs to keep an eye on them," Brett said, placing a hand on Jake's shoulder.

Jake nodded and turned on his heel. "Be safe."

"Let's go." Robert grabbed my hand, the heat of his skin warming my fingers.

I closed my eyes and pictured the stone walls and open sky the Brothers called home and let my Magic take over.

CHAPTER 6

IVIAN

DARKNESS SURROUNDED the three of us and I wondered if my Magic had failed me. Looking to the heavens, millions of stars dotted the night sky along with all the worlds belonging to the realms the Brothers protected.

"Is this the right place?" Brett said under her breath.

"Yes," I answered. "But it's not as I remember."

"*Inlihtnes,*" Robert cast an illumination spell and the stone walls brightened around us.

"Where are we exactly?" Robert asked as he looked around the stone corridor.

"This is the realm in which the Brothers survey all other realms," I said. "If truly they were attacked—"

My heart skipped a beat and then raced forward as if I were running for my life. Gripping my chest, I took a deep breath and leaned against the stone wall.

"Are you alright?" Robert's hand reached out to me, but he pulled back at the last moment.

"Fine," I managed through gritted teeth. "If all is not well with the Brotherhood." I took another deep breath and ignored my heart, trying to leap out of my chest. "We should see some sign of it here."

"The stars," Brett said under her breath as she stared at the sky.

"Violet said something about a night sky in her vision." Robert looked up as well. "Maybe this is what she saw."

I couldn't recall Violet's vision, though the satisfied feeling spreading through my chest indicated he may be right.

"I believe she may have," I said.

The sound of stones tumbling across the ground caught our attention and, without hesitation, Robert and Brett raised their shields.

"I think it best I refrain from using my Magic, lest we get stranded here," I said, stepping behind them.

"I think that's a great idea," Brett said.

"Shall we?" Robert nodded in the direction the noise had come from.

As we moved forward, the illuminator orbs bobbed ahead of us, lighting the path and leading us further into the labyrinth.

"Is it always this quiet?" Robert whispered as we came to a fork in the path.

"It can be," I said faintly. "To the left." I directed them.

Violet's anxiety squirmed inside me, leaving me with a lump in my throat as we continued.

"I've never known someone outside of the Brotherhood to have been here before," Robert said, keeping his shield firmly in front of him.

"That's because no one knows where we are, exactly." My eyes drifted to the sky, and Merlin's voice echoed in my head.

"Every realm has a path to this one. Every world a link to the Brothers and their protection."

"And only those who've been invited are able to access this place," I finished.

"You were invited?" Robert asked as Brett moved further ahead of us.

"Many moons ago, after my split with Nimue."

Brett turned the corner ahead of us and yelped.

"What is it?" Robert ran toward her, his footsteps echoing in the darkness as I followed close behind.

Rounding the corner, the shape of a man pressed against the wall came into focus.

"I thought he was standing guard." Brett's hand covered her mouth as she stared at him.

As I moved closer, I noticed the daggers punched through his flesh all the way to the stone, keeping him upright. His eyes were still open, but the blood on his body had dried some time ago.

"Help me get him down," I said.

Brett and I shuffled to either side of the man and braced for his weight. Robert pulled the daggers from his body one by one until he was free and slumped over us. Guiding him to the floor, Robert's hands went right for his jugular and his Magic lit up his fingertips.

"Dead," Robert said as he closed the Brother's eyes. "May you find peace," he said, placing his hand on the man's chest.

Another sound of something being dragged across the ground reached our ears. There was someone, or something, still here.

Robert stepped in front of us and raised his shield.

"We should keep moving," his words were barely a whisper.

I nodded, and though I knew I should refrain from using Magic, I pulled the familiar power to my fingertips.

"Descendit," Robert spoke in a hushed voice and the light from the illuminator orbs dimmed.

Navigating through the narrow passageway, the hairs on the back of my neck prickled as a memory that was not my own flashed across my mind.

Pushing past Robert, I knelt in the shadows and there was another body.

"How did you know he was there?" Brett asked.

"Because Violet saw this before. She was here." I looked up at Robert. "She did see the attack."

A strangled breath sounded up ahead, and I rushed toward it.

"Vivian," Robert called after me, but I ignored him.

The passage opened into a large circular room with an altar off to my right. Bodies littered the floor, and the starlight twinkled off of the dark crimson pool of blood in the middle of the room.

"Show yourself," I called out, and my voice echoed off the silent stone walls.

"We're here to help," Robert said. The illuminator orbs brightened as they swirled around the chamber, and the horrors of what happened here came into full focus.

"By the stars," I said under my breath.

The gurgling sound of someone choking on their own tongue caught our attention.

"Over here," Brett yelled, waving frantically.

Robert moved swift and agile, crossing the room in the blink of an eye.

"Keep your guard up." I searched the room for any other signs of life, friend or foe.

The sound of Robert and Brett struggling to free the half-dead man reached my ears, but my eyes stayed glued to the crimson pool of blood ahead of me. The calm surface of the

Brothers' torment rippled as if a breeze passed through the room, but I knew better.

Magic danced to the surface of my skin and white sparks sprung to my fingers.

"Can you hear me?" Robert's voice echoed around us. "We're here to help," he said to the lifeless Brother.

"I don't think he understands," Brett argued as I took a step toward the now pulsing pool of blood.

"It's not working," Robert's voice barely met my ears as each of my senses tuned into the hum emanating from the center of the room.

"Try again," Brett's muffled voice sounded like she was talking in slow motion.

Another step forward and I was standing at the edge of the Brother's lifeblood, staring at my reflection.

The ripples halted, and my reflection morphed into a face that was not my own. Her eyes were black as ink and every feature was a hard line, as if she'd been etched from stone.

"Vivian, what a long time it's been," Nimue smirked up at me.

"Not long enough," I sneered.

Her lips twitched into an unnatural smile. "Still harboring resentment, I see."

"What do you want Nimue?"

"I want to offer you a chance to fight on the side of the victors."

"You won't win this war." I shook my head.

"Still so naïve." She clicked her tongue in disapproval.

"Vivian, we need to get him out of here." Robert's voice reached me, but I ignored him.

"It's not naïve to fight for what's right. It takes strength and power to march against adversity no matter how dim things may seem."

"Save your breath. Your desire to nurture the weak has

always been your downfall," she barked. "Accept my offer of mercy or suffer the same fate as your precious mortals."

"I will not bend to the darkness that consumes you."

Her lips curled into a smile. "Very well."

Her reflection shimmered, and she was gone.

"Vivian?" Brett yelled, snapping me back to the present.

"I can't heal him," Robert said. "We need to get him to Merlin."

"Merlin can't help him," I said.

"What do you mean?" Robert's eyes snapped in my direction.

"When death finds them, only the Brothers can sway the scales and save a life."

"We have bigger problems," Brett said, walking toward me, her arms outstretched, with Magic crackling up and down her limbs.

Following her gaze, I turned back to the pool of blood. It moved of its own accord, rising into the air like a curtain.

"Is this a Brotherhood thing?" Brett asked.

"No." I squared my shoulders and started to draw on my Magic. "This is Nimue."

I raised my hands high above me and released my shield. The white gold brilliance washed away all other colors as Nimue's Magic searched for a way past my barrier.

"I don't know how much time I have," I yelled over the roar of Magic. "You don't want to end up stranded here."

"I can't leave him behind," Robert yelled as the blood rose to the height of the stone pillars and pressed against my Magic.

"Bring him if you must," I yelled over my shoulder.

The full weight of Nimue's Magic forced itself against my shield and my knees buckled.

Violet stirred inside me, her Magic pulsing to life, but now was not the time. We needed to make our escape, or they'd be stuck in this realm until my return.

With every ounce of strength I had in my body, I forced

Violet into the background and let my Magic erupt from every pore.

Shaking with the effort, I kept Nimue's torment at bay. I tried to call for Brett and Robert to hurry, but no words escaped from my lips. My vision started to blur and the edges of my shield began to fracture.

"Let's go." Brett placed a hand on my shoulder.

I closed my eyes and let my shield drop. The violent roar of Nimue's Magic galloped toward us and with my last shred of strength, I let my Magic take us.

The stench of death was quickly replaced with the smell of wood and vanilla as my knees hit the floor with an audible *thud* and I lost myself to the abyss.

VIVIAN IN THE DARK

Nimue is too strong...

I have to warn them...

I can't stay here...

I have to go back...

CHAPTER 7

IOLET

I woke to the sound of muffled voices and a splitting headache. My body throbbed in places I didn't even know could feel sore. Pushing myself upright, I looked around Robert's bedroom.

Okay, we're still at the Maxwell estate, I thought. But why on earth did it feel like I've been in the gym for twenty-four hours straight? I pressed my palms against my eyes to rub the sleep from them and even my eyeballs were sore.

Forcing myself out of bed, I made my way to the window and pulled the curtains open. Looking out over the water, a grey blanket of clouds hovered in the sky, making it impossible to tell what time of day it was.

The sound of someone hitting a mat reached my ears, and I noticed Becky sparring with Robert in the backyard. Robert helped her to her feet, and she swung toward him. Turning on his heel, he blocked her punch effortlessly, but she kept at it, pushing him around the blue mats and keeping him on the defense. I had a sneaking suspicion he was going much easier on her than he ever did with me. Still, I'd have to thank him later for training her. What with everything going on, I was glad he still took it to heart that I wanted her safe.

Crossing the room, I wondered if maybe Vivian had been training too, getting her sea legs, so to speak. It would account for the knot taking up residence behind my right shoulder blade.

Opening the medicine cabinet, I grabbed some ibuprofen and caught a glimpse of myself in the mirror.

The shadows under my eyes were a deep purple and my cheekbones looked sharper, harder than I remembered.

I tossed a few pills into my mouth and turned the faucet on. Scooping a handful of water into my mouth, I washed them down in one big gulp.

The sound of people arguing somewhere beyond the bedroom door reached my ears. While I should probably find out what was going on, the throbbing in my head kept me from moving.

Taking another long look at my reflection, I decided a bath was the only thing I could handle at the moment. And it would allow the medicine to kick in before I had to face everyone.

I turned the water on and threw some bath salts into the tub. Wincing as I lifted my shirt over my head, again I wondered what the hell Vivian was getting up to and how long had I been out? Hours? Days?

Dipping my toe in the water to test the temperature, I eased into the hot bath. The steam made the tiny hairs on my arm stand up and beads of sweat started to form on my brow as I lowered myself into the tub. The tightness in my chest eased as the heat of the water sunk into my bones.

The familiar hum of my Magic slowly pulsed through me like waves crashing and receding on the shore and I closed my eyes.

I was alive. Against all odds, I was still here to fight another day, even if I was sharing my body with an ancient mythical figure. It wasn't ideal, but at least I still had a fighting chance instead of being lost to The Lady forever.

Grah- Merlin may have an interest in what happens to me, but if I'm going to survive this, I couldn't count on anyone but myself. This was my life and my fight. Vivian and I couldn't live like this forever.

Turning the faucet off with my toes, I settled back and let my senses take over.

Searching for the Artognou Magic inside me, I came across something foreign and unnatural curled in the pit of my stomach.

Vivian, I thought.

There was something sinister about her Magic as it churned through me, stronger than I could ever have imagined. A shiver pulsed up and down my skin despite being submerged in the hot water and I turned my focus away from her waiting Magic.

Searching for my connection to Robert, relief washed over me the moment I touched our Artognou Magic. I didn't know how to get out of this mess, but maybe our connection might lead me in the right direction.

Taking a deep breath, my chest rose above the water line and dipped back into the hot bath, sending goosebumps across my neck and chest. Grabbing hold of our Artognou Magic, I started to put up my mental walls one by one, shielding me from external and, in this case, internal influences, too.

If I could keep Vivian at bay for longer periods of time, then I might have a chance to pull myself free of her influence. It was worth a shot, wasn't it?

Deliberately, I cleared my mind the way my aunt taught me.

Just like always, Robert was the only thing left once I cleared my mind. Moving across the empty space of my mind, I kept my entire focus on him, the shape of his shoulders, the stubble on his cheeks, the shadows under his eyes. Most importantly, I held onto the warmth that radiated off of him.

As I reached out to touch him, his hand made an identical movement, as if he were my reflection. My eyes flicked up to him and he placed his index finger over my lips to keep me from speaking.

A fluttered passed through me, faint but sure as his finger left my lips. Chasing the familiar feeling, I reached up and placed my hand on his chest. The hum of our Magic bloomed under my rib cage and I let out a shaky breath.

His fingers wrapped around my wrist and he pulled me closer to him. Our eyes held onto one another and a breeze brushed my hair over my shoulders. I wanted to see what was causing the surrounding wind, but I couldn't move.

A bright bluish glow bloomed somewhere to my right, lighting up Robert's face and sending goosebumps across my skin.

A knock on the bathroom door and someone clearing their throat brought me crashing back to reality.

"Yes?" I called out, deflated. It would seem my alone time was up.

"Violet, is that you?" Robert asked through the door.

"It's me, at least for the moment." I pushed myself up and grabbed a towel.

"Everything okay?" He sounded anxious on the other side of the door. "I felt something."

Standing with my body exposed to the elements, I wrapped a towel around myself.

"Sorry," I said, opening the door. "I was trying something."

His body filled the frame of the doorway as his eyes danced up and down the length of me. There was a sheen of sweat across his brow and he was still in his workout gear.

"Care to fill me in on your experiment?" He stepped to the side, granting me passage into the bedroom.

"I need to fix this setup, Vivian, and I have going on," I said. "I mean, I don't know how long I've been out or why my body feels like I was hit by a truck. Let alone what's been happening while I've been…" I wasn't sure how to finish that sentence. I wasn't away or sleeping exactly. I just wasn't conscious or in control for periods of time.

"It's been about four days since you were last yourself," he said, following me into the bedroom.

"Four days?" I turned on my heel and he stopped a few inches short of me. "Four days," I said again under my breath.

His lips formed into a tight-lipped smile. "And a lot's happened. Your vision of the Brothers, it wasn't something from the past."

The image of a wall of blood barreling down on me flashed before my eyes.

"Nimue and Morgana slaughtered the Brotherhood of The Realms," Robert continued. "The few that escaped arrived here a few nights ago."

"You were there," I said as another of Vivian's memories pulsed through me.

"Yes." He reached out and touched my arm. "It was awful. Nimue and Morgana, they—"

"We have to stop them, I know," I said. "But we have to fix this," I motioned up and down my body.

"I don't know how." Robert's eyes were bloodshot, as if he hadn't slept in days, and my heart ached for him.

"I was thinking maybe our bond might help."

"I don't think Magic can fix this," he sighed. "It only seems to make you both weaker." His hand reached out and traced my cheekbone.

"There has to be a way to manage when we slip in and out of control."

"From what Merlin said, this is uncharted territory. I don't think anyone knows what is and isn't possible, not even Vivian."

"I have to try something. I can't just stand by—"

"I know," Robert interrupted me. "And we will. But I need you to promise me, you won't use Magic until we know more."

I opened my mouth to argue, but just like in my vision, he placed his finger over my lips to keep me quiet.

"Vivian's stronger than anyone I've ever met, and she barely got us back home before she lost her hold on reality." His eyes bore into mine, rooting me in place. "Whatever this is, it's beyond our scope of understanding. Until we figure this out, promise me you'll refrain from using Magic."

It was a request, but I could hear the desperate demand in his voice. I wanted to tell him what he wanted to hear, but I couldn't lie to him. I wouldn't.

"There's no way we'll be able to stop Morgana and Nimue if I can't use Magic. It defeats the whole point of waking Vivian."

"I know." He ran his hand through his hair.

A knock at the door startled us both, and we jumped a part.

"Come in," I called over Robert's shoulder.

Brett stepped into the room. "He's finally awake, and they want to speak with you."

"Who is?" I asked, searching for something to wear.

"You haven't caught her up yet?" Brett's eyes bounced between the two of us.

"I was getting to it," Robert retorted.

"Mm-hmm." She rolled her eyes.

"We'll be down in a minute," I said, wiggling into a pair of jeans under my towel.

Brett made her exit, closing the door behind her.

"Who's awake? What's she talking about?" I asked as I picked through a pile of clothes.

"We found one of the Brothers still alive when we went to their realm."

"You did?" With my back turned to him, I slipped into a sports bra and let the towel fall around my feet.

"I couldn't heal him, but I couldn't just leave him either."

"Of course you couldn't," I said, keeping my voice light. "Even if it was only half as bad as my vision, seeing that first-hand had to be awful." Pulling a sweatshirt over my head, I asked, "Out of curiosity, why did you go to their realm?"

"After everything with Annabel, we can't be sure who we can trust," he said, motioning me toward the door. "I thought it best we find out what happened in their realm. If they were really attacked or not."

Making our way downstairs, a flutter of nervous energy ran through me. Would everyone treat me differently now that Vivian and I shared a body?

"And you trust them now?" I asked as we reached the bottom of the stairs.

"Trust is a strong word," he whispered into my ear and placed a hand on the small of my back. "But I believe the story of what happened to them."

"The question is, how could something like this happen?" Jake said, catching up with us at the bottom of the stairs. The dark circles under his eyes and cold, hard stare made me do a double-take. Losing Annabel was taking its toll and though I wanted to ask if he was okay, it was clear that he was barely holding it together.

"What do you mean?" I asked instead.

"The Brotherhood is meant to protect all realms, and yet they couldn't protect themselves?" Jake raised his eyebrows high on his forehead and tilted his head.

"Like I said, trust is a strong word," Robert reiterated.

Jake shrugged, and his jaw flexed.

"If you ever need anything," I gave his arm a gentle squeeze.

"Actually..." Jake hesitated and his eyes shot to Robert. "Maybe I can pick your brain later." The desperation in his voice quaked deep in my heart.

"Of course."

A handful of men stood around the living room, watching

and waiting. They looked just like the men I'd seen in my vision and I froze mid-step. Their stoic expressions were impossible to read, but I knew first hand the pain they had endured. Unease settled in my stomach as they watched me move across the room, and their screams echoed in my memory.

The leader cleared his throat and everyone in the room went silent, as if they didn't want us to know what they were discussing.

"It's about time," Merlin's voice boomed. "I trust you're well, Violet?" His eyes met mine with a fierce intensity I wasn't prepared for.

"Fine, thanks," I said, moving around the couch. "Where are Ethan and Elodie?" I asked.

"They've gone to take care of other business," Merlin said, turning away from me. "Cian, this is the man who saved you." Merlin gestured awkwardly at Robert.

"That's a bit of an exaggeration."

"You brought him to us and that was more than enough," the older man by the fireplace spoke. "As you know, it is not our way to divulge information or interfere with the goings-on in any realm." He leveled his eyes at Robert. "But we will make an exception in this case, as thanks for saving Cian's life."

The man nodded once to Cian, who was sitting alone on the couch.

"Very well," Cian said as his eyes scanned me from head to toe before turning to Robert. "You may've wondered why Morgana and Nimue would attack us?" His eyebrow rose on his forehead.

"It crossed my mind," Robert said, keeping all emotion from his face.

"We guard many secrets," he paused and leaned forward. His forearm flexed as he leaned on his knee and again his eyes shot in my direction. "Secrets that, in the wrong hands, would do great harm."

"I'm aware of what the Brotherhood's role is." Robert folded his arms over his chest.

"Then you understand it comes at a great cost to reveal what we keep in the shadows."

"I do," Robert nodded his head.

"They seek a means to make Nimue's escape from the Shadowlands permanent."

"We assumed as much," Robert replied, as if he were ten steps ahead of Cian.

"There's only one way she can shed the chains of the Shadowlands." Cian's jaw flexed like he was struggling to get the words out. "She must find the Holy Grail and partake in the gift of immortality."

CHAPTER 8

IOLET

"The Holy Grail?" I leveled my eyes at Cian. "That's real?" I scanned the room and everyone's eyes were on me.

"Yes," Cian said, rising from the couch and stepping forward. "Though it's quite different from the tales your realm has portrayed." He took another step in my direction. "And so are you, Waker." He stopped a few inches away, forcing me to look up at him. There was something familiar, something that drew me to him.

"Cian," the leader of the group scolded him.

"My apologies, Halvar." Cian inclined his head and took a step back.

"Tell me you kept the Grail's location a secret," Merlin demanded.

The leader shook his head, and the floor began to shake as Merlin's hands balled into a fist.

"What have you told them?" Merlin said through gritted

teeth and while the rumbling settled, there was a charge to the air that made the hairs on the back of my neck stand at attention.

"They know as much as we do," Halvar said.

"Which isn't much," Cian chimed in. "The Grail's been unreachable for two hundred years. It's anyone's guess where-"

"You think that'll stand in her way?" Merlin barked.

"We don't imagine it will," Cian said. "That's why we're passing this information onto you."

"You're only disseminating this knowledge because you lack the ability to keep the Grail and this realm safe any longer," Merlin seethed.

Cian winced at Merlin's words and his eyes flicked to me like he knew I was watching him. His honey-colored eyes searched my face as if he was trying to see through me to the woman within, to Vivian.

"Where are they headed?" I asked Cian, pushing my shoulders back and shaking off the nerves from his gaze.

The corner of his mouth twitched, and he sat back down on the couch.

"The Valley of the Draig," Cian said, looking at his nails.

"What in the devil's name do they want with the Draig?" Anger radiated off of Merlin in waves, making the air in the room thick and uncomfortable. "They have nothing to do with the Grail," Merlin said.

"Don't they, though?" Halvar's words sounded like a challenge and something unsaid passed between him and Merlin.

"The Draig, who are they?" Robert asked.

"Warriors, unlike anything this world has seen for centuries," Cian explained. "They'd do just about anything to get their hands on the Grail, and they have. Whole worlds have been destroyed in their hunt for immortality."

"Morgana doesn't stand a chance against the Draig. Let them fight it out and we'll stay out of it," Merlin huffed.

"You mistake our warning," Cian mumbled. He glanced at Robert for a fraction of a second, then back at me.

"Then enlighten us." Robert stepped forward, placing the left side of his body in front of me, forcing Cian to look at him.

"Nimue and Morgana do not seek a war with the Draig. They want their help."

"Help?" I blurted. "What on earth do they need help with?"

"Their bloodline was wiped from this realm," Merlin snarled. "Without Draig blood, the gate can't be opened, I saw to it myself."

"What's he talking about?" Robert looked from Merlin to the leader of the Brotherhood.

"Are you really that naïve, Merlin?" Halvar asked, folding his arms over his chest.

"Tell us what you're getting at," Robert snapped.

"The Draig were once a plague on this realm," Cian began. "They took what they wanted without consequence. Burning whole villages, enslaving hordes of people to do their bidding and taking the women of this world for sport."

Listening to Cian's words, I could feel the terror rising inside me as if I could feel the pain and sorrow of every life the Draig touched.

"Their reign created a generation of Draig that were native to this realm," Cian continued. "A generation of offspring whose blood is both human and bound to the Valley of the Draig."

"As I said," Merlin snarled. "I took care of them."

"You killed them?" I turned to Merlin and, for the first time, fear crept into my heart as he stared back at me.

"Yes," Merlin said without hesitation. "They didn't belong here."

"But you failed in ridding this realm of said offspring," Cian said.

"There were survivors?" I asked.

"Three," Cian nodded. "And it is their blood, diluted through the generations, that will open the gate and unleash the Draig on this world."

"A common goal won't align them," Merlin interjected. "The Draig will not follow orders from anyone other than their own."

"Why does Morgana even need an army to find the Grail?" I asked.

"Do you want to tell them, or should I?" Halvar looked past me to Merlin.

All eyes swiveled toward Merlin, waiting for another of his secrets to come to light.

"The Grail was brought here for safe keeping," Merlin sighed. "After the Draig destroyed numerous realms in the hunt for the Grail."

"We thought the Grail would be safe in a realm where Magic only lived in the shadows," Cian explained.

"The Draig are hunters, trained and skilled beyond your understanding. If they're allowed into this realm, they'll find the Grail and take the immortality they've sought for thousands of years," Merlin explained.

"Then we shouldn't go after Morgana," I said. "We should go after the Grail."

"If the Draig are allowed into this realm, they will destroy everything you hold dear." Cian said, and his eyes flicked to Robert and back to mine.

"If Morgana and Nimue are left unchecked, they will use a Draig offspring and open the gate to the Valley of the Draig," Halvar said. "And they will find the Grail." His words settled over me, and the pit of my stomach felt like a rock.

Cian's eyes held mine as each word his elder spoke sunk into my bones. He knew something they weren't telling us.

"About that," Jake said. "Isn't this the type of situation you lot normally handle?"

"Yes, but given the circumstances, were not in a position of power at the moment."

"Because Morgana and Nimue found a way to your realm and killed most of you," Jake said, studying Halvar.

"I assume you have a point?" Halvar raised his chin in defiance.

"The Brotherhood are protectors of all realms, but conveniently you couldn't defend yourselves from Morgana and Nimue." Jake took a step forward. "Not only that, but somehow Morgana was able to gain access to your realm without your knowledge."

Halvar gritted his teeth and the muscles in his jaw flexed.

"I want to know how they accomplished the impossible so easily?" Jake folded his arms over his chest.

"That's something we'd like to find out as well," Halvar seethed.

"You want to know what I think?" Jake held the leader's glare and his hands balled into fists.

"I'm sure you're going to tell me."

"I think you have a rat amongst your ranks."

"Jake," Merlin's voice was a warning.

"And I don't think we can trust you," Jake finished.

"That's enough," Merlin barked and grabbed Jake by the arm.

"No," Robert whirled around on Merlin. "He's right. This shouldn't be our fight. This is bigger than us, and yet somehow we're being dragged into it."

Merlin stared at Robert for a pregnant moment, his eyes dancing back and forth.

"You may be right, but there's nothing to be done." Merlin let go of Jake's arm. "Morgana and Nimue must be stopped."

"At what cost?" Jake fired back. It didn't take a genius to deduce that he was talking about Annabel. He's already lost the love of his life to this war. A war he's only a part of because of me.

"You're right," I said, placing my hand on his chest. "This isn't your fight."

His chest heaved under my hand with each breath.

"It's mine and Vivian's. Whatever the cost, it's ours to pay."

"No," Robert argued.

"It's why I was meant to wake her. So others wouldn't have to suffer the cost."

Jake's eyes met mine and his head fell to one side.

"Violet, I didn't mean—"

"I know," I interrupted Jake.

"This isn't your fight either," Robert argued.

"It is," I said, turning to face him. "You and I both know it's what I'm destined for." The weight of what was to come sat heavy in my heart as I held Robert's eyes. I was already half gone and if I could help it, no one else would lose their life in this fight.

"No," Robert shook his head.

"We should head out as soon as we can." I turned to Merlin.

The corner of his mouth pulled up. "We'll need Vivian for this."

"I know," I said, reaching for my Magic.

Pulling the familiar sensation to the surface, I let my Magic crackle over my skin as my shield came into focus.

"Violet, don't do this," Robert pleaded.

I reached for our Artognou Magic and let the flood gates open. Robert took a deep breath as his Magic poured into my veins. I could feel him fighting me, willing his Magic to stop, to break the connection. But he didn't know how. It never occurred to either of us that we might want to block our Magic from one another.

"We can find another way." Robert held my eyes as Vivian's Magic stirred deep within me.

"It has to be this way," I replied as Magic bloomed on my fingertips and I let down my mental walls.

The world around me swirled into a multitude of colors as the ground disappeared beneath my feet.

Nimue stood before me. Her image almost transparent as she paced back and forth. She was talking to someone, but I couldn't hear her words. It was as if she were on mute. As I stepped closer, her eyes zeroed in on me. Storming in my direction, she raised her hand, and the vision swirled into darkness.

"Please... someone," a woman's shaky voice caught my attention in the darkness. Reaching out, my hand found something solid as my eyes adjusted to the emptiness surrounding me. Edging forward, a figure huddled in the corner came into view. Her dark hair swirled around her bronzed skin and almond eyes.

The floor was ripped out from under me and my vision shifted once more.

"I won't do it," Robert's voice reached my ears before the vision came into focus.

"You have to," my voice was soft and encouraging.

Still, I couldn't make anything out. It was like I was wandering around in a fog bank.

"Violet..." Robert's voice trailed off.

Reality pulled me back to the present, but as the world reshaped around me, darkness pulled over my eyes like a blanket.

My knees buckled and Robert's arms wrapped around my waist to break my fall.

CHAPTER 9

IOLET

"Is she alright?" Cian's voice echoed in my head like he was at the end of a tunnel.

Vivian stirred inside me, distant and weak, and I realized I wasn't being pulled into the space between life and death.

"Something's wrong," I groaned as I opened my eyes.

Robert helped me to my feet, but kept his arm around my waist.

"Vivian?" Merlin asked.

"I can feel her, but only faintly." I shook my head. My legs were like jello and my lungs burned with each breath.

"Time is running out," Merlin said under his breath.

"So, what now?" Robert asked.

"Your task is the same, with or without Vivian," Halvar said.

"How do you—"

"He's right," I interrupted Robert.

"This isn't your fight," Robert stared me down. "You were

only meant to wake Vivian." His brow furrowed as he shook his head.

"It's her fight now," Cian said matter-of-factly, and crossed his arms over his chest.

"No one asked you," Robert snapped.

Untangling myself from Robert, I locked my knees in place. "You're right." I scanned the room. "Whether Vivian can help us or not, we can't let Morgana and Nimue destroy the Magical world as we know it. It may've taken me a while to accept all of this." I waved my hands around the room. "And accept who I am." I placed my hand against my stomach. "But now it's being threatened and I know, without a doubt, I'm right where I'm meant to be."

Vivian's magic pulsed through me, a gentle reminder that no matter what happened next, I wasn't alone.

"I don't know why I'm still here and Vivian isn't, but if I've learned anything," I looked back at Robert and took his hand. "It's that plans never go the way you think they will. This is the hand we've been dealt." I held onto Robert's gaze and squeezed his hand. "We can't walk away now."

Robert's head nodded once, and he turned to Merlin.

"Any ideas on how to get to the Valley of the Draig?"

"If I may," Cian stepped forward and looked to his leader.

The leader nodded, and Cian took another step toward us.

"We may not be able to take on this war ourselves," Cian started. "But we can get you there."

"How?" I asked, as the pain in my legs began to subside.

"We are the Brotherhood of the realms, are we not?" He looked around as if waiting for someone to argue the point. "Our ability to protect the realms relies on us being able to move around them freely."

I stepped toward Cian. "Let's go, then."

The corner of his lips turned up as he held his arms out to the side.

"All those who wish to make the journey." He swirled his arms around him. "Step inside the circle."

Gold tendrils slithered out of his hands like shadows and curled around the room like a snake.

Merlin's shoulder brushed mine as he took his place next to me. Cian flicked his wrist, and a symbol appeared in the middle of the circle.

Robert took my hand and stood beside me, followed by Brett and Jake.

Another flick of Cian's hand and several more symbols surrounded us.

"Ready?" Cian's eyes held mine, and I nodded once.

He raised his hands to the ceiling, and the symbols swirled around us like a slow-moving twister. The tendrils of golden light began to glow, making it difficult to see anything outside of the circle. As the Maxwell house fell into the shadows, the symbols moved around us faster and faster until they were nothing but a blur.

I felt like we were on a carnival ride. The force of the swirling symbols pressed into my lungs, making it difficult to breathe. I forced my head to turn to the side so I could see the others. Robert stood stoic next to me, the muscles of his jaw flexing was the only sign that any pressure was being put on his body. Jake looked just as still as his brother and Brett had her eyes closed with a small smile on her lips, as if she was enjoying the ride.

The symbols started to slow, and the pressure on my chest eased as the world around us shimmered into focus.

Trees sprung up out of the surrounding ground. Lush, wet grass covered the earth under my shoes as a stream formed behind Cian.

The symbols swirling around us halted and fizzled into nothing.

"We're here," Cian said.

Looking around, I saw nothing out of the ordinary or Magical. It looked like Cian had dropped us in the middle of a forest.

"This way," Merlin said, moving toward the moss-covered mountain side a few feet away.

"Are you sure we're in the right place?" I asked.

"It's a bit of a hike, but we're close," Cian answered.

The pungent smell of mud and freshly rained on flora filled my nose as we followed Merlin along the stream.

"Couldn't you have gotten us closer?" Brett asked, and she pushed a low-hanging branch out of her way.

"The mountain is protected and not accessible by Magic," Cian explained.

"It makes me feel slightly better, knowing Morgana would have to make the trek as well," I admitted.

"It shouldn't," Merlin said. "She grew up hiking and foraging in the wilderness."

"I thought she lived in Camelot," I said.

"She did for a time, but Camelot was not the glamorous castle television makes it out to be," Merlin explained.

"So, keep an eye out," Cian warned.

"What if she beat us here? What if she's already opened the gate to the Valley of the Draig?"

"Do you remember what it was like when you plunged the sword into the stone and brought Vivian back?" Merlin asked.

I shivered at the thought. The pain and power that filled my body was something I would never forget. "Yes."

"You were given the tools to harness the Gate's energy and call Vivian to you. Without the proper tools, that energy has nothing to focus on," Merlin explained. "And without any guidance, it will destroy everything in its path."

"So, we'll know," I said flatly.

"Without a doubt."

Merlin came to a stop and waved his hand over the rocks

jutting out of the cliff. Pulling a knife from his pocket, he dragged the blade across his palm.

The earth rumbled under our feet as cracks crawled down the cliff side like vines. The rocks shifted and fell away, revealing a tunnel into the mountain.

"Valley of The Draig," I exhaled and Vivian's Magic snarled inside of me.

"Shall we?" Merlin pointed to the opening as illuminator orbs flittered from his hand and rushed through the archway and into the mountain.

I followed Merlin with Robert right behind me and I was glad I was neither at the front of the line nor pulling up the rear. There is an energy to this place that was giving me the heebie-jeebies. It was the first time since learning about the Magical world I could actually sense Magic so strongly in one place.

"When was the last time you visited, Merlin?" Cian asked, bringing up the rear of our little party. His voice bounced off the walls and echoed through the long tunnel.

"I was here when the fortress fell," Merlin replied. "I sealed the tunnel from prying eyes hoping no one would ever be able to reach the Valley of the Draig again."

The illuminator orbs pulsed brighter, lighting Merlin in a soft, candle-like glow. As he turned to the side, I got a glimpse of the man he once was, the Mythical Merlin.

"What happened the last time?" I asked, as the last bit of outside light faded behind us.

"Vortigan was a foolish man."

"That's an understatement," Cian scoffed.

"He was desperate to have a keep of his own," Merlin continued.

With each step, the ceiling and walls of the tunnel opened up, making it feel much less claustrophobic.

"He made a deal with the devil himself to gain the fortress

he'd spent his whole life fighting for. What he didn't account for, was how ruthless the Draig would be."

"I don't know why you ever placed any faith in Vortigan," Cian said.

"He was a victim of his own ego, but I can't blame him for something he didn't understand."

"You were always one to forgive," Cian said.

The sound of rushing water grew louder as we moved deeper into the mountain. The air was thick with humidity and with each step, dew collecting on my skin. Thankfully, the temperature was on the lower end of the thermometer.

"How was Vortigan able to access the Valley of The Draig?" My boots slogged through a thick puddle of mud.

"Same way we are, I'd guess," Robert's voice came from behind me. His hand grabbed my elbow and guided me around another goopy section of the ground.

"Yes, well. This cave was once open to any and all who passed by. But when Vortigan opened the gate to the Valley of the Draig, they ran through every village within a hundred miles and eradicated any signs of life."

"What, why? On Vortigan's orders?" Brett asked.

Illuminator orbs passed close to the wall on my left and tiny critters skittered away from the light. It took everything in my power not to shutter at the thought of what other slithering, crawling creatures might live in this mountain.

"It's what they were trained for. The Draig are unlike any warriors history has ever known. They leveled whole villages in a single blow, leaving nothing but a pile of bodies and a ruin in place of a once-thriving village."

"It was believed at the time that a Dragon was responsible for the devastation," Merlin finished.

"The legend of the Red and White Dragon's," Jake mumbled.

The temperature dropped another few degrees as a breeze of fresh air moved through us.

"What stopped them?" Brett asked from behind me.

Robert's hand shifted from my arm to my lower back and I could feel his breath on my neck.

"It was Merlin," Cian said.

"Just him?" I said over my shoulder. "That's impossible."

"Haven't you learned yet?" The lilt of Robert's voice was teasing. "Nothing's impossible with Magic."

"Legend says," Robert continued, and I turned to look at him. "That the White and Red Dragons battled it out until only one was left standing. The Red Dragon." His eyes shifted from mine, and I followed his gaze to Merlin.

I felt like he was telling me a bedtime story, and I realized it probably was a story he'd heard many times as a child.

His eyes returned to me full of light and excitement.

"It's said that the Red Dragon swore to stay in the mountain to protect the villagers from any other threats until the day he should meet his end," he continued, and a small smile played on his lips. "The villagers worshiped the Red Dragon and to this day they fly his image on their flags."

"And the Red Dragon was you," I said, turning to look at Merlin.

"You know how stories get warped over time, always changing to suit the storyteller." Merlin brushed off the story.

Someone screamed up ahead, and we all froze mid-step.

"That can't be good," Jake whispered.

"You think?" Brett shook her head.

"Violet?" Merlin turned to me. "Any chance we can expect Vivian to make an appearance?"

"I don't know," I shrugged. "I can try," I said, reaching for my Magic.

"No," Robert whispered into my ear. "If Morgana's here, you need to save your strength. Neither you nor Vivian are any good to us if you're not at full strength." His eyes pierced through me, daring me to argue with him.

"He's right," Cian said. "You're of more use to us in your current state."

Robert nodded once in Cian's direction, and the tension between them seemed to dissipate a bit.

"Very well," Merlin said through gritted teeth. "Let us proceed with caution." He snapped his finger and the illuminator orbs vanished.

It took my eyes a moment to adjust to the darkness, and when they did, there was a bluish-white light up ahead.

As quietly as possible, we made our way toward the light and toward Morgana. With each step, my heart picked up in tempo and I held my breath, nervous that my heavy exhale would give us away.

Merlin knelt down as he reached the edge of the cave and motioned for us to do the same. As I reached the end of the tunnel, I looked down and I sighed, thankful we were only about ten feet off the ground.

I looked out over the massive cavern in awe. It was huge, almost as big as a football stadium. A body of water the size of a small lake stretched out in front of us. The midnight black water looked like a sheet of glass, despite the waterfall flowing into the lake.

"I've never seen water so still before," I said under my breath. It wasn't so much the stillness of the water that unnerved me. It was the heavy presence of Magic, allowing the water to stay frozen in time and absorb the constant flow of the waterfall without any evidence of its presence.

I've always known water to have a heartbeat of its own, the cadence of the waves crashing on the shore, the gentle sloshing of pool water in the breeze. But this lake looked as if it hadn't been alive since the fall of the Draig.

Looking up, the ceiling was twenty or thirty feet above us and tiny beams of light broke through the natural skylight and foliage above.

On the far right side of the water, I could just make out Morgana and Nimue's ghostly figure. Standing in a huddle near Morgana were a dozen people in varying degrees of despair. Their clothes, if you could call them that, looked like rags, dirty and falling apart at every seam.

"Next," Morgana shouted.

Ian grabbed a woman by the back of the neck and shoved her forward.

"Please," she whimpered. "This isn't the way."

"Do it," Nimue seethed.

Scooting up to Merlin, I whispered, "Are we just going to sit here and watch?"

"A moment," he said. "We must time our entrance carefully."

The woman Ian shoved forward raised her arms hesitantly out in front of her. Even from this distance, it was easy to see, she was shaking with fear as she began to recite a spell.

"On three," Merlin whispered.

Sparks ignited on her fingertips and a gust of wind blew back the hood of her sweater as an archway began to form in front of her.

"Oh, God," Jake breathed, and my blood went still.

"Two," Merlin said, holding up two fingers.

"You can't help them," one of the other prisoners yelled at the terrified woman.

"Jake, what is it?" I asked, turning to look at him. He was pale as milk and his eyes were fixed on one point in front of him.

Following his gaze, I saw what caught his attention, and my heart stopped as Merlin jumped over the edge of the cliff.

"Annabel?" I said under my breath.

CHAPTER 10

IOLET

"It's not her," I said. "It can't be."

"Jake, we have to jump," Robert said.

"Another trick," Jake breathed. "That's not Anna, it can't be Anna," Jake mumbled to himself and his hands shook as he stared at the woman.

"It's now or never," Cian placed a hand on Jake's shoulder and Jake nodded.

"It can't be her," Jake said under his breath as he jumped over the side of the cliff.

Robert nodded at Brett, and she jumped along with Cian.

"Ready?"

I nodded and jumped over the edge.

A crash of lightning boomed through the cavern as I fell. My knees buckled as my feet connected with the uneven surface and I pitched forward.

"Are you injured?" Cian asked

"I'm fine," I said, picking myself back up and limping to the others hiding behind a group of rocks.

Robert's hand wrapped around my elbow and without skipping a beat, his Magic moved through me, seeking the pain in my ankle. The throbbing quickly disappeared, and I rolled the joint to be sure I could stand without limping.

A deep howl erupted from one of Morgana's prisoners, catching our attention. Peering around the rocks, an elderly man was on his knees, while the woman, who bore a resemblance to Annabel, held her arm against her chest and shivered.

"You don't know what you're messing with," one of the prisoners pleaded as the woman continued the spell next to Morgana.

Morgana sneered over him and, in one swift motion, she pulled the man's head back and slit his throat.

"No," I gasped and my hand covered my mouth in shock. How could she kill someone so casually?

"Let that be a lesson to you all. Get in our way and suffer the consequences."

"No one else will die today for her sick and twisted cause," Jake growled as he observed the woman who looked like his wife.

"Jake." I reached for him. "It's not her."

"You think I don't know that," he snapped.

"You two need to change the trajectory of the gate." Merlin nodded to Robert and me. "We'll distract them."

"Us? How're we supposed to do that?" I asked, surprised it wasn't Merlin or even Cian who would deal with The Valley of The Draig.

"With your Artognou Magic," Cian said. "One of you will have to go through the archway to The Valley," he said, coming to a stop in front of us.

"I'll go," Robert said without hesitation. His eyes met mine, giving me a look that dared me to argue with him.

"When you're on the other side, you must not hesitate. The Draig keep sentries on their gates and you'll be spotted if you don't move quickly."

"Got it. Tell me what I need to do," Robert said eagerly.

"Take this." Cian held something wrapped in an old piece of leather. "It will give the gate a new focus and point it in another direction."

As Robert plucked the item from Cian's hand, he grabbed Robert's wrist. "Don't unwrap it," he warned. "Not until you're on the other side. Once you expose the element, you'll only have a few moments to make it back to us."

"It doesn't sound like we need our Artognou Magic for this to work," I eyed Cian skeptically.

"Whoever crosses into the Valley of the Draig becomes one of them."

"What?" I shook my head. "Robert, you can't do this." I pulled at his arm to stop him from taking a step toward his death.

"We both know I have to or Morgana will rain hell on earth." He reached out and took my hand in his.

"Don't worry, he'll be fine," Cian said nonchalantly. "Had you let me finish, you would know that your Artognou Magic will keep the gate open long enough to stay the effects so he can complete his mission and return as himself."

"You're not making me feel all warm and fuzzy about this," I said through gritted teeth.

"You don't have to feel good about it, you just have to do it." Cian leveled his eyes on me and his gaze pierced right through me, making me squirm.

"Tell me, how do I keep the gate open?" I demanded.

Cian smirked. "Just stay connected. It's your bond that will guide him back. Without the connection of your Magic calling to him, he won't know which way is home and will be lost to the Draig."

My mouth went dry and my stomach bottomed out as another crash of lighting burst through the cavern.

"I'm not strong enough for that, not after—"

"You are," he said. "I know you are." Cian gripped my shoulder. "I know the strength of your will, the power of your Magic and the love in your heart." His eyes met Robert's. "You can and will keep that gate open for him to return."

His confidence in me was surprising. We only just met, and he had more faith in me than I had in myself.

I nodded, still unsure but determined to keep Robert alive. Robert squeezed my hand and said, "Ready when you are."

"How do we open The Valley?" I asked.

Cian smiled, "Did you think I just came along for the ride?"

Voices echoed around us, as another of Morgana's prisoners tried to open the gate and unleash the Draig on the world.

"We have to be quick," Cian said. "We won't have the element of surprise for long."

I let out a heavy breath and nodded.

"Stop this madness," Merlin's voice boomed through the cavern as if he was speaking through a microphone.

"Merlin, how kind of you to show yourself," Morgana cooed. "I assume you're not alone." She turned in a circle, searching the cavern for others.

"You'd be correct," Brett said, stepping out from behind a boulder. My stomach churned at the thought of her facing Morgana, and my heart almost fell out of my chest.

Follow me, Cian mouthed and waved us forward as we stayed hidden on the opposite side of Merlin and Morgana's show down.

"And where's Vivian?" A high, lyrical voice chimed.

Vivian stirred inside me, angry as her Magic pumped through my veins, making my heart race. She was coming back and when she did, it would be with a vengeance.

"Nimue, you're looking a little worse for the wear," Merlin

shifted the focus as we crept toward a wooden boat sitting on the edge of the lake.

"Not all of us are immortal, not yet at least," Nimue snarled.

"Search the area," Morgana ordered and footsteps scraped against rocks.

"Run," Cian yelled.

Robert's hand wrapped around mine and we made a dash from our hiding place toward the boat.

"Stop them," Morgana howled.

My eyes met Merlin's, and he nodded once as sparks ignited on his fingertips.

"Your shield," Cian yelled as he hopped into the boat in one leap.

"Don't," Robert turned to me. "Save your Magic," he said as his shield fell around us like a warm blanket.

Jumping in the boat with Robert right behind me, Cian reached out his hand and the boat lurched forward into the water, heading straight for the rocks Morgana and Nimue were perched atop.

Thunder rumbled above us and Robert's shield took a direct hit.

"*Ian,*" Robert cursed.

Ian was like a bad cold you couldn't shake, and my Magic bubbled under my skin as his eyes met mine. My heart shuttered at his gaze and Vivian's Magic sparked to life inside me, aching to be released.

"We need to hurry," I said, looking over my shoulder.

Brett stood at the edge of the lake, electricity coursing over her body as she directed a blow at Nimue just ahead of us.

Nimue dodged the spell and refocused her energy toward Brett.

"We're almost there," Cian yelled over the sounds of the battle.

Morgana pelted us with cinder orbs, bombarding Robert's

shield with enough Magic to take down a building. The vibrant maroon fabric protecting us began to fade as a hole opened above us.

"If you're going to do something," Robert said through gritted teeth. "Now would be the time, Cian."

Cian began to sing an incantation in a deep, guttural voice that was reminiscent of a Tibetan monk.

A burst of blue light flew over our heads and erupted a few feet ahead of us. Water from the lake shot into the air and fell down on us like a torrential downpour.

Another explosion sounded from somewhere behind us and a bright flash of light filled the cavern like a thousand camera flashes going off at once. I closed my eyes, trying to block out the light, when Cian stopped his chanting.

Blinking the world into focus, I said, "Do you see that?" Hidden just under the rush of the waterfall in front of us, there was a stone arch taking shape.

"Valley of the Draig," Robert said under his breath.

My hands started to shake with nerves as the boat slithered through the water effortlessly. As we drew closer, symbols engraved into the stone archway began to light up. The hot white light burned my eyes and I had to look away from the archway.

"Don't let them near the gate," Morgana bellowed.

The boat accelerated the last fifty yards and came to an abrupt halt just under the archway.

Crawling out of the rocking boat and onto the nearest rock, I made my way up the slimy surface, and Robert followed me.

Cian hopped out of the boat with little effort and up to the arch as if he'd done this a thousand times.

Thunder roared through the cavern as Merlin did his best to keep Morgana and her gang occupied. I wanted to look, to see how much time we had, but we didn't have a second to waste.

Pulling myself up to the next rock, the glow of the arch made me squint, and I slid a few inches down the stone.

"I gotcha," Robert said, gripping my hip and pushing me back up the rock.

I took a deep breath and crawled up and onto the next boulder in front of the arch. The heat radiating from the stones was oppressive, and I turned away from the gate.

In the back of my mind, I wondered if the blinding light and overwhelming heat was meant to ward people off.

"You ready?" Cian asked, looking between us.

"Ready," Robert said as lightning crackled across the lake.

"Ready as I'll ever be."

Cian placed his hand on one of the symbols decorating the archway and spoke one final word to open the gate.

The symbols on the stone began to pulse in time with each step we took, like they wanted us to cross over, wanted us to become one of them.

As I reached the archway, Cian took my hand and placed it on the symbol he'd used to open the gateway to the Valley of the Draig.

"Whatever you do, don't break the connection." Cian's eyes held mine with an urgency that made my pulse race. "The gate will shut the moment you break away."

I nodded and turned to face Robert. His lips were on mine instantly. The heat of his kiss searing through my core as he tapped into our Artognou Magic. His lips moved against mine, eager and desperate, as if he was trying to hold on to this single moment in time. He pulled back and our Magic hummed beneath the surface.

"Hold on as long as you can," he said, cupping my face.

"Don't die," I demanded.

The corner of his lips turned up, and he kissed my forehead. He wouldn't promise me he would come back. We'd both learned that life and Magic never went as planned.

Without glancing backward, Robert stepped through the arch into another world.

As his figured faded, our Artognou Magic burst to life inside me, forcing my head back as the symbol burned into the palm of my hand.

The connection between us seared through me, stronger than ever before. I could feel the rhythm of Robert's heartbeat, and the blood rushing through my veins was electric as the Valley of the Draig called out to him like a siren.

Dread and fear like I've never felt before poured into my heart. This wasn't right. He shouldn't be doing this.

The symbols pulsed again, and I fell to my knees. Pain radiated through my palm from the symbol and down my arm, into my chest. My teeth hurt, my bones ached, and I felt like my skin was being stretched to the point of ripping.

The gate wanted to close. Wanted to take Robert as their own. Magic was being sucked from all corners of the cavern and a surge of white hot panic forced me to my feet.

"I won't let you take him," I said, pulling on our Artognou Magic.

Using my other hand to keep my palm pressed to the archway, I willed our Magic to keep the gate open. The symbols etched into the stone flickered and pulsed again, this time to the beat of my heart, my faltering, weak heart.

The heat of the gate overwhelmed me. Sweat dripped down my forehead and I couldn't see anything beyond my own hands.

The cavern rumbled under my feet, rattling my bones, and I heard a deep, guttural scream somewhere behind me.

"Children of the Dragon, I call upon thee." Morgana's voice cut through the pain.

"End this, now," Merlin said behind me. "Close the gate."

"Give him a minute," I yelled back, and a spell hit the cavern wall and rocks fell down around me.

The ground beneath me rumbled, and then I heard it. The sound of a thousand boots marching toward us.

"We don't have a minute,"

"Oh, God," my lips trembled.

Another electric shock fired from the archway and I screamed as the pain settled deep in my soul.

"Violet, you—" Merlin started.

"No," I growled. "Robert's in there and I won't let you kill him."

His eyes widened and his jaw flexed as my words settled over him. Looking over his shoulder, he glanced at Jake and Brett, who were struggling to fight off Morgana and Ian.

One of Morgana's men walked into the water and began to swim. As he reached the middle of the lake, he disappeared under the surface of the water. I gasped as I watched, waiting for him to resurface, when I noticed Merlin was chanting a spell under his breath.

As the bubbles disappeared, the lake settled and Merlin turned to me. "Do what you must. But hurry."

I nodded once and forced my Magic to the point of breaking.

Please, please don't be too late, I said to myself.

My fingers traced the symbol and the Artognou Magic poured out of me like a faucet. It was as if the Valley of the Draig was feeding on my Magic and trying to drain me completely.

I let out a ragged breath, and I dug deeper, holding onto the threads of our Magic. I could just barely feel the tenor of Robert's Magic and I let out a sigh of relief knowing he was still alive.

"Merlin," I heard Cian yell, and a brilliant flash of light erupted all around me. A violent wind rushed through my hair as gravel and dust pelted my skin.

My grasp on our Artognou Magic was slippery as I tried to

hold on. But it was like trying to hold a fish out of water. Every time I grabbed hold, it wiggled free, slipping through my fingers.

"You can do this," Cian said.

Exhaustion set in and Vivian's Magic began to take over.

Reaching for every shred of my Magic, my body shook as I held on for dear life. If saving Robert was the last thing I did, I could die without regret.

Our Magic ripped through me as the symbols on the arch pulsed slower and slower. The air was ripped from my lungs and my heart rate began to drop. Darkness started to pull on me as my eyesight blurred at the corner.

Come on Robert, I thought.

Another round of explosions rattled my body as I desperately kept my hand on the symbol.

The shadowy figure of a man appeared in the archway, and I breathed a sigh of relief. Then another figured appeared and another. Men and women covered head to toe in sleek, black, metal armor that resembled dragon scales ran through the archway like a stampede. The light from above glistening off of their armor as they darted past me by the dozens.

I gasped for air and the symbols flashed once more, this time more slowly, as I searched for Robert. I couldn't let the Draig into this world. I couldn't let them fall under Morgana's control, even if that meant letting Robert go.

Every muscle in my body convulsed as I tried to hold on to our Magic.

Sparks started to dance from every one of the symbols and I had to drag myself away from the archway to keep from getting burned by the Magic being expelled from the gate.

Cracks started to form in the arch and the stones began to separate as my vision blurred and my body went limp on the rocks. A pair of arms lifted me off the ground as I fell away, back into the darkness, back into the nothing.

VIOLET IN THE DARK

I clawed at the abyss, desperate to get back.

Robert...oh God, ROBERT!

I have to fight,
I thrashed against the nothing.
I have to save him,
I searched for any shred of strength.

Fear gripped my heart...I couldn't breathe...I couldn't think...

CHAPTER 11

IVIAN

THE FIRST THING I registered was a high-pitched ringing in my ears. My eyesight moved in and out of focus as the world blurred around me. A pair of arms around my waist pulled me forward as rocks and dirt rained down all around us.

"Nothing like waiting until the last second," a man's voice broke through the ringing.

"We have to get her out of here," Robert's voice sounded to my left.

Scanning the area, everything around me was in complete chaos. People half covered in dirty rags ran for cover. Electricity pulsed off of Brett, and half a dozen men and women in shining black armor charged her.

Draig. I cursed.

Looking to my left, rocks broke apart and reformed all around Jake, taking out the Draig warriors one at a time as Merlin and Morgana exchanged blows.

"I have to help," I croaked and tried to pull myself free.

"No disrespect, but you're in no shape to fight," the man next to me said.

"And who might you be?" I asked.

Robert jumped in front of me, summoning his shield just in time to block a spell.

"Cian," the man replied curtly. "And it's time we depart." He released his hold on me.

My legs wobbled and exhaustion pulled at my soul, but I held myself up. My body may be broken and weak, but the strength of my will and Magic would be enough to propel me forward.

"Lead the way," I said, as another spell hit Robert's shield in front of us.

Summoning my Magic, I came up behind Robert, placing my arms on either side of him.

"On my mark," I said, and he nodded.

My Magic galloped down my arms, hungry for release. The force of it almost knocked me to the ground. Whatever Violet had done before she faded away had left our body in dire need of rest and repair.

I locked my knees and said, "Mark."

Robert's shield dropped and my Magic fired on either side of him, striking the Draig in front of us. They were both blown off of their feet, their bodies hitting the surface of the lake like stones as they sunk beneath the surface.

"Go," I yelled. "They won't stay down for long."

Robert held out his hand for me, and I gratefully accepted the support as we made our way down the rocks.

As we reached the water, an explosion erupted around us, throwing dust and rocks into the air and making it impossible to see anything beyond our own feet.

Quickly summoning my shield, the hailstorm of jagged rocks rebounded off the barrier. As the dust cleared, Robert's hunched form came into focus.

A large shard of rock protruded from his right side.

"Are you alright?" I asked.

"Fine," he said, pulling the knife-like stone from his flesh. Blood rushed through his fingers and he grabbed onto the wound. "We need to keep moving."

Jumping down from the rocks, a deep, animalistic groan filled the air as Robert toppled into the boat.

"Can't you heal yourself?" I asked, and I placed my own hands over his wound to help stop the bleeding.

"Apparently not. Violet must have drained both of our Magic keeping the gate open."

"Get us out of here," I said to Cian.

He nodded, and the boat shot off into the water.

Pulling my shield up around the three of us, I closed my eyes and focused on nothing but the strength of my Magic.

"Not to sound alarmist, but we could use the Lady of The Lake right about now," Cian said.

The blood in my veins turned to ice as I looked across the water and saw Morgana standing on the shore.

"Shit," Robert said through gritted teeth.

I looked down at Robert, bloody and broken, and back up at Morgana, who was only getting closer.

A crooked smile played on her lips as the boat settled against the sand.

"Well, well. What do we have here?" She purred as she stared at us like easy prey.

"That's enough, Morgana," I said. "You got what you came for," I nodded toward the Draig around her.

"Hardly," she sneered. "Out of the boat."

"If you want to kill us, just do it and stop playing games," Robert barked at her.

I turned and leveled my eyes on him. *Don't tempt her,* I thought.

Robert forced himself to his feet and, though he kept most of his weight on his left side, he still reached for me for support.

Sliding out of the boat, it rocked back and forth, splashing water up my legs.

Morgana's head cocked to the side as she watched me help Robert onto dry land.

"A healer with the inability to heal himself. How useless you truly are," she mocked.

"Leave him out of this," I stepped in front of Robert. This was my fight, what I was brought here to do.

Morgana cocked her head to the side the same way she did when she was a child trying to figure out a puzzle. "What do you care what happens to him?" she asked.

She extended her arm and her Magic dragged Robert across the sand to her. She grabbed him by the neck, her nails digging into his skin, and he winced as her other hand found the wound on his side.

"Let him go," I said each word with measured fury.

"Make me," she seethed. Sparks danced across Robert's neck and down his torso as her grip tighten on him.

"Gladly," I smirked.

A bolt of hot white light shot from my hand directly at Morgana's chest.

Tossing Robert to the side, she squared her shoulders as her shield appeared before her, blocking the spell.

"This should be fun," she cooed as the spell ricocheted off her shield.

Raising her hands, the cavern above us started to quake. Rocks and weeds rustled free and fell toward us like stars falling from the sky.

"Make your exit," I said to Cian and nodded in Robert's direction. "He needs your help."

Placing my hands together, the tips of my fingers itching to destroy Morgana. My Magic bubbled over, creating a sphere the size of a large pumpkin. Red and black currents pulsed over the orb, blowing the hair out of my face.

"Time to prove your worth," Morgana ordered. With her attention on her newly acquired army, she left herself wide open.

Putting my thumbs and forefingers in a triangle position, the spell burst from my hands toward Morgana.

"Vivian," Merlin's voice yelled over the roar of Magic.

Looking over my shoulder, I saw Nimue barreling toward me, her Magic pulsing off of her like an electric storm.

Turning away from Morgana, I met my counterpart head on.

Making a sweeping motion with my hands across my body, a brilliant sword made of blue fire and white light appeared in my hands. My knees shivered at the brute force of Magic I called upon, but I locked my legs in place and held myself tall.

Mid-run, Nimue made the same motion. Only her sword burst to life with black and green flames.

Without missing a step, she raised her sword over her head, swinging toward me with a snarl plastered across her face.

Her blade struck mine, sparks of Magic flying in every direction. I kicked at her chest, freeing my sword and spinning around in time to block the spell Morgana had directed at me with the flat side of the blade.

Adrenaline kicked in and the weariness in my bones faded to the back of my mind. With my free hand, I called up a stunning spell, and without skipping a beat, I directed the spell at Morgana.

Turning on the spot, I caught Nimue's blade with my own. Forcing her back, I went on the offense, pushing her closer and closer to the shadows.

"You can't stop what's to come," Nimue's voice slithered into my brain as she moved to strike again.

Umbra-Kai crawled along the sides of the cave, moving freely in the shadows.

"You forget yourself," I smiled. "For I am not the one who is hunted."

I jumped backward as the tip of her blade slipped across the fabric of my shirt. I was unscathed, but I couldn't say the same for Violet's clothing.

Tightening my grip on the sword, I took a step toward Nimue. Out of the corner of my eye, I saw another of Morgana's spells. Raising my left hand toward the spell, a burst of light surrounded my palm, deflecting the spell into the rocks above us.

Magic poured out of me, directing itself at Morgana in a searing beam of light. Splitting my focus wasn't ideal, but manageable so long as I ended this quickly.

I raised the sword in front of me. The hilt at my belly and the tip raised to the sky exposed above us.

Lightning struck the sword and in one smooth movement, I arched the blade toward Nimue, lighting her up for the Umbra-Kai to see.

Her blade caught the brunt of my attack, deflecting the lightning. Even still, the shadows closed in on her faster and faster with each breath.

My legs began to shake and for the briefest moment, I thought I was losing my hold on reality. A boulder fell to my right, splitting open like an egg, and I realized it wasn't reality shifting around me. It was the cavern itself. My eyes did a quick scan. Morgana was nowhere in sight, but I knew there was no way she'd just given up and fled like the rat she was. The others had all escaped, including the Draig. A problem for another time, I thought as I turned back to Nimue.

She was on her knees, the sword held above her.

"I never wanted this for you," I said as the Umbra-Kai closed in around her.

"I don't want your pity," Nimue snarled.

Kneeling next to her, I couldn't help but feel the loss of my other half all over again.

"Vivian," Merlin's voice called to me.

Standing, I turned to reply when a spell hit me square in the stomach.

I doubled over and crumpled to the floor.

"Merlin," I yelled and pulled a shield around me.

"You were always the weaker half," Morgana said, standing over me.

"True strength has nothing to do with brute force," I said, trying to sit up, but my legs were useless.

A paralyzing spell, I thought.

"Spare me the lecture," Morgana said, pulling Nimue to her feet.

"Inlihtnes," Nimue said, and illuminator orbs surrounded her, keeping the shadows at bay.

"You don't belong in the light," I said.

Angry flames galloped over me, their heat oppressive as they forced Morgana and Nimue back.

"That should buy us a moment," Merlin said, appearing at my side.

"My legs," I nodded.

He placed his hand on my hips and warmth spread through my limbs.

In one swift motion, he helped me to my feet and though my legs were still coming to, I moved one heavy foot in front of the other and we made our escape.

CHAPTER 12

IVIAN

I STUMBLED out of the tunnel a few feet behind Merlin. My legs felt like they were filled with a thousand nettles, and each step took considerable effort, as if I had stones strapped to my ankles.

Fire shot over our heads as we made our way under the cover of the trees. The ground began to shake and a deep rumble that can only be born from the earth settling under us. Rock, dust, and weeds spewed from the mouth of the tunnel, surrounding us in a cloud of debris as the cavern collapsed behind us.

"She's not coming with us," Robert pointed to the curly redheaded woman, shielding herself behind a tree as the Draig fired at our group.

"Not to interrupt this little reunion," Cian pointed between the woman I'd never seen before and Robert. "But my part here is done," Cian said.

"Thank you for your help," Merlin nodded, as electricity pulsed off of him.

Cian nodded in return, and with a wave of his hands, he disappeared.

"Where are the others?" I asked, eyeing the woman.

"We weren't able to stop them," Brett said from her position on the ground. Her arm draped across her body, gripping a wound at her side. She looked as bad as I felt. "They—" she winced as she deflected a spell.

"They killed Morgana's prisoners," Jake finished for her as one of the Draig ran directly at him.

"Not all the prisoners," the woman Robert had been arguing with said under her breath.

"*Sanguis ignis,*" I fired the spell at the Draig, about to knock Jake to the ground.

The whites of the Draigs eyes burst with blood as his skin set ablaze and he hit the ground like a stone falling through water.

"We're not discussing it." Robert cradled his wound.

"You don't get the final say in this," Jake moved next to his brother, keeping his shield raised.

"Now may not be the time for this conversation," Merlin said, extending his arms and raising a wall of fire between us and the Draig.

"Agreed, we need to move to safety," the woman unknown to me said.

"I don't believe we've been properly introduced," I said, raising my shield in front of the woman and myself as a spell spiraled through the air toward us.

"Alyssa," she said, adjusting her shoulders and lifting her chin as she recomposed herself. "And shouldn't you be dead?" Alyssa eyed me with curiosity. Everyone's attention swirled in my direction.

"I assume, you mean Violet?" I cocked my head to the side as I directed her behind a large tree.

Alyssa looked at the others and back to me, "Aren't you Violet?"

"Vivian," I said casually. "I share Violet's body at the moment." A spell hit the tree at our backs and shook the leaves from their branches.

"Fascinating. Would you—"

"Absolutely not," Robert snapped from his hiding place across from us.

"This is a once in a lifetime—"

"I said no." Robert's words were final. "I don't want you anywhere near them with your little bag of horrors."

"I think Vivian and Violet can speak for themselves," Alyssa said with an air of authority.

"You're right," I smiled. "And I'm not interested in anything you have to offer."

"You may not know me but I have a gift with these sorts of situations." Her eyes crinkled as an overly friendly smile curled her lips.

Somewhere behind me, I heard the faint sound of leaves crackling. Allowing my senses to take over, I turned on the spot and my Magic galloped into the bushes.

The telltale *thump* of a body hitting the ground reached my ears as I turned back to Alyssa.

"And did your gift have a hand in returning Nimue from the Shadowlands?"

Her expression changed in an instant as she pushed her shoulders back and her chin up.

"Though this conversation is thrilling," Merlin twist his arms in front of him, producing a ward, "you need to have it elsewhere." He slammed his hand into the dirt.

A rush of air blew through the surrounding trees, signaling that the ward had taken root.

"She wants to come with us," Jake said.

"And I said no," Robert said. "She works for Morgana; we can't trust her."

"Sort it out," Merlin ordered. "The ward won't hold for long." He pointed to the opaque wall glowing from the earth. On the other side, the silhouette of the Draig stalked back and forth, hitting the invisible wall between us and waiting for their opportunity.

"I've told you." Alyssa leveled her gaze at Robert. "I work for no one."

Robert huffed. A sheen of sweat covered his face. He was in pain, but hiding it well.

I could see her anger and frustration bubbling under the surface, but she kept a level head.

"What business do you have with us?" Merlin inquired.

Her eyes shifted to Jake, then back to Merlin.

"The Draig didn't kill all the prisoners. There's one they won't dare touch."

"Who?" I asked.

"Annabel."

It was as if she'd thrown a poisonous snake in the middle of our group.

Jake flinched at the name. Robert sneered and my own heart fluttered with Violet's emotions.

"Why won't they hurt Annabel?" Merlin asked as he looked back at the delicate ward.

"She's one of them," Alyssa nodded to the Draig.

Robert shook his head. "You've caused enough pain, we won't sit here and—"

"Just listen to her," Jake interrupted him and the Draig banged against the ward.

"I did enough listening while I was her prisoner," Robert snapped, his face curling into a grimace as he shifted his hand over his wound.

Taking in the woman in front of me, the sharp lines of her face, her tightly fitting pants and jacket, her flawless cinnamon skin and fiery hair made her seem more suited to scholarly work than a prison cell mad scientist.

"Robert," Brett cocked her head to the side. "I know you don't trust her, but if Annabel really is alive…" she looked at Jake.

Robert crossed his arms over his chest and said, "No good will come of this."

"Annabel can't be one of the Draig," Jake said.

Alyssa nodded, "Her bloodline traces back to the Draig before you ended their reign." She pointed to Merlin.

"Do you have proof that it's really Annabel?" Brett asked. "We've been fooled by your Magic before."

"I apologize for the part I played in that. It was never my intention—"

"Save it," Robert barked.

Alyssa sighed and reached into her coat. "If it's proof you require," she held a device out to Jake.

"When Annabel was taken, she was put under my charge," Alyssa began. "Morgana instructed me to create a way for Emilia," she looked around our group. "The woman pretending to be Jake's wife," she explained. "To take on the form of Annabel so she could slip into your ranks undetected."

The Draig rushed the barrier, the bodies and weapons thrashing against the ward between them and us. It held, if only barely.

"You need to strengthen the ward," I said, turning to Merlin.

"We need to leave," Merlin barked.

"It appears they need a moment," I said, pushing Merlin toward the barrier. "Do what you can to strengthen it. I'll hurry them along," I said.

"She more than looked like Annabel." Jake's voice was low. "She had her memories too."

"That would be the bonding spell," Alyssa said proudly. "They were connected, mind, body, and soul. Emilia, for all intents and purposes, was Annabel."

"She may have played pretend well, but she was not Anna. She'll never be Anna." Jake gripped the device in his hand as I moved to his side.

"The Draig will be on us any moment," I said. "However you need to resolve this, do it now."

"The passcode is 0000," she nodded at the device.

With a shaky hand, Jake pressed the numbers into the device. Collectively, everyone held their breath as we watched and waited for Jake's response.

"What are you playing at?" Robert huffed.

"It's Annabel," Jake's said. His voice was barely a whisper as he looked down at the screen.

Robert moved stiffly to his brother's side and took the device from Jake. His eyes widened, and he said, "When was this taken?"

"Vivian," Merlin yelled.

I looked over my shoulder. The ward was failing and if we didn't leave now, we wouldn't get out of this alive.

"Take a look at the metadata," Alyssa instructed with a wave of her hand.

Robert held Alyssa's gaze for a pregnant moment, then turned his attention to the device and clicked for the information.

Robert's brow furrowed, and Jake grabbed the device from him.

"Well?" Brett asked.

"She was there, the whole time?" Jake choked. "I could have saved her." The color drained from his face. "I could have saved her," he said again as tears filled his eyes.

"What do you mean? When was the photo taken?" Brett looked between Robert and Jake.

"The date on the photo is the same date we stole Excalibur from Morgana," Robert said, placing a hand on Jake's shoulder. "We couldn't have known," he said under his breath.

"There, you have your proof," I said. "She comes with us until we can learn more." I moved to help Brett to her feet when Jake fell to his knees.

"Robert, help him," I ordered

Jake looked up at Alyssa, a tear falling from his eye, and asked, "Where is she now?"

"Jake," Robert said, trying to pull him to his feet. "We need to go."

"No," Jake pushed his brother away as Brett put her free arm around my neck.

"I'll tell you everything, I swear it," Alyssa placed a hand on his arm as she looked to the failing ward. "But I can't tell you anything if we're dead."

Jake's eyes followed hers and he nodded.

"Now that's settled," Merlin thrust both hands into the dirt. "We should take refuge." The ward wobbled into view once more, pushing the Draig back another few feet.

Merlin turned on his heel and started into the woods, "Follow me," he yelled.

"Can you do this?" I asked Brett, hanging at my side.

"Do I have a choice?" She smirked and gripped her wounded side tighter.

"No," I said, pulling her along with me. "Afraid not."

CHAPTER 13

IVIAN

OUR GROUP MOVED QUICKLY through the woods. My legs wobbling with each step. Holding up Brett was taking a considerable effort.

Alyssa, untouched by the battle, moved gracefully in front of me, keeping pace with Robert and Jake. Their stiff figures marching on either side of her reminded me of the knights who used to walk in line with Arthur.

My eyes moved past them to Merlin. Grey sunlight poked through the canopy of trees, brushing his shoulders as he led the charge. Some things never changed, I thought as I watched him jump over a fallen tree and make an abrupt right turn.

"Milady?" Brett asked, keeping her voice hushed.

I glanced down at her, half expecting her to need a rest. The blood staining her shirt had grown from a few drops to a giant splotch and her face was pale as snow.

"You should have Merlin look at your wound when we settle." I eyed her pale complexion.

She gave me a tight-lipped smile and nodded once.

"There's something I wanted to ask." Brett kept her eyes on the path in front of us.

"Yes?"

"You and Merlin have a history," she said, out of breath.

"Yes," I acknowledged.

"And you trust him?"

I looked at her out of the corner of my eye. "Of course."

"It's only," she grunted with the effort to step over the fallen tree at our feet. "There's so much he hasn't been forthright about," she continued as we picked up our pace once again. "I worry what the truth might do to my brother."

"Jake?" I asked, unsure where her line of questioning was leading.

"Robert." Her feet faltered, and we both stumbled forward. I caught my weight on a nearby tree and we both took a deep breath.

"Because of Violet," I guessed.

She nodded. "Both of my brothers love beyond reason, and if they think there's a chance to save the one they love… there will be no stopping them."

The faint flicker of Violet thrummed under the surface of my breastbone as I readjusted my grip around Brett and continued on down the path.

"Do you not love as fiercely as your brothers?" I wondered.

"I know the consequences of loving someone to the point of madness." A wet cough escaped her throat.

"You've lost someone," I said, understanding her pain all too well.

She nodded.

"And you worry their loss will consume them." I looked at

the two men in front of me. "Should Annabel and Violet be lost to them forever?"

"Jake is surviving one day at a time. If we don't find Annabel, I don't know what it'll do to him." Her grip on my shoulder slipped, almost knocking both of us to the ground.

"Brett, you need to hold on, just a little longer."

She pulled herself upright, wincing as she did so, and her fingers dug into the thin fabric at my collar.

"And Robert… he… he hasn't even begun to process the loss of Violet," Brett continued. "How can he?" Her eyes searched my face, Violet's face.

"Save your strength," I said. "We can discuss this once Merlin's healed you."

"If Violet's gone," her voice cracked as she ignored me. "If she's never coming back," she managed. "He needs to know."

"I'm afraid I'm just as much in the dark as you are," I relented.

"Do you think," she coughed again and blood fell into the dirt at our feet. "That Merlin will try to save her," she continued. "Or is he using hope to get us to do his bidding?"

"Merlin's been known to bend the truth to fit his agenda, but in this case, I believe he means to help Violet in any way he can." I gripped her side tighter, pulling her against me.

She nodded, exhausted, as her eyes fell back on her brothers.

"May I ask you something?" I inquired.

With the amount of blood she was losing, I wanted to keep her mind engaged, keep her talking as long as I could.

"You and the Promised One, Matthew?" I looked to her for confirmation. "You're together, are you not?"

She looked ahead, but her eyes were distant and the corner of her lips tipped up ever so slightly.

"We are," she sighed.

"And do you not love him beyond what is rational?"

"I do. And it's terrifying." A tear fell from her eye.

"Hearts mend over time," I said delicately. "Should either of your brothers lose themselves to grief, take comfort in knowing it won't last forever."

"We're here," Merlin announced in the middle of an empty clearing.

"Thank the stars," I sighed. "Merlin, she needs you."

Robert and Jake turned toward us, and without skipping a beat, they were by our side.

"You're gonna be okay," Jake said, taking her into his arms and I fell to my knees.

"Are you—"

"Fine," I said, waving off the help. "I'm fine." My body ached to the bone and my soul felt like it was being pulled in two once again, but I'd survive. I had to.

"We need shelter before they reach us," Merlin said, raising his hands in front of him. Magic danced on the tips of his fingers, and under his breath, he uttered a spell. His Magic moved through the trees like woodland creatures ferreting out their hiding place.

As he reached into his pocket, his Magic moved through the empty space. Merlin pulled out a blade and in one swift motion, he slipped the knife through his closed hand. Holding his palm away from him, he let the blood drip into the earth.

"*Ostium patitur,*" Merlin said.

A few feet in front of him, a door faded into existence. The sparks of Magic moving through the trees came to a stop opposite of the door and began to pulse. Like a ghost, the shape of a cabin became visible until his Magic fizzled out and a small wood cabin stood before us.

"After you." Merlin turned the handle and pushed the door open.

Jake carried his sister into the house, and Robert escorted Alyssa behind them.

"It's good to see some things never change," I said, stepping up to the cabin. I let my hand linger on the wood banister leading up to the porch to support my weight.

"If only we could visit her under better circumstances." Merlin looked up at the cabin that had been our safe haven on multiple occasions.

"One day," I said, stepping inside.

"Right, everyone," Merlin said, closing the door behind us. "Make yourself at home and get some rest."

"What is this place?" Robert asked, taking a seat at the large table in the middle of the room.

"One can never have too many hideaways." Merlin walked across the room and gripped Robert's shoulder. The tension in Robert's face eased and his shoulder relaxed as Merlin's Magic stitched his wound back together.

"When the Draig first plagued this world, and it became clear, they wanted nothing but death and destruction, I stationed myself close by." Merlin released Robert and moved to Brett's side. Placing his hand on her wound.

"Thank you," Brett sighed, as Merlin's hand moved over her battered body.

"We should be safe for now. I've cloaked the cabin and only those who've been invited in are aware of its existence."

The color returned to Brett's face as she sat up, and Merlin released her.

"First things first," Robert said as he pulled out a chair next to Brett. "Have a seat," he motioned to Alyssa.

"What're you going to do?" Jake's brow furrowed as he studied Alyssa, and she hesitantly took the chair Robert held out for her.

"Find out the truth."

"And how do you intend to seek the truth?" I asked, unsure of how far he was willing to push the issue.

"Merlin," Robert called. "You performed a spell on Lila once."

His voice caught on the woman's name. "I'd ask that you do the same now."

"Very well," Merlin said, moving to Alyssa's side. "May I?" Merlin held his hand out to her.

She nodded once and placed her hand in his.

Wisps of blue and green smoke formed on each of his fingers and wrapped around Alyssa's wrist. The smoke roamed over her like snakes slithering up a tree.

"Ask away," Merlin said.

"Is Annabel still alive?" Jake asked.

"Yes." Alyssa held Merlin's gaze as the smoke pulsed over her chest and continued to roam over her body.

"Good," Merlin said.

"And does Morgana know you've come to us?" I asked.

"No."

"Anyone else know you're here or that you were coming to find us?" Robert jumped in.

"No," she answered.

The smoke tightened around her torso, pulsed, and then released its grip on her.

"Very well," Merlin said, pleased with her answer. "And lastly, have you come here under false pretenses to gain our trust?"

"No. Everything I've told you is the truth."

The smoke coiled around her neck and pulsed as it read her true intentions. The spell throbbed once more and the tendrils of smoke resumed roaming over her body, waiting for the next question.

"I think that'll do it," Merlin said as the smoke began to recede.

"Tell me where to find Annabel." Jake moved to sit across from Alyssa.

"Jake." Robert shook his head.

"You know I have to."

"I can show you," Alyssa interrupted the hard stare between the brothers.

"I won't let you lead us into a trap," Robert sneered.

"I'm going, with or without you," Jake said, turning away from his brother.

"I'll go with you," Brett said, reaching her hand across the table to grab Jake's.

Her eyes met mine for a moment and her words echoed in my head. *Jake's surviving one day at a time. If we don't find Annabel, I don't know what it'll do to him.*

"This is madness. You can't honestly tell me you think this is a good idea?" Robert stared at his sister.

"It's Annabel," she said, and her eyes fell on Jake. "We have to try."

"No one is in any shape to travel," I argued. "At the very least, we should wait to regain our strength."

"Tell us where they're headed and we can come up with a plan of attack?" Merlin suggested.

She shook her head. "I won't give up my only bargaining chip."

"What is it you're bargaining for?" I asked.

"Protection." She looked down, unable to meet my eyes.

"Why do you need us to protect you?" Jake asked.

"I don't... I wasn't born with Magic." She forced herself to look up, but her cheeks flushed. "I can only manipulate the Magic of others."

"Curious," Merlin said.

"Morgana will know soon, if she doesn't already, that I've left," Alyssa said. "I've no doubt that she'll send someone after me."

"So, you're asking us to risk our lives for you?" Robert folded his arms over his chest.

"If you want Annabel back, then you don't have a choice," she shrugged.

Robert scoffed, "And you want to trust her?" He looked at Jake.

"No one said anything about trust, brother."

"Mark my words, this will be a mistake," Robert's voice was clipped and sharp.

"If she's lying, I'll handle her myself." Jake turned to look at Alyssa, and she adjusted in her chair.

"Might I make a suggestion?" Merlin looked at everyone.

"She's proven Annabel is alive, and that Morgana is unaware of her whereabouts." Merlin walked across the room and stood behind Alyssa. "I believe she's earned the right to our protection until she proves otherwise."

"Earned the right—"

"Oh, get off your high horse," Jake interrupted. "You brought Lila into our home, Lila," he shouted. "You asked us, asked Brett to trust her," Jake shot out of his chair.

"That's hardly the—"

"You're right, it's not the same," Jake got in Robert's face. "So far Alyssa hasn't killed any of us."

"No, she just tortured me, and tortured Annabel for her own edification," Robert barked. "That's so much better."

Jake's jaw flexed. "If it was Violet, you'd put any one of us in harm's way to save her, and you know it."

"Jake," Brett scolded her brother.

"No," Jake barked. "I'm sick of him acting like he's the only one that has something worth losing."

"I've given everything to help save the Magical world," Robert took a step back like he'd been slapped.

"Yeah well, maybe you should stop worrying about the big picture and worry a little more about your own family."

"I see." Robert's shoulders slumped. "Glad to know how you really feel." He turned and walked down the narrow hall.

"Robert," Brett called after him. "Was that necessary?" She turned on Jake as she moved to follow him.

I placed my hand on her shoulder and said, "I'll go."

"He needed to hear it." Jake sat back down across from Alyssa.

"Maybe," Brett said, as I started down the hall after Robert. "But Robert's not wrong either."

CHAPTER 14

IVIAN

I COULD STILL HEAR Brett and Jake arguing as I walked down the narrow hall. There were three doors leading to bedrooms, each with memories and secrets of their own. The door at the end of the hall was closed, and it was easy to assume Robert had barricaded himself behind the thick slab of wood.

My knuckles rapped against the door, but there was no response. I tried the handle, and the latched clicked over and I edged the door open.

"Robert, it's Vivian," I said before stepping into the room.

"If you're here to make me understand Jake's side of things, there's no need," he sighed and sat down on the edge of the bed.

"I only came to check on you," I said, pushing the door open. "I thought you might need a friend."

The corner of his lips twitched, "He's right, you know."

"About?" I asked, leaning against the doorjamb to help keep me upright. Bruises covered my arms and the muscles in my back were so tight, I could barely move without pain shooting down my spine.

"If it was Violet…" his eyes met mine, and he looked straight through me to the woman lost inside.

Love, pain, and concern swelled inside me. Not for the first time, I was envious of their connection.

"It would appear that you and your brother are cut from the same cloth," I said, stepping into the room.

A humorless laugh escaped his throat. "Sometimes to a fault."

"I know you can't trust Alyssa," I said, sitting next to him. "But will you not trust Jake?"

There was still so much I was learning about the Maxwell's family dynamic. But their devotion to one another was never something that came into question.

Robert shook his head, "Jake doesn't understand who he's dealing with."

"It seems to me that you're both choosing to see what you want to in Alyssa." A muscle in my leg twitched and a sharp pain fired up my spine.

Robert looked up at me and again the familiar stir of Violet moved within my rib cage.

"I just don't want him to get hurt," he sighed. "If he has Annabel ripped from him again… I don't know if he's strong enough to come back from that."

"And what about you?" Brett's words rattled around in my head.

"I'm not sure what you mean?" His brow furrow and his eyes danced back and forth.

"Brett mentioned that you and Jake love fiercely," I eyed him. "You've already lost one person you seem to care a great deal for. Can you come back from that?"

"You mean Lila?" He guessed and his eyes drifted to the floor. "Honestly, I've had little time to process that she's gone."

"And Violet?"

His eyes shot back to mine and his face paled.

"She's not—"

"I assure you, she's still here," I blurted to dissuade his concern. "But she shouldn't be." I placed my hand on his. Warmth spread through my fingers as my hand lingered on his, and I relaxed at his touch.

"But she is." He turned to face me, taking my other hand in his. "Do you feel that?" His thumb moved back and forth and their Magic purred inside me. "That's her, that's me, and that's us."

I kept my eyes on our hands, taking in the sensation of their bond. If I had my own heart, surely it would break. Brett was right when she said Robert hadn't started the process of letting go of Violet. What I hadn't realized was that Violet hadn't let go of Robert, either. I could feel it now, her steadfast resolve to get back to him, his undying loyalty to her. It was all-consuming.

"She's growing weaker. We both are," I admitted. It was obvious, but no one realized just had bad it was. Time was running out and realistically, it was looking less and less likely that Violet would survive.

"I'll find a way," Robert shook his head and a sad, tight-lipped smile spread across his face.

"And so will Jake," I said. There was no point in arguing with him about Violet. Not when it was clear he would never give up on her.

"I know," he sighed and got up from the bed. In three long strides, he came to a stop in front of the window and peered into the forest.

The sunset threw a kaleidoscope of colors across the sky and warm light flooded into the room.

"Robert?" His shoulders stiffened, but he didn't turn around. "You can't let your brother do this on his own. If things don't go as planned, he'll need your support."

He rubbed the back of his neck, and I wasn't sure if he had the capacity to forgive Alyssa.

"He has Brett," he said, keeping his eyes locked on the window.

"I see," I said, pushing myself off the bed. It took much more effort than it should have to push myself upright, and my legs shook as the full weight of my body settled on them. "To be honest, I didn't think you were the type to walk away from your family." I ignored the pain radiating through me with each heartbeat.

He turned from the window and stalked toward me. "You have no idea who I am. You wear Violet's face and speak with her voice, but you don't have her knowledge of me or the type of man I am." The coldness in his voice made it clear he was finished talking.

"Very well." I moved toward the door. If he wanted to push everyone away, that was his prerogative, and it wasn't my place to get in the middle.

"Wait," he sighed as I reached for the door handle. "I'm sorry. This isn't your fault."

"No need to apologize." I turned to face him. "What would you do, if it was Nimue standing out there asking us to trust her?"

My blood stilled as I thought of her mingling with the Maxwell's, asking me to trust in her, to join her.

"That's different," I said coolly.

"Is it though?" Robert took a step toward me. "You have a history with her and that makes you question her motives."

"I'm very clear on Nimue's motives and I don't believe Alyssa shares in Nimues vision of the future." I kept my voice calm and even. "I don't envy the decision you have to make. But either you move past your history with Alyssa and judge her on her merits in the here and now, or you hold on to your judgments and drive a wedge between you and everyone else."

His eyes held mine for a pregnant moment and his shoulders slumped. I could see my words settling over him as his lips pursed. He looked past me to where his family sat in the other room and sighed.

"What would Violet say about all of this?" I pointed out as I held onto the door handle for support. I'd underestimated my strength and needed to lie down before my legs gave out on me.

"She would want Annabel back," Robert sighed.

"As does everyone else here. You have a choice to make," I said, opening the door. "And I suggest you choose wisely. Some things can't be fixed once you've picked a side." I walked out of the room and closed the door behind me.

Stumbling into one of the other vacant rooms, I made my way to the bed. Throwing myself onto the plush mattress, every muscle in my body tensed and slowly relaxed into the soft surface.

"Will the boy help us?" Merlin's soft, deep voice came from behind me.

Sitting up, I said, "You know him better than I do."

"Yes, but I'm not inhabiting the love of his life." He stepped into the room and closed the door.

"I think that's part of the problem, to be honest. It's too hard for him to look at me and see her."

"I may have a solution to your predicament." His lips curved at the corners and his eyes sparkled like they always did when he had some half-cocked plan.

"That look has gotten me into more trouble than I care to remember," I laughed and shook my head.

"Oh, come now, it always works out in the end." He rocked back and forth on his heels.

"Do you think maybe you could do some healing while you talk?" I patted the bed next to me.

He crossed the room in two short strides and placed a heavy hand on my knee.

"It's to do with Alyssa," he started. "Given her popularity, I think it best we keep this between us for the moment."

"What do you make of her?" I asked, closing my eyes and rolling my neck.

"I like her."

I shot him a quick glance.

"She has a fire in her I recognize well. Always willing to push boundaries despite the cost. And the fact that she can only manipulate the Magic of others is fascinating."

"She sounds like someone else I know." I gave him a conspiratorial grin.

His Magic settled deep into my bones and the aches and pains subsided some. Still, I felt battered and weak in every corner of my soul. Magic would only help so much. We needed to stop Morgana and end this before I was no longer strong enough to be effective.

"All I'm saying is that I recognize her potential." He patted my knee. "Better?"

"Some." I adjusted and sat back against the headboard. "Now, tell me your plan."

CHAPTER 15

IVIAN

The chirps of a songbird broke through my dreams and pulled me back to reality. A good night's sleep restored my energy, and though I was far from feeling like myself, the aches and pains were better than yesterday. That was progress, at least.

The gentle murmurs of the others in the main room reached my ears, and I forced myself out of bed. Today would be full of challenges and, quite honestly, I wasn't sure I would see the end of this day.

Leaving the comfort of my room, I made my way out to the others.

"Good Morning all," I said as I walked into the main room.

"Vivian." Merlin nodded his head.

Alyssa sat at the far end of the large table, paper strewn out in front of her as she made notes in the margins. No doubt Merlin had already put her to work on his insane plan. Though I couldn't fault the man for never giving up.

"How're you doing today?" Robert's voice broke through my thoughts.

"Better, thank you. And you?" I was only mildly surprised to see him here with everyone. Though he was stubborn, he didn't strike me as the type to turn his back on his family.

"Same." He gave me a small smile as he walked over to his brother and clapped a hand on his shoulder.

"You sure you're ready to do this?" Robert asked Jake.

"Thank you," Brett mouthed as she sidled up next to me.

"I did nothing," I said, as Jake looked up at Robert and nodded.

"You did," she smiled. "Whatever you said," she nodded in Robert's direction. "It helped some."

"I don't know that I can lay claim to his shift in perspective."

"Trust me," she put her hand on my shoulder. "You helped more than you realize."

"Morgana was planning to leave first thing today. We must hurry if we're going to catch them," Alyssa spoke up. "That is, of course, assuming nothings changed since you interrupted her plans at the Valley of the Draig."

All eyes shifted to her. If she minded the attention, it didn't show.

"The Draig will be with them," she emphasized. "Which will make this more difficult."

"We understand what we're up against," Jake said.

"Then let's get going." She pushed away from the table and looked around at everyone.

"Not so fast," Robert said, moving across the room toward her. "If you're going to lead us into a dragon's den, then I need some assurance of your intentions."

"What are you suggesting?"

"A binding spell," Robert said. "I can't trust your words, but I can trust what you're feeling."

"Do what you must." She held out her hand to him and looked away.

Robert recited the spell that connected him to Alyssa, and Violet squirmed inside me. My stomach turned, and I felt like I'd eaten a boulder as the spell settled over Alyssa.

"After you." Robert motioned for her to take the lead.

"Like I said last night." Alyssa turned to face everyone. "I won't fight with you, I can't."

"We understand," Merlin said.

"Once we arrive, I'll head back—"

"No," Robert interrupted her. "You won't be going anywhere without us. Merlin will stay behind with you."

Merlin nodded in agreement; apparently, this arrangement was already agreed upon. My curiosity piqued, and I wondered what he was planning with Alyssa, since he seemed keen to stay out of the fray.

Alyssa looked at the others, waiting for someone to come to her defense.

"Fine." She didn't seem too pleased with the arrangement, but she was smart enough not to argue the point.

"Let's go then," Jake said. He rolled his shoulders and, though he kept a neutral expression on his face, the tension in his body was visible and his brow had formed into a permanent furrow, aging him at least ten years.

We made our way out of the house, single file into the forest and back toward the Valley of the Draig, or what was left of it.

Beams of sunlight flowed through the canopy of leaves above us, lighting up the forest. Everyone was quiet, lost in their own thoughts about what this day would hold. Though I didn't know Annabel myself, seeing everyone rally to her rescue made me just as committed as her family.

Jake moved in time with Alyssa, following her every step with exact precision. Brett and Robert walked side by side in companionable silence while Merlin and I took up the rear.

We arrived at the Valley of the Draig much quicker than I thought we would. Yesterday, it felt like we'd been running through the trees trying to escape the Draig for miles.

"I'd suggest keeping an eye out going forward," Alyssa said as she passed what used to be the opening to the cavern in the mountain. "I wouldn't put it past Morgana to have scouts all the way to their camp."

Keeping to the trees and bushes, we edged forward. Each step I took felt heavy, and unease settled in my heart. The likelihood of us fighting our way out of this wasn't high and every time we go up against Morgana is another chance, someone will be lost to us.

The Maxwells may understand what they are doing in theory, but in practice, I don't think any of them are equipped to handle the death of a loved one.

Out of nowhere, Jake grabbed Alyssa by the shoulder and pulled them both into a crouching position. We all followed suit, and my eyes scanned our surroundings.

The sound of boots crackling through the fallen leaves reached my ears and every inch of my body stilled, as if I was frozen in a block of ice.

Robert quietly moved into the bushes, disappearing as we listened for any more movement. A rustling in the trees to my left made my heart stall in my chest. Without missing a beat, I pulled on my Magic and circled behind a tree.

Whoever they were, whether Draig, those loyal to Morgana or some unsuspecting passersby, they needed to be dealt with before they gave our position away.

As I stepped around the other side of the tree, I placed my hand in the dirt and cast a stunning spell. The ground between us sparked to life as it spread toward the person like veins reaching for a heart.

The spell grabbed hold of the person's feet and before they could topple over, I had my arm around their waist.

Guiding them to the ground, I sat them upright against the trunk of the tree and looked under the hood they were wearing. Draig, she was not, but that didn't mean she wasn't loyal to Morgana.

"Alright?" Merlin whispered.

I nodded and rejoined the others.

"Anything?" I said under my breath as Robert stepped into our tight circle.

"A man, not Draig. I left him unharmed but he won't be a bother for quite some time."

"Same with her," I nodded toward the boots sticking out from behind the tree.

"This is a bad idea," Robert started to argue.

"We're not stopping now," Jake said, and nodded for Alyssa to keep moving.

Alyssa turned and pushed through the bushes without a word. Whether she wanted to continue or not, she didn't let on. That made me curious. She kept her emotions closely guarded, which was not a trait any of the Maxwells exhibited.

As we moved through the trees, the morning dew started to rise with the heat of the sun. Wisps of fog moved with our every step as beads of sweat began to form on my forehead.

It wasn't warm. In fact, there was a chill to the air despite the sweat building up on my brow. Scanning the others, I noticed that none of them seemed as winded as I was. I immediately attributed my decline to the presence of Violet and again I worried about how much time we had left like this.

I could feel her more this time, as if she never fully fell into the darkness after her fight in the Valley of the Draig. Her energy hummed just beneath the surface of my skin and when Robert touched me, her Magic was too quick to respond.

Alyssa came to a stop at the top of a small hill and waved us forward.

"Down there," she pointed. "The church off to the right, on the far edge of the village."

My eyes scanned the small sleeping village below.

"They were there the last time I was with them." She turned to Jake and said, "The last time I saw Annabel."

"I guess this is it," Brett said, stepping up to her and Jake.

"Merlin," Robert called, and nodded toward Alyssa.

"You need not worry about us," Merlin said, smiling at Alyssa as he placed a hand on her shoulder.

Robert didn't look convinced as he shook his head. His brow furrowed, and he quickly stepped to my side.

"Are you sure you're up for this? It isn't your fight." He watched me from the corner of his eye.

"Love is always worth fighting for," I smiled. "It's what makes us different from them." I nodded toward the church.

A small smiled played on his lips, but it didn't reach his eyes. He was worried and doing very little to hide it.

"Anything else you want to tell us?" Jake asked Alyssa.

"Last chance," Robert emphasized each word, turning them into daggers as he watched their meaning settle over Alyssa.

"They won't be expecting you, but they will be ready for you. Don't for a minute believe you have the element of surprise on your side," Alyssa warned.

"Understood," Jake acknowledged and started down the hill.

Brett, Robert and I followed Jake out of the cover of the trees and into the open air. I felt like a thousand eyes were watching us as we moved forward.

"We shouldn't dawdle," I said, picking up the pace.

We made it to the edge of the village in a matter of minutes, all of us breathing heavy. If someone saw us, no one had sounded any alarms, at least none that I could see or hear.

Walking through the gate that surrounded the village, we made our way toward the small, unassuming church. The chill in the air did little to cool my sticky skin, and my heart raced with each step. Was is just adrenaline or something more sinister?

"What if she's not here? What if we're too late?" Jake rambled for the millionth time.

"Either way, this is a step in the right direction," I tried to reassure him.

"And no matter what, we'll keep going until we bring her home," Brett said.

Jake nodded, but I could see the haunted look in his eyes. I don't know what scared him more, not finding Annabel here or finding her and seeing the mess Morgana had turned her into.

Very few people were out and about and mostly they kept their heads down, barely registering another person. Either this whole village was afraid of their own shadows, or Morgana had made it clear who was in charge.

As we rounded the corner of a building, a man with broad shoulders and muscular arms smacked right into Jake. They both went down in a pile of limbs, but Jake was quick.

He rolled to his feet, pulling the man up with him and putting him into a headlock. Brett and Robert reacted just as quickly and though they didn't raise their Magic, a trained eye could see the Magic just barely on the tips of their fingers.

"We don't want any trouble," Jake said, keeping his voice low and cool.

"Aye, nor do I," the man croaked. "I'm only deliver'n tis morn'in bread ye ken?" He pointed to the toppled-over basket.

"Let him go," I said, and Jake did without hesitation. "Morgana and her followers?" I asked, and his body went stiff. "Ahh, so they are here."

"Please, I beg ye—"

"You need not worry yourself about us," I said, stopping him from launching into his plea. "You never saw us and we never saw you." I held his eyes and the color in his cheeks began to pink back up.

"Go," I nodded for him to take his leave.

"You sure that was a good idea?" Robert asked.

"That man was terrified, he's not with them."

"What if he's scared enough to warn them?" Brett asked.

"There's no need to warn them." My Magic blazed to life on my fingers. "They already know we're here."

Electricity crackled off my palms, cutting through the air like an arrow toward the dozen of Draig standing ahead of us.

The others turned. Without skipping a beat, they raised their shields as the Draig charged forward.

CHAPTER 16

IVIAN

Jake took a knee and planted his hands in the dirt. Robert summoned his Arcane Magic and Brett's fingertips crackled with electricity.

Raising my shield, I swept my arms across my body, summoning the brilliant sword made of blue fire and white light once again.

My Magic pulsed up the blade as I held the hilt in both hands. Turning and swinging the sword, a rush of Devil's flame leapt from the tip of the blade toward the Draig a few feet from me.

Deflecting the flames, The Draig kept her full focus on me and she pulled her own blade from her hip.

Jake's deep voice boomed around us as he recited a spell to bring the earth to life. Dirt and dust swirled around us as if a tornado had touched down in front of us.

Sparks flew past my head as the Draig raised her sword and

swung with all her might. Our blades connected, and the sheer force of her swing almost knocked me to the ground. The Devil's flame circled back around, searching out its target. Ducking out of the way, her blade swung over my head, barely missing my scalp.

Shifting into a crouching position, I summoned my Magic and thrust my palm toward the Draig's chests. A flash of light threw her several feet back into the tendrils of the Devil's flame and fire consumed her.

"Jake, we can't see anything," Brett yelled, as another spell collided with Robert's shield.

"That's kind of the point, sis," he said.

"We need to get to the church before we lose them," Robert said, punching one of the Draig and dodging a fist himself.

"Go," I yelled. "I'll cover you." I flipped the sword in my hand, end over end.

"I'm staying with you," Robert's shield deflected a cinder orb as he marched over to me.

I nodded, grateful for the help and faced the Draig head on.

"Find Annabel and bring her home," Robert said to his siblings as his shield engulfed me.

I could feel Violet starting to stir, their Magic hungry for release. I wondered if I, too, could tap into their Artognou Magic.

"Give me your hand," I said, holding out my free arm to him.

Without hesitation, he gripped my palm and their Magic burst to life inside me.

The corner of his lips turned up. "Do your worst."

Pulling on my Magic along with their Artognou Magic, my sword began to glow bright blue.

Raising the blade to the sky, thunder rumbled overhead. Lightning struck the steel sword, and the shadows crept out of their hiding place.

Robert sent a Galvin spell galloping forward, catching one of the Draig off guard, and he went down like a sack of potatoes.

The heavens opened up and rain poured down on us in heavy sheets of water. In one swift motion, I arched the blade over my head, summoning every shred of Magic within the three of us and let it pour off of the blade in one massive burst of energy.

The Draig disappeared behind the brilliant light, as did everything and everyone else.

"Run," I squeezed Robert's hand, and he pulled me along with him.

I bought us a few precious minutes and knew if we played our cards to perfection, we could get to the church before the Draig had time to regroup.

Robert was fast, his legs punching the ground like a racehorse as we dodged and weaved between buildings. My breath was shallow and my legs felt fuzzy, as if they were no longer attached to my body.

"We're almost there," he reassured me, as if he could sense I was losing my strength.

As we reached the gate of the church yard, we stumbled through the small over grown cemetery and up to the stone building. Vines crawled up the church and over the headstones unchecked.

With our backs to the cold stone, I scanned the area for anyone. Jake, Brett, Morgana, the Draig, but all was quiet.

Chills ran down my spine and though I couldn't see her, I could feel Nimue close by.

An explosion rattled inside the church and, without hesitation, Robert pulled the door open and rushed inside.

Taking a deep breath, I followed behind him, shield raised and ready for a fight.

Bits of dirt, dust, and stone formed a cloud around me, and I coughed as I inhaled a mouthful of debris.

"You made it," Brett sighed, as Robert and I knelt behind one of the upturned benches.

"Is she here?" Robert asked.

"I don't know." Brett shook her head as another spell exploded in front of us.

I took a quick peek at what we were up against. "We need to gain the upper hand."

"We're all ears," Jake said as another round of Magic battered his shield.

"How many are there?" Robert asked.

"Five, maybe six," Brett answered.

"Okay," I nodded. "The two of you head that way and pull their attention away from us." I motioned toward the front of the church. "Robert, follow me." I moved without waiting for a response.

Keeping low to the ground, I made my way toward the back of the church.

"I hope you have a plan," Robert said behind me.

"I have half a plan and that's something," I fired back.

As we skirted around several other over turned pews, another explosion sounded behind us and I ducked behind the overturned bench. My vision blurred and my breath caught in my throat as Violet grew stronger.

Doing a quick scan of the room. Jake was out in the open now, deflecting spells, but Brett stayed hidden in the shadows.

"Stand down," Morgana's voice echoed through the church. Everyone stilled in the room as her boots crackled against debris and stone.

"Well, well, we meet again."

"For the love of newt," I swore under my breath.

"I want my wife back," Jake demanded.

"And what makes you think we have your wife?" Morgana cooed.

My spine stiffened as if someone had poured ice water down my back.

"Stay here," I whispered.

"What about you?" Robert asked.

"I'll be fine," I said, pushing him into the shadows and moving around the over turned furniture.

"I have it on good authority she's alive and still your prisoner," Jake seethed.

"Prisoner's such a strong word," Morgana mused as I kept my back pressed against the wall. "Maybe your wife doesn't want to come back to you."

The distinct crackle of Magic reached my ears as I crept along the back of the church.

Hold on, Jake, I thought. I just needed another minute to figure out a plan of attack.

"Quite the temper you have," Morgana clicked her tongue as she walked up and down the line of her followers.

Looking up at the rafters and the surrounding furniture, a plan started to form.

"I'm not leaving here without Annabel," Jake growled.

"I thought you might say that." The laughter in her voice sent a chill down my spine. "Bring her forward."

"Jake," a woman cried.

Stepping up onto a wood desk, I caught sight of Robert and Brett hiding just out of sight. Robert's eyes met mine, and he nodded once. Whatever I was going to do, I needed to do it fast.

"You have something I want," Morgana said as Annabel was thrown onto her hands and knees. The chains around her wrists and ankles flared with Magic.

I pulled myself up onto an exposed beam that ran the length of the church.

"And what might that be?" Jake asked.

"Alyssa. Can I not assume it was she that told you your wife was still alive?"

Morgana's followers stood on the left side of the church, watching the exchange as if they were discussing the weather. There were only a few of them, but the Draig would be here soon and we would be outnumbered.

"I don't know what you're talking about." Jake's shoulders stiffened, but he kept his voice even.

"Oh, but I think you do." Morgana knelt next to Annabel and grabbed her face. "You give me Alyssa and you can have your precious Annabel."

It was now or never.

Balancing on the beam, I moved out of the shadows and said, "We don't make it a habit of trading human lives."

"I was wondering when you would show your face." Morgana looked up at me.

With everyone's attention on me in the rafters, I hoped Robert, Jake, and Brett would take advantage of the opportunity.

Magic sprung to life in the room, each person ready to strike at the slightest movement.

"Now, now." I raised my hand to her followers. Magic crawling along my skin. "Give us the girl," I seethed.

"Are you so naïve to believe you have any power here?" Morgana snorted.

"There's something you're forgetting," I smiled. "I'm not alone."

As if we had planned it to the second, Brett, Jake and Robert sprang into action. A Galvin spell tore through the room, cinder orbs exploded on impact and electricity crackled through the tight space, making the hairs on my arms stand on edge.

"Have it your way." Morgana grabbed Annabel's chains and started to drag her out of the church.

"Anna!" Jake yelled after her.

Jumping from the beam, I dodged a nasty looking spell. Using the leverage of one of the benches, I launched myself forward, kicking a man in the chest and sending him toppling to the ground.

With half of Morgana's followers occupied with Robert, Brett and Jake, I was able to slip closer to the exit Morgana had just dragged Annabel through.

My shield flickered as a spell hit me on the right side. Looking over my shoulder, I saw the Draig file into the church one by one.

"By the stars," I cursed under my breath.

My shield faltered again, and as I looked back toward the exit, Nimue stood in front of me.

"Robert, the Draig," I warned him.

Without skipping a beat, Robert shifted gears and focused his attention on the hoard of Draig piling into the church.

"When are you going to learn?" Nimue stalked toward me.

Morgana's followers moved around her like fish skirting a shark. They were afraid of her, and rightfully so.

"Do you ever shut up?" I seethed and summoned my blade once more.

"Very well," Nimue smiled. Magic crackled on her palms as she held her hands in front of her chest.

"Jake, no," I heard Brett scream, but I didn't have time to look.

Nimue's Magic barreled toward me like a cannonball.

I raised my blade, and the spell hit the flat side of my sword and Magic deflected around me in waves. I could just barely make out the silhouette of Nimue through the curtain of Magic.

She was even stronger than the day before, and the worry in my heart doubled. With each passing day, she was growing in strength while I was slowly fading away. I couldn't let her win, not again.

I shifted my weight and was able to get out of her direct fire. Shifting my wrist, the sword dropped forward and Nimue's Magic fired into the back of the Church while I rolled to safety.

The bench I was hiding behind began to rattle and I quickly made a run for it.

I only got two steps away when I was confronted with a Draig woman. Her fist swung toward me and I ducked. Swinging my blade, I connected with her armor, but it was as if she couldn't even feel the blow.

Pulling a crude looking dagger from her belt, she took another swing at me. Dodging her blow, I turned just as Nimue cast another spell.

With my left hand, I cast an absorption spell while I fought the Draig with my right hand.

Nimue's Magic hit my palm and my wrist almost buckled. Her Magic was tainted and dark. The feel of it seeping into me made my head spin.

The Draig's blade moved for my throat. My eyes blurred, and it was as if two blades were coming at me. I dodged out of the way, but the edge of the knife caught my cheek. Pain seared through me, but I didn't have time to let it in.

Near exhaustion, I dropped to my knees and Nimue's spell hit the Draig head on.

"You have one more spell in you?" Robert asked as he reached my side.

I wanted to say no, but looking at him, the trust and hope spurred me to my feet. It was my job to protect them, to end this war with Morgana. Even if I didn't have anything left to give, I had to find a way.

I nodded.

His hand gripped mine and his shield fell around both of us.

Nimue stalked toward us, her Magic strong and pulsing off of her as it tested the strength of Robert's shield.

"Coward," she growled.

Their Artognou Magic stirred in me once more and I held onto it with everything I had left. Robert squeezed my hand and his Magic poured into me. My heart struggled against my ribs, trying to free its self as the sensation of all of our Magic ripped through me.

Violet, Robert and I were one.

Meeting Nimue's eyes, I called all of our Magic to the surface. The stones beneath our feet began to rattle and all the windows shattered into a million tiny shards. The air felt thick with our Magic as if the ozone itself was being forced into this small church.

The veins in my arms were glowing under my skin and my body felt light as a dust mote.

Nimue's eyes danced around the church before focusing on me again.

"You'll never learn," I said over the steady rumble of stone and wood being ripped apart. "Darkness will never win."

Magic rushed out of me with such force that my head fell back. It took everything in my power to keep me upright.

A high-pitched ringing noise blotted out the sound of our Magic colliding with Nimue's. The stones falling from the ceiling hit the ground without a sound as my knees gave out.

I felt like I was falling in slow motion. Falling forever into the darkness, into the empty void of nothing.

Robert's arm wrapped around me before I hit the ground and he threw me over his shoulder.

With the last bit of strength I had left, I produced a destruction orb and threw it at the roof.

A curtain of stone, wood, and dust fell between Nimue and us as my body jostled against Robert.

Cool air touched my skin, and I took a deep breath. The control I'd been holding onto snapped like twigs, and the abyss took me once more.

CHAPTER 17

IOLET

THE CONSTANT TAPPING of fingers on a keyboard pulled me out of my dreams. I cleared my throat and coughed. My dry and cracked lips ached and the side of my face throbbed with each heartbeat. My eyelids fluttered open and the only light came from the computer screen to my left.

"Robert," I croaked. "Is he?" I couldn't bring myself to ask the question. If he died, if I lost him, I didn't know how I would face his family ever again.

Becky's fingers froze over the keys and she looked at me. A pregnant moment passed as her eyes danced over my face and then she leaped on me.

"Oh, thank God," she squeezed me into a bear hug. "I was so worried about you."

"Did Robert make it?" I asked again, as she continued to crush me. When I lost control, I was sure I lost him and I hoped beyond hope she wasn't about to break my heart.

"He's downstairs." She held me at arm's length. "He's alright."

I let out the breath I'd been holding. He made it out of the Valley and he was alive. My heart swelled and if it could, it would have flown right out of my chest. Robert's alive.

"How'er you feeling?" She asked, her eyes searching mine like I might disappear at any moment.

"I'm fine," I said, clearing my throat. "A little worse for the wear," I winced as I adjusted myself on the bed. "But I'm alright."

"When you guys got back," her eyes fell, and she shook her head. "I thought you..." she trailed off and hugged me again.

"It couldn't have been that bad," I said, patting her back and unwrapping myself from her grip.

"You haven't seen yourself." Her eyebrows rose precariously on her forehead.

Pushing myself into a comfortable sitting position, my muscles strained against the effort.

I reached for the glass of water off of the bedside table I took a long drink. The cool water soothed my dry, scratchy throat, making its way down my torso and into my empty stomach like a cool stream navigating through my body.

"How long this time?" I asked, placing the glass on the nightstand.

"Only two days," Becky said.

"Oh, well, that's better. Though I'm not sure if that's a good thing."

"It's not," Becky sighed. "It means Vivian is getting weaker."

"What are you, an expert now?" I asked.

"Merlin and I are totally best friends. He tells me everything." She joked, trying to break the tension in the room like always.

"I guess this means we don't have much time left," I said, more to myself.

"They'll find a way," Becky tried to reassure me. "They have to."

I gave Becky the best smile I could muster. She didn't need to know how desperate my situation had become, or that it was unlikely Merlin could form a crazy plan to save Vivian and me.

"So, what'd I miss?" I asked, changing the subject.

"Annabel's back," Becky bounced with excitement.

"Are you serious? Is she - I mean, *how* is she?"

"Everyone's been a little out of it since you got back." Becky shrugged. "I'm not clear on all the details, but it sounds like you guys had a tough time getting her out of there."

"That would explain why I feel like I've been hit by a bus."

"You look like it too," Becky frowned.

"Rude." I leveled my eyes on her and we both laughed. The tightness in my heart lifted some. Spending time with Becky was always so freeing, and her humor was a welcome reprieve.

"Also," Becky leaned in as if she was about to let me in on nuclear secrets. "Some woman named Alyssa, who Robert hates by the way, came back with you."

"Alyssa?" I balked.

"Mm-hm," Becky nodded. "And she and Merlin have been working on something very hush, hush."

"What do you mean?" Curiosity bloomed in my chest.

"They're all whispers until someone comes around and then they clam up faster than a turtle slipping into its shell."

I laughed at the image she painted. "What on earth could they have to talk about?"

"Not sure, but Robert's not having it." Becky leaned back against the headboard. "There've been multiple arguments on why she's even still here."

"I can imagine," I said. "After everything she did to Robert..." I trailed off. I didn't know how much Becky knew, and it wasn't my story to tell.

"And Annabel," Becky continued. "How Jake and Annabel can stand to be in the same house as her, I'll never understand."

"How is Annabel?" I asked again. If she was here, really here, it meant I failed her. Failed to *see* she still needed our help.

Becky pursed her lips and said, "Okay, I think. I mean, she's not the same, that's for sure."

"I would imagine not." Visions of her being tortured flashed before my eyes, and I felt sick to my stomach. There isn't a person alive who wouldn't be changed by the kind of pain she endured.

"Jake hasn't left her side," Becky said. "It's kind of amazing, seeing that kind of love and devotion up close."

"Are we sure it's Annabel this time?" I worried my bottom lip.

The fact that Morgana tricked us at all the first time haunted me. If this was a repeat situation, who knew what kind of damage that would do to Jake, to all of us.

"Merlin did his thing." Becky waved her hand. "And confirmed it was really her."

"His thing?" I eyed her and cracked a smile.

"I don't understand it, but it's ironclad and Annabel really is Annabel." She pulled her laptop back onto her lap, but kept it closed. "Also, can we talk about how crazy it is that there was even a 'fake' Annabel in the first place?" She used air quotes to emphasize her point.

"Right? Who would've thought something like that was even possible?"

"I guess anything's possible with Magic." She shrugged as if what we were talking about was normal every day gossip. "I shouldn't hog you," she frowned. "Robert wanted me to let him know the moment you were up." She swung her feet off the bed.

"Wait," I said. "I'd like to feel more like myself before I see anyone."

"You want to get all sexy for him, I get it." She wiggled her eyebrows.

I laughed. "Not exactly, but a shower and some food would be nice."

"You know you don't have to lie to me," she teased.

I rolled my eyes and pushed myself out of bed. My legs were sore, but they felt sturdy at least. That was something.

"When I get out of the shower, I expect a big plate of cinnamon rolls waiting for me," I called over my shoulder as I made my way to the bathroom.

"Hey, I'm not here to serve you just because you're some fancy Waker or Lady of The Lake," Becky called after me. "You're just plain, old, boring Violet to me."

"Thanks, Beck," I said as I closed the bathroom door.

The Maxwells kept a supply of Old West Cinnamon rolls in the freezer. So, I knew without a doubt a plate of them would be waiting for me when I got out of the shower.

I turned the shower on and shed my tattered clothing. The last time I looked in the mirror, I was horrified to see how thin and wasted I looked.

I forced myself to look up at my reflection, and the person I saw standing in front of me shocked me to my core.

A large, angry, red scar cut down the right side of my face. My collar bone and ribs were much more prominent, as if I'd been starving myself over the last few weeks. Bruises in various states of healing covered my body in purple and yellow splotches.

I shivered, despite the room being filled with hot steam from the shower.

Turning away from the mirror, I stepped into the shower and let the hot water pelt my sensitive skin. The heat felt like coming home, and I closed my eyes as the water washed away my worries.

So much had happened since I was last myself. Knowing that

Jake no longer had to live with a hole in his heart brought me peace as I thought of Jake and Annabel being reunited.

My future was grim at best, but knowing that the people I cared about were happy and loved made all of this worth it. My only concern now was for Robert. He'd already lost Lila in this war and although their past was fraught with complications, she was still important to him.

If I died too… I shook my head. I didn't want to think about what that would do to him.

I let my head fall back into the water. Magic tingled over my skin. Something pulled at me and I could feel the vision starting to take hold.

Robert stood a few feet away in the quiet place of my mind. Moving closer to him, I looked for anything new or different from the last time.

As I reached out to touch him, his hand made an identical movement again. This was like déjà vu, only with visions.

My eyes flicked up to him and he placed his index finger over my lips to keep me from speaking.

I reached up and placed my hand on his chest. The hum of our Magic bloomed under my rib cage and I let out a shaky breath.

His fingers wrapped around my wrist and again the wind started up. This time I could look around for the source when a hole opened up to my right and blue sparks flew in every direction.

"Please don't make me," Robert's voice pleaded, and I turned to face him.

His lip was split open, blood oozed down the side of his face, and his hair and clothes were torn and burned at the edges.

"What happened?" I reached to touch his face, and I felt like someone punched me in the stomach. Air was ripped from my lungs and I doubled over as I was thrust back to reality.

I opened my eyes, but the only thing I could see was the pain in Robert's eyes before he vanished. He didn't speak the first time, and I wasn't sure what his words meant this time.

"Don't make you do what?" I said under my breath.

Unease settled deep in my heart that even the heat from the shower couldn't wash away.

Turning off the water and wrapping a towel around myself, I thought over every detail again.

Never had there been so little to go off of with my visions. Where were we? Why couldn't I see anything but us?

Walking into the bedroom, I pulled some clothes from the dresser and got dressed lighting fast.

There was a knock at the door just as I slipped into a t-shirt. "Come in."

As if he knew I was thinking of him, Robert appeared in the doorway.

"I heard you were hungry," he said, showing off a plate of cinnamon rolls.

"Starving," I said, as he walked into the room and closed the door behind him.

"How're you holding up?" His eyes passed over me. He has to have noticed how frail I'd become, but his expression didn't betray him.

"Alright. Better after my shower," I said, digging into the hot, gooey cinnamon dough. "And I hear Annabel's back."

"I'm sorry, I couldn't do any better," he reached out and touched the scar on my cheek.

"I'm alive." I took his hand in mine. "That's what matters."

He pulled my hand to his lips and kissed my knuckles. "That you are," he said.

"And you heard right, Annabel's home, safe and sound." Robert smiled from ear to ear.

"And Alyssa?" I peeked a glance at him and pulled apart the cinnamon roll.

"She's here too." His smile faded, and he crossed his arms.

"Why?" I asked bluntly.

"Good question," he sighed. "Merlin's got his claws into her."

"About what, do you think?" I shoved a gooey piece of dough into my mouth.

"I have no idea," he shrugged and took a deep breath. Clearly, this was a tough subject for him.

I popped another bite into my mouth, savoring the sweet frosting and spicy cinnamon.

"So what happened?" I looked up at him. "I mean, do I at least have a good story for this?" I motioned to the scar on my face.

Robert frowned and said, "After the Valley of the Draig, Alyssa told us Annabel was still alive." He ran his hand through his hair. "We barely got out of there. After Vivian tapped into our Artognou Magic—"

"She what?" I said through a mouthful.

"Yeah, it's kind of incredible, actually." A small smile played on his lips. "Her Magic is strong, stronger than anything I've ever felt," he continued. "What she's able to do with our Magic, it's unbelievable."

I had to admit, I was a little jealous she was able to connect to Robert in that way, but I was also jealous that I wasn't there to see any of it.

"It sounds like the two of you are getting along." I took a large gulp of water to wash down the last bite of the cinnamon roll.

"If her very existence wasn't threatening yours, I might actually like her."

A soft knock on the door caught our attention.

"Come in," I called over my shoulder.

"You're looking well," Merlin said from the doorway. "I was hoping to steal a moment with you."

"Of course, what is it?" I asked, looking between him and Robert.

Merlin looked at Robert. "If you don't mind, I'd like to speak to Violet in private."

"Whatever you—"

I cut Robert off, "It's okay. Give us a minute." I placed my hand on his chest.

"Keep your guard up," Robert whispered as he leaned in close. "He's up to something," he said, kissing my forehead.

In a few short strides, Robert crossed the room and closed the door behind him.

"I don't mean to be indelicate, but I need your blood," he said without preamble.

CHAPTER 18

IOLET

"My blood?" I repeated.

Nothing came as a surprise anymore. But this was an odd request by anyone's standards, and I didn't know how to react.

"We're working on a way to save you, but we need something from you to manipulate," Merlin explained.

"Who's we?" My eyebrows perked up on my forehead.

"Pardon?"

"You said *we* are working on a way." I folded my arms over my chest. I don't know what he's playing at or what he's avoiding, but I'm not having any of it, not anymore.

"Alyssa," he said bluntly. "She's working with me to—"

"I don't trust her," I said without waiting for him to finish.

"No one said anything about trusting her," Merlin smirked. "But I can't deny, she has a gift for turning Magic inside out and creating something new."

"Yeah, that's the part I'm worried about," I argued. "She

manipulated Robert's ability to heal. She turned another woman into Annabel. I can only imagine what she might do with my blood. I won't work with her."

"Even if it's the only way to save your life?" Merlin's eyes met mine and all the pleasantries fell away.

My heart skipped a beat and the cinnamon rolls turned to stone in my stomach. "Is it the only way?" I asked.

Merlin crossed the room and sat on the edge of the bed.

"Maybe, maybe not," he shrugged. "Since your situation," he looked me up and down, "is one we've never encountered before, it makes it difficult to know what is and isn't the right lead to follow."

"I get that we're shooting in the dark, but Alyssa?" I stared at him, willing him to understand my hesitation. "I mean, there's no way she's in this just to help me."

"I don't disagree with you." His voice was void of emotion and he kept his expression neutral.

"What did you promise her?"

"Protection, to start with. So long as she behaves herself, I'll grant her safe harbor."

"And?"

"And, she will have access to me."

"Do you think that's wise?" I asked.

"She'll not cross me if she knows what's good for her," Merlin chuckled, and it grated against my nerves.

How could he be so caviler with someone who's repeatedly shown us how dangerous she is?

I shook my head and rubbed the back of my neck, "There has to be another way that doesn't involve giving her my blood."

"What's your real concern here?" He studied me.

"How do we know she won't turn on us and run back to Morgana?"

"That wasn't the question." Merlin crossed his legs and cocked his head to the side.

"She tortured Robert and Annabel." I reminded him.

"Did she?" Merlin's eyes narrowed.

"Are you joking?" I balked.

"Robert admits that she never harmed him. As for Annabel, that was Morgana's doing and part of the reason Alyssa finds herself with us now."

"Still, her actions have caused more than enough pain without adding my name to the list."

"She's also brought joy to the ones you care about. Without her knowledge, Jake wouldn't have Annabel back."

I opened my mouth to argue, but I couldn't fault her for bringing Jake and Annabel back together.

"No one is claiming Alyssa to be a saint, but she can help. In times of great need, only a fool walks away from those who can offer another way of looking at a problem."

"I'm not a fool, Merlin."

"I know," he smiled. "And if it makes you feel any better, Alyssa doesn't have Magic of her own. She can only manipulate the Magic of others," he said. "Should things move in a direction I'm not comfortable with, it's easy enough to pull the plug on the project."

"If she doesn't have Magic, then how on earth is she supposed to stop what's happening to me?"

"She sees Magic in a way we cannot; from the outside. Her ability to look at a problem from her vantage point and have an intimate knowledge of how Magic works is remarkable. She may have the ability to unlock this situation with you and Vivian."

"What is it she thinks she can do?"

It's hard to believe someone without Magic could solve the very real issue of the Magical being inhabiting my body.

"She's looking into a few options. Unfortunately, the only way to test our theories-"

"Care to elaborate?" I cocked my head and looked at him. If

he thought I would offer up my blood without any questions, he had another thing coming.

"Not particularly. They're only theories at best, nothing to write home about just yet."

"Robert doesn't know, does he?" I asked as I sat down next to him. The weight of what he was asking from me slumped my shoulders.

"No," Merlin patted my knee. "And it needs to stay that way." He leveled his eyes on me.

"Why?" My brow furrowed. "If you're trying to save my life, don't you think he'd want to help?"

The last time Merlin asked me to keep something secret, I regretted keeping it from Robert. And with the very real threat of death hanging over my head, I didn't want to spend whatever time I have left hiding things from him.

"He's blinded by his feelings. Even if Alyssa could solve all our problems with the click of a button, he still wouldn't allow her the satisfaction."

"I don't like the idea of lying to him. Not after everything she's put him and Annabel through."

"If you live, he'll forgive you. If not, well then, he can't stay mad at a dead woman forever."

I shot a glance at Merlin, shocked at his bluntness.

"I hate to be crass, but your days are numbered." His eyes were kind, but I could see the determination in the set of his jaw. He wasn't going to let this go.

"I know." I wrapped my arms around my middle and I could feel each rib. He was right. I was dying, and so was Vivian. Even if Alyssa betrayed us, there wasn't much she could do with a dead woman's blood, right?

"Why do I feel like Dr. Faustus?"

"Does that make me the devil?" Merlin smirked.

"You and Alyssa both," I sighed. "I'm going to regret this, aren't I?"

"I can't promise you won't." He gave me a sideways grin, "But at this point, I think you're out of options."

I nodded my consent, and Merlin pulled a kit out of his coat.

"You weren't planning to take no for an answer, were you?" I eyed him.

"You should know by now that I'm very persuasive when I need to be." He unrolled the kit on his lap and held his hand out to me.

Giving him my arm, he wrapped a tourniquet just above my elbow.

"Can I ask why you're trying so hard to keep me alive?"

He looked up at me through his lashes and cocked his head to the side.

"I mean, don't get me wrong, I'm more than grateful, but why do you care what happens to me?"

Tapping the vein on my chicken bone of an arm, he said, "I know what it is to have destiny thrust upon oneself unwillingly." His voice was soft and thoughtful as he inserted the needle into my arm.

"Sure you do," I scoffed. "I didn't even know there was Magic before any of this. You were born into this world," I said, motioning with my free arm.

"You assume you know my story because Hollywood has told it over and over again," he smirked.

"What're you saying?" I furrowed my brow as my blood began to fill the vial.

"Much like yourself, I wasn't born with Magic."

"But I thought all Magic stemmed from you?"

"While that's true, it's not as simple as you might think," he smiled. "Many, many centuries ago, I was just like you. I lived a life of simple pleasures, unaware of anything out of the ordinary."

He pulled the needle from my arm. "That should do for

now." Placing a cap on the vial, he slipped my blood into his pocket.

"What happened then? I mean, if you weren't born with Magic, then how..." He placed a hand on my arm and the tiny prick in my skin closed up, leaving only a small drop of blood.

"My wife and I took in a child who lost her family, her home, everything."

"I didn't realize you were married," I said sheepishly. In all the time we'd spent with Merlin, I never thought of him as having people of his own.

"It was a long time ago." A faint smile touched his lips. "We were unsuccessful in having children of our own. When the opportunity presented itself, we jumped at the chance to raise the girl."

He stared at the wall in front of him, but his eyes were a million years away. Sitting silently and fighting the urge to ask questions, I waited for him to continue.

"There was a fire. My wife, she didn't make it."

"I'm so sorry." My voice was barely a whisper.

"To be fair, I didn't make it out alive either." The corner of his lips twitched and a heavy sigh lifted his chest.

"Our daughter was not of this realm." He turned to look at me. "The Draig destroyed her home, and she was all that was left of her kind."

His eyes held mine, and I dared not blink. I had the distinct feeling this was a story he didn't tell often, if at all.

"She pulled me out of the house." His eyes fell to his lap, "And she brought me back." His face softened as he spoke.

Unconsciously, I reached for the tiny scar that was the only thing left from my stab wound.

"From that moment, not only did I have Magic, but my life-span has exceeded what one might expect."

"She was a healer?" I asked.

He shook his head, "She was something more, something unique and truly gifted." He smiled, but it didn't reach his eyes.

"So really, she's the birth of all Magic in our realm?"

He nodded. "It's a wonderful gift, but not something I actively chose."

"Do you wish she hadn't saved you?" My voice was barely a whisper as my own feelings surfaced.

I'd often wrestled with this question myself. Though I was glad to be alive, there were moments I wished Robert hadn't saved me, hadn't put me on this path.

"Not anymore. But in the beginning, it was hard to accept the change, so to speak."

"I get it," I sighed. "My entry into the Magical world hasn't been all that graceful."

"Some take to the Magical world as easily as breathing, much like your friend."

"Becky?" I furrowed my brow.

He smiled, "She was meant for our world, it suits her."

"She mentioned you were the best of friends now," I laughed and the tension in my heart disappeared. There was so much about all of this that's difficult, but seeing Becky step into her own within the Magical world made it easier.

"Do you think she'd choose this life if given the opportunity?" Merlin asked.

"In a heartbeat," I said without a doubt.

"I thought as much." A sly smile played on his lips.

"You're planning something, aren't you?" I guessed.

"Maybe," he shrugged and stood up. "Just know, unlike you and me, she'll have a choice in the matter." He paused at the door and met my eyes.

While there were many reasons to question Merlin's actions, there was a warmth to him when he talked about Becky and a glisten in his eye. He admired her.

"I don't think it is a choice for her," I said, rising from the bed. "As you said, she was made for this world."

"Quite right." His smile reached his eyes, and he opened the door. "We should join the others, it's quite the reunion down there." He nodded for me to follow him.

CHAPTER 19

IOLET

As I followed Merlin down the stairs, I could hear the others talking and laughing. It felt like ages since I could feel the happiness radiating through the estate and it warmed my heart, knowing they were all safe and together again.

Reaching the bottom of the stairs, my stomach did a double flip. I was nervous to see Annabel. Guilt weighed on me like a ten-pound bag of sand. I should've known she was still out there, still in danger, still being tortured.

What must she think of me? I wondered.

"Finally," Becky's voice carried over the others as we rounded the corner into the kitchen.

Robert stepped closer to me, reaching for my hand and pulling me into the fold of his family.

"Everything okay?" He whispered against my ear and played it off with a kiss to my temple.

"Mm-hmm." I smiled and wrapped my arm around his waist.

"You look about as good as I feel," Annabel's lyrical voice chimed.

"You should've seen her before her shower," Beck laughed.

"Had I known I was walking into the Violet Evans roast, I would have stayed upstairs."

"She's just jealous of your total badass, Waker status," Matty sneered at Becky.

Becky's hand went to her chest and her mouth fell open in mock surprise. "You wound me," she rolled her eyes, and again the kitchen filled with laughter.

"Joking aside, it's good to see you." Annabel smiled.

"I'm so sorry, I should've—"

"You have nothing to be sorry for," she shook her head.

"I just—"

"Just nothing. You had more than your fair share to deal with. All of you did." She looked around the room. "I don't blame any of you." She looked up at Jake and he reached out to touch her. He hesitated for the briefest of moments and shoved his hands in his pockets. I couldn't imagine how hard it must be for him to have Annabel so close, yet so far away.

"Besides, I hear you've got a whole Dr. Jekyll and Mr. Hyde situation going on." Her eyes searched my face as if she was trying to see Vivian.

"Hopefully not for long," Merlin said, his eyes meeting mine as Robert's hand moved up and down my back.

You can't lie to him, Violet. Not again. I thought.

"It's been interesting, that's for sure." I pulled a stool out from the island.

"You could say that again." A short, clipped laughed escaped Annabel's throat.

"Now that everyone's here," Jake started. "You wanted to tell us something?" he motioned for Annabel to take the floor.

"We can't trust The Brotherhood," she said without preamble.

"What do you mean?" Brett leaned forward and her brow furrowed.

"They're working with Morgana." Annabel met my eyes.

"That's impossible," Merlin chimed in. "They can't take sides in any realm. The Magic that binds them won't allow it."

"I'm telling you, it is possible," Annabel's hand balled into a fist on the counter. "I know what I saw, and they are taking sides." An angry welt around her wrist stood out against her pale skin, and fury bloomed in my chest.

"Why would they come to us for help and warn us about Morgana, if they were working with her?" Robert asked.

"They were here?" Annabel's eyes darted around the room.

"Yes, after Morgana attacked them, they came here for protection and to regroup," Jake explained.

"Everyone, outside," Annabel shot to her feet. "Now." She pushed away from the island and stormed out of the kitchen.

Jake shrugged and pursued Annabel.

Robert and Brett shared a worried glance, but still got up from their seats and followed her.

"Is she okay?" I asked Brett, as we all made our way to the backyard.

"Physically yes, but who knows what kind of mental toll her imprisonment has had on her," Brett answered in a hushed voice.

"The best thing we can do right now is to support her," Matty explained.

"Hey, what's got you spooked?" Jake asked in a hushed voice as we filed into the backyard.

"If they were here, they could've bugged the place," she raised her hand to stop anyone from speaking. "And before any of you say it, I know it sounds crazy, but I've seen and heard crazier."

"No one's saying you're crazy." Jake took her hand, and the gesture seemed to steady her.

"Tell us what you saw," Matty stepped forward, pulling Annabel's attention.

"The whole time I was there," Annabel sighed, "The Brothers would come and go at random. Sometimes they would talk to Morgana, sometimes they would just pass on a message."

"It's possible," Matty mumbled to himself. "They could-"

"What're you thinking?" Robert interrupted Matty's rambling.

"Maybe they were trying to intervene, stop Morgana from going down this path and that's why they ended up dead."

"No," Annabel shook her head. "They were helping her, guiding her toward The Draig." She shivered and gripped the scars on her wrist.

I watched Annabel as her eyes shifted to each of us. She was different now, changed by the time she'd spent away from us. Her edges were sharp and the lightness that used to emanate off of her was gone. It broke my heart.

"Annabel, I saw what Morgana and Nimue did to the Brothers. They weren't willing to help them." The vision I had of the Brothers being brutally killed one by one flashed before my eyes.

"You saw what they wanted you to see," Annabel argued.

"No, she didn't. We were there," Brett supplied.

"Where?" Annabel looked between Brett and Robert.

"We went to the Brotherhood's Realm," Robert explained.

"I thought no one—"

"Vivian was able to get us there," Brett explained.

"It was like a horror film." Robert pinched the bridge of his nose. "Everyone was dead, mutilated. They didn't stand a chance."

"That's not possible," Annabel shook her head. "I'm telling you, something's not right."

"Annabel's right." Alyssa's voice carried across the backyard.

"The Brotherhood did visit Morgana, though I cannot say to what end."

She leaned against the frame of the French doors, her arms folded across her chest. Her smug angles and bravado made my skin crawl.

Giving Merlin my blood was a mistake. I thought.

Annabel moved closer to her husband, and Jake squared his shoulders, blocking Alyssa's view of Annabel.

"She's the one we need to worry about," Robert said under his breath.

"When was the last time you saw one of the Brothers with Morgana and Nimue?" Matty asked, ignoring Alyssa.

"After the fight at the cave. One of them showed up at the church, where you rescued me."

A cold trickle trailed down my spine as his name escaped my lips. "Cian."

Everyone turned to look at me.

"But he helped us." Brett shook her head.

"Who's Cian?" Annabel jumped at the thread.

"When we visited their realm, we saved one of them. Cian." Robert's jaw flexed, and I knew he was thinking the same as me.

"He helped us get to the Valley of The Draig, and he helped us stop Morgana," Jake explained.

"Did he?" I asked as I thought about the sequence of events that led us to the Valley of the Draig.

"What're you saying?" Jake asked.

"Whose idea was it to *shift* the gate?" I used air quotes to emphasize my point.

The Maxwells went quiet, each searching for the truth about what happened.

"It was Cian," Robert said. "He's the one who opened the gate."

"He used our bond to—"

"He used our connection against us," Robert sighed. "Cian

wanted one of us to get stuck on the other side or kill us both in the process. He wanted the Draig to make it into this realm."

"Well shit," Becky sighed.

"If that's true," Matty started, "And Cian was a plant, then they had to know you'd visit their realm and rescue him. It seems a little farfetched, doesn't it?"

"Actually, no," Merlin sighed. "Based on what happened with Annabel, it's easy to assume you'd be suspicious of anyone showing up unannounced."

"Still, it's leaving a lot to chance," Matty argued.

"Morgana doesn't leave anything to chance," Alyssa said.

"She's right," Merlin agreed. "Everything Morgana does is calculated."

"But how could she know how we'd react to the Brotherhood showing up here?" Brett asked.

"Because of Annabel," Alyssa said matter-of-factly.

Annabel's eyes widen and her face paled.

"Our - I mean Morgana's Annabel," Alyssa clarified. "Her secondary purpose was to collect as much information on all of you as possible."

"Know thy enemy," Merlin said.

"She knew your guard would be up after Annabel was exposed as a fake. She knew you wouldn't trust anyone, and she knew you couldn't refuse to help someone in need."

"I'm confused," Becky shook her head. "So is the Brotherhood with us or Morgana?"

Everyone's eyes fell on Alyssa.

"I was never privy to their conversations. You lot know as much as I do now."

"Maybe we're just talking about a few rogue Brothers who turned and are helping Morgana," I mused.

"Maybe, maybe not," Alyssa shrugged. "Maybe the men you met weren't Brothers at all."

"Wouldn't you have known?" Robert rounded on Merlin. "If they were impostors?"

"They were marked," Merlin argued. "Only those who have pledged their soul to protect the realms are capable of wearing The Helm of Awe."

"Why do I get the feeling you're not telling us everything?" Robert said through gritted teeth as he turned to Alyssa.

She chuckled, "Your inability to see the bigger picture has always been your weakness."

"Care to enlighten us, then?" Brett asked.

"Morgana isn't playing just one hand of poker," Alyssa moved through our group, looking at each of us, studying us. "She has every card at her disposal, guaranteeing her victory." She moved around our little circle and cocked her head. "Hate to break it to you, but the deck is stacked against you in every way imaginable."

"Wow. I've met a lot of guys who talk in circles like it's an Olympic sport." Becky shook her head. "But you put them all to shame."

A small grin pulled at Robert's lips.

"You have a fire in you," Alyssa smirked. "You're going to need it."

Becky rolled her eyes. "And now you just sound like a Bond villain."

"So, what do we do?" Brett asked.

"I think it best we operate as if they've betrayed their oath," Merlin offered. "But we mustn't tip our hand."

"Maybe I can try to see something," I offered.

"No," Robert and Merlin said in unison.

Their eyes met and I could see the questions building just under the surface.

"You need to save your strength," Robert said.

"He's right," Merlin agreed. "Each time you shift, so to speak, it makes you weaker, both of you."

"Isn't it worth finding out the truth?" Alyssa asked.

"I don't recall asking for your opinion," Robert leveled his gaze at her.

She raised her hands in surrender. "Do as you will, but the sooner you learn the truth, the sooner you'll know what you're up against."

"She's right," Annabel said. "We can't just sit here and hope for the best."

"Of course not," Robert said. "But you haven't seen how her Magic drains her."

"Everything has its price," Alyssa commented.

"This doesn't concern you," Robert snapped.

"You're right. I only came out here to speak with Merlin." She walked past us and stopped in front of Merlin. "Shall we?"

"We'll continue this later," Merlin said, placing a hand on Alyssa's back as they moved toward the house.

"Is it just me, or are they being a tad too secretive?" Becky watched Merlin and Alyssa disappeared into the house.

"We need to make sure the house is clear, set up wards," Annabel said, ignoring Becky.

"We already have wards in place," Jake said, trying to reassure her.

"Like we had in place when I was taken?" Annabel's eyes were cold as she looked up at him. "It's not enough."

CHAPTER 20

IOLET

"Anna, I..." Jake trailed off, the pain clear in his eyes.

Annabel sighed, "I'm sorry, I shouldn't have-"

"It's okay," Brett said. "You're right. We could use a little more defense."

Annabel gave her a small smile, and the tension eased a bit.

"You two clear the house, make sure the Brothers left nothing behind," Brett ordered Jake and Annabel and they started toward the house. "I'll take care of the wards."

"Want some company?" Matty asked.

"Always," Brett smiled, reaching for his hand.

"What should I do?" Becky asked.

"Find out what Merlin's up to," Matty said. "You're right, there's something going on with him and Alyssa and we'd all sleep better knowing what that is."

"Say no more." Becky started toward the house. "Violet, you coming?" Becky looked back in my direction.

"We'll be there in a minute," Robert answered, grabbing my hand and pulling me in the opposite direction.

"Sure you will." Becky wiggled her eyebrows.

"Come on," Robert said, "There's something I want to show you." He pulled me toward the pool house.

"Shouldn't we be helping them?"

"They can handle it." Robert's eyes met mine and his lips curled into a mischievous smile.

"With everything going on, what Annabel said, how can you just push it all aside?"

He stopped in his tracks and I slammed into him. His arm wrapped around my waist, steadying me. "Because I've learned a valuable lesson since meeting you."

"And what's that?" I placed my hands on his chest.

"Jake almost lost Annabel, Lila's dead and I don't know how much time I'll have with you before Vivian takes hold again." He brushed the hair off of my face. "I don't want to waste what little time we may have worrying about what's next."

My heart swelled and as I looked up into his eyes, everything else disappeared. He was right, the here and now was too good to waste.

"Okay," I smiled. "What did you want to show me?"

Lacing his fingers through mine, he pushed the door to the pool house open and flipped on lights as we made our way into the small sitting room.

The pool house was cozy and warm and I'd always loved coming in here. The boxy shape and tight quarters reminded me of an oversized tree house.

"I found these a while back," Robert said, digging through the closet.

"It's never seemed like the right moment to show you, but," he huffed as he pulled down a box and placed it on the tiled floor.

"But there's never a right time for anything nowadays," I finished for him.

I unfolded the lid of the worn cardboard box, and he reached in and pulled out a journal. "They belonged to William," he said.

"All of them?" Dozens of journals and loose papers filled the box to the brim.

"I had no idea he wrote this much." A small smile pulled at the corner of his lips as he sat down on the plush cream couch.

"I guess now we know where you get it." My chest warmed as I looked down at him.

There was still so much we were learning about each other. Little basic things about who we were. It was easy to forget sometimes that we were still in the beginning stages of our relationship.

"I was only ever given the one journal with the prophecy," he said, flipping through the pages of the chronicle in his hand.

"Have you read any of them?" I plucked one from the box and sat down next to him.

He shook his head. "I haven't had the luxury of spare time since I met you."

His eyes met mine and dipped to my lips for a fraction of a second.

"How did you find them?" I asked as heat rushed into my cheeks.

Still, with everything going on, one look from him sent a thousand little butterflies flapping around my stomach.

"A few weeks ago," he looked away from me. "You were..." he sighed. "Jake asked me to store some of their wedding gifts out here. He couldn't bear to deal with any of it."

I reached for his hand and laced my fingers through his. We'd all been through so much since the wedding, which felt like another life altogether.

"They were just sitting in here, all this time," he shook his head in disbelief. "You said that you felt connected to him, like you knew him through your visions."

He turned his body toward mine and draped his arm across the back of the sofa.

I chuckled, "Of everything I've seen and experience, he's always been the most clear and warm." I looked up at him and his dark hazelnut eyes stared back at me. "Kind of like you."

He reached out and tucked my hair behind my ear and let his fingers linger on my cheek. "Should you want to visit him, they're yours to read, anytime."

"Are you sure?" My words made it past my lips in a whisper as my heart raced at his touch. "Your family won't mind?"

"Considering they've been collecting dust in here, pushed aside and forgotten, I doubt anyone even cares about them."

"Still." I ran my hand over the leather cover. "It's your family's history, your legacy."

"You've been a part of this family since before we even met." He leaned in closer, his arm brushing against mine and sending a shiver up my skin.

A nervous laugh escaped my lips. "I remember meeting Annabel for the very first time."

"I was talking about the prophecy, but I *am* glad Annabel was your first introduction to our family. Brett can be..."

"Intimidating," I finished for him. "At first. But really, she's harmless."

"To you, maybe, but I wouldn't dare cross her."

"Are you kidding? The two of you butt heads more than any other people I know." I shook my head.

"Family's like that," he gave me a lopsided grin.

"Yeah, well, your family can be a tad overwhelming at times."

"Why do you think I live six thousand miles away?" He chuckled.

I sighed. "I never thought taking Annabel and Jake's wedding would lead me here." I shook my head in disbelief. Somewhere between accepting the job for Annabel's wedding and Robert healing the wound that Ian inflicted on me, my life took a sharp left turn.

"In a dodgy pool house, with a gentleman whose intentions are admittedly a little less than above board?" His cologne wrapped around me, pulling me under his spell and making my head swim happily in a rose-colored cloud.

Laughing, I nudged him. "I would hardly call this dodgy," I said, motioning around the lavish, albeit cozy pool house. "But all of this, it's been so much more than I ever dreamed for my life."

"Then you need to dream bigger."

"I think the time for dreaming might be behind me." I pursed my lips.

Tell him. I screamed internally. *Tell him about Merlin and the blood.*

"You can't think like that." His body invaded the space between us. The heat of his skin radiated off of him and my pulse quickened.

I wanted to tell him, blurt it out right then and there, but I didn't want to fight. Not now, not in this perfect moment. Who knew how many of these stolen quiet moments we had left?

"You're right, let's get back to your intentions," I pressed closer to him, bringing our lips a few inches apart.

"Don't get me wrong, I did want to show you the journals," he breathed against my lips and my eyes fluttered closed.

"Mm-hmm," I teased.

"But my motives for bringing you here are much more selfish," he said, leaning his forehead against mine.

"Care to enlighten me?" I mused as his fingers trailed up my arm, leaving goosebumps in their wake.

"Even if it's just for a moment, I wanted you to myself." He pulled an inch away and looked down at me. "It's been impossible, looking at you," he brushed my hair off my face. "And knowing it's not you looking back at me." His eyes burned into me, turning my bones to mush.

"It's me now," I breathed and placed my hand on his chest.

His heart beat with a fever, matching my own and making me lean closer in anticipation.

His eyes traced every inch of my face, every wrinkle, every freckle, as he stared at me. His fingers moved up my neck, over my thrumming heartbeat, to my chin.

"So it is." He tipped my chin up and his lips brushed mine.

An electric shock shot through me as his mouth moved softly, gently against mine. My heart threatened to beat out of my chest as he wrapped his arm around me and lifted me onto his lap. I pressed myself against him, deepening the kiss and drinking him in. He was warm, inviting, and I wanted to get lost in him, even if it was fleeting.

His grip on me was tight, keeping me rooted against him as his other hand found its way into my hair. Still, he was hesitant, like he was afraid to let down his guard and give into us.

"What's wrong?" I breathed as my skin burst to flames where our bodies touched.

"I've missed you," he said, kissing my neck and our shared Magic purred inside me.

"Then why does it feel like there's a wall between us?" I pulled away from him to catch my breath.

"I hardly think there's much between us at the moment," he looked down at our bodies pressed tightly together.

"You know what I mean." I wrapped my hand around the back of his neck and my thumb traced his jawline.

He lifted me off the couch in one swift motion and placed me on my back.

"I don't want to lose you again," he said, hovering over me.

"Robert, I'm here." I put his hand on my chest so he could feel the steady tempo of my heart. "I'm right here," I whispered.

His eyes held mine and with each passing second, his face softened.

He kissed me again and this time there wasn't anything between us. He was like a man starved for oxygen, and I was the only one who could save him. Any shred of restraint on either of our parts disappeared.

My body arched up to meet him and he quickly shed his shirt. The heat of his skin pulled me deeper and deeper into our little bubble, and the outside world ceased to exist.

My fingers dug into his shoulders, trailing down his back, and a low groan escaped his throat.

"I could feel you on the other side of the gate," Robert said, pulling his lips from mine and in one swift motion, he had my shirt off and on the floor. "The pain as you struggled to keep the gate open." His hand moved over my ribs, the heat of his touch making me shiver. "My only thought was getting back to you." He stared down at me as if I might disappear before his eyes.

"You did," I breathed, running my fingers through his hair.

His thumb traced the curve of my bottom lip as he hovered over me. "When I lifted you out of the rubble, I just wanted you to open your eyes, to look at me and know you were okay." He leaned his forehead against mine. "But it was Vivian's eyes that stared back at me." His words were like a knife in my heart. "I fought to get back to you and lost you all in one breath."

"I tried to hold on," I said as his hand moved down my side and settled on my hip.

"I know," he exhaled and his lips brushed mine again. "Promise me, we'll find a way out of this." His eyes pierced through me and guilt bubbled deep in my chest.

"That's a problem for tomorrow." I pulled him down to me and kissed him like it might be the last. If I was going to die at the end of this, I wanted to spend as much time as possible wrapped up in the man I loved.

CHAPTER 21

 IOLET

He broke our kiss, and my head fell back as I tried to catch my breath. His lips moved down my neck and over my collarbone, making me forget where we were, what was happening outside of us, and what my name was for that matter.

The sound of thunder boomed outside quickly, followed by a sizzle, and we both looked toward the door.

"A storm?" I breathed as I looked up at him.

Another boom, sizzle, and the pool house rattled like the ground beneath us was no longer stable.

"Not a storm," he said, getting to his feet and picking up our shirts.

"Moment's over," I sighed as he tossed me my shirt.

"It would seem so." He slipped into his shirt and held his hand out for me to grab.

"What do you think it is?" Another rumble and sizzle shook

the pool house as I pulled my shirt over my head and reached for his outstretched fingers.

"Only one way to find out." He pulled me into his arms. His lips crashed into mine and if he hadn't been holding on to me, my legs would have given out under me. "We'll finish this later," he smirked.

"Promise?"

His lips quickly brushed mine once more, and then he was pulling me through the door.

Inky black clouds swirled above us, whipping the surrounding air into a frenzy.

"What the hell?" Brett yelled as she raced out of the house.

Lightning struck the stone ground in front of the pool, leaving behind a dark scorch mark. Smoke started to rise from the mark, forming into something solid.

"That's not normal," Becky said as the others filed into the backyard.

"You shouldn't be here," I yelled, as Robert and I crossed the yard at a jog.

Another thunderous boom, sizzle, lightning.

Boom.

Sizzle.

Lightning.

Four figures rose from the ground, forming into solid creatures.

A kaleidoscope of colors flew up in front of all of us, our shields coalescing to form one giant wall against whatever these things were.

"Beck, get out of here," I said, as Magic crackled on my fingertips.

"Anyone know what this is?" Brett stepped forward, drawing on the elements as electricity hummed over her skin.

"Not a clue," Jake said. "Where the hell did Merlin go?"

"Are those hands?" Becky pointed at the figures taking shape in front of us.

The shape of a person stood before us. Where their eyes, nose, and mouth should be, there was nothing. A flat, unseeing surface, except I could feel their eyes all around me, making my skin crawl.

"Who are you?" Robert stepped forward. "What do you want?"

Their heads swiveled in my direction and I swallowed the lump in my throat.

"Your soul does not belong here," they spoke in unison and cold, hard dread poured into my heart.

"Answer me," Robert demanded.

And that's when I realized they hadn't spoken at all; they were in my head.

"They said my soul doesn't belong here." My mouth was dry as I spoke their words aloud.

"To hell with that," Brett leveled her eyes on the creatures, lightning moving down her arms and galloping toward them.

Her Magic passed right through their bodies and collided with the fence on the other end of the yard.

"You will come with us," they said. Each of them pointing a long ghostly finger at me.

"I'm not going anywhere." I squared my shoulders, my heart pounding and ready for a fight.

Another crack of lightning and the smoke swirled, losing its form and circling around us.

"Keep your guard up," Robert called over the howling wind.

"Get somewhere safe," I called to Becky over my shoulder.

"I'm not leaving you," she yelled.

Before she could argue further, Matty grabbed her by the waist and pulled her toward the house.

I'd have to thank him for that later.

"Any ideas on how to attack?" Brett asked as we moved into

a circle formation, our backs facing one another as the smoke swirled around us.

"Brute force won't work," Robert observed.

"We need to force them into a solid form, something we can fight," Annabel said behind me.

The smoke reverted in on itself, rushing into a single point a few feet in front of me.

"What's happening?" Jake asked from behind me.

I squinted at the orb of smoke floating in front of me, trying to decipher what it was and what it wanted.

Like a bullet, the smoke rushed forward, slamming into our shield with a force that rocked my bones.

Sparks erupted from the point of contact like a saw blade cutting into metal.

"It's breaking through."

"Hold it."

"How do we stop it?"

Everyone yelled at once as they all turned to face the smoke, trying to break our resolve.

"You were once her," the voices slithered in my head. *"When you were whole. Someone must pay the price."*

"Get out of my head," I yelled.

A wisp of smoke, no bigger than the plume from blowing out a birthday candle, slipped through our barrier. Wrapping around my wrist like a bracelet, it grabbed hold of me and pulled.

My body slammed into our shield as I fought to keep myself from being pulled through.

"Violet," Robert yelled.

"Grab her, we got this," Brett stepped forward, taking Robert's place by my side as his arms went around me and he put his body between me and them.

"I think they want Vivian." I struggled against their pull.

"Jake, I need you to freeze everything but me," Annabel said to my right. "I have an idea."

The grip on my wrist was like a zip-tie that had been pulled too tight. My fingers throbbed as my grip on my Magic slipped and I was pulled forward.

"Jake," Robert yelled as his grip on me tightened.

"A moment," Jake growled, and then everything went still.

My eyes started to blink, the wind disappeared and our shield moved in slow motion. Green sparks crawled down my arm toward the tendril of smoke holding me hostage. Pain seared my skin and my knees slowly buckled.

My eyelids were still in the process of blinking. Not even a second had passed when the spell latched onto the smoke like a predator lunging for its prey. Their grip loosened on my wrist as Jake's Magic faded and Robert caught me before I hit the ground.

"Sorry about that," Annabel sighed as I rubbed my arm where the spell had burned my skin.

The smoke screamed like an angry bird and swirled violently, reshaping into four human-like shapes again.

"We will have what's owed to us," the figures demanded.

"We don't owe you anything," I shouted.

Their heads snapped in my direction.

"Maybe don't piss them off," Jake said.

"You don't, but she does." Their figures vibrated and pulsed.

"Shit," Brett said under her breath, as they shot into the sky and lightning burst in slow motion, crawling across the midnight black clouds in bright angry branches.

Lightning struck our joint shield and my teeth rattled. Electricity crawled over our shield, searching for a way in.

"Brett, could you maybe?" I asked, nodding toward the Magic bearing down on us.

"I'll do my best." She placed her hand on the curtain

protecting us. Using her Magic, she pulled the web of electricity off of our shield toward her.

Another bolt of lightning struck us, but this time, Brett was ready. She absorbed the blast and stepped outside of our protective bubble.

"What're you doing?" I yelled.

Moving a few feet away from us, arms raised and Magic crackling across her body, she fired back at the clouds above us.

Two smoky figures shot toward her and I rushed forward.

"Violet," Robert yelled behind me, as I wrapped my arms around Brett and threw up a shield.

The figures swirled around us, testing my strength.

"Now what's your plan?" Brett shook her head.

"I thought you might have an idea," I smirked and looked up at the sky.

Three more figures fell from the clouds and rushed us.

"It's me they want." The faceless figures crowded us, pushing against my shield. My knees shook with the effort to keep my Magic steady and sweat formed on my brow.

"Don't you dare," Brett barked as I summoned a stunning orb. "Vi-" she flew backward, out of the protection of my shield across the yard.

Looking over my shoulder, my eyes searched for Robert through the figures surrounding me. I glimpsed his face for a brief moment before a wave of searing heat and light washed over me like a tidal wave.

The figures screeched as the entire backyard lit up in a warm summer glow. Through the haze of the light, there was a silhouette of a person walking toward me.

"What the..."

"Sunlight," Merlin said as he came into focus. "They can't survive in the light." He placed one hand on my shoulder, while the other kept the monsters at bay with sunlight.

"Are you hurt?" Robert asked, taking my hand.

"Brett?"

"Fine," she said, limping forward. "No thanks to you."

"I don't understand?" Robert looked between Brett and me.

"Your girlfriend's the one who blasted me halfway across the yard."

"I was trying to—"

"I know what you were trying to do," Brett cut me off. "But you have to stop trying to do all of this on your own. We're here to help."

"So what, I should let them kill you?" I argued. "No," I shook my head. "They want Vivian and I don't want you or anyone else risking their lives."

"Hate to break it to you, but that's what we do," Jake said, grabbing Annabel's hand.

"I wonder, what do they want with Vivian?" Annabel pursed her lips.

"And who or what are they?" Robert moved to his sister, placing a hand on her shoulder and healing the damage my Magic caused.

"I can answer that." Merlin's nonchalant attitude was so annoying sometimes.

"Where did you disappear to? We could've used your help." Brett crossed her arms over her chest.

"I think I did help; quite spectacularly, in fact." Merlin nodded toward the sky.

"Who are they and what do they want?" I asked.

"That, my dear, was the Umbra-Kai." He pointed toward the jet-black clouds as they started to roll in on themselves and fade away without a trace.

"I thought the Shadowlands was another realm?" Jake asked.

"It is," Merlin said, letting the sunlight in his palm dim and fade away, just like a sunset. "But something was stolen from them and they want it back."

"They want Nimue," I said.

"Or the next best thing," Merlin shrugged.

"Vivian," Brett guessed.

"But Vivian isn't the one who owes them a debt," Robert argued.

"No, but she's the other half of the soul who does," Merlin explained. "If they can't get to Nimue, Vivian is the next best thing."

"How do we stop them from coming back?" I asked.

"They won't stop until they have what is owed to them," Merlin said.

"Then how can we protect Vivian and Violet?" Jake asked.

"They're shadow creatures in the most basic form," Merlin started. "Shadows can't survive in the light, now can they?" He wiggled his eyebrows.

"If they're just shadows, then how were they able to grab Violet?" Robert asked.

I turned to Annabel. "And how were you able to shock them?"

"You did what?" Merlin turned to Annabel.

"When I was being held captive, they kept me from orbing with a modified Galvin spell and chains." She touched the welts on her wrist. "I figured if Jake could slow them down, I could target a Galvin spell to do to them what was done to me."

"Quick thinking," Merlin smirked.

"We have a problem," Alyssa yelled as she ran out of the house, her face pinched into a worried expression.

"What is it?" I asked.

"Becky and Matthew," she huffed. "They were taken."

I felt the blood drain from my face and I was pretty sure my heart was falling out of my chest. I pushed past her and ran into the house in what felt like slow motion.

"Beck," I called out for her. "Becky, where are you?"

"Matty?" Brett said right behind me.

Nothing.

"I'm trying to tell you," Alyssa said through heavy breaths. "They're gone."

"They left a fire message," Robert said behind me and crossed the living room.

"What's it say?" I grabbed the paper from him.

You have fifteen minutes to meet us under the pier before we take matters into our own hands.

-M

CHAPTER 22

IOLET

My stomach rolled, and I ran out to the backyard. Barely making it to the edge of the grass, my body convulsed, and the cinnamon rolls I'd eaten earlier rocketed out of me.

"Take a breath," Robert said as he rubbed my back.

"This is why I didn't want her involved in this world." I wiped my mouth with the back of my hand.

"We'll get them back," Brett said as she, Jake, and Annabel made their way over to us.

"How do we want to do this?" Annabel tossed me a bottle of water.

"Thanks." I took a big sip, swished the water around my mouth, and spit it out.

Jake turned to Annabel. "Are you sure you're up for this? After everything Morgana did to you?"

"I'm more than ready," she shrugged off Jake's hand. "If this ends up being a fight, I want to make her pay for what she did to me. To us."

"Robert and I should go," I said, meeting his eyes.

"You have another thing coming if you think I'm staying behind," Brett argued.

I held my hand up to her. "Of course not. But just because we might be walking into her trap doesn't mean we shouldn't be prepared."

"Better not to show all our cards at once." Annabel caught my meaning before the rest.

"Exactly. This is our home, our backyard. We know it better than Morgana, and we can outsmart her if it comes to that."

"We can take the high ground," Annabel motioned between her and Jake.

"I'm bringing Matty home," Brett's words were final. Brett was formidable at the best of times. Now, she looked like a woman ready to walk through hell to get Matty back.

"How much time do we have left?" I asked.

"About five minutes." Robert looked at his watch.

"It's now or never." Jake let out a heavy sigh and grabbed Annabel's hand.

I reached for Annabel's free hand, and Robert laced his fingers through mine.

Annabel's Magic took hold, and it ripped us from one place and time to another. I was glad I'd emptied my stomach a few minutes earlier. I'd forgot how violent orbing was.

Waves crashed on the shore in a thunderous boom, both calming my nerves and sending a thrill of panic through me in the same breath. The memory of being crushed under similar waves haunted me and though the beach had always been my happy place, now there was a darkness to it I could never quite shake.

From the roof of The Plaza, we had a perfect view of the beach below. A dozen and a half figures moved in and out of the pillars under the pier, and the street below was all but empty at this time of night.

"Do you think that's all of them?" Jake asked as he scanned the beach.

"Doubt it," Robert said. "I don't like the idea of walking into an ambush." He searched the surrounding area for any signs of life.

"It's not like we have much of a choice." I swallowed the lump in my throat.

"No, we don't," he acknowledged. "But rushing into this feels like a mistake."

"Shit or get off the pot," Brett whirled on her brother. "We're doing this and I don't have time for you to weight the pros and cons."

"Now's not the time," Jake moved between his siblings. "None of us like this, but we're not leaving here without them."

"If you drop us there?" I said to Annabel, pointing to the edge of the parking lot. "They won't be able to see us from under the pier."

"You're sure?" Brett asked.

"Like I said, this is my backyard."

"Alright, let's do this," Robert grabbed my hand.

"We should have a signal if things go south," Annabel said.

"I'll take care of that," Brett said. "Watch for sparks."

"Got it, sis," Jake clamped a hand on Brett's shoulder. "And don't do anything stupid."

Annabel reached out to Brett and Robert and we orbed off of the roof to the spot I'd just pointed out.

"At the first sign of trouble—" Annabel started.

"I know," Brett interrupted her.

"Good luck." She gave us a small smile and vanished.

"We can take the stairs." I moved toward the wood structure. "They'll lead to the beach and still give us cover."

The three of us moved down the damp wood stairs almost

silently as my heart raced. As we reached the sand, I ducked under the staircase and looked for my best friend.

"There," I whispered. Matty and Becky were on their knees, the water breaking around them, Magic crawling down their torso's. My breath caught in my throat and I swallowed hard as a chill ran down my spine.

"They're still alive," Brett let out a heavy sigh next to me.

"Let's get this over with." Robert stepped out from under the staircase.

Brett and I followed him. The gentle rustle of sand under our shoes, the waves crashing on the shore, and the wind whistling through the pillars under the pier made my nerves feel exposed and raw. Despite the frigid, damp ocean breeze, I felt like I was overheating. My skin tingled with Magic and Vivian stirred inside me with each step.

Everyone under the pier paused and turned toward us as we moved across the open sand. My heart beat against my chest with the heavy force of a mallet against a drum. My eyes met Becky's and my throat clamped shut, making it impossible to breathe. She was so helpless in this world of Magic and it was my fault she was in this position.

"So nice of you to join us." Morgana's playful tone made my skin crawl.

"What do you want?" I asked as a wave crashed against the pillars. The thundering of the water against the pier rattled deep in my bones.

"That's right, you're not one for chit-chat," she cooed. "Very well. I have a proposition for you."

"We're listening," Robert said, as the hiss of the water receding filled the air.

"Mordred, bring Emilia forward," Morgana called over her shoulder.

Mordred moved out of the shadows and out of the corner of my eye, I saw Robert stiffen. A woman was draped over his arms, her head hanging unnaturally. If not for the sound of her ragged breathing, I would have thought she was dead.

"Ian?" I looked the man up and down.

"It's Mordred actually," he winked. "Miss me?"

"If you're quite finished," Morgana shot Mordred a look, and he nodded once. "She's dying," Morgana explained, as the street lights from above splashed across the woman's face. Her complexion looked ghostly, blue veins snaking up her neck and disappearing into her snow white hair.

"And let me guess, you want me to heal her in exchange for our friends," Robert said.

"What a God complex you must have." She clicked her tongue. "Would it wound you to know your Magic may as well be a party trick compared to what Alyssa can do?"

"Alyssa? This is about her?" I furrowed my brow.

"She left us before her work was finished," Morgana growled. "And Emilia's condition has rapidly deteriorated without Alyssa's ministrations." She moved toward the woman and ran her hand over her face affectionately.

"What is it you want?" Brett asked.

"Alyssa, of course. But since that's unlikely, I'm willing to compromise."

She weaved in and out of the pillars, coming to a stop in front of Becky and Matty.

"You will take Emilia with you and Alyssa will reverse what's happening to her."

"You act as if we have any control over what Alyssa does and doesn't do," Robert said.

"Don't be so modest." She moved across the sand toward Robert. "I'm sure you can get creative," she leaned in and whispered in his ear.

Robert's jaw flexed and his hands balled into fists.

"There's that temper," she chuckled, and dragged a finger along his cheek.

"Enough with the games." I did my best to keep my voice even when really I wanted to rip her face off.

Her eyes met mine, and she took a step away from Robert. "That's right, you're an item. But fair is fair, Violet."

"What are you talking about?" I did my best to keep my voice even.

She ran a hand down Robert's chest. "You and Ian - that's what you called him, right? Well, I've heard all about your romantic interlude. And since you had a taste of mine," she squeezed Robert's face.

My skin flushed red hot, but now was *so* not the time for jealousy.

"We'll take Emilia back to Alyssa, but we want Becky and Matthew back right now." I refused to take the bait.

"You're not really in a position to make demands, now, are you?" She backed away from Robert and sauntered toward Becky and Matty.

"You want our help, then we want our people back," Robert demanded.

"Let's say I give them back to you." She crossed behind them so she was standing over Becky and Matty. "What incentive would you have to cure Emilia and send her back to me unharmed?" She placed a hand on each of their heads. "Now, I'm not without mercy." She cocked an eyebrow. "You can have one of them as a gesture of good faith."

"You expect us to choose between them?" I balked and my heart stalled in my chest. Was she insane?

"Not only do I expect you to choose," A Galvin spell crawled down Becky and Matty's necks to their chest. "But I expect you to choose quickly or they'll both die."

They convulsed under the spell, doubling over, and Becky whimpered.

Out of the corner of my eye, I saw tiny sparks dance on Brett's fingers behind her back.

"Let them go," Annabel's voice roared over the waves.

She held a knife to the throat of one of Morgana's men, and Jake was doing the same a few feet away.

"Ahh, so nice of you to join us again, Annabel," Morgana smirked as the spell flared and Matty slumped to the sand. "And it's Jake, right?" Her head cocked in his direction. "Emilia's told me so much about you." She looked him up and down, pausing at his waist. Her implication wasn't lost on anyone.

Brett's Magic ignited, lighting up the underside of the pier like a spotlight. "Let him go," she growled.

"Is that your choice, then?"

"If you kill them—"

"You'll what?" Morgana snapped at me.

"You think I won't kill your men?" Annabel sneered.

"No, I don't."

Morgana and Annabel stared at one another for what seemed like an eternity.

"But to prove I've not come here to fight," Morgana released them, and the Galvin spell quickly fizzled out. They both gasped for air, their bodies sagging with the effort to stay upright. "Now put your weapons down."

"Let them go first," Jake demanded.

"That's not how this works," Morgana said through gritted teeth. "I gave you something. Now it's your turn. Put your weapons down," she demanded. "Last chance."

Jake lowered the knife and shoved the guy he was holding hostage forward.

"Come now, Annabel, you wouldn't want to be the reason they die, now do you?"

"Anna," Jake said her name like a curse.

She removed the knife from the woman's throat and stepped to Jake's side.

"Very well then, shall we continue?" Morgana turned back toward me. "Which one will it be?"

"I'll stay," Matty yelled before anyone could answer.

"No." Brett took a step forward.

"Interesting." Morgana turned back to Matty. "It would seem we have a volunteer."

"What're you doing?" Becky shook her head.

"He's sacrificing himself for you, dear. Do keep up." Morgana looked between Becky and Matty and then up to Brett and smirked.

"No, we're both leaving here," Becky's eyes glassed over as tears threatened to spill over.

"I can take care of myself. This is my world, not yours," he explained. "And I won't make them choose between us."

"Tough words for the little lady," Morgana smirked. "Though it would've been more fun to watch them suffer the choice," she shrugged as she waved her hand over Becky and the Magical binds holding her to the spot disappeared. "You're free to go."

Becky stood cautiously. "This isn't fair," she croaked.

Morgana turned slowly back toward Becky. "Life isn't fair, and the sooner you learn that lesson, the better. Now go, before I change my mind." Morgana shoved Becky forward, and she stumbled toward us. I wrapped my arms around her the moment she was within reach and relief washed over me as I felt her heartbeat against mine.

Matty looked up at Brett, and the corner of his lips twitched into a small, sad smile. My chest tightened and I could only imagine how hard this was for Brett.

"Take him." Morgana waved her hand.

"Wait," Brett yelled. "This isn't his fight. Take me."

"Brett, no," Matty shook his head. "You can help them, I can't."

Morgana looked between Brett and Matty. "It's always such a shame separating lovers."

Morgana moved behind Matty and placed her hands on his shoulders.

"Tonight's gone better than I planned and so I'm feeling generous." She grabbed Matty by his restrained arms and pushed him forward. "I'll allow you to say your goodbyes."

Brett stepped forward, but hesitated as they drew closer.

"You have one minute," she whispered into Matty's ear from behind. "Mordred," she snapped her fingers.

Mordred shuffled across the sand, Emilia bouncing in his arms with each step.

"I can't leave you," Brett said under her breath.

"I won't be gone long," Matty placed his forehead against hers. "You'll find a way, you always do."

"This isn't how it's supposed to be."

"This is exactly how it's supposed to be. It's my job, my calling to protect."

As Mordred came to a stop next to Morgana, she shifted her attention to the woman in his arms. She looked worse than I would have thought possible, and I wondered if we really could save her.

"Come back to me," Morgana whispered against her hair and kissed her temple.

"You really care about her." I watched as Morgana let her hand brush the length of Emilia's hair.

"I'm not the monster everyone makes me out to be." Morgana closed the gap between us. "Would you not do anything to save your friend?" Her eyes moved to mine and Becky's joined hands.

"I would," I said, holding her gaze.

Morgana reached out and grabbed a few strands of my hair. "It's a shame we've ended up on opposite sides. We could have been great allies."

"I doubt it," I said through gritted teeth.

She took a step back and nodded to Mordred, who handed over Emilia to Robert. Her frail body shuffling like a rag doll between the two men.

"Let's go, Romeo," Morgana yanked on Matty's arms.

"I love you," Brett's hand fell from his face.

"Ditto," he smirked as Morgana dragged him away from Brett.

How she kept her composure, I'll never know.

"You have a fortnight to heal her. After that, all bets are off for your hero here."

She placed her hand against one of the pillars and said, *"Patentibus."*

A dark green portal swirled to life between two of the pillars. My hair whipped around me and sand kicked into the air. "Don't disappoint me," she yelled over the roar of the ocean as she stepped into the middle of the swirling chaos, pulling Matty with her.

Each of her followers stepped in behind her, one by one vanishing from the beach. As the portal whooshed to a close, Brett fell to her knees.

CHAPTER 23

IOLET

"Did you..." Merlin searched each of our faces the moment Annabel orbed us back. "Where's Matthew?"

"They took him," I said. "As collateral."

Brett stormed passed us and threw herself onto the couch.

"Who's the girl?" Merlin asked as Robert placed Emilia on the couch and laid a hand on her shoulder and hip.

"She's the one who walked around, pretending to be me," Annabel seethed.

"I thought she died," I said under my breath, and Merlin and Robert looked up at me.

"Emilia," Alyssa said from behind me. "My God." She rushed to her side and knelt next to her.

"That won't help," Alyssa nodded to Robert's hands.

Robert ignored her and continued to search for something, anything, he could mend.

"What's wrong with her?" Merlin asked.

"Excalibur," I said under my breath. The memory of her screaming as she held onto the sword flashed across my eyes.

"We're not actually going to help her, are we?" Annabel spat.

"We'll do whatever's necessary to get Matty back," Brett snapped.

"I didn't mean we shouldn't get Matty back," Annabel tried to clarify. "But after what she did, she doesn't deserve to live."

"Whether she does or not," Robert stood. "We have to help her."

"Excalibur wouldn't have this effect on someone," Merlin said.

"Bringing Nimue back from the Shadowlands took its toll." Alyssa reached for Emilia's neck with her two fingers. "Before I left," Alyssa started. "I was trying to help restore her strength."

"To what end? Hadn't she served her purpose?" I asked, folding my arms over my chest.

"That's an awfully callous outlook on someone's life." Alyssa's eyes raked over me.

"I just mean, Morgana got what she wanted. Why—"

"Why go to the trouble of saving her?" Alyssa finished for me. "Because solving the impossible is what I do." Her eyes met mine, and a lump formed in my throat.

To everyone else, she was still talking about Emilia, but her meaning was clear to me. I was no different to her than any other person at the end of their rope.

"Morgana must have run out of options." Alyssa placed a hand on Emilia's shoulder. "May I?" She held out her other hand to Merlin and looked up at him with a quiet determination.

He nodded once and without preamble, tiny particles, like the seedlings of a dandelion, burst from Merlin and floated toward Alyssa. She began to recite something under her breath, and Emilia gasped for air.

"What're you doing?" Robert looked between Merlin, Alyssa and Emilia.

"Making her comfortable," Alyssa said, keeping her focus on Emilia.

"This still doesn't make sense," I argued. "Why go to so much trouble to save her? Who is she to Morgana?"

"I don't have the answers to those questions. Only she knows." Alyssa nodded toward Emilia. As she stood, the wisps of Magic floating around her disappeared.

"It won't last long," Alyssa said. "I need to set to work if I'm going to have any chance of helping her."

"Wait," Robert stepped into her path. "There's still the matter of how you evaded capture."

Alyssa tried to move around him as she said, "We don't have time for this."

"I think we do." Robert stared down at her. "It's you Morgana wants, and yet she took Becky and Matty. Why?"

"I don't know." She snapped at him.

"Stop lying," Robert growled.

"She wasn't here," Merlin barked.

Everyone's eyes swiveled to Merlin, and Alyssa pulled herself free from Robert's grasp.

"I was wondering if you would step in," she scoffed.

"What do you mean she wasn't here?" I asked.

"I sent her on an errand," Merlin explained.

"You've got to be kidding me." Robert threw his head back and stared at the ceiling.

"There are matters to attend to, and I can't be everywhere at once," Merlin said matter-of-factly.

"She could have—"

"You may resent me for the part I played while Aiden detained you on Avalon, but—"

"Guys, can we not?" Jake sighed. "We have bigger issues at hand."

"I get that you have to help her, but I can't be a part of this, not after..." Annabel shook her head and orbed out of the room.

"Nothing's ever easy with you lot," Merlin sighed.

"I'm with Annabel on this," Jake huffed. "She knows too much about us already. If we fix her up and send her on her way, who knows what damage she could do."

"And if we don't, Matty dies," Brett shot up from the couch.

"Brett, you know I'll do anything to get him back. We'll find a way," Jake said.

"We already have." She turned to Alyssa. "Do whatever you need to save her."

"I don't even know if I can help her," Alyssa said. "What her body experienced, the transformation she underwent, isn't something that can be easily undone, if it can be undone at all."

"I know this is an impossible situation," I tried to reason. "But we don't have a choice. Leaving Matty's fate in Morgana's hands is not an option."

"Finally, someone with a little sense in their head," Brett sighed, and I gave her a small smile.

"I'm not saying what's happened to Emilia is fair or right," Jake argued. "But she took on the risk."

"Does that mean we shouldn't bother saving me either?" I asked. "I knew what I was doing, waking Vivian. I knew the risk and now I'm stuck in limbo."

"It's not the same," Jake argued. "And you know it."

"But it is," I said. "We all make choices we have to live with. Don't let this be something you have to live with. Don't let Emilia's death be something that sits with you forever."

"Fine," he nodded. "But she needs to stay under lock and key."

Alyssa exited before anyone could change their minds again.

"That can be arranged." Merlin turned on his heels and rushed out of the room.

"If anything—" Jake started.

"It won't," Robert interrupted him. "I'll do everything in my power to make sure of it."

"Let's just hope that'll be enough." Jake stalked out of the room to comfort Annabel, I presumed.

"Well, that wasn't awkward," Becky said, wide-eyed.

I sighed. "Everyone's been through a lot. How are you holding up?"

"I've had stranger nights," she half chuckled. "I just... Brett, I'm so sorry." She looked like she wanted to throw herself at Brett's feet.

"It's not your fault," Brett kept her voice even, but wouldn't meet Becky's eye. "He was right to protect you."

"Still, I wish there was something I could do." She pulled at her fingers nervously.

"Me too," Brett said under her breath.

"It may be a long shot, but maybe I can see something that'll help us," I mused.

Kneeling down, I placed my hand on Emilia's. Her skin was ice cold and sent goosebumps up my arm. Letting down my mental walls, a rush of Magic surged through me, pulling me into a vision as the Maxwell's living room swirled around me and reformed.

Giant, smooth boulders came into focus and I knew exactly where I was.

"You're going to be okay." Morgana stared down at Emilia. "I swear to you, we'll make this right."

Looking to my right, the altar rock I plunged Excalibur into was just a few feet away. I swallowed hard as the memory of the searing pain brushed across my skin. I was meant to wake Vivian, and still, I thought the process was going to kill me. I can only imagine the pain Emilia must have felt as she clung to Excalibur.

"Did...it...wor....work," Emilia managed to say.

"I believe so, yes."

Emilia smiled and closed her eyes.

The rocks swirled again, colors and shapes moving around me as they morphed into a different time and place.

"*Can you help her?*" *Morgana's voice came through crystal clear as the scene came into focus.*

Emilia lay on a small bed in the corner of a cabin. Alyssa and Morgana stood next to a large wooden table that took up most of the cabin space, and they spoke in hushed voices.

"I can try," Alyssa sighed, and looked over Emilia's almost lifeless body.

"That's not good enough."

"This isn't an exact science," Alyssa huffed. "And we have no idea what's causing her to deteriorate so quickly."

"I don't care what you have to do or who you have to do it to." Morgana closed the distance between her and Alyssa. "Am I clear?"

Alyssa nodded once, and Morgana turned on her heel and left the cabin.

"Time to work a miracle," Alyssa said under her breath as she pushed a few books around on the table in front of her.

Again, the vision faded and gave way to another setting.

Morgana paced inside a small, modern bedroom. The curtains on the window billowed with the cool breeze, and I moved closer to try to see where I was.

The bright green grass stretched out below me, all the way to the tree line that I knew led to a beach. A beach I'd once used to escape with Excalibur.

"I know you care about the girl, but there are more pressing matters to consider," Ian said.

"I'm well aware of the matters at hand, Mordred, and I'm perfectly capable of prioritizing my emotions."

"I don't doubt you." He stood and placed his hands on her shoulders, stopping her from wearing a hole in the carpet. "Alyssa will do her best; she always does." His voice was soothing, loving even. "While she does her job, you need to do yours."

Morgana reached up and touched his cheek. "Your fondness for Alyssa isn't appreciated at the moment." Her voice was ice cold, but he didn't flinch away from her. "Let us hope you're right about her, for both your sakes."

"My fondness for Alyssa is what allows her to excel."

"Don't give yourself too much credit. I've seen what the woman is capable of and it has nothing to do with you."

I blinked, and once again I was pulled in another direction. I stood in the dark, nothing coming into view. Looking around the darkness that seemed to go on forever, my heart rate picked up, and I moved around the empty space. Where was I?

The sound of someone struggling to breathe caught my attention, and I turned around.

"Where...are...we...going?" Her voice was raspy, but unmistakably Emilia's.

Another figure came into view next to Morgana, with Emilia cradled in his arms.

"You need more help than I can give you." The pain in Morgana's voice was clear as the scenery around me came into focus and the beach materialized.

"I don't.... want-"

"Save your strength," Morgana cooed.

"I don't want....to...leave....you," she exhaled.

"I know," Morgana sighed. "But we'll come back for you, I swear it."

As they walked a few more feet, the rest of the scene became clear and I recognized the stretch of sand they were walking across. Looking up ahead, the pier jutted out into the water, and the city lights turned the night sky a muted orange against the clouds.

"Give us a moment," Morgana said, and the man placed Emilia on her feet.

Morgana put her arm around Emilia's waist to keep her upright and walked up to the grouping of rocks against the cliff side.

Following them, I knew what would happen next, but still, I was curious about Morgana's behavior.

The woman carrying Emilia was not the Morgana I was familiar with. *Her eyes were warm as she looked at Emilia in her arms, and Morgana's voice was gentle as she whispered in Emilia's ear.*

"I know this is the last place you want to be again." Morgana held Emilia's chin between her fingers. "But if anyone can help you, it's Alyssa."

Emilia started to shake her head as a tear escaped her blood-red eyes.

"Yes, my dear." Morgana ran her hand over Emilia's hair. "This is in your best interest."

"What if," Emilia let out a heavy sigh. "What if...they...refuse?"

Morgana smiled and said, "You and I both know they won't. It's not in their nature."

"Please," Emilia managed to get past her lips as more tears fell from her eyes.

"If there was any other way, if there was something more I could do, you know I would." Morgana kissed her forehead and closed her eyes. "Let them help you and then come back to me."

Emilia nodded and slumped against the rocks.

"I...I." She grabbed Morgana's hand and squeezed.

"I know." She kissed Emilia's hand and stood.

As if we were on a stage, the overhead lights went out and the scene vanished into the darkness.

My Magic faded and the familiar sights and sounds of the Maxwell house wrapped around me.

"What did you see?" Robert asked the moment my eyes cleared.

I tried to stand, but my legs were weak after so many visions in a row. Pulling up my mental block was harder than it should be, and I felt dizzy as I tried to regain my bearings.

"I'm not sure what to make of it." A sharp ringing noise pierced through my ears and I stumbled forward.

"Are you okay?" Becky's voice was close to me, but I couldn't make sense of up and down.

"I think so," I mumbled as I plopped down in the chair next to the sofa.

Vivian's Magic churned within me and I could almost feel her beneath the surface. I felt like I was being smothered with one of those fifty-pound blankets as I sunk deeper into the chair.

"Violet." Robert's face moved in and out of focus in front of me.

I closed my eyes and said, "I think… I think I'm okay." I took a deep breath and opened my eyes.

Relief washed over Robert's features and his lips pulled up at the corner.

"See anything that can help us?" Brett asked.

"I don't know." I shook my head and looked at Emilia.

For whatever reason, she mattered to Morgana more than I would have thought possible.

"But her connection to Morgana is undeniable."

 IOLET

I WENT through each of my visions with them, explaining how tender and kind Morgana was with Emilia. Though I didn't understand how someone as cold-blooded as she seemed could feel so strongly for someone else.

"I still don't see why Alyssa is the only one who can help," I sighed. "It just doesn't sit right."

"I agree. It's all a little too convenient that she wasn't here when Morgana's men showed up." Robert looked over my shoulder to see if the coast was clear. "And now she's our only hope for saving Matty? Something's up."

"Alyssa aside, it's possible Emilia can still benefit us." Becky looked at Emilia.

"How so?" Robert asked.

"Emilia and Violet were exposed to the same Magic." Becky's eyes lit up. "If you solve one problem, maybe you solve the other." She shrugged.

"About that." I bit my lip.

"What is it?" Robert's eyes traced my face.

A lump formed in my throat and though I knew I had to tell them; I also knew this was going to suck.

"When Merlin came to see me earlier," I started. "We talked about how he and Alyssa might find a way out of all this." I motioned up and down my body.

"And how is that?" I could see the argument brewing in the set of Robert's shoulders.

"My blood." The words left my lips and my stomach hit the floor.

Robert leaned forward, placing his arms on his knees. "Can I assume you told him no?"

I licked my lips and took a deep breath.

"I gave it to him."

"You did what?" Robert shot up from his seat.

Becky flinched at the tone in Robert's voice. "We should give you guys some privacy." Becky pulled Brett by the arm. "And get you a drink." They made their exit; though if I had to guess, they were still within earshot.

"Robert, look—"

"Don't you dare try to play this off like it isn't a big deal."

"If you would listen," I snapped back. "I know you don't trust them, but what do we have to lose?"

"Everything!" he yelled as he closed the distance between us. "We have everything to lose. You don't understand what Alyssa is capable of."

"That's kind of the point," I argued. "Merlin thinks she has a real shot at figuring this out."

"Merlin thinks." Robert rolled his eyes and turned away from me. "He's the reason Alyssa wasn't here and why Matty's being held by Morgana as collateral. Had Alyssa been here when they showed up—"

"I get it, and I know you don't trust him. But I do."

"We didn't even know who he was until Vivian showed up and yet you trust him with your life?"

"If there was another way—"

"You didn't even try to find another way." Robert's cheeks flushed with anger. "Were you even going to tell me if this hadn't happened?" He waved his hand toward Emilia.

"I wanted to tell you earlier, but everything got out of hand so quickly." I took a step toward him, wanting to make him understand.

"What do they plan to do with your blood?" His eyes held mine like a heat-seeking missile.

"I'm not sure." I looked away from his gaze.

"Did you not think to ask what on God's green earth they were planning to do with your blood? Your *blood*, Violet."

"Of course I did," I fired back at him. "I'm not an idiot." My face flushed hot with embarrassment.

He folded his arms over his chest and shook his head.

"Just because I did something you don't agree with, doesn't give you the right to treat me like a child."

"This isn't about what I believe is right, Violet. Alyssa's dangerous and we don't know half of what Merlin is scheming."

"That may be so, but it's my life that's at stake, not yours," I yelled.

He flinched as if I'd slapped him.

"And what, because it's your life, I'm not supposed to care, not supposed to look out for what's best for you?"

"Whoever said you know what's best for me?" I snapped. "Ever since the day we met, you've acted like you're the only one who can act in my best interest."

"So because I care—"

"Caring is one thing, Robert," I yelled. "Trying to control everything I do is another."

He took a step back and immediately I regretted my words.

Guilt poured into me, making my stomach turn over and my heart sink to the floor.

"That's what you think?" His voice was low, each word measured. "That I want to control you." His dark coffee eyes held mine, and I swear I could feel his heart break.

"That came out wrong," I sighed. "I just don't know what to do. It's not like there's a playbook for this kind of thing."

"You think I don't know that?" He kept his voice calm and even, and that hurt me more than when he was yelling. "You think I'm not trying to find something, anything, that could help you?" He wouldn't meet my eye as he shook his head.

"I'm sorry." And I was. I really was. I hated that I'd hurt him, hated that he couldn't even look at me right now.

"You have nothing to apologize for. As you said, it's your life and you should get to live it however you please."

"Robert—"

"You'll excuse me if I don't sit by and watch you end it."

He stormed out of the room and as I moved around the couch to follow him, but Jake stepped in my way.

"Let him go," he said. "Give him some time to cool off."

I watched him turn the corner and each footfall on the stairs was like a bullet to my chest.

"Is it too much to hope you didn't hear all that?" I asked, holding back tears.

He nodded.

"For what it's worth, I would have done the same as you."

I furrowed my brow in surprise. "Really? I would have thought you'd agree with Robert."

"Alyssa may be a lot of things, and I'm not saying that I trust her, but without her, I wouldn't have Anna back. That's got to count for something." He nudged my shoulder with his own. "If anyone can help you, it might be her."

"If it was anyone other than Alyssa, he'd probably be encouraging me to do it." I rolled my eyes.

"He'll come around. His history with Alyssa is difficult, and he's not one to let things go easily."

"You think?" My brow furrowed as I looked up at him. "I debated telling him at all, but I don't know how much time I have left. I don't want to spend it lying to him."

"No matter when you told him, he still would have reacted poorly. He cares more than you know, he just isn't very graceful about it."

"I'm pretty sure he'd rather give up his Magic than put any faith in Alyssa," a short laugh escaped my throat.

"True," he smiled. "But you were right to stick up for yourself. It is your life. Even though he wants to protect you, he has to let you live by your own rules. It's the only way it'll ever work between you two."

"I didn't mean what I said, about him trying to control me." I bit my lip, ashamed.

More than anything, I hated that those words left my mouth. I didn't mean them, and I didn't feel that way. But in the heat of the moment, they just fell out of my mouth and landed on the floor like a grenade.

"You don't have to explain yourself to me. I know first hand how opinionated and persuasive my brother is." He rolled his eyes and a playful grin pulled at the corner of his lips. "And just between you and me," he lowered his voice. "He likes to think he has control over everything because the alternative is too daunting for him."

"Because of what happened with Lila and Chris back in school?"

"I think Chris' death made it worse. But even as a kid, he always tried to craft a life where he knew what the next step was. Not knowing what to do or how to help you scares him and he doesn't know how to deal with that."

"He's not alone. I'm terrified," I admitted. "And honestly, I don't know if I'll make it out of this alive. But I have to try, even if it is a long shot, to trust Alyssa."

"I know." He wrapped his arm around my shoulder. "And I get that you're used to doing things on your own, but you have people now. You don't have to walk this path alone."

"I'm still getting used to that," I admitted. "Speaking of not being alone, I should let you get back to Annabel."

"Yes, please don't let us interrupt your reunion," Merlin smirked.

"You know where to find me if you need someone to talk to," Jake said. He clapped a hand on my shoulder and headed toward the stairs.

"What do you have there?" I nodded toward Merlin's hands.

"It's pretty awesome, actually," Becky said, as she walked up to him. "He enchanted the pair of bangles to replicate a house arrest device."

"Jake wanted her under lock and key. But we're not animals, and I'm not putting her in a cage," Merlin explained.

"I've been working on a program that can track a specific signature of Magic." She flipped her tablet toward us. A small blinking light flashed on the screen and a wide smile spread across her face.

"How'd you figure out how to do that?" I stared at Becky in awe.

"Are you kidding?" She beamed. "That was the easy part."

"She's brilliant, isn't she?" Merlin beamed.

"It's also unlikely Emilia will do much damage in the condition she's in." Alyssa sauntered into the room carrying a tray full of crystals and a stack of books under her arms.

"What's all this for?" I asked Alyssa, as she pulled an iPad out from under the tray she was carrying and laid everything out on the table.

"Before I left, I was making some headway with her condition." Alyssa scrolled on the iPad. "Since I've stopped the treatment, it would appear that it wasn't a permanent solution." She motioned to Emilia's prone body.

"What was it you were working on exactly?" Brett asked as she sauntered into the room, a glass of amber liquid cupped in her hand.

"Her body took on more Magic than it can sustain," Alyssa explained. "I was attempting to dilute that Magic to make it more manageable for her."

"So, what're you going to try now?" I asked.

"I want to attempt to siphon the excess Magic she absorbed," she plopped the books down on the coffee table.

"Will that work?" Brett looked over at the various crystals on Alyssa's tray.

"Only one way to find out." Alyssa let out a heavy breath.

CHAPTER 25

IOLET

"Won't siphoning the Magic kill her faster?" Brett asked.

"It's a possibility," Alyssa said, without looking up. "Though I only plan to siphon some of the excess Magic, not all of it. That should allow her to survive."

"You don't know for sure?" Becky furrowed her brow and stared at Alyssa.

"Nothing like this has ever been attempted before, to my knowledge," Alyssa snapped. "It's not like I'm working from a tried-and-true recipe."

"If the Magic is killing Emilia, then where will you siphon the Magic to?" I wondered.

"Right, the Magic has to go somewhere, doesn't it?" Brett looked around the room. "Merlin?"

"In theory, yes." Merlin shrugged and looked back at the screen in Becky's hands.

"An elemental stone should be able to absorb the excess

Magic," Alyssa explained.

"That's if it even works at all." Merlin glanced at Alyssa sideways.

"I appreciate the vote of confidence." Alyssa rolled her eyes.

"Happy to have you prove us all wrong," Merlin beamed.

I turned to Brett. "Robert should be here for this."

"I think he needs some time to cool off," she said into her glass.

"You heard us too, then?" I grimaced.

"The whole neighborhood heard the two of you," she looked at me sideways. "Besides, you think he'd sit by quietly and let this happen?" She took another sip of her drink.

"No, but—"

"I know you want to make nice with him," she gave me a meaningful look, "But trust me, he doesn't need to be here for this."

"Brett," I touched her arm. "Are you okay?"

Her eyes met mine, and she took a deep breath through her nose. "No, but falling apart isn't going to do either of us any good."

"You know we'll get him back, right?"

"You can't promise that," she said, and drained her glass.

"Here we are," Alyssa said to no one in particular, as she stopped scrolling on her iPad.

Picking up a few of the crystals, she placed one on Emilia's chest, one above her head, and one on her stomach.

"Which one's need to go in her hands?" Alyssa mused as she grabbed one of the books off the table.

Opening to an earmarked page, she ran her fingers over the words. "Agate should be present in each hand to promote stabilization of one's aura," she read.

"Do we really think this will work?" Becky watched Alyssa and for the first time, she didn't seem to buy into all things Magic.

"Beats me," I shrugged.

Alyssa opened Emilia's hands, placing a piece of agate in each of her palms, closing Emilia's fingers around the stones.

"And the elements." She picked up five of the stones from the tray. "Earth is first," she said to herself. "Then air, Magic, water, and fire." She placed the book face up and turned toward Emilia.

Plucking the earth stone from her hand, she placed it just under the other crystal on Emilia's chest. I leaned forward, wanting to get a better look at the stone.

The color of the stone alternated between brown and green. Inside the stone, tiny leaves sprouted and died to an unseen cadence.

Alyssa laid the next stone, forming a line of down the middle of Emilia's chest.

Clouds swirled of their own accord, floating in and out of sights in the clear stone.

"I've never seen anything like this before." I kept my voice hushed, not wanting to disturb the Magic of the moment.

"Elemental stones are rarely used in today's modern Magical world," Alyssa said.

"It's old Magic from days gone by." Merlin sounded thought-ful, and he leaned in to look at the stones.

Alyssa laid the next one, and it looked nothing like the others. It was a crude and unfinished grey stone with specks of silver and all sharp edges.

Next was the water stone, with a whole ocean inside it, ebbing and flowing of its own accord. Then came the fire stone. Blue and orange flames licked at the surface as it lay on Emilia's torso.

Alyssa took a step back and let out a breath.

"Now what?" I looked between the Elemental stones and Alyssa.

"Now we hope this doesn't kill her," Alyssa sighed, and

picked up her iPad.

"If you know what's good for you, then you'll make sure it doesn't kill her." Brett's murderous glare burned into Alyssa.

"I'll need some Magic for this," Alyssa ignored Brett.

Again, Merlin offered his own, and the tiny blue seedlings of Magic floated toward Alyssa as she stared down at Emilia.

"Alright, here goes nothing," Alyssa exhaled.

Alyssa recited a few words from the iPad in her hand and touched the earth stone. It began to glow as if it were sitting on a flashlight.

No one moved a muscle as she recited the next few words and touched the air stone. The two elements sat on Emilia, glowing like elevator buttons, ready and waiting to fulfill their purpose.

Skipping the Magic elemental stone, she touched the fire and water stones with the last of the incantation.

"Is that it?" Becky's voice was barely a whisper.

Alyssa placed the iPad on the table behind her and rolled up her sleeve.

"*Purga animam aufert aliam.*" She held her hands over Emilia's body as she spoke. "*Et excoquam ad alia magicae.*"

The three larger crystals pulsed at her words.

"*Purga animam aufert aliam. Et excoquam ad alia magicae,*" she repeated the spell, and the crystals pulsed slow and steady again.

My heart began to race as I watched the Magic element start to glow from the inside out. It was almost as if there was a sun inside the stone, trying to break free of its heavy shell.

"*Purga animam aufert aliam. Et excoquam ad alia magicae,*" Alyssa said the spell again, and my head felt dizzy.

Bright orange sparks shot out of the agate in Emilia's hands, making everyone jump back. The sparks danced quick and jagged, coming to a point where Alyssa's hands had just been, forming a teepee over Emilia's chest.

The room filled with an orange glow, making Emilia's hair

look like flames curling around her and spilling over her shoulders.

Alyssa took a deep breath and stepped back into place. Putting her hands on either side of the buzzing sparks, she said, *"Purga animam aufert aliam. Et excoquam ad alia magicae."*

From the tip of the teepee, sparks burst toward Emilia's chest like a laser beam and connected with the Magic stone. The silver in the stone threw off dozens of tiny beams of light and cracks started to form along the grey surface.

My vision blurred, and I reached out against the wall to steady myself.

"You okay?" Brett looked me up and down.

"Yeah," I shook my head. "Just out of it after the visions, I think." I took a deep breath to steady myself.

Emilia's eyes shot open, and she started to whimper.

"Hold on, Emilia." Alyssa's eyes were wild as she stared down at Emilia. "You can do this."

"Please," she said through gritted teeth. "It hurts," she screamed.

"Purga animam aufert aliam. Et excoquam ad alia magicae," Alyssa ignored Emilia and continued reciting the spell.

Something burst deep inside me, forcing the air out of my lungs; my knees buckled. I felt like I was falling in slow motion. As my body crumpled to the floor, I could feel Vivian's Magic stirring inside me, poking and prodding for an opening to take over.

"Oh my God, Violet," Becky's voice was a million miles away.

I hadn't realized I was burning up until my skin touched the cool wood floor.

"What's wrong?" Brett said above me. "Is it Vivian? Is she taking over?"

"Alyssa, you have to stop," Becky pleaded.

"This is different," I said through gritted teeth as I rolled onto my side.

"Alyssa," Brett yelled.

I tried to take a deep breath, but the air filled my lungs quick and shallow.

"Merlin, do something," Becky yelled.

"Purga animam aufert aliam. Et excoquam ad alia magicae."

Someone else started to scream, their voice joining Emilia's in a cadence of pain.

"Violet, tell me what's wrong. Tell me what to do?" Brett's anxious voice reached me somewhere beyond the pain, and I realized I was the one screaming.

"What the... Violet?" Robert's voice carried through the room. "Alyssa, stop what you're doing or so help me."

"Robert, she needs you," Brett shouted at her brother.

His hands were on me a moment later and heat coursed through me as his Magic tried to find something, anything to heal.

"Purga animam aufert aliam."

"Alyssa, stop whatever you're doing! It's not working," Robert ordered.

"You don't know that."

"I know it's killing them."

A long, silent moment passed, the sound of Magic the only thing in the room.

"Et excoquam ad alia magicae," Alyssa said the second half of the spell.

Flashes of Excalibur burst before my eyes, the feel of the blade in the stone as Vivian's Magic poured into me echoed in my bones. I could feel her Magic, hungry and greedy, as it burned me from the inside out. Pain took hold of every cell in my body and I shivered as I lost control.

A flash of light bloomed behind my eyelids, everyone started yelling from every direction and the sound of furniture being blown apart was the last thing I heard as I fell back into the void, into the nothing.

VIOLET IN THE DARK

The shift was, **VIOLENT** *and* **SUDDEN.**
My soul was r i p p e d a p a r t

a n d,

I . . . S H A T T E R E D

i n t o — a

m — i — l — l — i — o — n

p — — i — — e — — c — — e — — s.

CHAPTER 26

IVIAN

"You should've put a stop to this. You know how fragile they are." Robert's voice pierced through the ringing in my ears.

"There's no way we could have known it would affect Violet and Vivian." Merlin's tone was dismissive.

"Maybe not before you started, but you saw what was happening to her and you stood by and did nothing."

"You want Matthew back, do you not?" Merlin leveled his gaze at Robert.

"Anyone care to explain what in the name of Newt just happened?" I asked, pushing myself to my feet.

"Viol- oh," Becky's face fell as she looked at me.

"Sorry to disappoint." I held onto the wall for support. "What happened?" I asked as I winced. Every part of me ached as if I'd been tied to a horse and dragged for miles.

The living room looked as if a storm had passed through, leaving no surface untouched. I looked at everyone in the room.

The tension was thick as they stared at each other, daring one another to speak.

"Are you feeling okay?" Becky asked me, the first real concern anyone had paid me.

"A little off-kilter," I admitted. "The transition was..." I hesitated as I thought about how to explain what it felt like. "Turbulent, violent, sudden. Not the easy passing of one soul through another."

Robert winced at my words as his eyes raked over me. "Violet? Is she...?"

"She's alright, I can still feel her," I reassured him. I'd gotten to know Robert well over the last few weeks. The set of his jaw and slant of his eyes was enough to tell me he was already on pins and needles.

His shoulders relaxed, and he swallowed hard as he nodded.

"Were we attacked?" I looked around the room and noticed a body on the couch. "Oh, and what do we have here?" I shuffled across the wood floors, testing my wobbly legs.

"She's the reason you feel so disjointed," Brett offered.

"Who is she?"

"Emilia," Alyssa gestured to the woman, "she was there when Violet brought you back. She's the one who took hold of Excalibur and allowed Nimue passage into this realm."

"How curious that she's still alive." I furrowed my brow. "How did she come to be here?" I looked between Robert, Merlin, and Alyssa.

"I think you should take a seat," Merlin sighed. "There's a fair amount to catch you up on."

Finding my way through the rubble, I waved my hand over a plush chair, flipping it back on its feet, and settled into the plush cushions.

"I'm all ears."

Alyssa filled me in on who Emilia was and, honestly, I was shocked the woman was still alive. Neither Violet nor Emilia should have survived the onslaught of Magic that coursed through them.

Once Alyssa finished explaining her part of the story, Merlin filled me in on the rest, one painful detail at a time.

Not only did we need to worry about Emilia and Matty, but now the Umbra-Kai are after my soul, and we needed to find the Grail before Nimue regained her earthly status and shed the Shadowlands for good.

"Is that all?" I asked once Merlin was finished.

"Violet also gave Alyssa and Merlin her blood," Robert said through gritted teeth. His jaw flexed as he folded his arms over his chest.

"To what end?" I asked Robert, and my eyes shifted to Merlin.

"We're trying to save you both," Merlin explained. "I hadn't realized she'd told you," Merlin addressed Robert.

"You seem disappointed that she confided in me." The anger rolling off of him was palpable, and it didn't take a genius to know why. After the explosive argument about Alyssa at the cabin and his complete distrust of the woman, it surprised me that Violet would agree to something he would be so fully against.

"Not disappointed, though I am surprised." Merlin pursed his lips. "She knew you wouldn't approve."

A short, clipped laugh escaped Robert's throat. "You told her not to tell me, didn't you?"

"I meant no disrespect, we're only trying to help."

"You almost killed her just now," Robert scowled. "How is that helping?"

"Okay, okay." Jake grabbed his brother by the shoulders. "This isn't going to solve anything."

Robert's eyes flicked to me and I could feel Violet's anguish. The heartbreak that emanated from the two of them filled the air, making it hard to breathe.

"We had no way of knowing it would affect Violet and Vivian," Merlin offered.

"That's the problem," Robert snapped at him. "You're letting Alyssa try things blindly, without questioning her intentions."

"What would you have me do?" Alyssa fired back at Robert. "You want Emilia saved, you want Matthew back, you want Violet to live. It takes a little risk and blind faith to create miracles."

"Saving a life at the cost of others is not a miracle," Robert said through gritted teeth.

"And I thought *I* was pissed," Jake said under his breath.

"Why don't we all take a moment?" I suggested. "Nothing will get solved if we're at each other's throats."

"Agreed," Alyssa said, sticking her nose in the air. "Now that we have a starting point, I can work on alternative solutions."

"Allow me." Merlin bent to pick up the tray of stones and the two of them quickly left.

"Not that I don't want to stay here and watch all the drama unfold, but someone should keep an eye on them." Becky pointed after Merlin and Alyssa.

"Thank you, Becky," Robert gave her a warm smile.

After a few minutes of silence, I leaned forward and took in the full scope of the damage. So much had happened since I was last in control, so much had changed and yet remained in limbo.

"Robert, I know you have your issues with Alyssa, but things can't go on like this. We need her if we're going to have a chance at saving Matthew," Brett finally spoke.

The pain in her voice cut through me as I remembered her words in the forest. She was so concerned about her brothers, about what a loss might do to them. And yet here she was, facing the question I'd asked her.

Do you not love as fiercely as your brothers?

"I can't trust her; I won't," Robert said. "But I can acknowledge we wouldn't have Annabel back without her." Robert's eyes met Annabel's and Jake's.

"I know you can't trust her. But for me," Brett crossed the space between them and placed a hand on his shoulder. "Can you stop living in black and white and let Alyssa do this?"

He let out a heavy sigh.

"For what it's worth," Annabel chimed in. "I had a front-row seat to what she's capable of, and it's a force to be reckoned with."

"All the more reason we should be cautious," I said.

"You think we should trust her?" Robert looked at me for guidance.

"I didn't say that," I leaned back. "Only that one shouldn't be fooled by her skill and forget her transgressions."

Robert nodded and said, "We need to come up with a Plan B. Just in case."

Brett let out a shaky breath. "I agree, I don't enjoy putting all our eggs in one basket, not when Matty's involved."

Robert wrapped his arm around Brett and pulled her in for a hug. "We'll get him back, I promise."

"I hope so," she whispered and pulled away from him. Even from a distance, you could see her heart breaking as she rushed out of the room, wiping the tears from her eyes.

"Brett," Annabel rushed after her, followed by Jake.

Emilia let out a soft moan, catching Robert's and my attention, and I couldn't help but wonder if she was in pain.

"Though I'm sure you've explored the option," I said. "Are you sure there's nothing you can do for her?" I nodded to Emilia.

He shook his head. "I tried, but my Magic couldn't latch onto anything. It's as if she's perfectly healthy and dying at the same time."

"I know what it is to feel helpless," I sighed. "But you can't give up, you can't let your frustration shut you off from the ones who care about you."

"You think I don't know that?"

"Do you?" I cocked my head. "You and Violet, there's something there. Hurt, heartbreak."

"How'd—"

"The transition was abrupt. Her feelings, her Magic, are much more present than they normally are."

He let out a sigh and ran a hand through his hair. "I know you trust Merlin." He stared into the empty fireplace. "But when it comes to Violet, he's hiding something."

"That's just his way." I tried to reassure him. "For as long as I've known Merlin, he's always kept his cards close to his chest."

"That's what I'm worried about." He closed his eyes. "If he can't save you both..."

My legs wobbled like a baby deer and I pushed myself upright and crossed the space between us.

"It's in times of great trial that you have to hold on to your faith." I touched his shoulder and his eyes met mine. "There's a reason Violet was spared when she woke me. If nothing else, trust in that."

"I need you to be honest with me." His eyes burned into me and for the briefest of moments, I understood their connection.

"I've nothing to hide from you."

"Do you think Violet will survive *you*?" His eyes met mine and for a moment, I felt like he could see right to the core of my soul.

"I don't know."

He turned and slammed his hands into the mantel. "That's not an answer," he growled as his head fell between his arms.

"When Nimue split our soul, leaving me deserted and alone, Merlin was the one who saved me." I reached out and placed my hand between his shoulder blades. "If Violet has a chance of surviving this, it'll be because of Merlin."

"You'd bet your life on him?" He turned his head to look at me.

"I'd bet all our lives on him."

"If it comes to you or her—"

"I know." The corner of my lips twitched. "As it should be."

He let out a heavy sigh and said, "I should get this placed cleaned up." He turned around and his eyes widened.

"What—" I followed his gaze. "By the stars."

Emilia's body floated above the couch, her hair and clothes moving around her as if she was underwater.

"Merlin!" Robert's voice carried through the house.

CHAPTER 27

IVIAN

"WHAT NOW?" Merlin rushed to Emilia's side.

Placing his hands on her shoulder and hip, sparks burst at his touch, making him take a step back and look her up and down.

"What's happening to her?" Becky asked as she, Alyssa, and Brett rushed back into the room.

"I don't know." Merlin's eyes bounced up and down Emilia's body.

"Vivian, are you alright?" Becky asked.

I nodded. "A little queasy, but whatever it is, it's not having a detrimental effect on me."

"It has to be the excess Magic." Alyssa shook her head as she looked down at the woman. "The spell must have brought it to the surface."

"You don't know that," Robert pointed out.

"True, but it doesn't take a genius to deduce we did something to her and now she's having a reaction," she glared at him. "Here, the Magic elemental, it might help." Alyssa held the stone out to Merlin and he took it.

Placing the crude rock on her chest, Merlin held his hands a few inches above the stone and began to recite a spell.

"Wait a minute." Robert crossed the room in a few strides and grabbed the elemental off of Emilia's chest.

A pulse of energy coursed through the room, sending my hair over my shoulder and a shiver down my spine. I recognized the Magic emanating off of Emilia; I'd felt it before when Nimue cast the spell to save Mordred.

"Rushing into things got us here." He brandished the stone like a scolding parent. "Don't you think we should—"

"Should what?" Alyssa snapped at Robert as she closed the gap between them. "Wait until she's dead?" She cocked her head to the side, daring him to speak.

"People die in war," I said, breaking the tension between the two of them. "Robert's right. We don't know how we can help her."

Another wave of Magic pulsed off of Emilia and I grabbed the edge of the couch as my stomach rolled. No one else seemed to notice or feel the Magic and I couldn't help but wonder why.

I let out a shaky breath and said, "Whatever's happening to her, it's tied to the Shadowlands."

"Of course." Alyssa threw her head back. "It's not just excess Magic. When she allowed passage for Nimue, she wasn't just exposed to feral Magic, but to the Shadowlands themselves."

"What does that mean?" Brett did her best to keep her voice even, but the fear in her eyes was unmistakable.

"I'm not entirely sure, but it gives me a better understanding of what we're working with." Alyssa's eyes were bright as she looked over Emilia's body.

"We can't leave her like this," I said, as another pulse of Magic moved through the room, forcing me to lean forward.

"What is it?" Robert furrowed his brow.

"The Magic radiating off of her is dark and painful."

"You can feel it?" Merlin studied me.

I met his eyes and nodded my head.

"Isn't there some sort of spell that'll put her in a coma or something?" Becky offered.

"A Stasis spell might do the trick," I said. "And it may just give us the time we need."

"It's not a solution," Merlin argued as his hands hovered over Emilia.

"No, but Robert's right, rushing into this without understanding the ramifications is asking for trouble."

Merlin rolled his eyes. "I think Violet's emotions are clouding your judgment."

"Quite the opposite." I pulled myself together and folded my arms over my chest. "It's your feelings for the girl that are making you reckless. Must you repeat history?" I said, hitting him where I knew it would hurt.

Merlin's mouth fell open to argue, but he quickly shut it.

"Fine," he snapped. "Stasis it is."

He began to recite a spell under his breath, and another wave of energy pulsed through the room, turning my stomach into knots.

I doubled over at the sensation and took a deep breath.

Robert's hand settled on the small of my back. "Are you alright?"

"I believe so," I sighed. "The Magic... she won't last much longer like this," I forced myself upright again.

"We'll do what we can," he sighed. "And I appreciate you backing me up," he whispered.

I gave him a small smile and said, "No need for thanks. You were right."

His eyes met mine and a small smile pulled at his lips. "Still," he sighed. "Sometimes I feel as though I'm always on the other side of these things."

"You're cautious." I placed a hand on his arm and he didn't flinch away. "Given the circumstances, you have every right to be."

The front door slammed open and footsteps jostled over the wood floors toward us. Robert and I raised our shields in unison and I could feel their Artognou Magic just under the surface.

"You're going to want to stop right there," Robert's commanding voice halted the intruders.

Magic danced on my fingertips, hungry and ready to strike.

"No need for theatrics, brother."

"Ethan?" Robert lowered his shield as two people stepped out of the shadows. "Elodie? Are you alright?"

"You look terrible," Brett rushed forward.

The tension in my shoulders eased and the Magic inside me uncoiled. I lowered my shield as Brett stepped around me and gave them both a hug.

"Well, hello to you, too," Ethan remarked as he wrapped one arm about Brett.

Both of them looked as if they'd been trampled by a herd of horses. Bruises and cuts covered their exposed skin.

"We've been better," Ethan answered as he placed a hand on Elodie's shoulder.

"Hold this," Robert tossed the Magic elemental stone to me as he stepped toward Ethan and Elodie.

The crude rock felt warm in my hands, as if it had been sitting in the sun all day. I felt uneasy, as if I were holding something that wanted nothing more than destruction. Placing the stone on the entry table, I wiped my hands free of the Magic and turned back to the others.

Robert held out a hand to each of them. Relief washed over their faces as his Magic flared to life and healed their wounds.

"Thanks," Elodie let out a heavy sigh.

"Anytime," Robert released them as the last bruise faded.

"We hate to barge in like - woah!" Ethan looked over Robert's shoulder, just now noticing Emilia's floating body in the living room.

"Looks like you already have your hands full," Elodie motioned toward Merlin and Emilia.

Merlin's words were hushed and unintelligible as the Stasis spell started to swirl around her body. The golden weave moved over her, wrapping her in a tight cocoon that would slow her heart and hopefully lessen the effects of the Shadowlands.

"It's always something." Robert ran a hand through his hair and invited them into the room.

"What happened here?" Elodie took in the destroyed living room. Her eyes lingered on Emilia as Merlin slowly lowered her body back onto the sofa.

"It's a long story," Brett sighed.

"Speaking of stories, care to tell us what happened to the two of you?" Robert raised his eyebrows.

"I wish we were here under better circumstances." Ethan clapped a hand on Robert's shoulder.

"But we need your help," Elodie looked between Robert and Brett.

"Anything," Robert said as the four of them made their way through the overturned furniture and debris.

"Do you remember when we ran into you at Merlin's cabin a few months back? Right before Morgana attacked Hearst?" Ethan asked as his eyes skated over Merlin.

There was a nervous energy to him that was making my skin crawl. Whatever happened to them, whatever they came here to tell us, had them worried and almost twitchy.

"Yeah, what about it?" Robert furrowed his brow.

"We weren't there to ask about a lost Promised One," Elodie admitted, and her eyes flipped between Robert and Merlin.

"Then why?" Robert asked.

Ethan leaned against the side of the mantel and Elodie looked at her feet like they held all the secrets in the world.

"They were on a mission at my request," Merlin answered for them as he stood and left Emilia's side.

"Will it hold?" I asked, looking over the couch at Emilia's sleeping body. Golden Magic spun around her, keeping her just on the edge of alive.

"Only time will tell," he sighed as he stared down at her. "But we need to come up with something quickly if we have any chance of saving her and Matthew."

"What mission were you on?" Robert refused to look at Merlin and instead kept his eyes glued to Ethan.

I watched Merlin carefully, the twitch of his lips, the set of his shoulders. He really was full of secrets. I used to think it was bothersome, but most of the time, there was a reason he kept his cards close to his chest.

"What is it, Merlin?" I wondered.

"Have you lost her then?" Merlin asked them.

"Lost who?" Robert demanded. "Ethan?"

"We were ambushed." Ethan let out a heavy breath. "These guys, they were..."

"Monsters," Elodie finished for him. "We tried, we really tried. But we were no match for them. They took her and there was nothing we could do." Elodie shook her head as she spoke, her frustration written in every line of her body.

"You had one job." Merlin let out a heavy sigh and pinched the bridge of his nose. "You should have called for backup."

"Gee, you think?" Ethan sneered.

"There wasn't time," Elodie said. "They were waiting for us."

"That's not possible." Merlin shook his head. "We took all the precautions."

"Clearly we didn't, because they knew exactly when and where we'd be with her," Ethan fired back, his cheeks flushed with anger.

"Merlin, how bad is this?" I asked as I continued to watch his every movement. To the untrained eye, he was calm, but if you looked closer, deeper, there was nervous energy crawling over his features. Knowing him for as long as I have, it was easy to tell this was much worse than anyone in this room realized.

"Who were you protecting?" Brett asked.

"Her name's Amara," Ethan sighed.

"By the stars," I exhaled. My blood stilled in my veins and I felt the color drain from my face.

"Who is she? Why were you protecting her?" Robert's hands balled into fists.

"Merlin, please tell me it's not who I think it is?" I grabbed the edge of the sofa to steady myself.

"Alas, I cannot." His jaw flexed as he held my eyes.

"What were you thinking, having them protect her?" I scolded him. "They don't have Magic; they wouldn't stand a—"

"You think I don't know that?" Merlin snapped. "The Draig can track Magic," he practically growled. "She was safest in their hands."

"Obviously not safe enough." I shook my head in disbelief.

"Wait a minute," Robert's eyes met mine. "What are we talking about here?"

"We don't have a minute to waste." I met his eye and his brow furrowed ever so slightly as he grasped the urgency in my voice.

"Elodie, who's Amara?" Brett kept her voice soft as she stepped toward her friend.

Elodie looked up at Brett, tears in her eyes as she said, "The Grail." Her breath caught and the words barely escaped her lips.

"I don't understand." Brett shook her head.

"Amara *is* the Grail," Ethan explained.

"The Grail is a woman?" Robert turned toward me, his eyes piercing through me, waiting for an answer.

"Yes," I nodded.

CHAPTER 28

IVIAN

A HEAVY TENSION settled over the room as everyone stared at me. Apparently, none of them knew the Grail was a woman, and I watched as they processed this new bit of information. Leave it to Merlin to keep them in the dark, I thought.

"You're joking, right?" The color drained from Brett's face.

"Not at all," I said.

"But all the legends?" Robert shook his head. "The cup, the knights. It was all a lie?"

"Not exactly." Merlin rocked his head back and forth. "The simple fact that the Grail is a woman is the only detail that was altered."

"But why?" Jake asked.

"Could you imagine living a life always on the run?" Merlin addressed Jake. "A life where you're always hunted."

"I get that, but why a cup?" Jake amended.

"Drinking the elixir of life has been a part of tales and

legends, even since I was a boy," Merlin explained. "It seemed only natural to tie Amara's gift to the stories that already existed, hence drinking from the cup."

"So, who is Amara then? How is she able to grant immortality?" Annabel asked.

I waited for Merlin to answer, but when it was obvious I'd lost him to his own thoughts, I said, "She's not of this realm. Amara's home was destroyed by the Draig and she was brought here for safekeeping."

"And the immortality?" Robert asked.

"Where she comes from, an immortal is born every few hundred years. It's just who she is; it runs through her blood, lives in each cell of her body," Merlin said, to no one in particular.

"And she can grant immortality to just anyone?" Becky asked.

"In theory, yes, but there's a catch," I said. "When she gives someone immortality, she's giving them a piece of her soul. There's only so much of herself she can dole out before there's nothing left to give."

"She also has to give it freely or it won't take hold," Merlin chimed in.

"Then we have nothing to worry about, right?" Becky shrugged. "I mean, who in their right mind would freely give Nimue, or anyone that deranged, immortality."

"You hit the nail on the head," Merlin said. "In the right frame of mind, Amara wouldn't grant Nimue eternal life, but there are many ways to break someone who can't die."

His eyes met mine and a thousand pains flashed over my skin. Nimue would do anything to have her way. I was living proof of that fact.

"They're ruthless," Annabel said under her breath. "There isn't a line they won't cross." Jake wrapped his arm around her as the life drained from her face.

"This all feels a little too... I don't know," Becky shrugged. "Perfectly planned out?"

"What're you thinking?" Robert furrowed his brow.

"First there were those shadow things."

"The Umbra-Kai," Merlin corrected her.

"Which ended up being the perfect distraction for Matty and me to get captured. Then we end up with sleeping beauty over here," she gestured to Emilia. "And if we don't save her, Matty's life is on the line. Oh, and let's not forget the Grail was being taken while all the rest of this was happening," Becky rushed to the end of her sentence in one breath.

"I tried to tell you," Alyssa said. "Morgana's always playing multiple hands at once."

"Emilia may just be a distraction," I said. "To keep us chasing a cure while they work on getting what they want from the Grail."

"She'll hold out," Merlin sounded hopeful, but his pursed lips told a different story.

"You and I both know that after enough pain and suffering, anyone would willingly give anything to make it stop."

"Amara is stronger than that," Merlin argued.

"Would you bet your life on that?" I held his eye, forcing him not to look away. "All our lives?"

"Even if she can withstand anything they throw at her, we don't know where to look for her or how to rescue her," Robert argued.

"Isn't there, like, some secret underground Magic network that we could tap into?" Becky's eyes lit up.

"The Magical world isn't the Underground Railroad," Merlin chided her. "And even if something like that existed, what good would it do in tracking Morgana?"

"First of all, I didn't literally mean underground, Grandpa." she stared up at Merlin like the ancient man he was. "Second, if there was a way to track Magic, or maybe the Draigs movement, we might be able to find them and save the Grail before they can do her harm."

Everyone stared at Becky as if she was Nostradamus giving another one of his half-baked prophecies.

"I could put you in touch with a few of my contacts," Robert offered. "They can get you in touch with the right people."

"And we know a few people who might be able to help get the word out," Ethan offered.

"If they can get me a lead, it may just be what we need." Becky's smile reached ear to ear. She was confident and strong with this type of work, and I admired her optimism. "And what about tracking the Draig or Magic?"

"Morgana and Nimue will have wards in effect to protect them," Merlin shook his head.

"Alyssa?" Becky looked to the woman for some guidance.

"Morgana never trusted me." Alyssa shook her head. "She placed those wards herself."

"Maybe we can drum up some info the old-fashioned way," Becky sighed. "The Draig will create a mess wherever they go; if I set the right parameters, we may get a hit." At this point, she was talking more to herself than anyone else.

"While she does that," Brett waved dismissively at Becky. "We need to come up with a Plan B to save Matty and hope Amara can hold out until we can find her."

"It's possible we can do a little more than hope," I smirked, and met Merlin's eyes.

"We could try," Merlin nodded. "But we'll need Violet and their Artognou Magic."

"I know." My heart sank at the thought of falling back into the darkness. But if it meant we could get a message to Amara and stop Nimue from gaining freedom from the Shadowlands, it'd be worth it.

"What is it?" Merlin's brow furrowed as he looked at me.

"Each time Violet and I move from conscious to unconscious, it takes something from us, drains us."

"You think you're running out of time?" Robert asked.

I nodded, "I don't know how many more times we'll be able to shift back and forth."

"So, the question becomes, do we take the risk?" Merlin mused.

"Maybe I can help make things easier." Alyssa looked me over thoughtfully. "What is it you're trying to accomplish?"

"We need Violet's Soothsayer Magic," Merlin said.

"Can't you just use yours?" Robert asked.

"Unfortunately, no," Merlin sighed. "The spell requires the Soothsayer to be bound by Artognou Magic."

"That seems pretty specific," Robert said.

"What will it do?" Becky asked.

"It's a form of astral projection," Merlin explained. "While you keep Violet grounded to the here and now, she can explore another time and place like she does in her visions and pass a message to Amara."

"Has this ever been done before?" Robert looked between me and Merlin.

My eyes met Merlin's, and I smiled. "You're looking at the man who created the spell for him and Arthur."

"I must say, you all are much more stimulating than your counterparts," Alyssa beamed. "I've been working on something, a tonic that may allow you both to be conscious for a short time."

"Don't you already have your hands full?" Robert nodded toward Emilia's resting body.

"She's not going anywhere." Alyssa moved closer to me. "And there's a fair bit of research I need to do now that we know it's the Shadowlands that's killing her.

"Shouldn't you be—"

"Robert, it's fine," I said. "Go ahead and mix the tonic."

"Right." Merlin clapped his hands together. "We'll need someplace quiet for you and Violet to perform the spell."

"The pool house?" Robert pushed off the wall.

"That should do nicely." Merlin smiled and motioned for Robert and me to follow him outside. "Alyssa, come find us when you're ready," Merlin said, without looking over his shoulder.

"I've always wanted to try something like this." Alyssa beamed with excitement.

"If you so much as—" Robert started.

"Yes, yes," Alyssa rolled her eyes. "You'll hang me out to dry and let the birds pick at my bones."

Robert stiffened as he ignored her and followed Merlin.

"One of these days, he'll thank me for everything I'm doing," Alyssa huffed.

"I wouldn't hold your breath," I said, following Robert.

CHAPTER 29

VIVIAN

MERLIN SPENT the better part of an hour drilling the spell into Robert while we waited for Alyssa to deliver what would hopefully make this whole plan viable.

"Could Violet have done something like this without knowing it?" Robert asked.

"It's unlikely." Merlin pursed his lips. "Why do you ask?"

"I think she may've, or at least I thought she was reaching out to me." Robert looked at his hands and pursed his lips.

"It's not a spell you just fall into," Merlin shook his head. "What makes you think she was trying to communicate with you through her visions?"

"When I was on Avalon," Robert started, "There was one night I could have sworn she was there with me. I could..." His eyes came back into focus and he looked at me. "I could feel her, and when the air stirred just right, I could almost hear her."

"Did the two of you ever speak of this moment? Confirm that she was reaching out to you?" I asked.

"No," Robert's eyes fell. "Things were less than ideal when I returned, and I chalked it up to wishful thinking at the time."

"It may be possible." I touched his shoulder. "The connection between you two, though it's still young, is undeniably strong and true."

"Either way," Merlin interrupted. "You'll still need to walk Violet through the process. Though it's not unlike her visions, it will be harder for her to stay in control. Especially since we won't have her full focus in this endeavor."

A knock at the door ended any further conversation.

"Come in," I called out.

Alyssa pushed the door open, a small bottle in her hands and a journal under her arm.

"Just in time," Merlin smiled.

He always admired those who dared to be different. Who dared to push boundaries and go into the unknown head-on. It was a quality I admired in him, though I also understood why his blatant favoring ruffled more than a few feathers.

"Are we sure about this?" Robert eyed Alyssa. "We don't know what it'll do to them, to both be awake, so to speak."

"If we always waited until we had the answers, nothing would get accomplished." Alyssa shook her head as she made her way into the room.

"Our only other option is to wait until Violet returns and we don't know how long that will be or how long Amara has." I gave him an apologetic smile. "I know this is hard for you, but this is the path we're on. We must do what's best for the Magical world."

"I don't need a lecture on duty," Robert sighed and ran a hand through his hair. "I just wish—"

"I fear the time for wishing is over," Merlin chimed in. "We need to take action. Now more than ever, or Morgana and Nimue will win this war."

"Understood," Robert said reluctantly. "Let's get this over with."

"Just a few drops under your tongue should do the trick," Alyssa said, handing me the tiny glass bottle. "I'd recommend taking a seat before you start."

I stepped around the coffee table littered with journals and took a seat on the small cream colored couch.

"Would you mind if I observe?" Alyssa's voice was soft and curious. "I've never seen anything like this and I doubt I'll ever have another opportunity."

"Of course," Merlin said. "If it's alright with them, it's alright with me."

I looked up at Robert, allowing him to decide. His eyes met mine and he let out a heavy sigh. "Just don't get in the way," he said, shaking his head.

He didn't send her packing, so that was progress at least.

Opening the bottle Alyssa gave me, I squeezed the plunger, filling the glass with the liquid she'd crafted.

"Bottoms up," I said, opening my mouth and letting a few drops hit the underside of my tongue. "How long should it take?"

Alyssa looked at her watch and made a note in the journal she was carrying.

"Your guess is as good as mine," she shrugged and watched me like I was about to sprout horns.

"Right then," Merlin clapped his hands together. "Robert, I know the two of you have had little practice with your Magic, but it must be you who drives Violet's vision."

"How do I go about doing that?" Robert sat down next to me.

"When you connect, you'll need to focus on Amara," Merlin explained.

"Okay, but I know nothing about her, what she looks like, who she—"

"You don't need to," Merlin interrupted. "It's about intentions. Once you feel confident in your goal, recite the spell and let Violet do the rest."

"I believe something's happening." I frowned at the sensation crawling over my chest.

It's like there were slugs under my skin and in my head. My body felt heavy, slow, and woozy as my heart started to race.

Alyssa moved closer, placing her fingers on my wrist and noting something down as she looked at me.

"Quicker than I expected," she mumbled to herself. "What exactly are you feeling? Can you feel Violet? Is she present more now than at other times? Do you still have a grasp of your reality?" Alyssa fired off.

"You'll get your turn." Merlin gently grabbed her by the shoulder and pulled her backward.

"What's...ugh...I feel like death," Violet sighed in my head.

"She's here." I nodded. "Though a bit groggy," I said through heavy breaths.

"Violet?" Robert touched my cheek and gently turned my face toward him.

"Robert?" Violet sounded confused. *"What's happening? Vivian, are you? Is that you?"*

"We need to try something, and we didn't have the time to wait for you to reappear," I said out loud so Merlin and Robert could hear at least my half of the conversation.

"Okay," Violet breathed.

Chills ran up and down our body and it was hard to keep my eyes in focus.

Closing my eyes, I spoke to Violet directly in our shared head. *"I know this isn't ideal, but you need to push through the fog and try to be more stable."*

"Easier said than done." Violet squirmed and I could feel her

Magic starting to mingle with my own. *"Alright, what are we doing?"*

"She's ready, go ahead and explain." I looked at Robert, hoping she would find her footing in him and the floating sensation would subside.

"We need to get a message to the Grail, who's a woman, by the way."

"Wait, what?"

"They'll fill you in later," I said aloud and nodded for Robert to continue.

"Her name is Amara," Robert explained. "With our Artognou Magic and your gift as a Soothsayer, there's a way you can see and talk to her."

"Right, I've been on the receiving end before," Violet said.

"How do you mean?" I asked her.

"What did she say?" Robert asked.

I held up a finger for him to wait so Violet could explain to me what she meant.

"Another Soothsayer spoke directly to me once, in a vision. It's like she knew I was there and warned me about what was to come."

I repeated what Violet told me, and Merlin seemed pleased that we weren't working from scratch.

"Are you both ready?" Robert asked as I sunk deeper into the couch.

"I believe so," I sighed. "Violet?"

"Let's do this," she said. I took a deep breath, nodded, and Robert took my hand.

"Vivian." Robert's voice was soft and his thumb traced the back of my hand.

"Hmm?" It was all I could manage in my weakened state.

"Maybe it would help if you pictured Amara as well, since you're sharing just about everything with Violet, anyway. She may get a better grip with your help."

I nodded in acknowledgment.

"Here we go." Robert closed his eyes and started to recite the spell.

I pulled up an image of Amara in my mind. Though it had been ages since I last saw her, I hoped it would at least help Violet.

Their magic flared to life inside me, warm like a summer day and overwhelming as it took hold.

"I'll lower my walls, are you ready?" Violet asked.

"Go on," I said.

It was as if we'd been hiding in a dark room and someone opened a door. Colors, sounds, and Magic pulled at me in every direction. Chaos filled my mind, and I wanted nothing more than to curl into a corner and shut it all out. If this was what Violet felt like every day, I was glad not to be a Soothsayer.

I let out a heavy breath as something started to take hold, and Robert continued to recite the spell under his breath. My eyes darted to Merlin as the entire room was picked up and turned on end.

Furniture disappeared, colors reshaped themselves as Robert's hand squeezed my own. Grass began to sprout under my feet and trees rose out of the ground where Merlin had just been standing a moment before.

Looking down, I realized I was no longer in Violet's clothes or body. I stood barefoot in the grass with Robert on one side of me and Violet on the other.

"Are you seeing all this?" I said breathlessly.

"Yes," Robert's voice was soft.

Violet stepped forward, leading the way as she moved through the vision effortlessly.

Just up ahead, a woman sat slumped against a tree, her dark hair matted and thrown in unnatural directions covering her face. Behind her and beyond the tree line, there was a crystal blue lake in the distance, but nothing that indicated where we were in the world.

"Is that her?" Robert asked.

"Yes."

Violet knelt next to the woman and looked back at us. "How's this supposed to work?" she asked.

The Artognou Magic flared to life inside me, and I saw the same light in Violet's eyes as she looked at Robert.

In the distant part of my mind, I could hear him reciting the spell once more.

"Amara?" Violet's voice was gentle, unsure. She reached out to place a hand on the woman's shoulder.

"Who's there?" Amara said, without looking up.

As I stepped closer, I noticed the dark purple bruises dotting her dark skin like angry blotches.

"Oh, Amara," I said, kneeling on the other side of her. "I'm so sorry."

"Vivian?" Amara lifted her head, her dark brown eyes peering into me. "How?" She looked at Violet and Robert.

"Do you know where you are?" I asked.

She shook her head and said, "We're on the move. I don't know where to. They keep me blinded most of the time with Magic."

"Merlin wanted us to get a message to you." Violet gave her a small smile.

"Merlin's with you?" Amara's eyes searched Violet's.

"He is," she nodded.

"I should have guessed," she smirked. "This," she waved her hand at the three of us, "It's got him written all over it."

Everything around me blurred for a moment, like someone was shaking me and distorting my vision.

Violet turned to me and, without having to say a word, I knew she'd just experienced the same thing.

"We have little time," Violet said.

"We're coming for you," I said. "I don't know how, but we will find you. Don't give into them, don't give them what they want."

She nodded and let out a heavy breath. "May I ask?" Her eyes darted between Violet and me. "Ethan and Elodie?"

"They're fine," I said quickly. "They came to us after they took you."

She let out a heavy sigh and her shoulders slumped forward in relief.

"There's something you need to know," she addressed Violet. "It's not just my immortality they're after." She paused and her eyes met mine. "They're looking for Elysium. They want to break down the barriers between our realms."

"But that would—"

"I know," she interrupted me. "And if it comes down to saving me or keeping Elysium sealed off—"

"It won't come to that," I blurted.

A sharp pain shot through me like I was being electrocuted, and Violet slumped forward.

"I don't think I can hold this much longer," Robert huffed.

"Do what you must," Amara said.

"We'll see you soon," Violet said, getting to her feet.

"Wait," I said, leaning into Amara. "Merlin wanted me to tell you, when smoke rises, the time for games will be behind you," I whispered. "I don't know what it means, but he said you'd know when the time came."

Her eyes met mine, and she nodded.

Everything around us began to rumble. The ground beneath my feet blurred and the world was ripped away.

"Did it work?" Merlin's voice called out from a distance.

"Yes," Robert sighed.

"We have a problem," I said through a haze as the pool house came back into focus.

Merlin stared down at me, his eyes boring into mine like he might burn a hole through my skull.

"She's going after Elysium," I breathed.

"William's mentioned it before, but I'm not sure what it is?" Robert looked between Merlin and me.

The fear in Merlin's eyes was unmistakable. Everything

we've been trying to protect, every precaution we've taken, every loss we've suffered was etched into the lines of his face.

"Elysium," Merlin cleared his throat. "Is almost like another realm, a Magical realm, but man created it, not the universe." He turned away from Robert and looked out the small window toward the midnight sky.

"It's all she's been after since the day she learned of its existence," I said, as my head started to throb.

"But why? What's so special about it?" Robert wondered.

"I wouldn't call it special, per se." I let out a heavy breath as my arms and legs started to tingle, and I shivered as I fought to hold on.

"If Morgana unleashes Elysium on this world, everyone, and I mean every soul who doesn't have an inclination toward Magic, will be killed."

"Oh God, no," Violet whispered as black fuzzy clouds began to crawl over my eyes.

VIVIAN IN THE DARK

Fear GRIPS my soul as I

F

A

L

L.

I want to scream,
but
I
can't.
Please don't let me fail.

CHAPTER 30

 IOLET

ROBERT'S VOICE broke through the fog next to me as he spoke softly to someone else in the room. The faint smell of chlorine made my nose tingle, and I took a deep breath and opened my eyes.

"How long was I out this time?" I asked.

"Maybe a half hour," Robert said.

"Have you told the others yet?" My head felt heavy against the back of the couch as I shifted my body toward him.

"We wanted to wait for you," Merlin said.

"How're you feeling?" Alyssa asked.

Robert's head snapped in her direction, but whatever he wanted to say, he kept to himself.

"A little groggy. Like I took a sleeping pill and I'm still trying to wake up."

"You may feel that way for a while," Alyssa said, taking down notes. "Though if you feel anything else, please do let me know right away."

I nodded and pushed myself upright so my arms were resting on my knees as she made her exit.

"You sure you're alright?" Robert placed a hand on my back.

I took a deep breath through my nose and exhaled through my mouth. "I'm starting to think we can't win this thing."

"Things may look bleak at the moment, but we can do this," Merlin said. "We have to."

"I don't know how much more Vivian and I can take." Tears stung my eyes as an overwhelming sensation of emotions flooded my heart. "It's exhausting going back and forth."

Merlin knelt down in front of me, one hand on my knee while the other lifted my chin to look at him.

"I know the universe has asked too much of you," he started. "I know you're tired and it would be easy to fade into the darkness for good, but you're still here for a reason. You may not have been born with Magic, or the knowledge that your counterparts have, but you're stronger because of it."

"How?" My voice broke as tears threaten to overtake me.

"Because, unlike them, you've chosen this life every step of the way. You could have walked away; you could have said no at any point. But you haven't, and that makes you truly unique."

"I'm so tired, Merlin."

"I know." He pulled me into the fold of his arms. "I know," he whispered again.

For a brief moment, I let myself feel it all. The fear of losing the people I loved. The weight of having to save the Magical world. The helplessness of being lost in my own body with Vivian. I let myself collapse against his chest and let the tears fall freely for just a moment.

Whatever came next, there wouldn't be time for weakness, there wouldn't be time for tears and heartbreak, not until this was over, one way or another.

"Okay," I said, pulling away from Merlin and wiping the tears from my face. "I'm okay."

"Violet, you don't—" Robert started.

"Yes, I do," I grabbed his hand and squeezed. "We should tell the others about Amara and Elysium."

"Yes, there is much to catch everyone up on." Merlin gave me a tight-lipped smile.

Robert helped me get to my feet, and I felt like I'd run a marathon. More than anything, I just wanted to sleep for a week. Leaning on him, we made our way into the kitchen where the others were gathered.

"How did it go?" Becky asked the moment we were through the back door.

"It worked," I said. "Though I'm pretty sure we've got bigger problems than the Grail being captured."

"What do you mean?" Brett asked.

"Morgana is hunting for Elysium." Merlin's commanding voice captured everyone's attention as Robert and I took a seat at the island. "If she finds it, she'll be able to wipe out the majority of life on this planet."

"How can something that powerful even exist? And why?" Brett shook her head.

"It was created eons ago as a haven for the Magical world. It was never meant to be destructive." Merlin explained.

"So, what happened?" Jake asked.

"The same thing that always happens," Merlin said. "Greed, lust for power, you name it. Instead of being a haven for the Magical world, it became a weapon." Merlin shook his head. "The more people took from Elysium, the more it took from this world."

"What do you mean?" I asked.

"The devastation was unlike anything this realm had ever seen before. Entire countries lost everything, millions of people fell ill and died horrible, painful deaths." Merlin paced up and down the kitchen. "The plight has been called many things throughout the centuries, the most notably the Bubonic Plague."

"Wait a minute," Becky pushed herself off the counter she was perched on. "The Plague was because of Elysium?"

"I'm afraid so," he confirmed. "We didn't realize how bad it had gotten until it was far too late," Merlin pinched the bridge of his nose.

"How could you not have known how bad it was?" Brett scowled.

"Because the Magical world wasn't affected," he said, frowning at the memory. "Once we realized what was happening, access to Elysium was banned and the realm was completely closed off," Merlin explained. "The Brotherhood was able to successfully move the gateway out of Central Asia to an unknown location and there hasn't been an incident since."

"But why would Morgana want to unleash another plague on this world?" Becky asked.

"Morgana has spent her entire life fighting for the freedom of the Magical world," Merlin explained. "She's never agreed that keeping our gifts out of the limelight has been the right thing to do."

"Yeah, but having Magic out in the open and killing more than half the world's population is two different things," Jake scoffed.

"It is, and it isn't," Merlin leaned on the counter in front of him and hung his head. "Rid the world of everyone without Magic, and what do you have left?" He lifted his eyes to meet Jake's.

"A world full of Magic where we don't have to hide who we are," Robert spoke each word carefully.

"Who would want to live in a world like that?" Becky asked. "I mean seriously, a world of nothing but the same sounds pretty boring to me."

"There are many who believe it's the only way for everyone

to truly learn what they're capable of," he said. "What they don't realize is that we need people like Alyssa, Matthew and yourself who help us look deeper and fight harder."

"How have we not heard of this before?" Robert asked. "You'd think if something this terrible happened, people would do anything to keep the memory alive so history doesn't repeat itself."

"There was a great debate on how the memory of Elysium should be treated," Merlin explained. "Some, like yourself, thought that we should pass down the story of Elysium as a warning. Others believed it would only lead to more temptation and yet another catastrophic event."

"So, this has been Morgana's plan all along?" Brett asked. "Wipe out the majority of the planet?"

"It's why we sentenced her Beyond the Veil in the first place," he said. "Le Fay should not have been able to bridge the gap between the Veil to bring her back."

"Why didn't you tell us about Elysium the moment Morgana returned?" I asked. If he knew all along what Morgana was after, why not warn us, give us a heads up?

"I was hoping it wouldn't come to this," Merlin sighed. "Vivian was meant to stop Morgana before it ever got to this point."

"But she didn't because you messed with the Waking," Robert said. "To save Violet's life."

"It would seem my meddling, though for a noble purpose, has made Vivian's task more difficult."

"You still should have told us." I shook my head.

"Maybe, but the memory of Elysium was not something I wished to invoke, if I could help it."

Robert placed his hands on the counter in front of him. "So if the Brotherhood moved Elysium, then they should be able to move it again, or at least tell us where to look so we can stop Morgana."

"I'm afraid not." Merlin pursed his lips. "The Brothers who were in charge of moving Elysium's gate to a new location didn't survive the journey."

"Of course they didn't," I sighed.

"It was thought best that no one knew where Elysium was," Merlin said.

"So, what? They were killed?" Jake balked.

"Their sacrifice has kept this world safe for the last seven hundred years. It was a small price to pay."

"So, how do we find it, then?" Annabel asked.

"Better yet," Jake said. "How do we stop Morgana from finding it?"

"All throughout history, people have been trying to find Elysium," Merlin explained. "There are clues hidden all over the world, some real, some fake."

"Has anyone ever come close?" Becky asked.

"Depends on who you ask. Some believe The Brotherhood destroyed Elysium altogether." Merlin leaned against the counter. "Others believe they've found all the right clues leading them home to the promised land."

"Knowing what Elysium can do to this world, why would anyone even want to find it?" Becky asked.

"Greed mostly," Merlin said. "The concept of unlimited Magic is quite tempting to the right sort of person."

"You mean a psychopath," Becky amended.

"It became more of a game than anything else," Merlin continued. "Everyone wanted to be the one to solve the impossible puzzle."

"If no one's ever found it, how can we be sure the Brothers didn't destroy it?" Jake asked as he wrapped an arm around Annabel's shoulders.

"There are many things in this world that have yet to be discovered," Merlin smirked. "Just because no one's deciphered the clues in the right order yet, doesn't mean someone won't."

"Le Fay got close once," Robert said. "At least, I think they might have."

"Care to share with the class?" Annabel asked.

"William mentioned it," I answered.

A short laughed escaped Robert's throat. "You were right all along. It's all connected," he finished under his breath.

"William?" Merlin cocked his head to the side.

"Our ancestor," Robert motioned between him and his siblings. "He kept journals and in at least one of them, he mentioned Elysium."

"What exactly did he say?" Jake asked.

"He and his wife were trying to prevent Le Fay from getting their hands on the coordinates. They had inside access to Morgana's support system and were trying to use that to stop them."

"I had no idea William was tangled up with Le Fay," Brett looked at Jake. "Did you?"

"Not a clue," he shook his head. "I always thought he was just the messenger of the prophecy."

"We're there any clues, any bits of information that we could use?" Merlin asked.

"I haven't read everything," Robert shrugged. "But there was mention of some Cook expedition. I didn't think much of it at the time, to be honest."

"Where's this journal now?" Merlin asked.

"It's with my things." I started to get up, but Robert put his hand on my shoulder and gave me a warm smile.

"I'll grab it." He pushed away from the counter. "Give me a minute." He jogged out of the kitchen, a newfound light in his eyes.

"Hopefully, he left behind some clues that we can track down," Brett said.

"What kind of clues are we talking about?" Becky asked. "I'm pretty good at cracking codes."

"This isn't some computer warfare that you can type your way through." Merlin rolled his eyes.

"So, what are we looking for exactly?" Jake asked.

"As I said, throughout history, people have been creating clues, tracking down other accounts and searching for Elysium at their own peril," Merlin said. "There isn't just one set of clues out there."

"So, it's kind of like the old treasure maps?" Annabel said. "Each one building on the other but all trying to lead to the same place."

"Precisely," Merlin nodded, and the corner of his lips twitched. "If you find the right clue, it could lead you to the next, or it could lead you on a wild goose chase. Hence, it's just about impossible to find."

"Maybe not impossible," Robert said, brandishing the journal as he walked back into the kitchen, only slightly out of breath.

"My dear boy," Merlin sighed. "Even if William did indeed stop Le Fay during his time, that doesn't mean it will help us today."

"When I first read the words, I felt something," I said as Robert tossed the journal on the counter.

"What do you mean?" Brett furrowed her brow as she stared at me.

"It was a gut feeling. Like, William wanted me to pay attention to his words."

"Why didn't you say anything?" Brett folded her arms over her chest. "We could have been looking into it all this time."

"Truthfully, I didn't think it was connected." Robert came to my defense. "And not that it's an excuse, but the Brotherhood showed up pretty much the moment we got back and well, there were other, more pressing, matters to deal with," Robert pursed his lips and his shoulders edged closer to his ears.

"There's no need to play the blame game," Merlin opened the journal and let the pages flip to the more worn out part of the binding. "There was no way for you to know that Elysium might be in play."

"If William's right, and I'm inclined to think he is, then Le Fay is already in possession of more than a handful of clues," Robert said, leaning against the counter. "He mentions an Ian," Robert pointed to the journal. "Who we now know as Mordred. If he had the clues back then, it's safe to assume he knows which ones are the real deal and which ones are fake."

"That does pose a problem." Merlin flipped the page in the journal and frowned. "Though if he had all the answers, Elysium would already have taken hold of this world."

"Merlin," I leveled my eyes at him. "We both know, you know more than you're letting on."

He held my stare but kept silent as he flipped through the journal in his hands.

"Now's not the time for keeping secrets." I tried pushing him a little further.

"She's right," Brett said. "There's way too much we don't know and you need to start sharing so we can end this once and for all."

"What do you want to know?" Merlin waved his hand out in front of him, inviting everyone to ask what they wanted.

"Do you know where Elysium is or where to begin looking for it?" Robert asked point blank.

"I don't know where it is, no," Merlin answered.

"But you do know where to start looking." I eyed him carefully.

"Yes." He nodded. "But only because you mentioned the Cook expeditions."

"What were they?" Jake asked.

"Thomas Cook charted the islands of New Zealand in the 1700s," Merlin said, looking at the journal as he flipped from page to page. "He made several expeditions to the islands during a time when travel was precarious and yet he was able to do more than anyone ever expected of him."

"He was Magical?" Brett guessed.

"Bingo." Merlin pointed at her. "Most explorers were during that time," he shrugged. "The risk involved was far less for those who are Magically inclined."

"Why New Zealand though?" Jake asked.

"It was undiscovered territory at the time, and the landscape is quite diverse. Even if someone did happen upon the islands, the chances of them stumbling upon the gate was slim to none unless they knew what they were looking for."

"Are we saying Elysium is in New Zealand?" Jake furrowed his brow.

"It's one theory, yes," Merlin nodded. "But there are about a hundred other theories as well."

"But you believe in this one," I cocked my head to the side, "Don't you?"

I watched him carefully. The corner of his mouth twitched ever so slightly.

"Of everything I've seen, every detail I've tracked down or been privy to, it holds the most clout."

"There are more journals we can go through." Robert reached for the one Merlin was fumbling through. "I was just showing them to Violet before the Umbra-Kai showed up." Robert glanced in my direction and I could feel my chest and cheeks start to flush.

"Looks like we have some work to do," Brett said matter of factly.

CHAPTER 31

IOLET

"ROBERT SAID you might need some help," Elodie said when she walked into the dining room.

"Where's Ethan and Becky?" I asked.

"Still trying to track down Amara," Elodie pursed her lips.

"Any luck?" Brett asked.

Elodie sighed, "Not yet." She took a seat at the table and grabbed one of the journals and aimlessly flipping through it. "Ethan's taking it pretty hard."

"There was nothing more either of you could have done." Jake pat Elodie's shoulder.

"You try telling him that," she scoffed.

Robert walked into the room carrying another box of journals and plopped them down on the table.

"He was prolific, wasn't he?" I noted as I pulled the leather-bound journals out by the handful.

"Have you read all of these?" Brett asked Robert as she picked up one of the tomes.

"None of them, actually." Robert shook his head. "I didn't know they existed until recently.

"Where should we start?" Jake asked. "It's not like we have the time to read through every single one of them."

Robert raised his hands over the table and recited a locating spell. One by one, the journals containing any mention of Elysium started to glow from the inside out.

"We can start with those." Robert motioned to the dozen journals lying on the table.

"Sorry to interrupt," Alyssa said as she rounded the corner. "But I require some Magical assistance. Anyone know where Merlin is?" Her eyes searched the room, to no avail.

"I just left him in the pool house," Robert said without looking up at her.

"How's everything coming along?" Brett asked before Alyssa turned to leave.

"Better," she sighed and leaned against the door frame. "I may have found a way to isolate the Shadowlands Magic that's infecting her."

"Do you think you can stop it?" Brett asked. "From killing her, I mean?"

"I won't know until I try," she smiled, but it didn't reach her eyes.

"Everything okay?" I asked as I studied her expression.

"Fine." She pressed her shoulders back and forced a smile onto her face, but I held her uneasy eyes. "A little frustrated," she admitted. "If only Morgana had listened to me."

"What do you mean?" My brow furrowed.

"I warned her that Emilia wasn't strong enough. That she wouldn't be able to survive that kind of Magic," she shrugged.

"Serves her right for what she did to us," Jake said under his breath.

"I know she hurt you, both of you," Alyssa address Jake and Annabel. "But she's not the monster you've made her out to be."

A short, clipped laugh escaped Jake's throat.

"She's no saint either," Annabel said. "You forget I was there. I witnessed firsthand the pleasure she took in my pain."

"No one is the villain of their own story." She took a step back. "To some, you lot are the ones who've caused all the pain and suffering. It would serve you well to remember that."

"Us?" Jake yelled. "We've done nothing—"

"As I said," Alyssa turned her back on us. "No one is the villain of their own story." She walked away without so much as a glance backward.

"Unbelievable," Jake shook his head.

"She's not wrong." Brett's voice was cold and emotionless.

"You can't be serious?" Jake balked at his sister.

"We've all done things we're not proud of." She turned the page of a notebook without looking. "Things that keep up us at night, things we have to justify to feel better about ourselves." Her eyes met Jake's and something private passed between them.

I looked over at Robert. The set of his jaw, the hunch of his shoulders and the pinched look of his eyes and mouth made me wonder what he was thinking.

"What is it?" I nudged him.

"Nothing." He looked up at me and smiled.

I leveled my eyes at him and he sighed.

"I know Emilia isn't in anyone's good graces." He ran a hand through his hair. "But I still wish there was more I could do for her."

"I know." I placed a hand on his back. His disposition to help others was so ingrained in him that I knew it pained him to not be more useful.

"Let's just focus on the task at hand for the time being." Brett handed a journal to Robert.

We all sat in silence for what seemed like days, reading William's words and trying to decipher all the clues he'd left behind. It was hard to tell which ones were real, which ones were worth digging into further, and which ones had nothing to do with our problem at hand.

Le Fay had been smart about their hunt for Elysium, and though William and his cohorts were tracking their every move, they still came up short at every turn.

"Is that all of them?" I asked as I stuck my last note card on the wall in front of us.

"I think so." Robert leaned back in his chair, stretching his arms. "At least, I'm not aware of any other boxes of journals."

"Okay, so what do we have?" I picked up a slice of cold pizza from the almost-empty box.

"It's like a jigsaw puzzle from hell." Jake cracked his neck from side to side.

I took a step back and stared at the wall in front of me. Taped to the wood panels around us, about a hundred note cards in every color decorated the walls.

It was pure chaos and not a lick of it made sense.

"We need to organize them into categories and work through them in groups," I said, scanning the cards in front of me.

"Okay, but what categories do we even put them into?" Jake asked.

"How about Elysium?" Robert pushed back from the table and stood. "Anything that specifically mentions Elysium should be gathered into a pile."

"Alright," I said, "That's a start."

Drawing on my Magic, I recited the locating spell and searched for the word *Elysium* on the cards. Magic swirled out of my fingertips, touching each card and lighting them up like torch lights in the winter.

Brett, Annabel, and Elodie started pulling the Elysium cards off the wall and grouping them together.

"What's next?" I asked as I stared at the wall.

"Cook," Brett said. "I ran across more than a few mentions of the Cook expeditions."

Reciting the spell again, all the cards relating to Cook lit up and again they compiled them into a group.

We sorted the rest of the cards into a Le Fay pile, Morgana pile, and a random pile of the clues that were still left over. We split into groups, each combing through a stack of cards, trying to make sense of it all.

"This is pointless," Robert sighed after reading through his index cards for the third time in a row.

"It doesn't make a lot of sense, does it?" I frowned at the clues William had left us. "I wish we could talk to William, find out everything he knew about Elysium and how close Le Fay was to finding it."

Robert chuckled and set the cards down in front of him.

"What?" I nudged him.

"You really want to meet the guy, don't you?"

"Jealous?" I wiggled my eyebrows.

"Of a dead man?" Robert leaned in close to me. "Not in the slightest," he whispered against my lips and gave me a quick kiss.

"This isn't getting us anywhere," Annabel huffed, and pushed away from the table. "There has to be a better way to find Elysium."

"To be fair," I said. "The fact that it's this difficult is promising. Look at all the data we have." I waved my hand over the piles of journals and note cards. "And yet, still we can't piece anything together."

"Let's hope they're having the same problem we are," Robert leaned back in his chair.

"I wouldn't count on it," Becky said from the doorway.

"Did you find something?" Jake asked.

"We think so," Ethan said, stepping into the dining room. "Although it could be a coincidence."

"Nothing is ever a coincidence with us." Robert's jaw flexed as his eyes pierced through Ethan.

"Merlin said the New Zealand theory was sound, right?" Becky said, placing her computer on the table and flipping it open. "Well, it just so happens," her fingers flew over the keyboard, "a small town on the South Island was abandoned overnight."

"When?" I asked, my heart racing.

"Last night," Becky said.

"But Morgana was here last night, so it couldn't have been her." I shook my head.

"That's what I thought," Becky replied.

"The Draig," Robert's face went ghost white.

"It looks like their work," Ethan confirmed.

"How'd it happen?" Annabel sat forward.

"The news is reporting a petrol station fire getting out of control," Ethan replied.

"Where is this town, exactly?" Brett asked.

"It's just off a lake called Takepo near Mt. Cook," Becky explained.

A chill ran down the length of my spine and Robert sat up straight.

"Mt. Cook?" Robert repeated.

"You're sure?" Jake asked.

"Yeah, look." She turned her computer toward us. A map of the area lit up the screen, showing the outline of Lake Tekapo, and to the west, the words Mt. Cook in tiny letters.

"Get this," Ethan said, folding his arms over his chest. "There's a military base camp just outside of town."

"You think they hit the camp and took out the town to cover their tracks?" Brett asked.

"It would make sense," Ethan shrugged.

"How can we be sure it's the Draig and not some freak accident?" I asked. "We can't read into every event happening all over the world," I tried to reason. I wanted to believe we were on the right track, but getting our hopes up was a sure-fire way of missing something.

"You know that underground Magical network I was talking about?" Becky grinned. "Well, we've got it working in full force."

"We were able to get in touch with a few people on the ground in New Zealand. They were two hundred miles north, but they're checking into it and should let us know soon what we're dealing with," Ethan said, clasping his hands together and cracking his knuckles.

A deep rumble rattled the house, followed by an explosion.

"What the hell was that?" I jumped to my feet, along with everyone else.

The smoke alarms blared to life, beeping all around us as smoke started to billow into the room.

"Alyssa," Robert cursed, and ran out of the room.

"Beck, are you alright?" I yelled over the alarms.

"All good," she coughed, waving smoke out of her face.

"Ethan, Elodie, stay with her," I yelled and ran after Robert.

Smoke filled the entryway and I could hear the crackle of flames coming from the living room.

"What the hell were you thinking?" I heard Robert yell over the roar of the fire.

Rounding the corner into the living room, pockets of clouds hung in the air, dousing the flames threatening to engulf the room.

"This is why I don't like experimenting with Magic," Brett grumbled under her breath. She made a motion with her hands, and the French doors flew open and the smoke rushed out of the living room.

"We just finished putting this place back together," Jake sighed.

"What happened in here?" The living room looked like a scene out of *Backdraft*. Everything was burnt to a crisp and covered in soot.

"We may have underestimated the hold the Shadowlands have on her soul," Merlin coughed.

"Is she okay?" Brett rushed to Emilia's side and looked her up and down.

"She's still alive, but I don't think she's coming back from this." Alyssa shook her head, her eyes wide as she stared down at Emilia.

"She's too weak," Merlin said. "I doubt she'll make it through the night."

Brett whirled on Alyssa and grabbed her by the front of her shirt. "She has to come back from this. Matthew's life is on the line."

"Brett," Robert's voice was a warning, but she didn't let go of Alyssa.

"I don't know what else to do," Alyssa continued to stare at Emilia despite Brett being inches from her face. "There isn't anything—"

"No," Brett yelled and shook Alyssa. "Fix this, you have to fix her," Brett's voice squeaked and for the first time, I saw the cracks in her perfectly crafted facade. If she lost hope of getting Matty back, I wasn't sure if she would make it through this.

"Alright Brett." I grabbed her by the shoulder. "We'll figure this out, we'll find a way."

She let me pull her off of Alyssa and took a step back.

"You're not listening to me," Alyssa snapped. "There isn't anything I can do."

"Giving up isn't an option," I said as I handed Brett off to Robert.

"There is one way we can get Matty back," Annabel said, stepping over a charred pillow.

"Anna." Jake looked like someone sucker punched him. "You can't," the words barely left his lips. "I just got you back."

"She's too far gone." Alyssa looked between Emilia and Annabel. "We need her alive for that to work."

"I know you want to help, but taking Emilia's place isn't the way," I said.

"What choice do we have?" She snapped. "We can't just give up on Matty, we can't leave him to their mercy." Tears filled her eyes, and she balled her hands into fists.

"We're not giving up on anyone," Jake folded her into his arms. "We never have and we never will."

"So, what do we do now? How do we save him?" Brett asked.

"Now we switch to Plan B," Robert said. "Take him back with brute force."

CHAPTER 32

IOLET

EXHAUSTED DIDN'T EVEN BEGIN to cover how I was feeling. Every inch of my body ached with the need to sleep, but no matter how hard I tried last night, I just couldn't quiet my mind enough to fall asleep.

I knew Robert was awake when his fingers started to trace a pattern up and down my side. I curled closer to him, enjoying the warmth of his body against mine.

"Do you think Brett's okay?" I asked.

His hand halted in its ministrations and his grip tighten on my hip.

"I don't know," he sighed. "She..."

Adjusting my body, I sat up on my elbow, so I was looking down at him.

"What?" I studied the tension in his jaw.

"After everything that happened with Chris, when he died," he shook his head as he stared at the ceiling. "She closed herself off to everyone." He turned his head to look at me. "Matty was the first one to break through her walls. I just don't know what it'll do to her..."

"I know." I touched his face. "Hopefully we won't have to find out."

"It changes you," he sighed. "Losing someone. You can't ever get that piece of you back. But I don't have to tell you that."

"We've all changed." I looked down at him. "We've all lost pieces of ourselves in this fight."

His fingers resumed the tracing of my spine through my cotton shirt, but his eyes stayed on the ceiling.

"I thought my destiny was to find you so you could wake the Lady and save the Magical world." He closed his eyes and let out a heavy breath. "From the moment I read William's words, my life changed forever. But for what?" His brow furrowed as he looked up at me. "Annabel might never be herself again. Lila's dead, Matty's behind enemy lines and you." He reached up with his other hand and touched my cheek. "I've all but ruined your life and hung the noose around your neck."

"You know that's not true." I placed my hand on top of his. "We all had a choice to make, and we stood by your side and fought with you. You give all of us the strength to keep pushing forward."

He sat up and rolled us both over so he was hovering above me.

"Where would we be if I hadn't let destiny decide my fate?"

"Well, we may not be here, right now, like this." I reached up and touched his face. The stubble on his cheeks was rough and his lips parted with my touch. A small smile tugging at the corner of his mouth.

"You have a point." He rested his forehead against mine.

"Terrible things happen all the time. People die and it's not your fault."

"I just hope we're not going through all of this for nothing." His nose brushed mine and my lips parted.

"It's not your job to worry about the future," I breathed.

"You're right," he lifted his head and his eyes found mine. "That's your job."

His eyes nailed me to the spot and my heart beat against my rib cage with a renewed ferocity. I wanted to tell him whatever he wanted to hear. I wanted to take his pain and worry away, but nothing about the future was certain or solid anymore. The world was in flux and the only thing I knew for sure was that the sun would rise in a few short minutes.

"Robert," I whispered, and curled my hand around his neck. "I know things look grim right now and I have no idea how the hell we're supposed to come out on the winning end, but whatever we do next, we'll do it together."

"I can get on board with that." His voice was husky as he curled a stray hair behind my ear.

His lips fell on mine in one swift motion and my heart galloped forward unbridled. His mouth moved against mine as if my lips held all the answers. His kiss was hungry and desperate and I gave into the frenzy as heat flushed my cheeks and moved down my chest.

Our Artognou Magic bubbled to the surface and the heat of his Magic poured into me as I pressed myself closer to him.

A soft knock at the door broke through our little bubble and he rolled to the side.

"When this is all over, we're taking a trip far away from any interruptions."

"I like the sound of that." I kissed his cheek and dragged myself out of bed.

Whoever was on the other side knocked again, this time a little more impatiently.

"Coming!" I yelled as I pulled a pair of jeans on.

While I pulled my hair into a ponytail, Robert answered the door.

"What's up?" he asked.

"Emilia's dead," Jake said. "You should come down." My heart nearly stopped and the heat of the moment was quickly replaced with cold, hard fear.

"Alright, be there in a minute," Robert said, closing the door.

My eyes met his, and I felt sick as I thought about what this would mean for Matty's chances. "What are we going to do?" Tears stung my eyes and I could only imagine how helpless Brett must feel.

"You have to stay strong." Robert grabbed my shoulders. "This isn't over yet."

"Brett won't sit by and wait for us to come up with a plan."

"No, she won't," Robert pursed his lips.

"You should head down," I said. "I'll see what I can see, maybe find where they're keeping him."

He nodded once. "Don't be too long."

He left the room, closing the door behind him and leaving me alone.

"Alright Violet," I said to myself. "Time to shine."

I laid down on the bed and stared up at the ceiling. Though the sun was starting to rise, dark clouds covered the sky, casting a heavy gloom over the room.

Closing my eyes, I let the barriers down in my head and slowly relaxed into the down comforter.

My Magic purred to life, stirring just under the surface and taking hold as I kept my thoughts on Matty.

I stood on a rocky shoreline, looking out over robin's egg blue water. The lake stretched as far as I could see and it was beautiful, unlike anything I'd ever seen before. The night sky glistened above me. Perfectly clear and showing off the millions of stars in our galaxy. I'd never seen the Milky Way before, but there it was right before my eyes, cloudy, colorful and shining down on me.

Stepping carefully over the rocks, I started to make my way up the shore, searching for something, anything, that would tell me where I was.

Looking away from the lake, I saw a small stone building rising out of the brush. Its steeple roof pointed toward the stars above.

Running toward the church, careful not to trip over the rocky shore, my chest started to feel tight, like I couldn't get enough air in my lungs.

"Come on, Violet," I mumbled to myself.

There was a large window looking out over the water. Lights flickered inside and hot white pain burst through my chest.

I doubled over in pain as my vision blurred.

"No," I yelled and forced myself to hold on to the magic that was quickly slipping through my grasp.

Taking a few deep breaths, I pushed myself closer to the edge of the building. Crawling up a few rocks, I peered into the window.

"Matty," I breathed a sigh of relief.

All the pews had been pushed aside and though he wasn't chained up, angry orange and yellow Magic crawled over him, keeping him in place.

"Where are you?" I whispered, and my breath fogged the window in front of me.

Crawling back down the rocks, I moved around the side of the building and up into the parking lot. There was nothing - not a single sign, tourist board, nothing.

Trees dotted the far end of the parking lot, all the way around the other side of the lake. The hairs on the back of my neck rose as I looked between the lake and the trees. There was something familiar about all this, as if I'd been here before.

My Magic faltered again, sending a wave of nausea through me and I stumbled on the pebble-covered path.

"Come on, come on," I said through gritted teeth.

Stumbling to the front of the little church, there it was. A tin plaque at the bottom of the stairs.

Welcome to the Church of the Good Shepherd.

I fell to my knees on the pebbled pathway and breathed a sigh of relief.

Jumping out of bed, I ran to the bathroom, barely making it to the toilet as my stomach convulsed. Resting my clammy head on my arm, my body shook, and I took a few deep breaths.

The same nagging feeling pulled at me, as it did in the vision.

Where had I seen that lake before? I wondered as I waited to see if my stomach would force anything else out of my body.

Pushing myself upright, I rinsed my mouth and brushed my teeth. My body ached like I had the flu. I wanted to lie down more than anything, but there was still too much to do before I could rest.

As I made my way down the staircase, the image of Amara flashed in my mind. Her battered body slumped against the tree. I could hear voices from a distance and I grabbed the railing to steady myself.

As quickly as she'd come, the image of Amara disappeared and I was left with that nagging feeling once more. Moving through the house, I could hear everyone talking out back. As I walked through the French doors, the cool air hit me and I sighed with relief.

My body felt hot and sticky after my vision and the subsequent throwing up.

"You're looking a little green around the gills." Becky's eyes widened as I walked up to the group.

"Just a little under the weather," I sighed.

"Did you get anything?" Robert asked.

I nodded. "He's being held in a church. As far as I could see, he was okay," I said to reassure Brett.

"Where's the church?" Brett asked, without skipping a beat.

"I'm not entirely sure where, but I got a name."

"Shoot," Becky said, pulling out her phone.

"Church of the Good Shepherd," I said, looking over her shoulder.

Becky typed the name into Google and a full list of results popped up.

"You're going to have to be more specific," Becky frowned.

"There was a lake," I said, recalling the crystal blue water. "It sat just on the edge of the water."

"Okay," Becky mumbled to herself and she added, lake to the search. "Holy crap," she looked at the screen and then at me.

"What?" I asked.

"Is this it?" She held the phone out to me, her eyebrows dangerously high on her forehead.

A small stone church sat on the edge of a bright blue lake. Just on the edge of the picture, I could make out a group of trees on the other side of the water and it hit me.

I nodded once as I stared at the photo on her screen.

"Where is it?" Robert asked, as my ears started to ring.

"Lake Tekapo, New Zealand," Becky's voice sounded a million miles away as she answered Robert.

"Looks like Merlin was right." Robert took the phone from Becky.

"Holy crap," I said under my breath.

"What is it?" Robert asked.

"Amara," I said as the ringing in my ears subsided. "This is where we met her, in the vision."

"Looks like we're going to New Zealand," Becky said.

"Then you better hurry," Cian came crashing out of the house.

"Cian," Merlin rushed to his side. "What is it?"

I still wasn't sure he could be trusted, as his eyes landed on me.

"Halvar forbid me from coming here." Cian dragged his eyes from me and up to Merlin. "But you're right, she's in New Zealand and I want to help."

"Why?" I asked. It was too convenient he was here, now, at the very end, when he could have told us this all along.

"You may not understand the gravity of Elysium, but I do. We all do as, Brothers." Cian's eyes bore into me. "Despite what Halvar may think, Elysium is our responsibility. I won't let him or anyone else stop me from protecting it."

"Very well," Merlin said. "Why don't you fill me in on the details while the rest of you prepare for the journey."

Merlin wrapped his arm around Cian and the two of them walked back into the house.

"We'll that was dramatic," Becky said wide-eyed.

CHAPTER 33

IOLET

WE MADE a plan to leave once Merlin had time to prepare Emilia's body for her burial rites. Cian performed a truncated ceremony, and he escorted Emilia's soul into the afterlife with the promise to meet us in New Zealand as soon as he could.

Emilia may have been a thorn in our side, and she caused Annabel and Jake a fair amount of pain, but I was there when the Shadowlands Magic took her and I wouldn't wish that kind of pain on anyone.

I wanted to lie down, to get some rest before we marched into battle, but Becky was like a dog with a bone, and she wouldn't let up until she said her peace.

"I'm coming with you," Becky yelled at me as I sat on the edge of the bed with my head in my hands. "You have no right to tell me to stay."

"Beck, this isn't a vacation," I tried to reason with her as exhaustion pulled at my every nerve.

"You think I don't get that?" She crossed the room and hovered over me. "Why do you think I've been training with Robert?"

A short, clipped laugh escaped my throat, "Learning self-defense with Robert won't help when you can't stop a spell that's meant to kill you."

"I know the risks involved," she said through gritted teeth.

"You don't understand how dangerous this is." I stood, leveling my eyes at her. "This isn't a game; we might not make it out of this and I don't want you getting hurt. I lost you once already and it damn near gave me a heart attack."

"This isn't up to you." She folded her arms over her chest and stuck her chin out like a stubborn child. "It's my life and if I want to be there to help you—"

"You can't help us this time," I practically yelled at her. "This isn't something you can fix behind your computer." I let out a heavy sigh, guilt seeping into my bones for snapping at her. "We already have to worry about getting Matty back," I grabbed her by the shoulders. "I can't do this if I'm worried about you too."

"And I can't stay home while my best friend goes off to fight a war she may not come home from." She pushed away from me, her cheeks flushed red with anger.

She wasn't wrong, and her words hit me in the chest like a knife.

The chances of me coming home were almost nonexistent. Vivian and I were never meant to live like this, and it was taking its toll. Even if we managed to take Morgana down, there was still the matter of having to kill me to set her free. Otherwise, all of this would be for nothing.

"This isn't your fight," I said, trying once more to reason with her and get her to stay here, where she was safe.

"Arguably, it's more my fight than it is yours." She cocked her head to the side as if she were stating the obvious.

"How do you figure that?" I furrowed my brow at how ridiculous she was being.

"If they get to Elysium, it's me and every other non-magical person who dies."

I opened my mouth to argue, but again, she wasn't wrong.

"Exactly." She nodded her head, sensing her victory. "So, I'm coming."

I pinched the bridge of my nose and let out a heavy sigh. "Fine, but you have to promise me something." I raised my eyebrows at her.

"Anything." She nodded like a happy puppy.

"If things go south," I reached for her hand. "And it's likely they will. Promise me you'll stay out of harm's way."

"Nothing—"

"Promise me Beck, or so help me, I'll tie you up in the basement."

She frowned. "Fine, I promise."

"Thank you," I sighed.

"But just so you know…"

I rolled my eyes and let go of her hand. She had to have the last word.

"Just because I don't have Magic, doesn't mean I'm useless."

"You know I don't think you're useless." I shook my head at her and sat back down on the bed.

She sat next to me and wrapped an arm around my shoulders. "If this is the end, really the end," her eyes met mine, "then I just want to be there and do whatever I can to help."

"You really should have been a Promised One." The corner of my lips turned up as I looked at her.

She was fearless and far more accepting of the Magical world than I ever was.

"I know," a short laughed escaped her throat. "It's so not fair you got all the Magic in this relationship."

"I've seen you work your Magic." I leveled my eyes on her. "I couldn't even imagine the pain in the ass you'd be if you had my kind of Magic."

A knock at the door interrupted the retort on the tip of her tongue.

"Come in," I sighed, realizing that my chances for a nap were quickly slipping away.

The door swung open and Robert poked his head in.

"You ready?" He asked, giving me a small smile.

"We are," Becky stood and Robert's eye's bounced between me and Becky.

He opened his mouth, but I shook my head, indicating it wasn't worth asking, and I got up from the bed.

"Ready as I'll ever be."

As the three of us made our way downstairs, the rest of the group filed into the entryway. Jake, Annabel, Brett, Merlin, Ethan, and Elodie all looked up at us from the bottom of the stairs.

They had become like family to me and as I looked at each of them, my heart felt like it would burst out of my chest. The Maxwells, Ethan, and Elodie all sacrificed so much for me, now it was my turn. Even if it meant I had to pay the price with my life.

"Ethan secured us a place nearby where we can stay and get our bearings," Elodie said as we reached the bottom of the staircase.

"Should anyone wish to stay behind," Merlin's voice carried through the entryway. "Now would be the time to bow out."

"Violet?" Alyssa said as she rounded the corner. "Can I have a moment?"

I looked between Robert and Merlin, and they both shrugged.

Leaving the others, I followed her out of earshot.

"What is it?"

"I still haven't been able to come up with a way to stop what's happening to you and Vivian."

"Oh, well, it was a long shot." I tried to keep my voice neutral, but inside my heart was breaking. I knew the chances were slim, but going into this battle without a solution didn't leave me with much hope.

"I wanted you to have this though." she held up a small vial of liquid. "It'll help when it comes time to facing Morgana."

"Thank you." I plucked the vial from her fingers.

"It was the least I could do after everything else." She tucked her hair behind her ear and it was the first time I've ever seen her look defeated.

"We all do the best with what's given to us," I said, touching her arm and slipping the vial into my pocket.

As I made my way back to the others, I hoped for Alyssa's sake she found her place in the world once all this was over. She may not be high on my list, but we all deserved a second chance to make things right.

"Everything okay?" Brett asked, as I stepped back into the entryway.

"All good." I nodded and slipped between Robert and Becky.

"Alright." Annabel held out her hands. "Let's do this."

Just like before, we each grabbed onto the other's hands. When we were all connected, Annabel's Magic ensnared us and the Maxwell estate fell away in a rush of colors.

The feeling of being turned inside out only lasted a few seconds, but it was enough to make my head spin and my stomach flip in on itself.

Landing in a heap of limbs, my ankle twisted under me, but I was grateful for the feel of solid earth beneath me.

"God, that sucks," Becky groaned next to me.

Without having to ask, Robert squeezed my hand and his Magic crawled over my skin, healing my sprained ankle and leaving me feeling a little less nauseous.

We walked up the stone path to a small bungalow style building. At the entrance, one of the wooden double doors was propped open, and we stepped inside.

"Hello," Ethan called out.

As we entered the bungalow, my heart started to race as I looked around the small living space.

"Do you think anyone's here?" I asked as we moved further into the house.

"There has to be, right?" Robert answered with a question of his own.

Looking up at the beautiful stained glass at the far end of the bungalow, a sense of peace washed over me. There was something so soothing about the colored glass as I thought of the careful hands that etched each piece.

"Ethan?" A man's voice broke through my reverie, startling me.

"Carter, I presume?" Ethan held out his hand. He towered over the rest of us, even Ethan, which was impressive.

"That's right," Carter shook Ethan's hand. "There isn't much room, but you're welcome to make yourself at home."

"We appreciate your hospitality on such short notice."

"It's what we're here for," Carter said, leaning against the wall closest to him. "You really think you can end this?"

"We're going to do our best," I said.

"You're Violet, right? The Waker?" He pushed off the wall as he looked me up and down.

"I am." I nodded my head at the title.

"I thought you'd be a little more formidable if I'm being honest." His eyes bounced between Jake and Robert before coming back to me.

"She's plenty formidable," Becky jumped to my defense.

"Looks can be deceiving." Annabel shot Carter a warning glance.

"I meant no offense." He raised his hands in surrender.

"We've all heard the stories, what you're capable of." He smiled and lowered his hands when no one else came to my defense.

Thunder rumbled overhead and the hairs on the back of my arms stood up.

"It's been storming like that since they took the camp." Carter moved toward the window and looked out across the lake.

Lightning cracked above the mountains, looming up in the distance, and thunder rumbled overhead once again. I walked over to one of the windows and stared at the mountain tops as the weight of what we were about to do settled in my heart.

"They're already up there, aren't they?" I asked as Merlin stepped up to the window next to me.

"I fear they are," he said gravely.

"Do you really think we can do this?" I kept my eyes on the landscape outside.

"The vial Alyssa gave you," Merlin said under his breath.

"What about it?" I asked. I could feel the tiny bottle against my thigh in my pocket.

"It'll allow Vivian to take hold when the time comes."

"I don't understand," I said, keeping my eyes on the mountains as the others made themselves comfortable in the house.

"The tonic we gave Vivian when the two of you reached out to Amara," Merlin began. "It was a test, to see if we could force the shift."

"Of course it was," I sighed. "Are you ever upfront with what you're planning?"

"I find people are more cooperative when they don't have the whole picture."

"So, what? I drink the vile and Vivian takes over?"

Merlin turned to look at me. "If you do, there's no guarantee you'll be able to come back from it."

"So this is it, then?" I looked up at him.

"I wish there was more I could do." His lips twitched into a sad grin.

"Everything's against us, isn't it?" I barely whispered.

"It's when your back's against the wall you fight hardest," Merlin said. "We have everything to lose and everything to gain with this fight."

Little drops of rain dotted the window as I stared at the snowcapped mountains. All of this, every moment since Robert saved my life, has been leading to this moment.

CHAPTER 34

IOLET

WE WASTED no time in getting the layout of the town from Carter. Our first priority was finding Matty and Amara, one of which we knew the exact location. If we had any chance of succeeding and not tipping our hand, we'd have to split up.

Robert, Brett, and I would head to the church on foot since it was less than two kilometers away. Annabel would orb Jake, Ethan, and Elodie to the military camp further up the road in the hopes of finding Amara, but also to create a distraction so we can slip in and rescue Matty.

"Merlin and I will try to triangulate where they are." Becky looked out the window to the mountain tops.

"We should have a location for you when you return," Merlin said confidently, and placed a hand affectionately on Becky's shoulder.

"Alright," I said, gathering my nerves. "Everyone ready?"

"Let's bring them home," Jake smiled and laced his fingers

with Annabel's. She looked up at him and the distance between them seemed to melt. Annabel would never be the same, but it warmed my heart to see her starting to heal.

"More than ready." Brett's voice was calm and even, but one look at her and anyone could see the tightness in her shoulders and the whites of her knuckles as her hands balled into fists.

Becky crossed the space between us and wrapped her arms around me. "Be safe," she whispered against my ear.

"Always." I squeezed her tightly.

Turning to Brett, Becky placed a hand on her shoulder and said, "Give them hell."

Brett nodded once, and the corner of her lips curled up.

"Remember, we have one shot at this," Robert said, looking at each of us.

"Once the element of surprise is gone, they'll know we're here. We won't get another chance at saving them," I said, my heart thrumming against my rib cage.

"We'll do our part. You do yours," Annabel said as she held her hands out for her group to grab hold.

"See you soon," I nodded, and without another word, they all shimmered and vanished from the living room.

"Ladies," Robert said, opening the front door and motioning to Brett and me.

The walk to the shoreline was quick, and we kept a safe distance from the main road. Under different circumstances, I'd love to perch up on the rocky beach with my camera and capture the natural beauty of this place. The still blue water stretched as far as the eye could see and the mountains rose up all around the lake.

"There it is," I said, stopping in my tracks.

The small stone church sat on its own little patch of land, isolated from the rest of the town. Like a lighthouse, it was a beacon at the top of the lake, looking out of the water for lost souls.

"You're sure he's in there?" Brett asked, without looking at me. All of her attention, all of her focus, was on the church. On Matty.

"It's where I saw him last." I did my best to keep my voice hopeful.

"Wait for the signal," Robert said, scanning the area. "We've got one chance at this." His fingers wrapped around my hand and he pulled me closer to his side.

"You sure you don't want to come with us?" I asked.

"If I can't be by your side," Robert said, placing his hand on my cheek. "I'd rather be making sure you're safe than wondering if you're alive." My eyes met his and I could see how much he hated letting me head into danger without him.

"We'll be quick." Brett nodded at her brother.

A deep rumble echoed off the mountains, and a breeze moved over the perfectly still lake, sending ripples through the glacial water as thick black smoke rose from the trees in the direction of the military camp.

"That's it," Brett said. "Let's go."

"Be careful." Robert gave me a tight-lipped smile.

"We will," I said, jogging to catch up to Brett.

"It's too quiet," she said when we were about twenty feet from the Church. "Something's not right."

The pit in my stomach was getting heavier the closer we got to Matty's prison. She was right. Something felt off-kilter about all this, but I couldn't put my finger on it.

"The window." I pointed to the back of the Church. "That's where I saw him."

Brett and I moved up the rocky beach, keeping close to the bushes that butted up against the Church.

My heart beat wildly in my chest. What if Matty wasn't in there anymore? Or worse, what if he was dead? My palms started to sweat despite the chill in the air and a sick, anxious feeling bloomed in my chest. If this went poorly, if Brett had to face a reality without Matty, I wasn't sure that I was strong enough to hold her together.

She moved toward the window and I grabbed her shoulder, motioning for her to stay back. For once, she didn't fight me on the point. Whatever we were about to find in this church, I didn't want Brett to be the first to see it.

Stepping around her, I kept my back against the stone building until I was at the edge of the window. I held my breath, waiting to hear something, see a flash of light, anything that would tell us we weren't alone.

Creeping off the wall, I peeked in the window. It was just like I'd seen in my vision. The pews had all been pushed to the side. In the middle of the room, Matty was on his knees, Magical binds keeping him in place.

"He's alive," I said, pulling away from the window. "He's okay." I exhaled and my head spun with relief.

"How many are there?" Brett's eyes lit up.

I looked back through the window and scanned the room.

"I don't see anyone." I turned away from the window again. "Shit."

"You think it's a trap?" I asked.

"Or they all went for the camp like we hoped." Her lips pinched together as she stared out over the water.

"There's no way it's that easy." I let out a heavy breath.

"Screw it." She stepped around me, placing her hand on the window, and the pane of glass shattered into a million tiny fragments.

"Well, that's one way to do it," I grumbled as we both hoisted ourselves up and through the window.

"Brett, Violet?" Matty's brow furrowed as he looked at the two of us.

"Is there anyone in here with you?" Brett asked, her shield raised and magic crackling along her fingers.

"No," he shook his head. "They only come by a few times a

day. Does this mean you were able to save the woman Morgana handed over?

I shook my head as Brett crossed the space between her and Matty. "She was beyond our help."

"Don't," he said as she reached to pull him to his feet.

"What is it?" I asked, as Brett froze in place.

"They're charged," Matty said. "If you move me, it'll go off like a bomb." His eyes met Brett's and his lips curled into a half smile.

"What on earth are you smiling about?" Brett shook her head at him.

"I told you, you'd find a way."

She dropped to her knees next to him and touched his face. "I'm sorry it wasn't sooner."

"Do you know what spell they used?" I asked, taking a cautious step closer to them.

"I was unconscious." he shook his head and looked down at the spell coiling around him. "But if I had to guess, it's more than one spell. Merlin maybe?"

"He isn't with us." Brett moved her hands over him tentatively, like she was searching for a weakness in the spell.

The front door of the church burst open, making every nerve in my body jump to attention as I raised my shield.

"We've got company," Robert said, closing the door.

My heart raced, heightening all of my senses as I braced for a fight. It was all I could do to block the familiar onslaught of a vision trying to take hold. *Now was not the time.*

Red and white wisps of Magic bloomed on Robert's palms as he moved to my side and turned to face the entrance.

"Whatever you're going to do," I said to Brett. "Do it fast."

"How bad is it?" I asked as my mental walls fell into place and the heaviness of the vision passed.

"Nothing we can't handle." The corner of his mouth turned up as his eyes met mine.

"Try a Galvin Spell," I heard Matty behind me. "It might disrupt the frequency just enough for me to push past the bindings."

"It's going to hurt," Brett warned him.

"It's better than the alternative," he pointed out.

The sound of footsteps crunching in the brush outside the church reached my ears and my body tensed.

"What're they doing?" I said under my breath.

The Church was almost silent as the sparks from Brett's Galvin spell burst to life.

"Do it," Matty whispered.

As if on cue, Brett's Magic struck Matty's bindings and the front door of the Church swung open. Hard, black metal filled the entryway, and The Draig rushed us.

Robert threw a blast of Magic as I summoned Devil's flame. My Magic licked down my arm and shot off my fingers as the spell galloped forward.

The Draig in the front of the pack was massive, and he deflected Robert's blow with his sword as he rushed forward. My spell bounced through the group, trying to find purchase as each of them deflected the spell with their weapons.

Matty let out a guttural scream behind us as Brett continued her efforts to free him.

"He's not going anywhere," one of The Draig shouted, and I jumped backward as his blade shot toward me like a bullet.

"Brett, look out," I said as the dagger skimmed past me toward her.

With her free hand, she held up her palm and Magic shot forward, turning the knife to dust as she continued to work on Matty's chains.

"It's working," he groaned.

"Violet," Robert shouted my name just in time for me to turn to block a stunning orb.

More of Morgana's followers filed into the tiny church behind the Draig, Magic flaring to life all around us.

"Nothing's ever easy," I sighed as my Magic pulsed on my hands, waiting to be released.

One of the Draig swung his sword forward, pushing me further into the church toward Brett and Matty. Using my shield to block the blade, I dropped to my knee and set off a distraction spell.

"Heads up," I yelled as a burst of light, like spotlights, erupted over my head. Jumping to my feet, I kicked out in front of me and the Draig standing nearest stumbled backward. Summoning a stunning orb, I threw the spell at the Draig woman, but someone jumped in front of her with a shield.

"Now that's not fair, is it?" The tall, spindly man said as sparks crackled over his shield.

"Brett," Robert yelled. "Where we at?"

"Almost there," Matty practically growled over the sound of Magic.

Electricity crawled off the man's shield in front of me, spreading like a web all around me. My eyes met his, and he smirked as he lifted his hand and squeezed his fist.

The electricity pulsed against my shield, leaving me winded but otherwise unscathed. Rushing forward, a cinder orb in my hand, I threw the spell at him as a Draig jumped from one of the pews and landed on top of me.

The building shook as I hit the stone floor, the glass shattering all around us as hot white light filled my vision.

I could feel Robert's magic just on the edges of mine and I pulled our Artognou magic to the surface as the Draig on top of me raised the blade in his hand.

Before I could summon a spell, the knife struck my shield, cutting through it like butter and sending a wave of bone-shattering pain through my body.

Don't lose focus. I chanted in my head and I held the Draig's wrist hovering above me.

"I can't," Matty screamed, his voice breaking through my own pain.

"Just a minute longer," Brett's voice was strained, determined as the Magic holding Matty arched up into the ceiling like a solar flare.

The hum of Magic now shooting in every direction caught my attacker's attention for a fraction of a second, which was just the opening I needed.

Using my hips, I bucked him forward and twisted his arm to roll him off of me and pinned him to the ground with my legs and forearm. Summoning my shield once more, the protective barrier wrapped around me and I swung my fist, connecting with the Draig's jaw.

An explosion behind me thrust my hair forward and I could feel debris hitting my shield.

Twisting his wrist with my other hand, I was able to get the dagger free and toss it out of sight as I summoned my Artognou Magic once more.

Pure, hungry Magic crawled over my skin, echoing, the Magic flaring wildly above me. My Magic pulsed toward the Draig under me and his body flinched as the spell took hold and he went limp as the fight went out of him.

"You alright?" Robert asked, helping me to my feet.

"All good," I said through heavy breaths.

Another spell shot through the air toward us as the few of Morgana's army still remaining charged into the church.

The floor rumbled, almost knocking me off balance, as small pebbles and dust fell from the ceiling.

"Brett, you have to stop," Robert yelled as a bolt of Magic erupted from Matty's chains, just missing Robert.

"I'm almost there," she said.

I looked over my shoulder. Matty lay in a heap on the floor, his body giving out from the pain while Brett stood over him, Magic erupting from the two spells like lava from a volcano. My eyes widened at the pure chaos surrounding Brett and Matty as dread crept over me. There was no way he was going to make it out of this alive.

Robert pushed me behind him as a spell connected with his shield.

"We need to end this, now," he said over his shoulder.

I nodded and grabbed his hand, letting our Artognou Magic course through us freely. My skin felt alive and uniquely aware of every sensation around me. The heat of Brett's Magic, the steady cadence of Robert's shield, the electric current running through Matty's chains.

The spell enslaving, Matty continued to fight Brett's efforts, throwing another flare of Magic into the air and taking out one of Morgana's men.

I could feel Robert pulling our Magic to the surface as another spell bounced off our shield and took out a chunk of stone to our right.

"Oh God," I heard Brett's voice, but it was the wide eyes of our attackers that sent a shiver down my spine.

Turning to look over my shoulder, a brilliant flash of light blotted out the sky and the surrounding air rushed toward Brett and Matty as her spell started to implode on itself.

"Get—" Robert's arms went around me and we tumbled to the ground in a heap of limbs as Brett's Magic burst forward and everything around us erupted in a fury of fire and stone.

CHAPTER 35

IOLET

A SHARP RINGING penetrated the haze around me. I opened my eyes and my vision glitched, sharp and jagged, as I tried to focus on the sky above me.

Sky? I wondered idly. *How'd... what happened?*

There was something heavy on my chest, making it hard to breathe, but I couldn't focus my eyes through the dust and smoke to see what it was. My nose filled with the acrid, heavy smell of fire and as I tried to push myself up, my shoulders barely lifting off the floor, my head spun wildly, forcing me to lie still.

I tried to take a few deep breaths, give my body a moment to come back to itself, but my lungs struggled against the weight on top of me and the smoke engulfing the space where the church used to be.

Staring at the white wispy clouds moving at a glacial pace

across the sky, the ringing in my ears started to fade, giving way to the crackling and popping of flames.

The weight shifted on top of me, groaning as the body rolled to the side, allowing my lungs to expand and my heart to beat normally.

"Violet?" Robert's voice was gruff, as if it took a large amount of effort to say my name.

"I'm here," I said, wincing as the blood rushed into my torso. "What—" I coughed as I inhaled a mouthful of smoke. "What happened?" I wheezed.

"Brett," Robert pushed himself to a sitting position next to me and looked around the rubble.

"Are they…" I was too afraid to finish the question. I couldn't imagine a world without them, but I also couldn't fathom how they might have survived when they were at the epicenter of the explosion.

Pushing myself upright, I looked around me. The church was gone, reduced to a pile of stone in a heap around us. Morgana's supporters lay next to us in the rubble, some dead, some regaining consciousness, but Brett and Matty were nowhere in sight.

"I don't know," Robert groaned as he stumbled to his feet and brushed the dust from his clothes.

Reaching out his hand to me, he pulled me to my feet and held me steady. A sharp, tingling pain moved up my arm and across my shoulders as I stared up at him. Blood caked the side of his head and dust clung to his eyelashes as he searched for his sister.

Scanning the surrounding area, I realized the lake was now on my right and where Brett and Matty had been a few moments ago was now just a pile of stones and wood. My heart constricted, and I stumbled forward through the rubble.

"Robert," I managed to choke out as tears stung my eyes. He turned and followed my gaze. Without skipping a beat, he limped over to the pile of stones and shattered wood beams. Raising his hands over the pile of debris, he began to recite a spell under his breath and the debris floated into the air piece by piece. Each stone moved through the air, light as a feather, as Robert moved his hands like an orchestra conductor, clearing a path to what lay beneath.

The tempo of my heartbeat echoed in my ears as I took a tentative step forward. I was almost too afraid of what I'd see, too afraid that Matty and Brett were dead.

"Took you long enough," Brett croaked as her shield glitched in and out before disappearing altogether.

"I thought you were..." I shot forward, grabbing her arm and helping her to her feet.

"We almost were," Matty's voice came from the rubble.

The hairs on the back of my neck rose as I felt Magic fill the room. Robert and I both turned as if we were one and raised our shields around the four of us.

"We saw the smoke and..." Annabel's voice trailed off as she and Jake shimmered into view.

"Man, are you a sight for sore eyes." I let my shield drop.

"We ran into a little trouble," Brett said, helping Matty out of the pile of stone and wood.

"I'll say," Jake looked around at what used to be a small, intimate church.

Someone, somewhere in the debris, moved, shifting a pile of rocks which caught all our attention.

"Care to get us out of here?" I asked, grabbing Annabel's hand.

Annabel nodded and grabbed onto Brett's shoulder. Her Magic wrapping around us and the church vanished in the blink of an eye.

"What the hell happened?" Becky yelled the moment my feet touched solid ground.

"We're fine, thanks for asking," I sneered at her as my

stomach did a back-flip from Annabel's Magic. Taking a deep breath through my nose, I fought the nausea that threatened to overwhelm me.

"We heard the explosion from here." Becky shook her head. "I thought—"

"I know, but we're okay." I wrapped an arm around her shoulder. "We're all okay."

"Matthew, I'm so sorry that—" Becky started.

"Don't." he held his hand up. "There's no need for apologies." Brett helped him as he hopped on one foot to the couch and sat down with a grimace.

Robert moved to his side without hesitation and placed a hand on Matty's shoulder. Matty's body relaxed into the cushions and the tension in his face eased as Robert's Magic went to work.

"Were you able to save Amara?" I asked, looking around the room.

Jake cleared his throat and said, "She wasn't there."

I felt like someone poured ice in my veins as I looked out the window and up at the mountain tops.

"We looked everywhere," Ethan said from the kitchen table without looking at any of us. Everything about his demeanor was somber, his expression, the set of his shoulder, even the tone of his voice. I'd never seen him so dejected.

"Do you think they were expecting us?" Robert asked, as he moved to Brett's side and placed a hand on her forearm.

"I don't think so," Annabel shook her head and wrapped her arm around Jake's waist. "They didn't seem to know what hit them when we showed up."

"It was barely even a fight; it was almost as if they thought they'd already won and had let their guard down."

"Who's Amara?" Matty got to his feet now that Robert had taken care of all his wounds.

"That's right," Becky said. "You weren't there when we

learned about her."

My whole being felt frozen and their voices barely reached me.

"Amara is the Grail, and Ethan and Elodie were protecting her before the Draig kidnapped her," Brett explained.

My Magic crawled under my skin at the mention of The Grail and my heart started to race.

"Okay, wasn't expecting that," Matty furrowed his brow. "So, if she's not here, then where?" He asked, taking the knowledge in stride.

"If it was me, I'd keep Amara where I could see her," Jake said, propping himself against the wall. "Where no one could get to her, without going through me first."

Reaching for the wall, I pressed my back against the cool surface as my head started to spin.

"You're probably right," Brett said. "But that doesn't make things any easier."

"And that's assuming they haven't already taken what they want from her," Robert amended.

"Here." Becky handed me a glass of water. "You're looking a little pale."

"Amara's stronger than you think. She won't give in if she has a choice," Merlin said.

"You have a lot of faith in her," Annabel said. "But faith alone won't be enough to stop Morgana."

"I know that better than you, my dear." Merlin's voice was cold as his eyes shot to Annabel. "That's why we need to end this now before it truly is too late."

"In case you hadn't noticed, we're a little worse for the wear," Robert said, as he finished healing Brett.

The walls in my head started to crumble and the glass in my hand shook as Robert moved to my side and laced his fingers through mine.

"What is it?" His brow furrowed as he watched me.

I let out a shaky breath, and the water slipped from my sweaty palm as a vision forced its way into my head. The glass hit the floor and shattered, water splashing on the front of my jeans.

"Violet?" Someone in the room said my name as ghostly figures appeared in front of me.

Amara was forced to her knees in front of Morgana.

"What'er you seeing?" A pair of arms gripped me.

"Are you ready to cooperate or shall we pick up where we left off?" Morgana's head twitched like a bird of prey.

"Violet." Someone shook me.

"It's Amara," I forced the words from my mouth.

Being aware in both the present and in my vision has never happened before. The Magic coursing through me was overwhelming as the two realities collided in front of me.

"You don't understand," Amara squeaked.

Mordred walked across the empty clearing, ignoring the woman cowering in the dirt. "Smoke's been spotted below."

Morgana closed her eyes and with what looked like a considerable effort, she swallowed her anger.

"They'll be here soon, no doubt. Prepare everyone," she said, waving Mordred away.

"What's happening with Amara?" Merlin's voice reaches me.

Turning her attention back to Amara, there's a fire in her eyes.

"I'm done playing games with you," Morgana snarls as she raises her hand. Magic crackles across her palm and lights up Amara's face.

"Alright," Amara squeaks.

"No, Amara, no," I yell.

Someone shakes me again, yelling my name as if from the end of a tunnel.

"She's giving in." Dread clawed at my heart as I watched a smile spread across Morgana's face.

"Finally, come to your senses?" Morgana raised an eyebrow.

"You'll never stop, never give up," Amara said, more than a state-ment than a question.

"You could have saved yourself a lot of pain," Morgana kneels next to her as Nimue moved out of the shadows. "Had you come to this conclusion sooner."

"Just get it over with," Amara bites back.

"This...can't...happen," I breathe and feel myself slide down the wall.

"Nimue, is she there?" Merlin asked from somewhere in the room.

"Yes."

Morgana stepped forward, pulling a knife from her belt as she ran the blade across Amara's palm in one swift motion. Doing the same to Nimue, Morgana grabbed both their hands and pressed their palms together.

"Do you give yourself freely?" Morgana asked.

"I do," Amara said, holding Nimue's gaze.

The air stirred around Nimue and Amara, rustling their hair and clothes. Where their hand connected, their skin started to glow and the color in Nimue's face pinked up.

"No." I shook my head as the vision started to fade. "No, no, no." Anger welled in my chest as my sense came back to me.

Everyone is the small living room stared down at me, silent and haunted. We failed again. First the Draig and now this.

"Nimue is immortal," I forced myself to say the words. "Amara...she...just gave it to her."

"No," Annabel whimpered, and Jake wrapped his arm around her.

"You're speaking to things you can't possibly understand," Merlin snapped. "Amara knows what she's doing, we just have to trust her."

"Trust her?" I pushed to my feet. "She just gave the enemy immortality. How'er we supposed to combat that? How are we supposed to win this fight?" I fired at him. "You think I don't understand what I just saw," I said without giving anyone a chance to speak. "You think I don't get we've all but lost?"

Merlin scoffed and took a step backward. "Such a young one." His lips curled at the corner and he placed his hands on my shoulders. "Your fire is admirable and you'll need if we're to win this."

"We've never backed down from a fight before," Brett jumped in. "We're not gonna start now."

"Even if it is a lost cause," Jake sighed. "We have to try."

Their willingness to run headfirst into a battle we know we can't win made my chest swell with pride. Of all the people that could have ended up in my life, I was grateful that it was the Maxwell's standing beside me in the end.

"Then I guess you'll be needing a location," Becky said, ignoring the tension in the room. Pulling up her computer, she turned it around for all of us to see. "It's not exact, but we were able to narrow it down to here." She pointed to the pin on the map that seemed to be in the middle of nowhere.

"You're sure?" I asked, still not understanding how she was able to track Magic.

"You doubt me?" Becky raised her eyebrows at me.

"Never when it counts." I nudged her affectionately.

"So, how do we want to do this?" Annabel asked. "How do we stop her?"

"Whatever the plan is," Ethan pushed back from the table and moved into the fold of our little group.

"Count us in," Elodie finished for him and stepped to her brother's side.

I started to shake my head and opened my mouth to argue.

"This is on us too," Elodie said. "Amara was our charge."

"We may not have Magic," Ethan said. "But we've trained for this moment our whole lives."

"We can't, we won't sit by and do nothing," Elodie folded her arms over her chest.

"Besides, I want to see you take down Morgana just as much as the next guy." A little of Ethan's light-heartedness returned, and I nodded at their willingness to fight by our side without Magic.

"We'll take all the help we can get," Robert said.

"Rest up and gather your strength. We'll need to leave as soon as possible and we'll need everything you have to give if we have any chance of winning this." Merlin said, turning his back on all of us and looking out the window. "We don't know how long she's been up there or how close she is to getting the barriers down between this realm and Elysium. We have to be prepared for any eventuality."

CHAPTER 36

IOLET

A FEW HOURS LATER, with everyone healed and as rested as we could be, we gathered in the tight living room. No one said much of anything as we wrapped ourselves in jackets, scarves, and gloves.

Matty and Brett stood on the other side of the room, their foreheads together, speaking in hushed tones. I could only imagine how hard it must be to have to say goodbye again after just getting each other back.

"The potion Alyssa gave you?" Merlin said, keeping his voice low enough that only I could hear him.

I reached into my pocket and pulled the small vial of liquid out.

"Good." He nodded. "I'll tell you when the time's right." He placed his hand on my shoulder and squeezed.

"Can I steal her for a moment?" Becky grabbed my hand and started to pull me away from Merlin.

"Of course," Merlin smiled. He placed his hand over mine, folding my fingers around the bottle. He gave my hand a gentle squeeze and turned and walked away.

"What was that about?" Becky asked.

"Who knows," I lied. "It's Merlin," I said, keeping the vial tight in my fist.

"Anyway," she sighed. "I know we've been here before." She paused and bit her lip. "But this feels different, it feels..."

"I know." I let out a heavy breath. "And I wish I could tell you it was all going to be okay."

"What you're about to do, everything you've become," she grabbed both of my hands in hers. "I think your parents would be proud of you. I know I am."

My heart swelled as a million emotions wrestled inside of me. "I hope so," I said, trying to keep the tears at bay. "No matter what happens up there, I need you to know—"

"I know," she smiled. "I'm the best thing that ever happened to you, you don't know what you'd do without me..." she trailed off with a chuckle.

Even in a life and death situation, she always found a way to bring light into my life.

"I couldn't have asked for a better sister." I pulled her in for a hug.

"I know this is your hero moment and all, but if there's a chance to get out," she held me at arm's length, "I won't hold it against you if you take it and run like the wind."

A short, teary laughed escaped my throat. "I'll do my best."

"It's time," Robert said, placing a hand on my shoulder.

"You take care of her," Becky turned to Robert, wiping a few tears of her own off her face.

"I will." He gave her a gentle smile.

"No," Becky said, pointing a finger at him. "I mean, I'm holding you personally responsible if even a hair on her head is displaced."

Robert nodded and grabbed my hand.

"And be careful," Becky dropped her pointed finger and wrapped an arm around his neck.

"I always am," Robert said, returning her hug.

"This isn't going to be easy," Merlin said as we all came together. "And in all likelihood, some of us won't make it out of this alive."

His words settled over the room like a heavy weight on all our shoulders. Robert's hand squeezed mine as Annabel wrapped her arms around Jake and Matty draped his arm over Brett's shoulder.

"Today, you fight not only for yourselves and the ones you love," Merlin continued. "But for the millions of people unaware of your sacrifice. This will be the hardest fight of your life. No matter the cost, we cannot fail." Merlin's eyes met everyone in the room. "We all have a job to do." His eyes met Becky's for the briefest moment. "So, let's get on with it."

Annabel stepped into the middle of our circle with Jake by her side as she held out her hands.

"See you on the other side," Matty said to Brett as he placed a kiss on her forehead.

"Not if I see you first," she said, leaning into him once more before stepping up to Annabel.

Ethan and Elodie stepped forward, and each placed a hand on Annabel's forearm.

"What about Cian?" I looked to Merlin for an answer.

"Don't worry, he won't miss the fight," Merlin smirked and again he looked at Becky.

"Ready?" Robert whispered against my ear.

I looked up at him, his dark brown eyes pouring into me and my heart shattered into a thousand pieces. I knew what had to be done. I knew we needed Vivian for this, and I knew the chances of me coming back alive were slim.

I reached up and touched his face. "I'm ready," I said.

Together, hand in hand, we stepped up to Annabel and the others.

"Good luck, everyone," Robert said, reaching for Annabel's hand.

I reached for Annabel's hand and before anyone else could utter a word, the floor beneath my feet melted away and impossibly cold air brushed across my cheek.

"We're here," Annabel said as my boots found purchase on the cold, hard ground.

The temperature was way below freezing up here and though the sun was shining, it might as well be just a decoration. Zipping my jacket all the way up and tightening the straps on my gloves, I took in the surrounding area.

"Which way do you think it is?" I asked.

"Over there," Merlin said immediately as he pointed across a ravine.

"How do you know?" Brett asked, as she looked out at the vast nothingness.

"I can feel it." Merlin's eyes narrowed as he studied the path ahead of us. "We need to hurry."

Merlin set off in front of us, leading the way. As we climbed over large boulders and down steep slopes, I realized how unnaturally quiet it was. There wasn't a single bird or animal in sight as we made our way toward Morgana's camp. Even the small bushes dotted between the rocks seemed to stand still, as if they too felt something unnatural in the area.

As we made our way over the next grouping of rocks, there was a charge in the air that set my teeth on edge, making me wish I was anywhere but here.

With each step, the thickness of Magic in the air built like an invisible fog. Every step was a little harder to take, every breath filled a little less of my lungs. My skin felt alive and anxious, as if the Magic of the area was trying to seep into my body.

"Are we almost there, do you think?" I asked, barely above a whisper. I felt self-conscious speaking out loud when we had been quiet for so long. My voice sounded like I was using a microphone in the deep silence of the mountains.

"It should be—"

What sounded like the roar of a jet engine broke through the silence, whipping the surrounding air into a frenzy.

"What the...?" Annabel flinched next to me and turned in a circle, searching for the source of the noise.

"Bloody hell," Merlin said, and he started running. Following him, we zig-zagged through boulders bigger than a house. The sheer force of the wind being whipped around us was almost impossible to combat. My feet tripped over one another and I was only able to keep myself upright by using the rocks around me for balance.

"What the hell is going on?" I yelled over what sounded like the mountain ripping apart.

"Nothing good," Merlin said over his shoulder.

Pushing forward, we reached the edge of the ravine and I thought my heart was going to fall out of my chest.

Morgana, Nimue, Mordred, and dozens upon dozens of Draig were just below us. Blue light filled the space and tendrils of electricity poured out of the gate.

I had to force myself to breathe as I realized the blue light I'd been seeing in my visions of Robert was not just some odd Magical anomaly. It was Elysium.

"Amara," Ethan said next to me.

I followed his gaze to a woman slumped over on the ground a few feet away from the others.

"We need to split up," Merlin said. "You two head over to the other side and make your way down to Amara." He pointed to Ethan and Elodie. "I'll create a diversion, give you a chance to slip in without them noticing," Merlin said.

"We should set up a perimeter," Robert suggested. "Fan out and close in on them."

"We'll take the far side," I said, nodding toward the other side of the ravine where the Elysium gate was closest to a large grouping of rocks.

"We'll move into position, just at the base of the ravine." Jake pointed out a new location for him, Brett, and Annabel.

"Keep your guard up," Brett said, as she started to move forward. "We don't know how many of them are up here."

Annabel reached for Jake's hand and the three of them disappeared.

"Let's head back this way." Robert started to backtrack when Merlin grabbed my hand.

"Violet?" Merlin stopped me before I could follow Robert. "The vial." His eyes held mine as I unzipped my jacket.

I twisted the cap off and in one shot, I downed the licorice flavored liquid.

"Violet?" Robert called after me.

"Take care of each other," Merlin said, giving my hand a squeeze and turning away from me.

I climbed over a rock and made my way to Robert. As I turned the corner of a large boulder, I was pulled forward by the sheer force of Elysium.

"I got you." Robert griped me by the elbow and helped me steady myself.

We ran as quickly as we could, following the curve of the ravine to the opposite side. By the time we reached the edge, I couldn't feel the end of my nose and my lungs burned as I tried to catch my breath.

As we made our way down a ravine, closer to Elysium, the wind picked up into what I could only describe as hurricane-force winds. The Magic coursing through the air was almost suffocating as my Magic ignited inside me, itching to be released.

Reaching the bottom of the ravine, we kept close to the ground and under the cover of the dried and bristly bushes. In the middle of the small clearing was a swirling well of violent Magic, engulfing everything in its vicinity. The light around Morgana distorted, almost bending and swirling at neck-breaking speeds, sending a sharp dagger of fear through my torso.

"I won't let you do this," Merlin yelled over the roar of Magic and wind.

"Merlin, how kind of you to join us."

Morgana nodded her head toward her henchmen and they moved toward him like predators.

"I'll handle this." Malice dripped off of Nimue with each word she spoke as she sauntered forward. It was hard to believe she and Vivian were ever the same person.

"This isn't the way to get what you want," Merlin growled.

Morgana smirked, "It's the only way."

Nimue turned toward Morgana and nodded her head once. Morgana raised her hand in the air, a bolt of lightning striking her arm as her lips mumbled a spell.

"Let's go." Robert pulled me to my feet, and we rushed forward.

Thunder cracked again and my ear started to ring as we raised our shields. Magic burned through me as my legs propelled me forward with a new found strength.

Out of the corner of my eye, a bright flash of yellow light caught my attention. Turning just in time, I was able to raise my shield just as a spell came hurtling toward my head.

Squaring my shoulders, I faced our attacker. Shield still raised, I formed a cinder orb in my hand.

"Mordred," Robert said through gritted teeth.

"This should be fun," Mordred smirked.

He ran at us full force, his finger sparking with electricity as he shot another spell in my direction. The electricity crashed into my shield with a deafening boom and I staggered back a few steps.

I wasn't sure if I was weak due to Vivian or if his magic was that much stronger than mine. I planted my feet to help balance myself and summoned a Galvin spell. Green Sparks ignited on my fingertips as he shot a spell at Robert, who quickly countered with his own.

Pitching the spell like a softball, the sparks danced across the space between us, searching for their target. Mordred bounced from foot to foot, jumping out of the way as the spell tried to wrap itself around him. Raising his own shield, the Galvin spell dissipated on contact.

"Son of a- " I started when someone crashed into me. We tumbled to the ground, a tangle of limbs and a Draig landed on top of me.

Feeling my magic bubble under the surface of my skin, I released it in a burst of raw magic, throwing the Draig off of me onto his back a few feet away.

The entire mountain rumbled and rocks slid from the edge of the cliff down the ravine all around us. Looking over my shoulder, I watched Nimue get to her feet, a deep scowl on her face as Magic bloomed to life on both of her palms.

My attacker got to his feet and wiped the blood from his face as he pulled a dagger from his hip. Over his shoulder, I saw Mordred and Robert's spell connect, throwing them both off balance and flying through the air. Spells flew in every direction as Annabel and Jake joined the fight. A cinder orb flew across the space, barely missing Robert's shoulder as he rolled out of the way.

My attacker ran at me, a knife in his fist like a bull charging a flag.

Summoning a stunning vine, I knelt to the ground, placing my hand in the dirt and discreetly allowing the spell to crawl through the pebbles and attack without his knowledge.

A slow smile spread across my lips. When he was just a few feet away, he paused at my expression and the stunning vine took hold, wrapping around his leg and dropping him like a sack of potatoes.

Puffy clouds moved above us, blotting out the sun as my attacker writhed in the dirt a few feet away. Summoning a cinder orb, I stood over him and fired the spell at his chest. His body went stiff in the dirt and turned to dust as I stepped over him without a backward glance.

Turning my sights on Morgana, my mouth nearly hit the floor. Elysium was twice the size it was a few moments ago, and she was standing at the opening, her arms raised and tendrils of smoke-like Magic pouring out of the opening.

Calling on our Artognou Magic, my fingers sparked with the need to release.

"Watch out," Robert yelled as he took Mordred down with a sweep of his leg and fired a bolt of Arcane Magic toward me. I hit the ground and rolled, the spell missing me by a few inches as it connected with another Draig, who collapsed next to me.

Shit. I thought as I got to my feet and three more Draig ran toward me.

CHAPTER 37

IOLET

FOCUSING MY SHIELD AROUND ME, I summoned a stunning orb in one hand and Devil's flame in the other.

Looking over my shoulder, there was a large boulder just behind me that would be a perfect spot to launch an attack.

Throwing the stunning orb at one of the Draig in front of me, I turned on my heel and didn't wait to see if it connected. Using the natural footholds, I was up on the rock in two quick steps and able to send Devil's flame down toward my attackers.

Lightning cracked a few feet away, striking the Draig closest to me.

"You holding up?" Brett asked as she rose to her feet, lighting sizzling all around her.

"I'm good," I said, throwing a cinder orb over her shoulder and taking down a woman who was about to attack Robert from behind. "Help Ethan and Elodie get to Amara?" I nodded toward the men guarding the Grail.

"You got it." A small smile touched her lips as she raised her fist to the sky and another bolt of lightning struck the Draig a few feet away.

Annabel orbed close by with Jake and the moment they materialized a burst of Magic erupted off of Jake, sending the row of Draig in front of us flying backward.

"Thanks for that." I jumped down from the rock.

"Don't thank me just yet," Jake said as Magic coiled around his hands and he looked up at the edge of the ravine.

Morgana's army lined the cliffside. Draig and Magical people standing shoulder to shoulder in every direction.

"You didn't think it would be easy, did you?" Morgana bellowed over the roar of Elysium. Her eyes met mine, and if looks could kill, she would have destroyed me on the spot. "This is for Emilia," she said as she raised her fist in the air and every last one of her army poured into the clearing.

My Magic flared to life and crawled over my skin. I could feel Vivian in the back of my mind, but I didn't have time to worry about how much longer I had.

I turned my back on Elysium and the others and faced the horde of Morgana's followers charging at us. Jake and Annabel flanked either side of me, and Magic bloomed to life all around us.

Red sparks galloped toward us, Cinder orbs pierced through the air as stunning spells and a hot blue fire burned a path in our direction.

Annabel orbed out of sight, reappearing on top of the Draig at the front of the group. Wrapping her hands around his neck, sparks burst from her fingertips and shot down the length of his body.

As I pulled on my Artognou Magic, Annabel flipped off of The Draig and disappeared midair. The Draig hit the ground and tumbled forward as his fellow men and women at arms pushed past him.

My Magic crawled down my arms, inky black smoke moving forward as Annabel appeared toward the back of the group.

Jake shot forward, arm stretched out in front of him as Annabel ripped a sword from a Draig woman and reappeared midair in front of Jake, dropping the sword and then disappearing again.

I shot my hand forward and twisted my wrist. The smoke responded like it was an extension of my arm, grabbing onto the nearest assailants and dragging them off of their feet.

Jake rushed forward, both hands wielding the sword as his blade connected with another sword. Magic pulsed up Jake's blade, and a wave of energy burst like a star erupting in the sky.

The sheer force of the explosion threw me off of my feet and sent me flying through the air as rocks and dirt pelted my body.

As my back hit the ground, the air was knocked out of my lungs and my vision glitched like an old home videotape.

Looking over my shoulder, I saw Robert and Mordred locked in a death grip, their Magic pushing against each other in a battle of wills. Rolling to avoid a wayward spell, I saw Nimue on top of Merlin with a nasty looking spell on the ends of her fingers, and Brett shot a bolt of lightning across the open space and threw Nimue off of Merlin.

"Violet!" Someone yelled my name from what felt like a thousand miles away.

I could feel Vivian's Magic starting to bleed into my own, the primal, untapped energy starting to course through my body. Pushing myself to my feet, I raised my shield and summoned another spell.

"Watch out." Jake grabbed me by the waist and pulled me off my feet as a spell shot through the space I'd just been standing.

Whipping around, Jake released me as he blocked a blow from another attacker.

The woman who just attacked me charged forward. Folding

her arms over her chest and in one quick motion, she thrust them forward. The ground split open under my feet and knocked me off balance as she jumped and kicked at my torso.

Grabbing her foot and sending a stunning spell up her leg, we both hit the ground in a heap of limbs.

Rolling onto my hands and knees, I took a deep breath and conjured Devil's flame. The fire charged toward the woman on the ground a few feet away from me. As the spell reached her, a shield materialized over her stunned body, forcing the flames to ricochet into a tree.

"Please," another woman squeaked. "Don't kill her," the woman begged as she threw her body on top of the other woman.

"Go," I said through gritted teeth. "And if I see you again..."

She lifted the other woman off the ground and the two of them limped out of sight.

"Violet," Elodie yelled.

Getting to my feet, I saw Ethan and Elodie coming toward me, a badly beaten woman draped between the two of them.

"Amara," I let out a sigh of relief as I rushed to get a better look at her.

"Elysium," Amara's lips barely moved. "You have to close it," she croaked, and her body went limp.

Lightning shot over our heads as Brett sparred with two of The Draig army. "Get her out of here," she said, keeping her eyes focused on her fight.

Robert ran to my side, out of breath, his lip cut open and bleeding. "How're you holding up?" His eyes scanned Ethan and Elodie behind me.

"We have to get to Elysium," I said, looking at the now building-sized gap in our world. Icy blue Magic swirled around the clearing, pulling everything in its path into the vortex.

"I can clear a path," Jake said, brandishing the sword Annabel stole for him.

Morgana stepped in front of Elysium once more, her arms outstretched. The ground rumbled, rocks broke away from the cliffside, and tumbled forward wildly. Lightning jumped out of Elysium, and the deep rumble similar to a jet engine about to take off blotted out every other sound in the clearing.

My feet were ripped out from under me, and Robert and I tumbled toward Elysium. My hands searched for something in the dirt to grab onto, but only weeds and small rocks scraped through my fingers. Robert swept past me, pulled in the same direction as my body tumbled recklessly through the sharp rocks and rough weeds.

"Hold on," Robert yelled.

Robert tugged on our bond and I could feel the Artognou Magic spring to life. I wasn't sure what he was planning to do, but I gave in to the call of the Magic, letting it flow through me freely.

Robert muttered a spell, and he came to a stop as I flew past him. Reaching out, he grabbed my wrist. The bones in my arm snapped, sending a hot wave of pain tingling down my arm. My legs flew out behind me as Elysium continued to try to suck me into its abyss, and I let out a strangled cry.

Brett came to a stop just ahead of us, both arms raised as she recited a spell. Wisps of smoke cascaded out of her open palms and the pull on my body lessened.

As my body relaxed into the dirt, Robert's hold on me relaxed and he knelt next to me.

"Are you hurt?" he asked, looking down at me.

"My arm," I said through gritted teeth and rolled over onto my back.

With a careful hand, his fingers traced the bones in my broken wrist.

"Could you speed it up?" Brett's voice was urgent above us.

"You guys okay?" Elodie rushed to my side.

Robert's Magic flooded into my arm, the warmth galloping through my broken bones and molding them back together.

I let out a sigh of relief as the pain subsided and then folded my arm over my chest. "Fine." I pushed myself to my feet.

"Guys," Ethan yelled.

We were surrounded by Draig and Le Fay alike, spells and blades drawn and ready to kill us all.

One by one, they grabbed each of us and marched us out into the middle of the clearing to stand in front of Morgana.

"Bring me the humans," Morgana shouted as the Magic from Elysium settled to a low rumble. "The Grail is yours, my dear Draig."

The Draig pushed Ethan and Elodie forward. Their eyes met as they were shoved to their knees. Amara was dragged back across enemy lines and handed over to I assumed was the leader of the Draig.

My heart battered against my ribs and my stomach churned with panic. I had to do something, anything.

The man restraining me let his Magic curl around my neck, making it almost impossible to breathe or speak. Out of the corner of my eyes, I saw Brett try to wiggle free from her captor and was swiftly knocked to her knees.

"Don't, Morgana," Merlin yelled.

"You have no power here." Morgana sauntered forward. "This world is ours now." Morgana motioned around the ravine. "It's a mercy to kill them now, rather than let them die in agony when Elysium takes over this world." She clicked her tongue, and I wanted to scream.

"Mercy?" Merlin snorted. "That's what you call this?"

"Would you rather they suffer?" She cocked her head toward him.

"I won't let you do this," Merlin said through gritted teeth. "We stopped you once, we'll do it again."

Morgana threw her head back and laughed. "This time is different,"

She reached her hand into Elysium, her eyes lighting up as the Magic crawled over her body. In one swift motion, she shot her other hand toward Elodie.

Magic crawled down Elodie's neck and over her heart and her body was lifted into the air, a strangled cry escaping her lips.

"EL!" Ethan yelled.

Morgana closed her fist and Elodie's chest collapsed, her ribs snapping with a sickening crack.

A whimper escaped my lips, and the Draig yanked on my restraints.

Elodie's eyes went wide as Morgana twisted her wrist and Elodie's head was crushed like a snail under a boot.

Everything felt like it was in slow motion. Elodie's body hanging lifeless for all of us to see. Morgana's sneer as she pulled more and more Magic from Elysium.

"I'll kill you," Ethan screamed, and I heard the snap of electricity as his captor exerted his dominance over Ethan.

I could feel my Magic boiling beneath the surface like a fury I've never felt before.

"Doubt it," Morgana snapped her head to Ethan and Elodie's body hit the cold, hard earth.

Oh God no, please no. I thought.

Magic roiled inside me, making my skin feel like it was on fire.

"Stop this," I managed to yell.

"Wait your turn, Waker," Morgana snapped.

Merlin stepped forward, Magic blazing on his palms.

"I wouldn't if I were you," Morgana said, holding out her palm to Elysium, and Magic crackled from the opening to her hand. "I'll kill them all in one shot if that's what it takes."

Merlin stepped back and his eyes met mine.

"Now. Where were we?" Nimue grabbed Ethan by the hair and thrust his head back.

This couldn't be happening! I shook my head and tears filled my eyes.

The soft click and rustling of rocks behind me pulled my attention from Ethan for a fraction of a second.

An explosion went off a few feet away, and I was tossed to the ground. Another explosion sounded close by, followed quickly by people yelling.

Boom.

Boom.

Boom.

Boom.

Bombs went off all around us, turning the clearing into complete chaos as I looked around wildly, trying to figure out what was going on.

No longer being bound by Magic, my own flared to life and sparks erupted from my fingertips involuntarily as I got to my feet.

"What the hell?" I said, looking down at the Magic coming off of me.

"You didn't think it was going to be that easy, did you?" Becky's voice reached my ears as the dust cleared.

Becky, Matty, Cian, and the Umbra-Kai stood in the middle of the clearing between us. Becky and Matty held up what I could only assume was a detonator and their fingers clicked the button. The entire cliffside behind Elysium collapsed.

"Violet. I'm going to need you to take a back seat now." Vivian spoke loud and clear in my head.

VIOLET IN THE DARK

GIVE

THEM

HELL

VIVIAN!

CHAPTER 38

IVIAN

VIOLET SLIPPED into the back of my mind easily, and my Magic burned over my skin. Whatever the cause of this sudden shift, I didn't care. I was just grateful to finally feel like myself, feel the power of my Magic coursing through me without the constant hum of Violet in the background.

"What the hell?" A rough voice said from behind me. I could feel him pull tighter on the binds that held me.

Magic danced across my skin and burst off of me in a wave of pure energy. My shackles were ripped free as I stepped forward, electricity burning at the tips of my fingers. Keeping my eyes on Morgana, I took another step forward, sparks firing from my hands to free the others beside me.

"This is the end of the line, Morgana," I yelled across the clearing as the dust settled.

"Vivian," Morgana sneered. "You've already lost." Her hand reached into Elysium and she pulled Magic into this world.

The Umbra-Kai stood before us, their bodies shivering as they held onto their form, waiting, watching.

"You owe us a debt." The Umbra-Kai crept forward. "You owe us a soul."

"I've paid my debt," Nimue snarled as Magic bloomed on her palms.

"Annabel, get them out of here," Robert said behind me.

Annabel appeared next to Matty and Becky, and the three of them vanished before our eyes. It was as if they were the only things holding everyone back, and when they disappeared, Magic cracked across the sky.

Nimue rushed forward and the Umbra-Kai lost their figures, turning to inky black smoke and flying toward her.

Taking another measured step forward, my eyes stayed glued to Morgana as chaos erupted around me. Cinder orbs flew over my head, Devil's flame licked at my shield, and dirt and stone burst into the sky as I closed the gap between Morgana and myself.

A handful of Draig stepped between us and electricity crackled off my fingers. Releasing the Magic boiling through my veins, my Magic cut through the air like a thousand arrows and removed the Draig standing between me and my target.

"Don't let him get—" Robert's voice was cut off as the earth shuttered around me.

"Robert!" Brett yelled from somewhere behind me. "That's my brother, you asshole." I fought the urge to look back. The only way I could help Robert, help all of them, was by ending this here and now.

The Magic Morgana pulled from Elysium glowed all around her, and I summoned my sword once more. The blade flared to life in my hands, bright orange and gold flames flickering over the edge of the sword.

"You die here today," I said through gritted teeth as fury filled my chest.

As I raised my sword and took one last step, Morgana unleashed her Magic on me.

A hot white light bleached out the clearing as I raised my sword, allowing the blade to absorb the brunt of the spell. My hands shook with the force of her Magic; she was strong and with Elysium, she was a force to be reckoned with. But she was still too arrogant, too reckless to win this fight.

Flipping the hilt in my hand and dropping to my knee, the Magic humming over the sword burned the skin of my palm. Directing the blade into the frozen earth, Magic rumbled across the ground in thick, heavy waves.

Morgana stumbled backward as I quickly got to my feet, raised the blade to the sky and brought down a hail storm of electric Magic on top of her.

Raising her arms, her shield went around her and the Magic fizzled out.

"Cian, it has to be Mordred," Merlin yelled somewhere in the distance.

"We need to close Elysium," Robert said, pulling on my arm.

"I need to kill her first," I snarled as I pointed the tip of my blade toward Morgana.

"We cut her off from Elysium. She'll be easier to kill," Robert reasoned.

"I'll keep her busy," Merlin said, flanking me. "Go."

Reaching for Robert's hand, I kept my eye on Elysium before us. A pool of ice poured out of the void, devouring the landscape in front of us as Morgana pulled more and more Magic from the other realm.

Robert squeezed my hand and I could feel his and Violet's Artognou Magic burst to life inside me like the sun. Every muscle in my body coiled with its strength. Their Magic combined with my own, making me feel uniquely alive.

Ice crawled toward us, destroying everything in its path as Merlin dropped to his knee, lightning erupting off of him in every direction. Thunder roiled above us, and Robert tightened his grip on my hand. Blocking the lightning with ease, we moved toward Elysium.

Hail started falling from the sky and immediately, Robert and I raised our shield over our heads to keep from being pelted. A tornado touched down in front of us, pushing Morgana and Nimue away from Elysium as we reached the other side of the clearing.

"Let's go," Robert yelled over the roar of Elysium and the wind from Merlin's Magic. Still holding hands, we ran as fast as we could through the thick air.

As we got closer, the howling from the other realm seemed to consume us. Now that we were up close, it took my breath away. So many times I'd heard the stories, so many times I recalled the faces of the dead. Now I understood it. The raw Magic clawing toward me was intoxicating. I could feel it drawing me in, wrapping around me, begging me to use the magic within.

"Vivian," Robert pulled on my hand. "Don't give in to it."

"I never understood the allure." I took half a step forward, the pull like a current I couldn't escape.

"Vivian." Robert stepped in front of me, and the allure of Elysium faded ever so slightly.

Exhaling a heavy breath, I held his eyes. Robert tapped into our Artognou Magic again, and my resolve rushed back to me. Each of my senses coming to life. I could taste the crisp cold air coming off of the ice. I could feel the wind move through each strand of my hair. My eyes homed in on Elysium in front of us, and I could see the shape of individual snowflakes passing into this realm.

"I'm alright," I said. "Let's finish this."

He turned away from me and started to chant a spell as an explosion erupted around us. I could feel the heat of the blast on my back and without hesitation, I raised a shield around both of us, keeping us out of harm's way as another blast rumbled through the ice.

"You need to hurry," I said, and the ice cracked and shifted. Mordred stalked toward me, a sickly smile spreading across his face as their Artognou Magic poured out of me.

Mordred thrust his Magic toward us, trying to stop Robert. Blocking the blow, I felt the shield around us rumble.

"Are you alright?" Robert asked.

"Just keep going," I yelled over the snap and boom of lightning behind us.

Throwing my blade to the ice, I held out both of my arms as Magic crawled over my skin.

"You really want to do this?" I yelled at Mordred.

"I really do," he growled as he swung his arm around and thrust spell after spell in my direction.

The strength of my Magic combined with their Artognou Magic pulsed through me like another heartbeat. I took a step toward Mordred. Black vines crawled off my arms and as they reached out to him, he stumbled backward.

Behind him, Brett moved across the clearing, dodging spells as her Magic shot her would-be assailants out of her path.

Mordred fired another spell at me, the orb exploding against my shield. Devil's flame flowed out of me, the fire burning a path across the ice as Brett leapt into the air and wrapped herself around Mordred, taking him down into a crouched position.

A part of me wanted to go to him and the piece of my heart that loved the boy he used to be broke. He was no longer the Mordred I knew. He died the moment the Umbra-Kai granted him eternal life.

"Go," she yelled at me. "I've got him." She dug her elbow into his spine and his head shot toward the sky. "Cian," Brett yelled as the Brother and the Umbra-Kai rushed the clearing, destroying everything in their path until they reached Brett.

"No," Nimue's blood-curdling scream ricocheted off the cliffside, drawing everyone's attention.

The Umbra-Kai morphed into their true form as they crept over Mordred and Brett. The midnight black haze and shadows curled around the two of them, blotting out their forms, leaving only the sound of their agony as the Umbra-Kai engulfed them and collected their payment.

"Vivian," Robert's voice cracked. "What's happening?"

"Just don't stop," I said, turning away from the rest of them and focusing on Robert.

I placed my hand in his once more and held my hand up to Elysium.

The edges of the rift in front of us became blurry and unstable. Sparks of energy flew off in wild directions as the tear began to heal and shrink. Flaming arrows bounced off our shield like darts, unable to find purchase.

Nothing would stop us. Nothing would stop me.

Searching for where the flaming arrows came from, I caught sight of a scrawny woman hiding in the tall grass about twenty yards away. Her lips pulled back into a snarl as her hollow eyes darted between me and Robert. Her cover was blown. Running toward us, her arm raised as she fired off another round of Magical arrows to stop us from closing Elysium.

This time, one of them stuck, and the flames went out as it released its poison into my shield. The inky, blood red poison spread across my shield like a pot of ink across a desk and I could feel it seeping into my bones.

"I can't hold the shield," I coughed and as I looked over at Robert, I noticed the color had completely drained from his face.

"You're almost there," I said under my breath, letting the shield drop. Instantly, I felt the poison dissipate as I turned toward the gaunt woman.

"Now we can play," she snarled, and a wisp of black smoke danced around her fingers.

I squared my shoulders and planted my feet. If she wanted a fight, she was going to get one.

Pulling some Magic from Robert, the raw hungry power of their Artognou Magic sizzled across my skin.

Robert continued the spell, but his words were a staccato beat as he struggled to win out over the power of Elysium.

Lobbing the stunning orb toward her feet, she jumped out of the way, grinning as if I'd foolishly missed.

The ice under her feet cracked, absorbing the blow and tossing her off balance. The smoke in her hand uncoiled itself and shot toward me like an explosion of flour. Calling on a freezing spell, I threw up my hands and my Magic turned the smoke solid mid-air and the blob fell to the ground with an audible *thud*.

Without hesitation, she threw another fire arrow at me and I slid out of the way on the slippery ice. Scrambling to gain my balance, I kept my eyes on her as she summoned another arrow and directed it at Robert.

With Robert's back turned to the woman, he didn't see the arrow as it arched through the air toward him and finding purchase between his shoulder blades.

Anger filled my heart as he fell to his knees, but continued with the spell.

"Robert," I yelled over the whistling roar of Elysium closing.

"I've almost got it. Hold her off," he grunted.

Chills ran over my entire body and I tapped into the core of my Magic. Making a beeline for the sniveling woman, I dodged another spell she threw my way. The whites of her eyes doubled as I closed the distance between us. Reaching out, I grabbed her hand before she could toss another spell in my direction and I kicked her legs out from under her.

My body moved almost without thought. The muscles took

over and performed the way they always should have. With the woman flat on her back, I hunched over her and placed my hand over her chest.

Without hesitation, I recited the spell that would drain her Magic from her body and leave her an empty shell. Blood ran from her eyes like tears as the Magic was ripped from her soul. She clawed at my hand and tried to buck me off of her, but it was already too late.

As her body went limp, I got to my feet and moved as fast as I dared to Robert's side. I knelt down next to him and pulled the fire arrow from his back as the last sliver of Elysium closed in on itself.

"Now go get her," Robert said through ragged breaths.

CHAPTER 39

IVIAN

PICKING UP MY SWORD, Magic bloomed on my palm as I moved across the ice toward Morgana and Merlin. A red and black sphere grew on my palm with each step and I could feel the pulsing Magic aching for release.

Twisting my wrist, the spell burst from my hand toward Morgana's back. Without turning to look, she raised her arm behind her and blocked the spell.

Merlin continued his attack, pulling a fraction of Morgana's attention.

"Vivian!" Jake yelled as a tree flew through the air. Nimue's spell crashed into the bark, sending a million tiny splinters into the air.

"I'll take care of her," Merlin snarled. A burst of light pulsed off of him, forcing Morgana to take cover and allowing him to move past me to deal with Nimue.

Adrenaline coursed through my blood, propelling me forward as I called up a stunning spell. Without skipping a beat, I fired the spell at Morgana, quickly followed by a Cinder orb. Swinging my sword above my head and letting my magic pour into the blade, I felt the fire take hold and charge forward.

Tightening my grip on the sword, I held Morgana's gaze as she got to her feet. Magic crackled off of her, spewing like lava with every flick of her wrist. Throwing her hand out, the heat of her Magic passed inches from my face as I dodged out of the way and into another spell.

My shoulder caught the brunt of the Magic, forcing me to my knee as liquid fire pulsed down my shoulder, over my chest.

Rage burned through me as I raised my free hand. A burst of light surrounded my palm as she fired another spell. Deflecting her Magic, I got to my feet, ignoring the pain and pushing forward. Magic poured out of me, and I kept the searing beam of light directed at Morgana, keeping her on the defense.

Raising the sword to the sky with my other hand, lightning struck the blade and my Magic pulsed up the steel. I was only a few feet from her now. I could see the fear in her eyes, taste it in the air.

She bared her teeth at me as she threw her arms out to her side, a rush of Magic rolling off of her like a tidal wave. Using the flat side of the blade, I pushed against her Magic and it pivoted past me as I tried to regain my position.

Morgana edged toward me, her Magic becoming untamed as it crackled against my sword and threw off embers that seared into my exposed skin.

Somewhere behind me, I heard the deep rumble and crackle of rocks being ripped apart as a scream tore through the clearing. I had no idea who was crying out in pain. I only hoped it wasn't the people I've grown to care for.

Just under the surface, I could feel Robert and Violet's

Artognou Magic hum through me. Grabbing hold of the bond, I pulled their Magic to the surface, using it to push back Morgana's advancement.

Holding up a shaky hand, I used every ounce of Magic burning through me. Light burst from my palm and collided with Morgana's Magic with a force that almost knocked me to the ground.

The cliffs surrounding us rumbled as rocks flew into the air and swirled around us.

"I won't go back," Morgana snarled as dark green smoke curled around her, lightning coursing through the Magic that slithered over her arms, waiting to be released.

"You don't have a choice," I snapped.

In a fraction of a second, the green smoke shot toward the rocks swirling around us and fired them toward me one by one.

I was slow to raise my shield, and a boulder collided with my chest, knocking the wind out of me. I could feel the warmth spread across my torso and a small tremor of panic pressed into my heart.

Gripping my chest, my fingers came away slick with blood as another boulder struck my shield. Violet's body was failing me and though the pain was almost too much to bear, I pushed to my feet, using the sword to keep my balance.

"I guess your Waker wasn't all she was cracked up to be." An arrogant, sickly smile flittered over Morgana's lips.

"She was everything I needed her to be," I said through gritted teeth.

Raising the sword to the sky, thunder rumbled overhead and lightning struck the blade once more. Golden flames crawled up the hilt of the sword, engulfing my hand.

In one swift motion, I arched the blade over my head and, in one massive thrust of energy, I sunk the blade deep into the earth beneath my feet. A massive burst of energy rolled toward

Morgana, and I rushed forward, still holding my chest as blood continued to seep out of my body.

The spell caught her off guard and I was able to get her feet out from under her. Toppling to the ground, I pinned her underneath me, my Magic poised and ready on my fingers. I raised both my hands above my head, the tips of my fingers touching as I pulled the Magic from my core. The power of it rattled between my palms over my head as I pulled every last shred of Magic out of my soul.

I released the spell as Morgana threw her hands up. Her own Magic collided with mine. The air stilled for a fraction of a second and everything froze as our Magic imploded and rushed forward with the force of a dying star. The earth-shattering blast threw me across the clearing and when my back hit the sharp, unrelenting mountain, everything went dark.

* * *

Ringing pierced the darkness, sharp and all consuming.

Thump-thump. Thump-thump.

I could hear the sound of my lungs expanding, as if I was listening from the inside out.

Thump-thump. Thump-thump.

Unrelenting pain fired through every cell in my body like hot knives digging into my skin.

Thump-thump. Thump-thump.

* * *

"Vi...can...me..." Robert's voice cut in and out somewhere outside of me. "Please."

"What..." I gasped for air as my vision flashed between the smoke-filled sky and the backs of my eyelids.

I felt like I was being crushed under a building as shallow breaths filled my lungs.

"I'm here, Violet," Robert's hand brushed my face as my hearing started to come back to me. A gash on the right side of his face was covered in dried blood, and dirt clung to his sweaty skin. "You're okay, you're going to be okay." His eyes moved over me wildly.

"I... did she?" I asked, as the ringing in my ears subsided. "Morgana?" I asked.

"She's dead," Robert exhaled. "Vivian did it."

"I can't feel my legs." I shivered as pain racked over my body.

Robert's hands fluttered over me, the heat of his Magic coursing through my veins.

An explosion sounded close by and Robert's shield flew up around us.

"What's happening?" I tried to turn my head, but a sharp pain shot down my neck.

"Nimue," Robert said. "Merlin's handling it."

I could still feel the warmth of his Magic trying to keep my body from tearing itself apart, but the cracks splintering my soul were starting to push back.

"Vivian," I coughed. "We have to..." I tried to take a deep breath, the pain in my chest making it almost impossible. "She's dying...we both are," I sputtered.

"I'm not giving up on you," Robert's voice was gruff and full of emotion as he stared down at me.

My face wrinkled in pain as the heavy weight on my chest grew stronger. "She has to—" my body convulsed against the rocky surface under me.

Robert's eyes traced the length of my body. "Tell me where it hurts most?"

"My," I gasped for air, "chest," I exhaled.

He placed both of his hands over my chest and his Magic flowed through my breastplate and into my struggling lungs.

"Better?" He asked.

I nodded. The weight had eased off a fraction of an inch, but was still achingly present.

The thought that Robert would be able to keep me alive long enough for Merlin or anyone to do something was ludicrous.

"You have to do it," I groaned through the pain. "You can't let…" I shivered as a wave of pins and needles prickled over my skin. "She can't die in my body. Not now, not after everything."

"Please don't make me," Robert begged.

"You have to free her so she can claim Morgana's soul."

My skin felt like it was being flayed off of me while my bones throbbed with every breath. I could feel Robert's Magic inside me, but it was no longer doing anything to dull the pain.

"I can't," he said through gritted teeth as he stared down at me, pain etched in the furrow of his brow.

My back arched off the ground as flashes of light erupted in my eyes.

"Robert," I exhaled as my body eased back to the earth and I searched for his face.

His eyes met mine, pinning me to the spot, and my heart shattered into a million fragments. I didn't want to leave him. He didn't deserve to lose another person. But what choice did we have?

"Thank you for everything," I said and reached up to touch his face.

"Don't. Don't say goodbye." His voice cut through me like a dagger as the pain built in his eyes and shrink-wrapped them in tears.

"You and I both know this is what I was born for." I gasped for air as a bone-deep chill settled into my limbs. "It's my destiny…what-" I coughed rattled through me. "What I was…meant to do. We…can't…fight it," I wheezed.

His hand cupped my face as tears streamed down my cheeks. He kissed me full and hard, and a wave of pure agony rolled through me. I loved him more than I could put into words, and now it was too late.

"Robert, I—"

"You don't have to say anything." He stroked the sweat soaked hair off my face.

"But I do, there's so much to say before..." my body shivered and the world around me spun out of control. "Before I can't," I said as I closed my eyes.

"I can't lose you. Not after everything we've been through," he said. His Magic pulsed through me at the intensity of his words and I looked up at him. "You promised."

"I love you. No matter," I took a breath to steady myself. "What happens now, no matter where...I end up, I don't regret a single moment that led us here."

The ache in my bones made me weary despite Robert's healing hands and I had to fight through the exhaustion.

"I do have regrets," Robert admitted. "You were happy. You had a life before all this and we took it away."

"You gave me a family, something I never thought I'd have again."

"They do love you, more than they love me." A tear-filled chuckle escaped his throat.

My lips twitched into what I hoped was a smile.

"Please don't make me ask you again," I sighed.

With what little strength I had left, I lifted my hand to his face.

Hovering over me, he looked into my eyes. Beads of sweat rolled off of my head, mingling with the tears rolling down my cheek.

"My..." my body flinched with each ragged breath I took. "Heart belongs..." I closed my eyes as I struggled to get the words out. The pressure in my chest was almost too much to bear. "To...you...always," I managed to open my eyes.

He was looking down at me, his brow furrowed, tears stinging his eyes. Leaning down, he placed his lips against mine. My heart swelled with the heat of his kiss and for a fraction of a second, the pain didn't exist.

"And mine is yours. Always," he breathed against my lips.

Pure white light filled the space around us as Robert summoned his Arcane Magic. I held onto his eyes, my body convulsing once more as a tear fell down my cheek.

"Forgive me," he whispered.

His other hand slipped under my body and he lifted me to him. He pressed his forehead to mine and I could feel the heat of Arcane Magic between us.

Hesitantly, he pressed his Magic against my chest. A fire burned through my veins like wild horses running through an open meadow.

My vision blurred, and I closed my eyes as images flashed before me:

Robert and I in the bookstore the first time we met. His crooked smile and curious eyes as he watched me.

Robert hovering over me, his eyes burning into my soul as he saved my life.

Us on the beach, my hand in his as he told me about the Magical world.

The Arcane Magic tore through me, my Magic flaring to life in an attempt to fight the invasion as the flashes continued.

Robert on my couch, his arm over his head, fast asleep.

The feel of his lips on mine the first time we kissed.

Our bodies pressed together in that tiny bathroom in Yosemite.

My body rocked, and the air was ripped from my lungs.

The way his Magic moved with mine the first time he showed me how to make a shield.

Our bodies wrapped together as we gave into our feelings at Caltome.

Darkness started to bleed into the flashes as my heart faltered.

Robert's smile from ear to ear as he danced with the flower girl at Annabel and Jake's wedding.

The heat of his kiss as he tapped into our Artognou Magic before heading into the Valley of the Draig.

The feel of his heartbeat as we lay in bed, my head on his chest.

The memories faded to black like an old Hollywood movie, leaving me alone in the darkness.

"What've I done?" Robert groaned as my heart beat one last time.

VIVIAN IN THE DARK

Though I will miss the Maxwell's, miss Robert.

I'm free once more.

May their world shine a little brighter, now that Morgana's in my charge.

Thank you, Waker for your sacrifice.

May your soul yet win delights on this, your death-day.

CHAPTER 40

IOLET

SCORCHING WAVES of pain crashed through me in the darkness. I couldn't see anything, couldn't hear anything. There was nothing but the pain of my body being ripped apart as an electric shock burst through me.

I could hear voices far off in the distance and I was vividly aware of how heavy my body felt as the emptiness around me started to glow.

Something, or someone, moved out of the darkness and into the light toward me.

"Robert?" I hesitated as the light brushed against his features, a small secret smile on his lips.

I kept my entire focus on him, the shape of his shoulders, the stubble on his cheeks, the shadows under his eyes. Most importantly, I held onto the warmth that radiated off of him.

As I reached out to touch him, his hand made an identical movement and my mouth fell open in awe. This was my vision, the one I'd been having since I woke Vivian. But how was any of this possible?

"I don't understand?" I shook my head. My eyes flicked up to him and he placed his index finger over my lips, just like I knew he would.

The pain disappeared, and a flutter passed through me, faint but sure as his finger left my lips. Chasing his warmth and comfort, I reached up and placed my hand on his chest. The hum of our Magic bloomed under my rib cage and I let out a shaky breath.

His fingers wrapped around my wrist and he pulled me closer to him. Our eyes held onto one another as the wind brushed my hair over my shoulders and a bright blue glow bloomed all around us, lighting up Robert's face and sending goosebumps across my skin.

He took a step backward, pulling me with him out of the light and in the darkness.

The smell of dirt and singed hair was the first thing that registered, but I couldn't place what was happening or where I was.

Forcing my eyes open, Robert hovered over me.

"Argh," I mumbled, turning my head. A flash of blue light swirled just beyond Merlin. The same blue light in my visions, the same blue light of Elysium.

"Oh, thank God." Robert crushed me to him. His arms wrapped around me and his body shook us both.

"I don't understand?" I croaked.

Holding me at arm's length, tears falling from his eyes, he looked at me. His eyes searching my face. "Vivian?"

Looking inward, I searched for the familiar hum of her Magic but came up empty-handed. Somehow, I felt lighter, but it was the emptiness that made me realize she was no longer inside me.

I shook my head and said, "She's gone."

Robert let out a sigh and his grip on me eased. "Can you move?"

"I think so." I pushed myself upright. It was strange not feeling Vivian anymore. I felt naked, alone, and exposed.

Robert helped me to my feet and wrapped an arm around my waist. His body was warm against mine and just beneath the surface, I could feel our Magic purring softly.

"How?" I tried to take a step but my legs gave out on me and Robert's gripped tighten around my waist.

"Elysium," Merlin said.

I turned to look at Merlin as a sheepish grin spread across his face.

"I thought using Magic from Elysium would—"

"The price was paid with Nimue's life. The world at large is safe once again." Merlin waved away my concern.

"But I thought she was immortal? Amara, she—"

"I ripped her Magic from her, made her human and thus, Elysium could take from her to give to you."

I looked back at Robert, his bright eyes and wide smile staring down at me.

"I'm...I'm alive," I said under my breath. "I didn't think, I was sure that..."

"I know," Robert's smile faded. "Me too."

"Elodie?" I searched the faces around me.

"She's gone," Ethan croaked as he carried her body toward us.

"But Elysium?" I looked at Merlin. "If it saved me, then it can save Elodie?"

"She was already too far gone by the time we were able to get Elysium open again." Merlin's lips formed a thin line.

"We tried," Robert sighed. "We really tried." He reached out and placed a hand on Ethan's shoulder.

"It's not fair," I said, trying to hold back tears.

"I know." Robert held me tighter.

"What now?" I looked between Robert and Merlin.

"We get out of here," Brett huffed. Her dark hair had turned snow white and her skin was pale and clammy.

"Are you—"

"Fine." She batted a hand at me.

I felt like my stomach was filled with stones as I looked her over. She wasn't fine, not by a long shot.

"Anna." Jake held his hand out to her. "Take us back."

Looking around the clearing, there was so much death and destruction. "What will happen to Elysium?" I asked.

"Cian's already trying to find a new home for it," Merlin informed me.

A breeze coasted over my skin, the cold returning as the adrenaline started to wear off.

"Cian, how did he—"

"All a part of the plan," Merlin smirked. "Once Halvar forbid the Brothers from going anywhere near Elysium, he knew something wasn't right."

"So it was Halvar all along?" Robert asked.

"Indeed. By going against his Elder and leaving their realm, he forfeit his right to ever return, and so he saw us through to the end."

"That's how Becky ended up. Wait, where is she?" I whirled around, looking for her.

"Back at the cabin with Matty, they're both safe," Annabel supplied.

"We did it, then," I said under my breath. "We actually did it."

"You did," Merlin smiled.

"Shall we?" Annabel asked, holding her hands out for us to grab.

The world warped around us and reformed into the living room we'd left behind only hours ago. Becky's arms wrapped around me; her words lost in my ear as I watched Brett collapse in front of me.

Matty grabbed her by the waist and slowly lowered her to the ground. "Brett, what is it? What's wrong?" He smoothed her hair out of her face as she shivered on the floor.

Robert let go of me and knelt next to his sister. He placed his hand on her shoulder and his brow furrowed as his Magic coursed through her.

"You can't help me," Brett said as she convulsed and grabbed her brother's hand.

"I can," Robert shook his head. "You just have to give it a minute."

"Robert," her voice was soft as sweat beaded on her forehead.

"Brett, please let him help you," Matty held her hand to his chest, worry etched into the lines of his face.

"It's the Shadowlands," I said, recognizing the same symptoms as the ones Emilia had. "Isn't it?" I asked.

Brett's eyes met mine, and she nodded once. "It had to be done." She closed her eyes and winced.

"No, no, this can't be. You have to do something," Matty's eyes searched the room.

"Alyssa tried," I said. "There wasn't—"

"You can't just let her die," Matty shouted.

"I don't understand," Becky said. "Emilia didn't die right away, why can't we-"

"Emilia was only exposed to the Shadowlands Magic when she took Excalibur," Merlin explained. "Brett was consumed by the Umbra-Kai when she held down Mordred and allowed them to collect what was owed to them."

"What about Elysium?" Robert suggested. "It saved Violet; we can use it to save Brett."

"My dear boy," Merlin sighed. "Even if we knew where to find it, this is the exact reason it can't be used. It's too tempting."

"We've done everything for the Magical world," Robert got to his feet and shouted.

"I know." Merlin grabbed him by the shoulders. "But that doesn't mean the Magical world owes you a debt."

"Can't you get Cian back here?" Jake moved to his sister's side.

"I can orb her—"

"Cian is no more," Merlin informed us.

"What do you mean?" I asked.

"Just like the previous Brothers," Merlin began. "He sacrificed his life to keep the location of Elysium hidden."

"What about that stasis thing you did with Emilia?" Becky chimed in.

"It would only prolong the inevitable." Merlin shook his head. "We don't know how to stop what's happening to her."

"There has to be something we can find a way to—" Matty rambled.

"It's okay," Brett exhaled.

"I can't lose you," Matty placed his forehead against Brett's.

Becky squeezed my hand as we watched Brett dying in the arms of the people she loved.

Emotion welled up in my chest and got caught in my throat as tears burned my eyes. It wasn't fair that I should live and Brett should die.

"You'll be okay," Brett said, placing her hand on Matty's face. "I love you more than all the stars," she exhaled.

"I love you, more than all the moons," Matty said through tears, his voice hitching on the last word.

"Brett, I—" Robert dropped to his knees.

"I know," she turned to look at him.

"I can't live in a world without you." Robert held her hand, and I moved to his side, placing a hand on his back.

"You can," she said. "You all can."

"You're the glue of this family," Jake said as he looked down at his sister.

"We need you," Annabel said over Jake's shoulder.

Her eyes moved over each of us and back to Jake. "Our family has never been stronger," she breathed. "You don't need me to hold us together."

"We'll always need you," Robert said as a single tear fell from his eye.

She closed her eyes as another shiver moved through her.

"Please don't go," Matty whispered as he laid his head on her chest, his tears staining the front of her shirt.

My own tears spilled over as I held onto Robert's arm. My heart split open as I looked at Jake, Annabel, and Robert. Their world, their family, was changing in a way that could never be put right again.

"Brett," Matty whispered as he clung to her, but she was already gone. "Brett," he lifted his head and looked down at her, shaking her to wake up.

"Matty," Becky grabbed his shoulders. "She's gone."

"No," he pushed her hands away.

"Matty," she tried again, and he collapsed against Becky, his anguish making his body shake as he stared down at the woman he loved.

EPILOGUE

"They're here," Merlin said, turning his attention to the pulsing symbol as I walked out into the Maxwell's backyard.

Orbs of light swirled around each other, creating a mesmerizing double helix. The outline of a man slowly appeared, as if he was materializing on the other side of opaque glass.

The orbs swirled upward and back-flipped out of their helix to create an arch.

"It's beautiful," I said as a calmness washed over me.

One of the Brotherhood of the Realms became solid on the other side and then passed through the archway with ease. His blond hair reached past his shoulders. Braids and dreads artfully placed throughout his mane were held together with silver bands. He wore a thick fur over his shoulders that reminded me of the History channel's version of the Vikings, and he was much younger than I expected.

I don't know why, but I'd imagined someone older, wiser, more equipped to handle the realm of death.

"Welcome, Brother," Merlin said, inclining his head. "I trust

Halvar has been removed from his position within the Brotherhood?"

"He has," the Brother acknowledged.

Another form came into shape, and a second man pushed his way through the fog and through the archway. Their brown leather pants clung to their legs like a second set of skin as they moved away from the arch to greet everyone.

The taller, clean-shaven Brother had a knife strapped to his leg and hieroglyphic tattoos running the length of his left arm. He held what could only be described as a tome while the other heavily bearded brother held an ornately carved animal skull by the horns. Engraved in the bleached bone of the skull was an intricate design of vines and circles that would be stunning if not for the fact that they were engraved on a dead animal's skull.

The Brother tapped his chest with his fist and nodded in Merlin's direction.

"Are the souls prepared?" The Brothers deep voice asked.

"Yes," Robert said from behind us.

Passing through the open French doors, Brett and Elodie's levitating bodies floated next to Robert and Ethan effortlessly.

"Very well," the brother said, motioning for Robert to take the lead.

Robert moved toward the pyre, Brett's body in tow, Ethan and Elodie behind him. They had both been cleaned up since the last time I saw them. Strips of cloth Merlin prepared were draped and tied over their skin in an intricate pattern, and their hair was slick with oil.

The Brothers followed behind Ethan and then the rest of the family fell into step behind them. Becky and I were the last in line, and my heart picked up with each step.

Robert raised his hand and Brett's body gently moved to the top of the pile of wood and settled against the platform. As Elodie reached the end of the aisle, Robert raised his hand again and she floated to the top of the wood pile and settled next to Brett.

Taking his place, Robert stood next to me and I looped my arm through his, pulling him close. Jake stood on the other side of Robert with Annabel wrapped under his arm as we waited for the Brothers to take their place.

The Brothers stood next to the pyre and turned to face us. Cracking open the leather binding, and flipped to a book-marked page.

"What is that?" Becky whispered next to me.

"It's called the Black Book of Carmarthen," I said, recalling what Robert had told me of Magical burial rites. "It contains spells and enchantments only the Brotherhood of the Realms have access to. It's how they are able to facilitate safe passage between realms."

"There's but one guarantee in life," the Brother began. "Death. Today we bid safe passage for Brett Maxwell and Elodie Kekoa from this realm to her final resting place."

The skull-wielding brother walked up the ladder of the pyre and placed the object in between Brett and Elodie. Once he descended the stairs, a glowing orb appeared in his palm. He looked at his counterpart, awaiting his cue.

The Brother kept his eyes on the page in front of him and began to recite a spell. His voice was low and almost lyrical when he spoke like he was singing a song long forgotten.

As the hymn came to a close, the Brother holding the orb cast it into the kindling of the pyre. Flames crawled up the sides of the wood and I could feel the heat on my face. The fire eagerly jumped toward their exposed bodies, and I flinched as the flames licked at their skin.

The Brother continued the sing-song spell and before I could look away, pure white smoke began to pour out of Brett and Elodie. The smoke curled timidly out of them, as if it was conscious and aware of its surroundings as the Brothers' words coaxed it out of them.

Watching Brett more carefully, I noticed there was a glow to the fog, like the sun lighting upon a spiderweb. It pulsed around her and expanded over the length of her body, swaying to the tempo of the Brother's song.

The second Brother, the one who'd placed the skull, began to hum deep in his chest. The flames grew taller, engulfing the pyre, leaving only a shadow of Brett and Elodie's figures as the white smoke rose above the flames and began to circle around the pyre like ghosts.

"Should you wish to say goodbye, now is the time."

Brett's parents stepped forward first, and their words were barely a whisper. Magic pulsed off of each of them, shooting toward the sky and bursting above us like fireworks.

Matty moved next, his steps unsure as he took a deep breath. I couldn't hear what he said, but I could feel his pain as his shoulders shook with his tears.

Keeping his head down, wiping tears from his face, he took his place again next to Annabel, and she wrapped her arm around him.

Robert stepped forward and without preamble, he said, "Sleep well, *cor meum*."

The brilliant light of Arcane Magic pulsed on his fingertips and he released a bolt of Magic into the sky.

Jake patted Robert's shoulder as he and Annabel stepped forward to say goodbye. His words were hushed by the crackling of the fire as he raised his arm above his head and a bolt of lightning cracked open the sky.

"Anyone else?" The brother asked.

Something inside me felt compelled to speak and, without realizing it, I stepped forward.

The acrid smell of the wood burning mixed with the briny

ocean air. As I drew closer, the heat from the pyre hit me like a wall and I came to a stop.

I didn't know what to say as I stood there. Brett had become a fixture in my life. Someone I could count on, someone who was a beacon of strength, and now she was gone.

"You were the light in all our lives, a true north," I said, calling upon my Magic. "I'll carry you with me always."

I turned to look at Elodie. I didn't know her well, but she had one of the purest hearts I've ever known. She never backed down from a fight, never gave up, and she always had a smile for her twin brother.

"You deserved so much more," I said. "I'll do my best to honor your sacrifice every day." The intense heat electrified my skin and a pulse of raw Magic burst from my chest.

I stepped back in line and Robert draped his arm over my shoulders.

Ethan stepped forward with his parents, and they each said their tearful goodbyes before stepping back in line.

"Whether you brought happiness or pains, may your soul yet win delights, on this your death-day," The Brother announced.

The fire sizzled and burned out, leaving nothing behind on the pyre. Brett and Elodie were gone.

* * *

"That should just about do it," Merlin said after everything was cleaned up from the funeral. "There is one last thing I'd like to do if everyone's up for it."

"What else could there possibly be?" I asked, emotionally spent.

"I believe someone has more than earned the right to be a part of our world." Merlin's eyes landed on Becky and a smile pulled at the corner of his lips.

"I think you're right," Robert said, picking up Merlin's train of thought and nudging Becky.

"Me?" she balked.

"Shall we head to the water?" Merlin asked. "Annabel?"

"I'd be happy to," she smiled and reached out her hands for all of us to grab.

Standing on the beach with the rest of the Maxwells, my hair whipped around my face with the ocean breeze. A wave crashed on the shore, sending a mist into the air that reached our party a few feet away. Another wave rushed toward the shore and the sound of the water hitting the sand bounced off the cliff and made my bones rattle.

Becky and Merlin stood in the middle of our circle. If she was nervous, she didn't show it. Not for the first time I wondered what kind of Waker she would've been had the prophecy been about her.

"Once the transformation to a Promised One is made, it cannot be undone," Merlin said, placing a hand on Becky's shoulder. "Your life will belong to the protection of the Magical world." As he stared at her, I wondered if he was trying to will her into understanding what being a Promised One was really about. She may have fun working with Matty, researching and hacking away, but the real life, day to day of this Magical world, was a whole other ball game.

"Should you wish to continue, you must acknowledge that you understand this, by willingly sacrificing your lifeblood."

He held out a crude looking dagger for her to take and, of course, she did it without hesitation.

Merlin smiled as she placed the blade in her other hand and closed her fingers around the metal. As she quickly pulled the knife across her palm, drops of blood fell to the sand.

"Let's get started," Merlin said. "Hold your palm out for me."

She turned her bloody hand toward the sky and reached out to him.

Grabbing her wrist with one hand, he pulled her closer to him and began to recite a spell over the open wound.

The blood from her cut slowly rose like a tornado, spinning

unnaturally suspended in the air. Merlin's voice grew louder with each word of the incantation. Letting go of Becky, he raised his face and arms toward the sky, where an angry, black cloud had formed and lightning struck the tips of his fingers. When he looked back at Becky, his eyes were glowing an icy blue and in one swift movement he threw his arms wide open and her blood froze in mid-air. As it hovered for a moment, I caught sight of Becky's profile.

She stared at Merlin in complete awe. She'd been around all of us to see her fair share of Magic, but this was something different; this was raw, all consuming Magic.

As he finished the spell, her blood began to spin again, slowly at first and then faster and faster until I could barely see it. With her palm still raised to the sky, her blood rushed back into her through the wound she had willingly given herself.

Merlin lowered his arms and the clouds disappeared. The sound of the waves replaced the roar of Magic and the seagulls resumed their cooing as if a person's life hadn't just been altered.

"Is that it?" Becky said, turning around in a circle to face me.

"That's it," Merlin said. "Welcome to the club."

Walking toward Becky, she met me halfway, and I threw my arms around her. I don't know how I got so lucky to have her as my best friend. So much in my life had changed, but Becky had always been a constant. Now she was a part of this crazy world with me and I honestly couldn't be happier.

"You're giving off some serious Magic," Becky said as she pulled away for me.

"You can feel my Magic?"

"I mean, I think that's what it is."

"You're right." Matty spoke for the first time since the funeral. "Now that you're a Promised One, you'll be able to feel the Magic rolling off a person. That's how you'll know who belongs to us."

"To endings and new beginnings," Merlin said, procuring a bottle of amber liquid from his coat.

"Now what? The prophecy is fulfilled?" I asked, as Merlin handed the bottle to Jake and he took a sip.

"My dear Violet," Merlin smiled warmly, like the parent figure I've been without for so long. "Now you get busy living."

"I can get on board with that," Robert said, pulling me into the circle of his arms. He smiled down at me, his hand smoothing back my hair. More than anything, I wanted to stay in this moment forever.

"Kiss me," I said, looking up into the dark brown eyes I'd fallen in love with.

His lips touched mine, soft and quick, as he pulled me closer to him.

"A good kiss," I breathed.

His arms wrapped around me, pressing me to his chest as he kissed me full and hard. His lips were soft as his hand made its way into my hair. Everything we'd been through bubbled to the surface and as he deepened the kiss, I let myself feel it all. All the love, all the loss, all the pain.

I could feel the tension in his body ease as he lifted me off my feet. The heat of his skin pressed against me and I melted into the warmth I'd become so accustomed to. My heart thrummed in my chest like a hummingbird trying to escape. The damp ocean air disappeared and time seemed to stop altogether as he placed me back on my feet.

I looked around at the people who'd become like family, and the cracks in my heart healed ever so slightly.

NEW ADULT NORSE MYTHOLOGY ROMANTIC FANTASY
REALMS SAGA
REALM OF FLAMES & STEEL
ALLISON SIPE
REALMS SAGA
REALM OF STARS & SHADOWS
ALLISON SIPE
AVAILABLE EVERYWHERE & ON KU

AUTHOR'S NOTE

I've started writing this about a hundred times now and nothing ever comes out right. So here it is, raw and unedited...

When I started writing Violet's story, it was just for fun. Something to keep my mind occupied while I sat in boring college classes. Something to do on those warm summer nights, when it was too hot to venture outside.

I never meant for anyone to read my story, other than a few friends and maybe a few family members. I never meant to find pieces of myself in Robert's words. I never meant to push myself outside of my comfort zone like Violet.

I just wanted to write the story I wanted to hear.

I've changed so much in the course of writing this series, I'm not longer in college, I've traveled the world, I'm no longer single or living in my family home. I grew up with these books in a way. And though I wasn't a child when I started writing Violet's story, I was still so young at heart and wide-eyed to the world.

Writing these books altered me forever. They pushed me and made me stronger. Sometimes writing was the escape I needed and other times, it was all I could do to escape the blank page. It's been said so many times, so many ways, by so many people, that writing is hard.

Writing takes pieces of you. Each character is a shade of who I am. Every setting is a slice of the world I live in. When I started writing, I didn't realize so much of me would end up on the page. My life, my sadness, my heartbreak, my loves. The things I've seen, experienced and fallen in love with, live in my books forever now.

It's incredible really. When I look at where I started and where we are now. When I first started writing, Violet didn't have Magic. She was never going to have Magic and what a shame that would have been. Her Magic is what made this story special and changed her in impossible ways through out the series.

Her Magic changed her for the better, much likes these books have changed me for the better. It hasn't always been easy and everyday hasn't been a picnic. But if Violet and I have anything in common, it's that we never gave up, no matter how difficult the road ahead seemed.

I've thanked many people over the years in my books. The ones who stood by and encouraged me, helped me and supported me. But there's one person I've yet to thank until now.

Violet Evans.

She jumped into my head all those years ago with a story to tell and it's been a privilege building this world with her for the better part of a decade. The Soothsayer Series has become such a big part of who I am now. I've learned so much, grown so much and it all started with her.

So thank you, Violet. Thank you for choosing me, trusting me with your story. I've carried you all over the world, in manuscript form, in notebooks, in my laptop and in my heart. Thank you for the adventure and thank you for being the story I wanted to hear.

Until we meet again my friend...

Dear Reader,

I hope you enjoyed *Elysium.* I have been with these characters for many years now and it's such a privilege to share them with you. Though this is the end of Violet and Robert's story, I do hope to see them again. *wink wink*

If you've made it this far, we're basically best friends now! I know you'll want to hear about my next series so don't forget to sign up to my mailing list. Realm Of Flames and Steel has all the good stuff, Magic, Love (and it won't fade to black this time) adventure, found family and of course a strong woman who saves the world.

For up to date details and launch dates for my upcoming series, head over to allisonsipe.com and sign up to my mailing list!

I love to hear from my readers, so please feel free to email me with any questions or just drop me a line at, allisonsipe.com

Until Next Time, Embrace Your Magic!

ABOUT THE AUTHOR

Allison Sipe lives in Southern California with her boyfriend and two adorable dogs. She has a degree from California State University Northridge in English Literature and is very proud to have gone to school for something she loves.

When she's not reading and writing, she loves to travel. She's been around all around Europe, London is one of her favorite cities and the little island of Kauai is where she gets a lot of her writing done.

If you'd like to contact her, you can message her on her website of find her on most social media platf